W9-AVE-893

ROBERT J. BROWN OR
PATRICIA I. BROWN
3345 MAINE AVE., LOT 282,
SEBRING, FL 33872

CLOTH *of* HEAVEN

B.J. HOFF

CLOTH of HEAVEN

SONG of ERIN No 1

Tyndale House Publishers, Inc.
Wheaton, Illinois

Visit Tyndale's exciting Web site at www.tyndale.com

Copyright © 1997 by B. J. Hoff. All rights reserved.
Author photo taken by Bill Bilsley © 1996. All rights reserved.
Cover illustration copyright © 1997 by Laura Stutzman. All rights reserved.

Unless otherwise indicated, all Scripture quotations are taken from the *Holy Bible*, New Living Translation, copyright © 1996. Used by permission of Tyndale House Publishers, Inc., Wheaton, Illinois 60189. All rights reserved.

Scripture quotations marked NIV are taken from the *Holy Bible*, New International Version®. NIV®. Copyright © 1973, 1978, 1984 by International Bible Society. Used by permission of Zondervan Publishing House. All rights reserved.

Edited by David Horton
Cover design by Andrea Gjeldum

ISBN 1-56865-843-5

Printed in the United States of America

CLOTH OF HEAVEN

Weaver of time and infinity,
Who fashions the intricate tapestry
Of all my life—my days and years—
I bring to you my smiles and tears,
My hopes, my dreams, my memories,
My triumphs and my tragedies.
I bring them, every one, to you,
Who takes all things and makes them new.
Lord, take my life and weave for me
A garment for eternity.

B. J. HOFF

ACKNOWLEDGMENTS

So many special people play a part in the development of a book that it's impossible to thank them all. But to mention a few:

As always, my deepest thanks to my family: my husband, Jim, for his *endless* patience; and my daughters, Dana and Jessie, for always being there for me, even in the midst of those frantic deadlines.

To Ken Petersen and David Horton, my editors, for believing in and sharing the vision and for going the extra miles to bring the book to fulfillment. Thanks to Ron Beers for all the encouragement and for offering so many authors like myself a climate in which we can do our best work. To Travis Thrasher—there must be ten of you to accomplish so much for so many and to do it all with such a cheerful spirit!

A continuing note of appreciation to Dr. Eoin McKiernan of St. Paul, Minnesota, founder of the Irish American Cultural Institute, for everything he has done for the Irish on both sides of the Atlantic—and for this writer, who is deeply grateful.

B. J. Hoff

PART ONE

The Big Wind

And a mighty windstorm hit the mountain.

It was such a terrible blast that the rocks were torn loose,

but the Lord was not in the wind.

After the wind there was an earthquake,

but the Lord was not in the earthquake.

And after the earthquake there was a fire,

but the Lord was not in the fire.

And after the fire there was the sound of a gentle whisper.

1 KINGS 19:11-12

The Silence

Deadly still was the heavy air,
Horrible silence was everywhere. . . .

THOMAS D'ARCY MCGEE

IRELAND, JANUARY 6, 1839

On this day in Ireland there were those who searched the sky with anxious frowns, as if they half expected to see an omen or perhaps a hint of some dark, unnatural force lurking behind the clouds. The warm stillness of the winter day was unnerving, no matter how welcome a change from the bitter cold.

Epiphany Sunday had dawned upon a hushed world of white, blanketed by the heavy snowfall of the night before. By afternoon, the day had warmed to unthinkably mild temperatures. Men stood at the crossroads in their shirtsleeves, making conjectures about the odd weather and what, if anything, it might forebode.

The women across the island had no time for such speculation. Instead, they busied themselves throughout the afternoon preparing what few savory dishes they could manage, given their meager budgets. Cottages grew steamy from hours of baking, and children turned more restive by the hour in anticipation of the coming evening. If entire villages seemed to hum with excitement, it was to be expected, for festive occasions were all too rare in the Irish countryside. Of late, the sound of the funeral dirge had become far more familiar than the lively tunes of merrymaking.

On this day, even in the most remote and primitive counties, every warm moment seemed a gift, a respite from winter's gloom and the

general climate of dread that had long clutched at the very heart of
Ireland. For a few hours this evening, those families fortunate enough
to still have a roof above their heads would gather around the hearth
fire and enjoy their blessings, blessings all the more precious for their
scarcity. Tonight, at least, Irishmen would lay aside their worries
about rising rents and unnerving tales of eviction while their women
donned brave smiles and bright colors as they, too, attempted to forget their fears. There would be laughter and songs and prayers for
God's keeping, and at the heart of it all, the deep music of living—
a music created from centuries of sorrow, a longing for freedom—
and hope.

Yet there were some whose hope rested not in the evening's lighthearted festivities nor in the ancient land of their birth—nor even in
the God of their fathers or in the faith that had sustained their families
for ages past. Instead, their hope clung solely to the idea of escape.

These were not always the ones who spoke most often of leaving
the "poor old island" behind. They did not necessarily shudder by
the fire at the thought of forsaking home and country for a harrowing
voyage across the sea in search of a better life. More often they *had*
no homes or at least knew the threat of eviction upon the daily horizon, and they shuddered more from the reality of winter's cold and
encroaching starvation than from any fear of crossing the great Atlantic.

For these, escape had become their hope. For many, it was their
only hope.

1

Terese

But the haunted air of twilight is very strange and still,
And the little winds of twilight are dearer to my mind.

EVA GORE-BOOTH

INISHMORE, ONE OF THE ARAN ISLANDS
IN WESTERN IRELAND

Terese Sheridan stood in the hulking shadow of Dun Aengus, watching night gather over the ocean. The day had been warm, unnaturally warm, and so close that the flame of a candle wouldn't have flickered. But now a light breeze had picked up and was playing along the stones, while in the distance a random flare of lightning illumined the sky.

The huge stone fort towering overhead had been there forever— since long before the coming of Patrick, according to the Old Ones in the village. With its vast rings of stone walls and what must surely have been thousands of jagged stones placed upright to ward off ancient attacks, it loomed over Inishmore and the island's people like some colossal, magnificent creature risen from the sea, turned to stone by its long centuries of vigil.

In its permanence and hovering immensity, the fort had somehow become to Terese not only a sentry to the entire island but a kind of personal guardian as well. Dun Aengus was the only thing of any real stability in her life. But tonight she was bidding it farewell. She had walked out from her aunt's cottage in the village to say good-bye to the fort and to Inishmore; before first light dawned tomorrow, she would be gone.

She and her best chum, Peggy O'Grady, had been planning their departure from the island for months. Tomorrow they would go. Yet, despite her eagerness to get away, Terese could not entirely ignore the heaviness of heart that had settled over her throughout the evening. There had been many partings in her life—too many by far— and for all the bitterness and sorrow she had known in this place, there were memories here, whispers of her life, of the family she had lost, the all-too-rare times of love and warmth they had known together.

At seventeen, Terese was the only one of her entire family left on this side of the Atlantic. Both her father and her brother, Cavan, had made the crossing to America more than six years ago, leaving behind nothing more than a promise that within a year they would send for the rest of the family to join them.

The streets in America, however, had turned out to be paved not with gold, as was rumored, but with animal droppings instead. The fine jobs that were to have ensured ship passages for the family— and perhaps even a house in the new land—had never materialized. Their father had died less than a year after leaving Ireland, and Cavan had ended up in a place called Pennsylvania, digging coal below the ground with their uncle Tibbot and his sons.

Within a year of her father and brother's leaving, Terese and the rest of the family, unable to keep up the rent, had been evicted. Forced to spend most of the winter living in a rock cave by the shore, baby Mada and Terese's older sister, Honor, had both died of exposure and pneumonia. Within a week of their passing, their mother was also dead, leaving Terese, not quite twelve years old at the time, completely alone.

Ill from the cold and nearly dead from starvation, Terese had gone to beg a bed with her aunt Una in the Field of the Horses, a tired little village close to the sea. The first time she went, her aunt had turned a deaf ear to her plea for shelter. "And how would I be making room for one more mouth to feed?" Aunt Una had asked. "There's no room and no food. You're a fine big girl now. You'll have no trouble finding work to keep yourself."

There had been no work on the starving island, of course. More desperate than ever, Terese had finally swallowed her pride and gone to Aunt Una again. This time, whether out of guilt or some newly remembered trace of family feeling, her aunt had relented, allowing her niece a smelly pallet in the corner where the pig sometimes slept and a cramped place at the table among her five cousins.

Not a day had since passed that her aunt had not reminded Terese of what a burden she was and her incredibly good fortune in having Christian kin willing to give her a roof over her head, and at such a sacrifice to themselves. And not a day passed in the ensuing years that Terese did not burn with resentment as she counted the money that had finally begun to arrive from Cavan, carefully hiding it away with the intention of amassing enough to escape Inishmore and her aunt's "Christian charity."

There had been times during the worst of her loneliness when she wondered if she might have been better off to have died in the cave with her mother and sisters. But she could always rouse herself from the temptation of self-pity with the reminder that there was something better in store—something out there, across the Atlantic, just waiting for her to claim it. She had only to endure her aunt's spitefulness, her uncle's indifference, her cousins' ridicule for a time, not forever. Repeatedly she told herself that she could endure *anything* so long as there was hope for something better.

In truth, Terese had kept herself alive through hope. It was all she had, this fierce hope of hers, the anticipation of a time when she would finally escape the squalid poverty of her existence for that "something better."

Now that time had come. By this hour tomorrow she and Peggy would be in Galway City. From the money Cavan had sent her over the years and her earnings in the kitchen at Corcoran's Inn, Terese had managed to squirrel away almost twice again the amount she customarily handed over for her keeping. At last she had enough for her passage to America. Enough for a new life.

Suddenly, the melancholy that had been pressing in on her through-out the evening lifted, almost as if hope itself had come swooping down and borne it away on the wings of the wind. Terese felt a sense of release, of deliverance, that made her want to shout her impending freedom to the entire island.

At that moment, an unexpected squall of wind came wailing across the shore, followed by a crash of thunder and a stunning display of lightning. The air turned sharply chill, and Terese wished she had worn her coat instead of her cousin Nancy's thin sweater.

She realized it was growing late—surely past eight by now—and with a last glance at the stone fort, she turned to start back toward the village. Without warning, another gust of wind, this one stronger, roared in on her, howling like a banshee over the treacherous stone walls of the fort.

Terese looked to the sky, ink dark and heavy with the threat of rain, then back to the shore, where the tide had risen. Farther out, waves surged and rolled with mounting fury. A storm was blowing in, and with incredible swiftness, it seemed. The wind slapped at her face and shoulders, and she hugged her arms to herself against the cold as she turned to run toward home.

2

Brady

"I am of Ireland. . . ."

W . B . Y E A T S

GALWAY CITY, WESTERN IRELAND

After a long day in Galway City, Brady Kane wandered into the district called the Claddagh. He had read about the place, had heard Jack speak of it through the years, but nothing could have prepared him for its strangeness.

He felt as if he had stepped into another world, another age. Here, in this southernmost quarter of the town at the mouth of the harbor, lived a colony of fishermen and their families that time and the world seemed to have forgotten. Everything about the area and its inhabitants spoke of the past. Winding lanes and squares of thatched-roof dwellings, the quaint, colorful clothing of the inhabitants, and their language—Brady had heard more of the Irish spoken today than he had heard during his entire month in Dublin—gave the observer a sense of a people and a culture unchanged for centuries.

He stopped and looked over the bay. A few small boats were in the water—the small, primitive curraghs mostly, and a couple of brown-sailed rigs—but for the most part the harbor was deserted.

The sudden puff of wind blowing in off the water felt good. The day had been surprisingly mild until an hour or so ago, but now the waves were beginning to churn as the breeze picked up, and Brady welcomed the cooler air.

This was his first trip to Ireland, and he had had to fight Jack all the way for it. Brady wasn't sure why his brother was so set against the idea, but he had his suspicions. Somehow he didn't think Jack's opposition had anything to do with the flimsy excuses he'd been mouthing for months—*We're too busy at the paper; I can't possibly spare you, not now.... Don't forget I'm going to be in Boston for two or three weeks soon, and you'll have to take over for me at the paper and at the publishing house as well.... We have manuscripts coming in, authors to meet with.... Then there's all the work at the Committee....*

In the end, it was the Committee that had won it for Brady. He had finally managed to convince Jack that he would be far more effective in helping to raise money on behalf of Ireland if he could see for himself what the conditions in their homeland really were, if they had been exaggerated or not. How could he possibly be effective with the Committee, he had argued to Jack, unless he was acquainted firsthand with Ireland and its people?

"If the conditions there are really as intolerable as we're told, I'll come back with the proof to support our work—sketches, paintings, and a full account of the truth. Come on, Jack," he had pressed. "I need to go, and you know it."

"You *want* to go is more like it," his brother had countered.

"You said yourself we need to establish some European reporters, Jack. Why can't this be the first step?"

The black scowl eased slightly, and the long Irish sigh that followed told Brady he had won.

"Two months," Jack finally agreed. "Two months, and not a day longer, mind!"

Brady suspected that Jack's reluctance to grant him leave to Ireland had something to do with concern that he might end up wanting to *stay* in Ireland. He had to admit that his brother's instincts were sound. They always were. It had been over a month now, and Brady seldom thought of home.

It was true that he had squandered much of the time indulging his fascination with Dublin City, rather than exploring the Irish countryside as Jack expected. The old city had drawn him in almost immediately, with its gypsylike charm, its heady, almost intoxicating, variety of sights and sounds, its buildings, and its fine bridges—and its even finer women.

Ah, the women!

Still, when he hadn't been playing the rake or cultivating all things Irish in a fevered attempt to rid himself of his more obvious "Americanisms," Brady had sketched and painted like a madman, often working until dawn. He had also managed to rationalize his preoccupation with Dublin by telling himself that it was Ireland's principal city, after all, and so it was only reasonable to make a thorough study of it.

Indeed.

Finally, however, when he had lingered as long as he dared without sabotaging the rest of his expedition, he left Dublin and headed for Galway, in the west of Ireland. He had arrived in the city of his birth yesterday but after settling in had been too fatigued to do any real exploring. Today, though, he had wandered much of the town, making some interesting sketches of its different quarters and its people in the process.

The wind was whipping up harder now, the spray off the water stinging his face. Brady turned away and stood studying the small, rough-hewn houses about him, many already darkened for the night. Every now and then a man would go in or out, occasionally a woman as well. The men seemed a reticent lot, for the most part: dark and taciturn in their old-fashioned breeches and jackets—and those surprising light blue stockings. As for the women—well, he had seen a beauty or two, barefoot, decked in their peculiar short cloaks with red petticoats swirling about bare legs as they darted in and out of the lanes.

He stretched, breathing in the tangy sea air that was laced with the strong, acrid odor of a quayside fish market. It was a curious feeling, standing in this place knowing that his parents or even Jack might have ventured among these peculiar people at one time or another in the past. Perhaps he even had relatives in one of those small thatched houses.

He doubted it. He hadn't seen many Spanish-looking faces since he entered the Claddagh—faces like his own and Jack's, common enough in Galway City. His gaze went to one of the aged Spanish archways off to the left, then back to the nearest dwellings. No, Brady thought it unlikely that there would have been much intermarriage here. These people had remained independent over the centuries, an isolated, exclusive settlement. Why, they were said to even have their own king, who governed them, claimed dominion over the bay for the community, and flew his own personal sail and colors from the masthead of his boat!

Outside the Claddagh, Brady had seen abundant evidence that Galway had once been a busy trading port with Spain. The black Irish— like his own family—could be seen everywhere. He spied more than one black-haired, dark-eyed lovely so exquisitely formed and graceful that she could have served as the ideal artist's model.

Their mother had been raven haired, according to Jack. Brady hadn't known her, of course, nor his father. His mother had died giving birth to him, and his father hadn't lived much longer before being hanged as the result of a midnight raid on a British post, apparently by one of those secret societies. Whiteboys, Thrashers, Ribbonmen—the Irish had boasted countless numbers of them over the years.

Jack had done his best to keep their parents' memory alive as Brady and his sister, Rose, were growing up, and perhaps he had been more successful than he realized. Brady had come to feel an uncommon closeness to the young mother who died giving him life, and to Sean Kane, his doomed father.

Jack had instructed him not to "waste time" in Galway, claiming that there was nothing of any real interest to be found in the "city of the tribes." But for Brady, it was enough that his parents had once lived here, worked here . . . died here. In some bizarre fashion, that tragic duo had continued, even in death, to play a significant role in what he had become. His fierce, ongoing desire to see the country of his birth; the elemental streak of rebellion that seemed to fire his spirit, no matter how vigorously Jack tried to dampen it; and the unaccountable attachment he held for this small, struggling island and its people—somehow those two shadowy figures of the past were a part of his passion.

Perhaps what accounted for the difference in the way he and Jack felt about the country was the fact that Jack at least had his memories of Ireland—he had been almost fourteen when they emigrated—whereas Brady remembered nothing.

But he was here now, and he intended to see it all. He had gotten himself lost several times during the day, wandering along the narrow, winding streets of the city before ending up here in the Claddagh. He supposed he should be getting back to his room instead of standing here staring out at the sea. The wind had begun to churn up in earnest, and it held the distinct threat of a rainstorm on the way.

Shifting his sketchbook to the other arm, he started off. He had just turned onto one of the narrow lanes leading away from the harbor when a small girl with a merry laugh darted out from between two crude huts, nearly colliding with Brady.

"Whoa!" he cautioned the child, putting out a hand to steady her. She was a wee thing, no more than four or five, surely: barefoot, reed thin, and none too clean. But her eyes danced with lively mischief, and when Brady smiled at her, she laughed in pure delight.

At that instant, another girl—no, not a girl, but more a young woman, he realized after taking a closer glance—emerged from the same dirt path. She, too, wore no shoes, but a bright blue cloak flew about her in the wind, and her kerchief had slipped to reveal a wild mane of black hair.

She turned on the child, firing a stream of what Brady took to be Gaelic invective as she wagged a scolding finger at her charge. It took her another second or two to notice Brady. When she did, her impatience seemed to give way to alarm. Grabbing the little girl's hand, she tugged her close and began to pull her down the lane alongside her.

The wind blew her kerchief free with the movement, and Brady flung out a hand to catch it, returning it to her with a small flourish. Her eyes narrowed—wonderful eyes, enormous in her thin, delicate-featured face—but she gave a grudging nod of thanks.

A blast of wind swept down the lane at that instant, surprising Brady with its force.

The child squealed, but obviously not in alarm—the odd little creature was laughing again!

Her guardian, however, was not amused. Her gaze went to the harbor, and Brady turned to look. There was thunder now, and the peculiar closeness of the day was gone, broken by the wind and an accompanying drop in temperature. Lightning streaked over the water, and the child cried out in glee. The older girl seemed not to notice. Her finely sculpted features had gone taut, and although she spoke not a word, Brady could sense the tension gripping her.

Was she the child's mother? he wondered. She appeared awfully young herself and, like the little one, somewhat peculiar.

As he watched, the older girl ducked and hauled the child up in her arms, though she was obviously too slight for such a burden.

Strangely reluctant to see her leave, Brady put a hand to her arm. "Wait, please."

She looked at his hand, then raised her gaze to his face. Brady actually flinched at the anxious look she turned on him. "Sorry," he said, releasing her. "But I thought you might be able to help me with some directions. Do you speak English?"

The girl made no attempt at a reply, but instead stared at Brady as if he had suddenly grown horns.

He tried again. "English?" he repeated. "Do you understand?"

The wind slammed against his back, nearly knocking him into her. The girl froze, her gaze going to something over Brady's shoulder, and the raw fear he saw in her eyes caused a sudden burst of panic to spiral up in him. He whipped around and saw for himself the dizzying charge of lightning hurtling across the bay, as if a heavy arm from heaven had unleashed an assault of fiery arrows.

At that instant, Brady realized that there was something far more treacherous on the wind than a rainstorm.

3

In Search of Shelter

Oh! thou, who comest, like a midnight thief,
Uncounted, seeking whom thou may'st destroy . . .
JOHN KEEGAN

A shrieking gale caught Terese up, nearly tossing her off her feet. For the first time she realized that this was more than a winter rainstorm, that something unthinkable was happening and she might actually be in danger. Instinctively, she threw herself to the ground, crouching behind the stones and shivering as much from fear as from the suddenly frigid air.

For a moment she could do nothing but lie, dazed and shaking, against the rocks. A rumbling deeper than thunder rushed in off the sea to sweep the cliffs and the fort like a fury. Never had Terese heard such a sound, as if the wind would tear the earth itself asunder. Lightning streaked wildly, arcing over and around her.

The sky released a deluge of hail and rain, slashing her head and arms like a storm of needles. Terese screamed in pain, throwing her arms up to shield her head as she scrambled to her feet and began to run.

She felt the savage wind slapping at her, shoving her, as if to lift her from the ground and into the deadly maelstrom. Panicked, her heart thundering so violently she could no longer distinguish the pounding of her blood from the roar of the wind, Terese practically threw herself at one of the taller stones, wrapping her arms around it and clinging desperately as the downpour of rain continued to pummel her without mercy.

She screamed into the night, but the storm stole her voice, dashing her cry against the rocks before finally carrying it out to sea.

Every muscle in Brady's body went rigid as yet another blast of wind slammed against him. On instinct, he threw himself in front of the two girls, trying to shield them. "Over there!" he yelled, pointing at the low ditch running between two of the houses.

The black-haired girl stared at him, clutching the child in her arms even closer. It occurred to Brady in a split second that she might be slow-witted, for she seemed not to understand, even when he grabbed her arm and began tugging her toward the ditch.

She fought him, shaking her head violently, hugging the child to her as she twisted free of Brady's grasp. At the same time, she made a sharp motion that they should run in the opposite direction. Not waiting for Brady to follow, she bolted off.

At that instant, another furious gust of wind hurtled over them. There was a crash, then the sickening sound of something tearing and splitting as the roof on one of the houses just ahead lifted completely free and blew apart, sending clumps of thatch flying wildly into the night.

Before, Brady had merely felt dazed by the unexpected onslaught of the storm. Now he knew his first stab of real fear. This was no ordinary wind, and he knew that there was no time to lose in finding shelter.

There were others now, spilling out from the houses in a flurry of panic and bewilderment, sending up a chorus of wailing and screaming as they poured into the streets. Many seemed in a state of shock. Others, nearly naked and marked with bruises and lacerations, stumbled through the crowds calling for family members and loved ones.

As Brady reached the girl, he could hear her muttering something in the Irish, repeating it like a litany. It struck him then how slight she was. He slowed her with a restraining arm and, without giving her a chance to protest, moved to take the child from her. Those enormous dark eyes challenged him for a split second as she retained her hold on the small girl in her arms. Even when she finally relented and handed the child over to him, she eyed him closely, as if to make certain he was not an abductor.

"Where?" Brady shouted above the wind as he bundled the child to his chest. "Show me!"

Again the girl pointed, and they started off at a hard run. The night had become a tempest. The wind caught them up from behind, threatening to drive them to the ground as a sudden deluge of cold rain burst from the sky. Lightning rent the darkness, stabbing wildly at houses, piercing everything in its path in a dizzying assault.

Brady looked for some sign of shelter, but the small houses were clearly more hazard than haven in this kind of storm. Besides, the girl seemed to know exactly where she was going. At least he hoped she did.

He glanced down at the child in his arms, surprised to see that her expression was more bemused than frightened. As if sensing Brady's gaze, she looked up—and actually smiled at him!

She was odd, no doubt about it!

Nearly blinded by the rain and pummeled by the merciless wind, Brady had all he could do to keep up with the dark-haired girl racing down the quay ahead of him. She was as fleet as a deer, and he had the feeling that if she hadn't been so intent upon keeping the child well within range she would have easily left him behind and fled into the night.

They charged on, the baleful wind shrieking at their backs, in their faces, all about them now—for it was moving inland at incredible speed, like a horde of demons unleashed from the very pit of hell. Brady cried out a warning as a wooden pail came flying at them, barely missing the girl's head before banging against a yard pump and splitting into pieces.

Slates and stones flew in all directions, creating even more danger. Brady thought himself to be as fit as any man, but now he became keenly aware that the exertion of the hard run and the burden of the child were beginning to tell on him. When a particularly vicious gust of wind seized him, shaking him and sweeping him forward, he came treacherously close to sprawling headfirst in the street.

Brady saw that the girl was heading toward a small, thatched-roof cottage at the other side of the street. When he realized her intention, he stopped her with a firm hand while bracing the child tightly against himself with his free arm. "That'll do us no good!" he shouted, suddenly angry that she had led him past stone buildings and harbor businesses to what looked to be a worthless refuge.

There was fire in her eyes when she whipped around to face him. She jabbed a finger rapidly in the direction of the cottage, then opened her hand and beckoned furiously for Brady to follow with the child.

Brady snapped another look at the small dwelling, with its crumbling chimney and thatched roof. He wouldn't have been surprised to see it lifted from its very foundation and flung aloft. He gave a violent shake of his head. "Are you daft, girl? We'd be better off in the streets!"

But she had already started off and was leaping over the debris in the street, making her way toward the hut. Brady swallowed a cry of disgust, then followed, tripping over stones and jagged pieces of metal as he pressed the child to himself, all the while wondering why he hadn't simply left both of them standing in the street and saved himself.

4

Terror on the Wind

A great storm from the ocean goes shouting o'er the hill,
And there is glory in it and terror on the wind. . . .
EVA GORE-BOOTH

Terese knew her very life depended on the stone wall withstanding
the wind. The shock of the storm and the cold, slashing rain had
temporarily paralyzed her and dulled her senses. But on the threshold
of her foundering consciousness lurked the awareness that the walls
of Dun Aengus were her only hope.

So she lay, drenched and freezing, clinging to the jagged piece of
rock as if by the very force of her own weight she could anchor it
and herself to the earth. For a time, anger displaced her terror. The
bile of bitterness rose in her throat at both her father and her brother
for their abandonment. But when she tried to scream her rage into
the wind, she found her voice locked inside her, her teeth clenched
in a vise that shot searing flashes of pain through her jaws and up
her temples. Too dazed to think, she could only lie, stricken, in the
darkness, engulfed by the fury and horror of the storm.

Once, she tried to pray, but the effort was futile. In the mind-
numbing terror of the storm and the sheer misery to which her body
was fast succumbing, she could think only of surviving.

Besides, if her aunt Una was right, God was in the midst of this
tempest, in control of the madness that had been unleashed upon the
island this night. Terese felt only outrage at a God who would wreak
such savagery upon the very land and people he had created.

She could not fathom a God of such wanton devastation. She could
not plead with such a God. Certainly, she could not *trust* such a God.

She could only resist him. Her arms tightened about the cold, slippery rock. No doubt her aunt would say that God was the only anchor in the storm, even in a storm such as this. But to Terese, God had somehow *become* the storm. . . . He was in it, over it, all around it, a part of it. Her anchor, her *only* anchor, was this ancient, rugged piece of rock. The rock, at least, she could touch and embrace and cling to.

A low groan now tore from her, a bold, primitive cry in the face of this God of destruction. If she survived this night of horror—and in that moment Terese vowed that survive it she would—then she would know herself capable of surviving anything, and surviving it on her own, without any help from God or anyone else.

Suddenly, the wind hurled what seemed the full force of its fury at her. The gale hammered at her, whipping and slashing, pelting her with hail, pressing her into the earth, yet threatening to sweep her up and over the rocks. Terese shook with such violence she thought all the bones in her body would surely shatter. Blinded by hail and bruised by the merciless wind, she could do nothing but cling to the rock.

At last, she began to scream . . . terrible, wild cries, not of fear, but more of rage—rage, and a desperate, almost savage, shout of defiance. And with each bitter cry, she seemed to absorb the force of the storm, claiming it and making it her own.

Brady felt as if his clothes were being ripped from his back, so fierce was this wind that seemed to have come out of nowhere. He knew about hurricanes only from books, except for what he'd been told by Ransom, the black carriage driver Jack employed, who claimed to have survived such a tempest somewhere in the Caribbean. As he blundered up the path toward the miserable little dwelling that was clearly his guide's destination, he reasoned that this storm could be nothing less than one of those terrifying gales.

As he recalled, a hurricane could supposedly lift a church right off its stone foundation and send it hurtling across town. Yet this wild-eyed young woman thought they would be safe inside that pitiful cottage just ahead.

She was daft, no doubt about it!

Disgusted with himself for following the simpleminded girl to his own destruction, Brady could see nothing for it but to change course and look for more suitable shelter somewhere else. He stopped, digging his heels into the ground against the force of the wind as he looked this way and that. To his dismay, none of the other thatched houses nearby appeared any more substantial than the one in front of him.

He felt a rough yank at his sleeve and looked to find the girl tugging at him, her dark eyes snapping. She began to jabber something at him in the Irish. The word *amadon* was the only thing that registered, and that was because he'd heard Jack apply it to any number of his business acquaintances in New York.

If he wasn't badly mistaken, the word meant "fool."

Brady stood his ground, refusing to follow her into that thatched death trap. The next thing he knew, the wild girl was trying to wrest the child out of his arms, all the while scalding him with her Gaelic diatribe, most of which was immediately swallowed up by the wind.

They were nearly at the house, but they had to struggle mightily now just to keep their footing. Brady still had the child anchored securely in his arms, but his chest felt as if it were about to explode, and fatigue and the battering wind were threatening to bring him down at any moment. He knew they had no time to lose, so when the girl would not be deterred, he gave in and followed her.

At that instant, a towering hulk of a man, lantern in hand, appeared in the doorway of the cottage. He looked to be hewn from stone, a colossus with hard, craggy features and a rugged frame, a full head of jet black hair laced with silver, and a riot of black beard. It struck Brady that all the behemoth needed was a pike in his hand and he could have easily been taken for one of the ancient warrior-chiefs who had once gone roaring into battle sporting little more than a kilt and brandishing a rough-hewn spear.

Without warning, the fierce-looking creature rushed at them, whipping the child out of Brady's arms as if she were no more than a twig and at the same time hauling the older girl to his side. Before Brady could even react, the big fellow hissed something in the Irish at the little girl locked against his chest. She chirped a response, and the man turned a blistering scowl on Brady.

The giant gave the dark-haired girl a tug and moved to turn away, clearly intent on leaving Brady to his own resources. But the girl snapped a quick look over her shoulder, then grabbed the big man's arm, gesturing insistently in Brady's direction.

The man's look dripped suspicion, but with a hard jerk of his head he indicated that Brady should follow. Brady hesitated. There was no telling what might lie in wait inside this great oaf's dwelling.

But then another wall of wind slammed him in the back, shaking him like a rag doll and propelling him forward. He followed the three inside, reasoning blackly that if this was his day to die, he might just as well have a bit of company in the passing.

⁂

Only once did Terese dare raise her head to look about her. Wicked bolts of lightning still pierced the night with abandon, but even with the intermittent light she could scarcely make out her surroundings through the wind-tossed sheets of ice and rain.

The stones and ground were glazed with sleet, as were her own face and hands. Even her hair felt stiff and weighted with a thin layer of ice. Still clinging to the stone, she pulled herself up just enough to look toward town. A hail of icy rain struck her like a whipsaw, slashing her skin. She cried out in pain, then screamed again at the sight of a table, all four legs intact, scudding across the fort only to be dashed to pieces against one of the taller stones.

Lightning knifed the sea, the fort, the cliff, revealing momentary glimpses of things Terese would have expected to see only in night-mares. Boats had been smashed to pieces, their debris now bobbing wildly in the water. A poor, terrified hen, feathers plucked from its body, went screeching into the sea, carried by the wind. Torn rem-nants of clothing whipped across the shoreline like a macabre parade of boneless corpses. Other objects flew by: crockery, bits of wood, clumps of sod and thatch, shrubbery ripped free of its roots—even animals, pathetic, broken creatures swept up from the earth and flung out upon the night.

Terese knew she was weeping, but her tears were lost in the down-pour of sleet and rain cascading over her upturned face. When a vicious blast of wind seized her, her hands slipped free of her stone anchor. Panic barreled through her, but she clambered to regain her hold, fastening herself once more to the ancient rock of Dun Aengus.

Still the baleful wind continued to shriek and hurl its wrath, as if hell itself had been loosed and would this night claim not only its own but whatever innocent might chance upon the march of its deadly destruction.

⁂

As Brady passed through the open door into the small dwelling, he was surprised—and vastly relieved—to note the thickness of the walls, far sturdier than they had seemed upon first glance. Inside, the cottage was not quite as wretched as he might have imagined—but it didn't miss by far.

There looked to be no more than two rooms, partitioned by a

curtain that hung between them. He saw only one window, and this too narrow to allow much light. No doubt the place would be gloomy both night and day. A beeswax candle burned weakly in the middle of a deal table, and the wild flickering of the flame revealed the force of the draft blowing through cracks in the walls.

Brady took in the furnishings in one quick sweep. The turf fire, flanked by stone benches, had been allowed to go out; no doubt this break in tradition was in deference to the dangerous wind. There was a painted dresser of surprisingly good craftsmanship, two three-legged stools, a wicker basket half-filled with potatoes, and a good-sized but badly sagging bed pushed against one wall. The floor was dirt, but well swept. In one corner was a pool of water, apparently the result of a leak in the thatched roof above.

He had seen enough of the cottages of the poor to imagine that beyond the curtain probably lay little more than a straw pallet or two, covered with thin blankets for the girls. He heard a scurry in the corner nearest the hearth and saw three or four chickens scratching in the dirt. It had taken him a long time to grow accustomed to the sight of fowl or pigs inside even some of the better Irish dwellings, but now he found the sight strangely comforting, as if this sign of domesticity meant the inhabitants might not be quite so peculiar after all. It was clearly the home of poor but ordinary people, not a charnel house where unsuspecting sojourners might disappear.

He was allowed little time to appraise his surroundings, however, for once inside, the big fellow shoved the table out of the way and drew up a large, wooden slab door from the dirt. He said nothing but merely made a sharp gesture to the girl and the child, then to Brady, that they should all descend.

A huge wave of relief washed over Brady. They were going below ground! It seemed that his guardian angel had not abandoned him entirely!

Thick walls aside, the little house was shaking like a creature caught up in the grip of a violent palsy. Brady hurried to join the others. When he would have stopped long enough to offer a word of gratitude to the man holding the door, the unfriendly giant froze him with a dark glare and an impatient snap of his head. Those cold blue eyes left no doubt whatsoever that he thought Brady a fool—an un-welcome one, at that—and that Brady's bid to share their under-ground shelter was granted grudgingly.

Despite the man's churlishness, Brady gave a quick nod of thanks as he prepared to descend a hemp ladder leading below. At the instant he turned to lower himself into the pit, a screaming blast of wind roared in on the small dwelling. There was a deafening shriek, then a groaning overhead, followed by the terrible sound of something splitting.

Brady hesitated, shooting a glance upward only to see the thatched roof begin to rock, then whip madly up and down just before it lifted completely free and went flying off into the furious night. For a split second he locked gazes with the big man holding the slab door open and saw his own terror reflected in that hard blue stare.

He watched the giant reel and stagger, losing his balance in the furious gust of wind that now came howling through the house. The door fell away from those large, rough hands, and in one lightning flash of clarity Brady realized what was about to happen just before the heavy slab came crashing down on his head.

5

The Weary and the Wounded

Solomon! where is thy throne? It is gone in the wind.
Babylon! where is thy might? It is gone in the wind.
Like the swift shadows of Noon, like the dreams of the Blind,
Vanish the glories and pomps of the earth in the wind.

JAMES CLARENCE MANGAN

The madness had gone on until nearly dawn. Even after the storm finally subsided, Terese had remained sealed to her rock of anchor, half-frozen and numb from the relentless battering of the wind and icy rain.

Now she stood on the shore, watching the sea. After the deafening, seemingly endless roar of the storm, the present silence was somehow unnerving. The waves were still turbulent but not so violent now, mostly roiling crests keeping harmony with the morning wind.

The harbor teemed with floating debris: broken boats, dead animals, pieces of furniture, and clumps of shrubbery and other vegetation. All around her, the smell of smoke mixed with the acrid odors of salt water and dead fish.

Exhausted from her night's ordeal and still dazed by the unthinkable devastation she had found upon returning to the village, Terese could do nothing but stand and stare, letting the spray off the ocean bathe her face. The nightmare of the past few hours had totally depleted her, drained her last vestige of strength. Her skin still tingled from the long exposure to the elements, and she felt the onset of a head cold. More than anything else, however, there was merely the somber awareness that the storm had passed, that she had survived it only to find herself more alone than she had ever been in her life.

Behind her, the small village had been nearly decimated. What few houses remained were without roofs. Most had either been burned or leveled or swept away altogether. Many villagers had already declared their intention to go on the road, to make their way to Galway City and seek refuge with relatives. Terese suspected that by the end of the day the town would be virtually deserted, except for those who had vowed to stay and rebuild. As to whether these few were brave or merely foolish, she couldn't say. She knew only that she did not intend to remain with them.

She turned slowly away from the sea and stood staring at the village. There was nothing there for her. Her aunt's house had been razed, crushed to random heaps of thatch and rubble. Like countless others, the entire family was now homeless.

Aunt Una had wasted no time in announcing, with an unmistakable hint of spite in her tone, that Terese need not expect to accompany the rest of the family to Galway, where they would shelter for a time with Uncle Felim's aging parents. No doubt by now they had already started off, and without so much as a final farewell.

Earlier, her mild, subservient uncle had made a halfhearted attempt to assuage his conscience by seeking out Terese to explain. "You understand, lass? The old man and woman, they haven't the room for us as it is, much less yourself. Your aunt is fearful lest they turn us all away."

Terese had never found it in her to either like or dislike her uncle. Even though he was the only member of the household to favor her with a kind word now and then, he was so cowed by his wife that he always seemed a mere shadow of a man. She could not respect him, and so she could not feel any real affection for him. Most of the time, she held no more than a faint contempt for him, tempered only slightly by the awareness that Uncle Felim was not a bad man, really, nor an unfeeling man. He was simply a weak man.

Terese had no use for weakness.

So even though she was trembling inside at the time, she had brushed off his feigned concern, telling him she would manage well enough, that he was not to worry. "I'm seventeen years old, after all. 'Tis time for me to be on my own."

"You won't be holding it against us, then?" he said, glancing around as if to make certain his wife was well out of earshot.

Terese assured him that, far from holding it against them, she thought things would work out perfectly fine for her. She carefully refrained from divulging her plans to go to America, however; if they suspected that she had money put aside, they would be after her like starving dogs at a kill.

Now, as she watched the procession of the displaced that had already begun to file out of the village, their few remaining worldly goods tied upon their backs, she wondered if Galway might also have been struck by the past night's storm. Was there any cause to believe that the evil wind had confined its destruction to Inishmore?

Well, then, and what of it? America was her destination, and the sooner the better. So long as there was a harbor where she could board a ship, she was not long for this wretched island.

If she felt a prickling of fear at the thought of launching into such an adventure alone, she suppressed it. In the aftermath of the storm, her friend Peggy had decided she could not leave her family now. Her father had hurt his back, and her mother, she said, could do nothing but stand and weep; she must stay and help however she could.

At first, Terese had been angry, and they had exchanged bitter words. But not for long. She had no strength left to waste on anger. Besides, Peggy was only doing what she thought she must do, after all. And it would be *her* loss, would it not? She would be the one left to Ireland's mean poverty while Terese went on to prosper in America.

She could fend for herself well enough. She had her wits, the dress on her back—a dry one, thanks to Peggy, whose personal belongings had fared somewhat better than Terese's—and the money she had buried in the ground behind the henhouse. She needed nothing more, at least not for now. Once she reached Galway, she would try to purchase a better dress for the crossing. But for the present, she looked as respectable as anyone else she was likely to encounter this day.

Stooping, she retrieved her weathered *pampootas*—her shoes—and slipped them on. Earlier she had found a piece of a shawl, which she now knotted about her shoulders, savoring the warmth against the chill air. Finally, she cinched the *crios*—the bright sash she had made for herself—at her waist and lifted her face for one final look at the towering eminence of her old friend and protector, Dun Aengus.

Then, squaring her shoulders, she turned her back on her past and went in search of a shovel.

Pain.

Hard, red explosions of it in his head, down his neck . . .

Brady had been dreaming that he was standing on a bleak shore, alone and shivering as he suffered the attack of dark-featured sailors who hurled massive stones at him from a ship that bobbed up and down in the bay.

Behind him and all around, there was nothing but barren land. No houses, no shops, no trees, and no people. The unknown waters were silent, as were the sailors on their battleship. Nothing broke the stillness except for the splitting of his skull beneath the onslaught of the stones. . . .

He felt nothing but the pain as the sound of whispering crept in on him, prodding him awake—short, harsh whispers and utterances he couldn't make out. Meaning to ease the pain, he tried to turn but stopped, gasping as a white-hot bolt of agony shot through his skull.

Someone was holding his hand. He felt the warmth, the slight pressure. He forced his eyes open, groaning as the dim, flickering light set off another sharp wrench of pain in his head.

On a stool close beside him sat a dark-eyed little girl, gripping his hand. When she saw him turn toward her, she smiled.

Brady stared at her, recognition gradually dawning. The fey child squeezed his hand as if to encourage him.

He blinked several times against the pain as his eyes finally began to focus. He was in a cold, dark hole of a room, the air thick with dust and mildew. He could make out a slight, womanly figure in the corner, bent low as she rolled what looked to be a piece of cloth. She glanced up at the tall, dark form hovering over her and murmured something in the Irish.

Brady tried to speak, but when he opened his mouth nothing came, only a blinding slam of pain at his temples and the back of his head.

Again, the child pumped his hand a little, then turned to the others and chirped something at them. The hulking form emerged out of the shadows and stood scowling down at Brady. Memory rushed in on him, driving through his confusion: the storm, the violent wind, the rickety little house—the heavy door crashing down on his head.

His ears rang, and nausea surged in him, then ebbed. He touched his head and became very still. Bandages swathed his forehead and a portion of his skull. He wondered how bad his injuries were. He tried to sit up, but a hand the size of a bound book thrust him back.

He stared up into the dark-skinned face looming over him, realizing now that the granite-visaged man was younger than he had thought upon first sight of him. Younger, but a hard man all the same, he sensed, harder even than Jack, who had his soft spots once you knew him. He doubted that this towering stranger in his garb of homespun had many soft spots.

Brady wanted to ask what time it was, if it was night or day, then remembered that these people spoke the Irish. Though he might recognize bits and pieces of the old language from Jack, he didn't know enough of it to communicate.

He glanced over at the older girl and saw her watching him, but she made no move to rise from her place in the corner. The child finally released Brady's hand but stayed seated at his side, her curious gaze following his slightest movement.

"'Tis a bad blow. The door fell square on top of your head. You will need to lie still for now."

Startled by the deep, resonant voice and even more by the English, Brady gaped at the man. "You speak English?"

The man merely lifted one dark brow at Brady's surprise. "Who are you?" he bit out. Something in that drumroll of a voice seemed to carry a hint of a threat.

Still taken aback, it took Brady a moment to recover. "Kane," he finally replied. "Brady Kane."

The other's eyes narrowed slightly. "American."

In one clipped word, the black-bearded giant had managed to convey a monumental contempt.

"Irish American," Brady shot back, his head throbbing with the effort.

The man's expression didn't change, and Brady had all he could do not to squirm under the full force of that burning stare. "The girl says you helped with the wee wane," he said, giving a small jerk of his head in the child's direction.

"They were more help to me than I to them," Brady offered. "I might have been blown out to sea if they hadn't come along and led me here."

"What would you be doing in the Claddagh, Yank?" Something about the way the giant flung the words at him made Brady feel as if he had committed some sort of heinous offense simply by showing up in Galway.

Weak as he was, he refused to be intimidated by this bad-tempered Irishman. "Business," he said, grimacing at the furry thickness of his tongue. "I'm here on business."

His interrogator crossed his massive arms over the broad expanse of his chest. "And what sort of business would it be that brings a

rich Yank to Galway City? It's a poor, backward people we are, after
all.''

Brady found himself wondering if that mocking brogue might not
be somewhat affected. He had caught a glint behind that hostile stare
of what appeared to be a keen wit, perhaps even a formidable intelligence. Was the man deliberately goading him? But if so, why?

"Newspaper business," Brady answered. "An assignment of
sorts." He paused, deliberating as to how much he ought to tell this
stone-faced stranger.

The man's gaze held steady for a moment more. Finally, he lifted
one large hand and gave a tug to the kerchief about his neck, twisting
his mouth as if Brady merited no further interest. "Are you seeing
me clearly, Yank?" he snapped with a sudden change of subject.
"Any blurring of your vision at all?"

Brady shook his head, instantly regretting the movement. Pain
struck his skull like a well-sharpened ax, and he couldn't stop a groan
of protest.

"Be easy," said the other. "There was no real damage done, I'm
thinking. You'll be fit enough in a day or so. But for now, you'd
best lie abed." His tone left no doubt that he found the situation less
than desirable.

"Where—what is this?" Brady asked, glancing around the dark
room.

"You've never seen a cellar before, Yank?"

Brady twisted his lip, again irked by the man's seeming dismissal
of him as a fool. "What time is it?" he hurried to ask before the
other could turn away.

"'Tis morning. Well past first light. The storm has gone, but we
will stay below for a time, all the same."

"Your house—"

"It still stands, except for the roof."

Brady glanced at the girl in the corner, who had turned back to
her occupation with the bolt of cloth on her lap. "I'd like to thank
her," he told the man hovering over him. "I don't even know her
name." He paused. "Nor yours."

The giant's eyes went hard as stone. "Don't be making more of
it than it is," he said, his tone harsh. "The girl is soft. She would
bring a wolf into the house if the beast followed her home."

His dark look seemed to imply that perhaps this was exactly what
had happened. Caught off guard by this unexpected rudeness, Brady
could manage no response.

The man started to turn, then stopped. "She can't hear you when you speak," he said, the words hard as driven nails. "The girl is deaf."

The giant walked away without another word, leaving Brady to stare at his back. After another moment, he again felt a small hand close about his own and looked to find the child watching him. She squeezed his hand, then mouthed a word he didn't catch.

He frowned at her, and she spoke again. "Gabriel," she said clearly, giving a jerk of her head toward the big man who had planted himself on a stool near the older girl. "His name is Gabriel." She pronounced it *Gah-brul.*

"I'm Evie. Eveleen," she added smartly. "And that—" she nodded toward the older girl in the corner—"is Roweena."

So the child also spoke English. He wouldn't have expected as much. The books had led him to believe that most of the Claddagh's fishermen and their families spoke only the Irish, and he had already heard much of the old tongue in the streets of Galway.

"Roweena," Brady repeated, studying the child. "She's your sister, is she?"

The little girl shook her head. "Gabriel found her. Her was lost, like me."

The child's speech was remarkably clear for one so young. "I don't understand," he said. "What do you mean, lost?"

She pursed her lips. "Lost, don't you know? I was put out, but Roweena, her was in a fire when she was a babe. Most everyone died, except Roweena."

Brady dragged his gaze from the dark-haired girl in the shadows back to the child. "So, then—this man, Gabriel, he's not your father?"

Again the child shook her head. "We don't have a da, Roweena and me. We have Gabriel."

The man snapped something at the child just then, his words cracking like a whiplash. The little girl pressed her rosy lips into a tight line but couldn't seem to resist explaining. "Gabriel says I'm not to blather, that I must leave you to your rest," she whispered hurriedly, leaning closer to Brady. "I will thank Roweena for you."

Brady reached out to stop her. "Wait. He said the girl's deaf, yet she speaks."

The child—Evie—regarded him as if he were dim-witted. "Her's clever, Roweena is," she said with a trace of childish indignation. "Gabriel taught her to talk. Like this." She framed the small column of her throat with both hands and worked her jaw up and down.

Still confused about the relationship of the two girls and the grim-faced giant, Brady glanced across the room, where Gabriel was now holding the bolt of cloth while the girl wrapped it over and over again.

After a moment he turned back to the child. "You live here with him, then?" he asked. "You and . . . Roweena?"

She nodded. A quick grin revealed a noticeable gap where both front teeth should have been. "Gabriel is our angel," she said matter-of-factly.

Brady stared at her. "Your angel?"

She nodded vigorously. "Roweena says Gabriel is like God's angel who looks after us and keeps us safe."

While he knew very little about angels, Brady could not imagine a less likely example of one than the dour colossus who sat scowling at him from his shadowy corner across the room.

Near the remains of Aunt Una's house, Terese found a shovel, its handle broken down almost to a nub. Gripping what was left of it with both hands, she went at her task with a vengeance, lifting the dirt away.

By the time she reached the pouch that contained her secret savings, she was in a fever. Her ordeal of the night before had left her more shaken than she cared to consider. She was intent only on retrieving her money so she could be on her way while the morning was still calm—in the event that the wind should come back.

She drew in a ragged breath. The pouch was intact, still neatly tied, just as she'd left it. She gave the shovel a toss and with shaking hands lifted her treasure from its nest in the ground.

The moment she touched it, she knew. Her hands began to tremble so violently that she could scarcely untie the string.

She upended the pouch, then sat staring at what was left of her years of saving. Not quite two dollars. There had been nearly twenty when last she counted it only three nights past. Twenty American dollars.

Every hope of her heart drained slowly out of her. She felt as empty as if her lifeblood had been sucked from her body.

Aunt Una.

She knew immediately who had stolen from her. No doubt her aunt had watched her at some time in the middle of the night, when she had gone to check the pouch or to add the latest sum from Cavan.

Two dollars would not take her to America.

She didn't know how long she sat there, hunched over the hole in the ground, rubbing her fingers over the pouch as if it were something that had once lived but was now cold and lifeless. Anything could have transpired about her, and she wouldn't have known. She heard no sound save the beating of her own heavy heart, felt nothing but a sick disgust at her own carelessness.

After a long time, she blinked and looked about at her desolate surroundings. Gone. Everything was gone. And she should have been gone, too, gone from Inishmore.

She should have known her aunt would snoop. She should have taken more precautions, hidden the money farther away from the house, even taken it to Dun Aengus—

No! This wasn't her fault. *She* wasn't the thief. *She* hadn't robbed her own kin, hadn't spied on her own blood in order to commit so vile a deed.

Slowly, she came to her feet, propelled by a fierce surge of rage rushing up within her. What—or *who*—was responsible for the misery, the injustice of her life, the trouble that had plagued her ever since she was a wee wane?

Her mother would have claimed it was the will of God, that Terese must "persevere" and "endure the Lord's chastening." Aunt Una, no doubt, would blame the devil, would say that old Satan himself was behind life's mischief and torments, working to discourage and destroy "the innocent."

Aye, and if that be the case, then, sure, her deceitful aunt was one of the devil's own helpmates.

Terese didn't know who to blame, but she desperately needed to blame *someone*. Someone should answer for the wretchedness of her life, shouldn't he? And for the lives of so many others. Someone had to be responsible.

With a sudden cry of fury, she lifted the near-empty pouch toward heaven. "You won't stop me!" she screamed. Without knowing the real object of her rage, she went on screaming into the hushed morning. "Whoever you are ... wherever you are, I'm going, do you hear? I am leaving this wretched island, and I am never coming back! I'm going, and there is nothing you can do to stop me!"

She fell silent as quickly as she had given vent to her rage, gasping for breath and clutching the pouch close to her heart. "I'm going," she announced again, this time in a whisper. Then she turned from the empty hole in the ground and walked away.

6

Jack

Brother, son, beloved one,
Your absence mocks my heart.

ANONYMOUS

NEW YORK CITY, MID-FEBRUARY

The sun had yet to rise as Jack Kane sat in his study, outlining ideas
for his editorial. Most of his time was spent on the business end of
the newspaper, but he had refused to relinquish the editorial page. If
there was one thing an Irishman enjoyed more than politics and pretty
women, he was fond of saying, it was spouting his opinions. If he
happened to be in a position where he could inflict those opinions on
an entire city, so much the better.

These early hours before dawn had always been Jack's favorite
time of the day. He relished the quiet, the stillness of the house before
Addy set the kitchen help to stirring and started her morning forays
in search of offending dust mites. Normally, Ransom would be showing up in another hour or so. Although he knew full well Jack never
left for the office before seven-thirty, the crafty old stableman always
came early with the sole intent of enjoying a biscuit or two and a
slice of ham. No doubt he would be thoroughly put out by Jack's
instructions not to arrive before noon today.

Jack was having a hard time concentrating this morning. His feelings about the city being "overrun with filthy, debauched immigrants"—as asserted in an anonymous letter received by the paper
earlier in the week—were somewhat difficult to express, given the
fact that "filthy, debauched immigrants" referred almost exclusively
to the Irish.

Even though there were twenty-five years and an ocean between Jack and old Ireland, he tried never to deceive himself: He was as Irish as any of those poor souls who made up the city's plague of poverty. So even though he had tried for balance in his current editorial, he'd ended up scratching most of it out, recognizing that the tone was far too defensive, even petulant. No doubt he sounded a bit like an irascible drunk.

Perhaps he should simply ignore the diatribe this anonymous writer had directed at the refugees pouring into New York Harbor. Nothing chafed a small, self-important man more than being ignored, after all.

He got up and went to stand at the window. The street lamps were still flickering, casting only enough light to reveal shadows from the large old trees and ornamental fences that fronted Thirty-fourth Street's gracious mansions. A trace of snow from the night frosted the street, while tree limbs swaying in the wind promised another bitterly cold day.

The stirring of the wind took his thoughts to Brady. Ever since word had come of the devastating storm that struck Ireland in early January, Jack had tried to convince himself that his precocious brother, always resourceful, would fare perfectly well, even in a hurricane. Even so, if he didn't hear from the young jackanapes soon, he was going to send one of the lads from the paper across to look him up.

His brother's infuriating recklessness, his inclination to think only of the moment—and only of *himself,* Jack reflected with a sour twist of his mouth—was nothing new. It never seemed to occur to Brady that people worried. Under normal circumstances, Jack wouldn't have been alarmed if no word arrived for weeks at a time. But surely Brady realized that news of the storm would have reached the States by now. The least the irresponsible whelp could do was drop a post as to his whereabouts and his circumstances.

He turned away from the window and crossed the room to stoke the fire. The study was one of the smallest rooms in the drafty old house and as such should have been one of the warmest. But the ceiling was high enough to clear an oak tree, and the windows were anything but tight; consequently, there was always a chill.

Poker in hand, he straightened and turned his back to the fire. Of late, he had given an occasional thought to selling the place. He had bought the rambling old horror a few years past on a whim. At the time, he had still been young enough—and crass enough—to enjoy flaunting his success. An Irish upstart with a bank account large enough to stake his claim on Thirty-fourth Street was a scandal and an affront, and he had thoroughly enjoyed outraging the gentry nearby with his "vulgarity."

But now the sprawling old mansion, by the very fact of its immensity and flamboyance, was almost an embarrassment. Certainly, it was an annoyance, and an expensive, inconvenient one, at that. Yet he was loath to give it up because it was the first home he had ever owned. Besides, he still rather fancied the idea of offending the carriage trade.

Black Jack Kane: a pig plopped down in a palace, he thought with a grin.

Still grinning, he glanced at his pocket watch when Addy appeared in the doorway. As usual, she had given him no more than thirty minutes alone. The woman couldn't seem to endure a man having himself a bit of peace and quiet.

Jack feigned a scowl at her. Unmoved, she stood, hands on angular hips, square jaw thrust forward, black eyes snapping.

"A pity you won't stay abed like most respectable men," the Irish housekeeper challenged. "No doubt we're the only household above the Bowery that serves breakfast before sunup."

"Don't start on me, woman. Even if I slept until noon, you'd still come prowling about before dawn, just so you'd have something to harp on."

As was always the case, his contrived crossness didn't faze her. "Didn't you say you weren't going to the office this morning?" she reminded him, the perfect point of her slate gray widow's peak puckering with disapproval.

"I did."

"Well, now, had you told me you'd changed your mind, I'd have seen that your breakfast was ready earlier."

"Did I say I had changed my mind?"

She glared at him. "And why else would you be all slicked up at this hour of the day?"

"As it happens, you sour old woman, I am *not* going to the office this morning. But I do have appointments *here,* beginning at ten."

The dark brows arched, and the hatchet jaw lifted a notch more. "Appointments, is it? Here at the house?"

Jack nodded, replaced the poker, and went back to his desk. "I'm seeing applicants for the driver's position. You can show them in here one at a time as they arrive. I thought I'd see them here so if I find a likely candidate he can have a look at the stables."

She tightened her mouth. "No telling what sort will show up, I expect."

Jack bent over the desk and began stacking his papers to the side. "Don't worry a bit, Addy," he said straight-faced. "There's a gun right here in the top drawer. Naturally, I'll protect your virtue with my life."

He glanced up and saw her narrow her eyes. The dear invariably narrowed her eyes when she was bent on baiting him. Addy was nothing if not predictable.

"And what's to become of old Ransom, the poor man? You'll be sending him out on his keeping with the ragpickers, I suppose."

Jack bared his teeth at her. "You know perfectly well that Ransom has asked for a position here in the house. Faith, woman, he must be at least a century or more by now, wouldn't you say? He's only a step short of being crippled by rheumatism, and he's all but deaf. We could be run down in the street by a stampede of horses, and he'd never hear them until they'd flattened us." He paused. "He will work as a handyman about the house from now on."

The housekeeper made a short sound of disgust. "Handyman, indeed! The old fool is about as handy as a drunken sailor."

"You'd know more about drunken sailors than I, you outrageous woman," Jack said evenly as he went to the door. "I believe I will have my breakfast now, Addy. If you please."

She sniffed and started off ahead of him. The tight little bun at the back of her neck didn't budge—Jack half suspected that she anchored it with chicken wire in the mornings—as she took off down the hall toward the kitchen, muttering to herself all the way.

Jack smiled as he followed, knowing full well that she was smiling, too—rather like a she-wolf at the thought of its next kill.

Addy O'Meara had been with Jack since he and Martha rented their first flat, after their marriage. Formerly a part of Martha's household, Addy had come to assist the newlyweds—and never left. She had nursed Martha through the long months of illness that ended in death two years later, all the while helping Jack to raise "the wee brother"—Brady, who in truth was more son to Jack than brother—with an eagle eye, a firm hand, and an Irish mother's heart.

Addy had been mother, friend, and confidant for so many years that Jack no longer thought of her in any other way except as family, and he quite simply could not imagine life without her.

Unfortunately for him, the cantankerous old woman was well aware of the fact.

7

An Encounter between the Strong and the Strong

And because I am of the people, I understand the people,
I am sorrowful with their sorrow,
I am hungry with their desire. . . .

PADRAIC PEARSE

Cavan Sheridan stood, cap in hand, studying the fine room into which the prickly housekeeper had directed him. "The *Study*," she had called it, her Irish tongue lingering on the word as if the study were a holy place. "Mr. Kane will see you in the *Study*."

The room was spacious but not immense. The quiet decor was a surprising contrast to the somewhat gilded furnishings he had glimpsed beyond the open doors flanking the great marble corridor. The windows were shrouded in velvet, but the draperies had been drawn to admit the weak morning light. Green damask covered the walls in those places where there were no bookshelves, and Cavan had a sense of a forest retreat, dense and calm and sheltered. The man who had chosen the sturdy furniture of leather and rosewood, the fine paneling that gleamed like aged honey, and the thick, richly textured carpet that silenced each footfall would be a man who favored comfort over luxury, he mused—contentment and warmth over opulence.

The room didn't fit the stories he had heard about Black Jack Kane.

Although he'd been in New York City for only six weeks, Cavan had already heard numerous tales—some conflicting—about the "Irish black bear" who allegedly showed no restraint in flaunting the wealth and power of his newspaper empire. Depending on who happened to be giving the account, Kane might be depicted as a rogue, a scoundrel, an upstart, an infidel—or a genius. Some described him as ruthless, others as arrogant, wily, and cold-blooded. Most, however, tended to agree that, whatever else he might happen to be, Kane was brilliant.

At the sound of a soft whistling outside the door, Cavan turned. His curiosity had heightened to the point that he had all he could do not to gape at the man who entered the room. Kane's acknowledging nod was neither condescending nor rude, but strangely cavalier—as if he had more important things on his mind than this interview but intended to be good-natured about it all the same.

For a moment he stood behind the desk, fixing Cavan with a gaze too dark to register any hint of emotion. Kane was younger than Cavan had expected, given the man's colorful reputation and the influence he apparently wielded; he might have been forty, but scarcely more. And if he was indeed the rascal he was reputed to be, his appearance was deceiving. Where Cavan had anticipated a middle-aged, overweight swell with the florid face of one accustomed to excess, Jack Kane was tall and trim—a dark, lean man with an air of hard elegance and the arrogant good looks of the black Irish.

Cavan, who at an inch or two over six feet seldom found himself at eye level with other men, noted that Kane probably topped him by another inch or so. Below the coal black mustache, Kane had the long lip of the Irish. His not-quite-swarthy skin and raven hair bespoke a trace of Spanish descent seen mostly in the west of Ireland.

Cavan had done his homework on his prospective employer. He knew that Kane, an orphan, had come across while still a boy, along with a younger brother and sister. According to rumor, he had attained his present level of success by a combination of hard work, an almost legendary shrewdness, and a brassy kind of courage that took chances most men would run from. In less than two decades, Jack Kane had risen from sweeping floors at an upstairs print shop on Chatham Street to an apprentice position, eventually going on to become the owner and publisher of one of the country's largest, most influential newspapers. There was also speculation about a political career in the making. Despite his youthful appearance, the man was practically a legend.

Cavan meant to be "the legend's" newest employee. He had been without funds for nearly a week now, had not eaten more than a few stale crusts of bread in all that time, and was virtually reeling on his feet. The latest in a series of temporary odd jobs had ended nearly two weeks past; since then he'd been sleeping in alleys among the newsboys and ragpickers, using discarded papers to ward off the wind.

He was desperate, indeed had never wanted or needed anything quite so much as this job with Kane's newspaper. At the moment, it represented the difference between starvation and survival.

Yet, as his eyes met and held the black gaze of Jack Kane, it was something more than desperation that fueled his resolve to work for Kane's paper, the *Vanguard.* In a way he couldn't have begun to define, Cavan sensed that the man across the desk from him held the power to change his life, to offer him something more than a respite from hunger and humiliation.

He had been hoping, searching, praying for this moment—his crossroads, as he had come to think of it—since he was a small boy. He had always known he would recognize it when he came upon it.

Now that it was here, he knew he must hurry to claim it before it slipped away.

⚜

Jack was curious and even a little amused to feel himself scrutinized as thoroughly as if he were the applicant rather than the employer.

The lad had brass, that much was plain.

The boy had caught his interest immediately. He was almost as tall as Jack himself, with shoulders broad enough to balance his height, even though his frame was all angles and sharp turns. In truth, he looked as if he had not sat down to a full meal in a very long time, if ever. But it was the fiery glint of intelligence behind that startling blue gaze that intrigued Jack.

"The name's Sheridan, sir," the youth volunteered. "Cavan Sheridan."

"And where are you from, Cavan Sheridan?" Jack asked him, at the same time glancing down at the surprisingly legible handwriting on the paper the youth had thrust at him.

"Pennsylvania, sir."

Jack glanced up. "What in the world are you doing in New York?"

The boy shrugged but made no reply.

"On the lam, are you?" Jack pressed.

The other bristled visibly. "No, sir! Nothing like that."

The accent was right out of the west: western Ireland. One of the islands, more than likely. "Then why did you leave Pennsylvania?"

"To get out of the mines." The brogue thickened perceptibly. "I couldn't stay in the mines."

Jack felt an unexpected softening within. He knew a fair amount about the conditions the country's coal miners worked under—abominable conditions, for the most part. His eyes went to the thin scar that traced the right side of Sheridan's face, from eyebrow to long, lean jaw. "Got yourself banged up a bit, did you?"

The youth hesitated, then nodded. "There was a cave-in. Broke my shoulder and my collarbone. But I would have left the mines in any event."

"How old are you, lad?"

"Nearly twenty, sir."

Older than Jack would have thought. Perhaps because of the lanky frame or the light band of freckles running across his nose, Sheridan looked scarcely more than a boy. Or was it something in those unsettling blue eyes? Some hint of vulnerability that didn't quite go with the hard line of the mouth or the scar.

Jack studied the youth for another moment, then motioned him to a chair. "How long did you work the mines?" he said, sitting down at the desk.

The wide mouth tightened. "Since I was fifteen, sir."

"That's a bit young for such a place."

"Not really, sir," Sheridan said, hesitating another second or two before lowering his long frame into the chair across from Jack. "Lots of boys go down before they're ten."

Jack leaned back, locking his hands behind his head. "Can't imagine that's much of a life."

Sheridan's gaze darkened, and the earlier hint of youthfulness and vulnerability seemed to fade. "No, sir. It's not. In truth, it's no life at all."

Jack studied him. "You're from the islands," he said, making it more statement than question.

Sheridan looked surprised. "Aye, sir. The Big Island."

"Inishmore?"

The lad nodded.

"How long since you left?"

"I was thirteen when I came across, sir."

Jack had been fourteen. At the time he had believed himself to be a man. Now he realized how very young he had been. "So—you've been here in New York for how long?"

Sheridan sat on the edge of the chair, large hands knotted on his knees. He looked stiff and uncomfortable with his surroundings, Jack noted.

"Not long, sir. A few weeks is all."

"Where are you staying?" Jack could almost anticipate the answer. He knew all too well where penniless immigrants kept themselves when they had no place to go. New York could be brutal to its poor, relegating them to the worst of its slums or the mean streets themselves.

The boy glanced away, looking more awkward than ever. Something pricked at Jack's heart. "I've been down that road myself, lad," he said gruffly. "There's no shame in it."

Sheridan expelled a long breath. "I'll have me a place, once I hire on somewhere."

Jack lowered his arms, took a cheroot from its box, and lighted it. "I'd be interested in knowing what qualifies you to be my driver."

Sheridan wiped his hands over his knees, first one, then the other. "I drove the coal wagons at the mines for the past two years, sir. I'm a good driver. I'm strong and do well with the horses."

Jack's eyes flicked to the youth's hands, large and chapped, with a faint residue of coal dust under the nails. In spite of his leanness, the lad did give the appearance of strength, even a kind of restrained power.

"Not exactly the same thing as driving a buggy," Jack pointed out.

Sheridan leaned forward still more. "More than likely, you'll be seeing a fair number of applicants for this job, Mr. Kane. But you won't be finding one better suited, and that's the truth." He paused. "I'd also be good to have around in the event of trouble."

"Well, now, I'm not hiring a bodyguard, lad. It's a driver I'm needing." Jack heard his own brogue slip out but made no effort to curb it. It came and went, and nothing evoked it so much as a fit of temper or a boy, like this one, fresh off the boat.

"Still, I'm the best man."

"Sure of yourself, eh? That's all right. No harm in it, unless there's nothing but air behind the starch." Jack considered him for a long moment. "Tell me the truth now, lad: Are you running from the law? I'll find out soon enough, so don't lie to me. I don't hire trouble. It finds me easily enough as it is."

Sheridan shook his head with convincing vehemence. "I'm in no trouble, and I'll be bringing you none, Mr. Kane. All I'm wanting is an honest job and a fair wage."

"Are you a drinker?"

Again the youth shook his head. "No, sir. I can find better ways to spend my wages."

"Curse of our people," Jack muttered, as much to himself as to young Sheridan. He held a bitter resentment toward the gross exaggerations of his countrymen's drinking habits, yet he was forced to acknowledge that the caricatures were not without some substance. Many of the Irish *did* drink to excess, there was no denying it. They drank to drown their troubles and their sorrows, seemingly blind to the fact that they were only borrowing even more grief for themselves and their loved ones.

To Jack, the whiskey was a beast—a beast that fed upon the soul as much as the body. For that reason, he had not lifted a glass of the stuff in over twenty years. Nor would he knowingly hire a man who couldn't stay out of his cups. It was his contention that if a fellow couldn't control his appetites, whatever they happened to be, he could not be relied upon as an employee.

He looked at Sheridan. "The job pays four dollars a week."

Actually, he had been prepared to offer only three, but something in the rangy youth sitting across from him prompted a more generous figure. "You would be required to either live here, on the premises, or remain as late as you're needed each night—which wouldn't usually be very late at all, but on occasion could run past midnight. You could take your meals here, in the kitchen, so long as you're on time and don't inconvenience the cook."

"I could stay here?"

Jack noted the quickening of interest and nodded. "There's a comfortable room above the stables. You could have that, if you like. My present stableman, who'll still be coming in to help out some about the house, has his own quarters elsewhere."

"Are you offering me the job, then, sir?"

There was no mistaking the eagerness in his eyes, the hunger. Not only hunger for a decent meal—though that, too, no doubt—but hunger for opportunity. Perhaps in a way, Jack thought, it was a hunger for hope itself.

"You be straight with me, lad," he said sternly, deftly shifting his cigar from one side of his mouth to the other. "Is there anything else I ought to know about you? Any reason at all I shouldn't hire you?"

Sheridan seemed to consider the question carefully. His reply was a surprise. "I left the church," he finally said.

Whatever Jack might have expected, it certainly wasn't this. "Indeed," he said evenly.

The boy nodded. "I couldn't stomach the way the priests treated the miners. Some of the men tried to protest the terrible conditions in the mines, the way the owners took advantage. Working us like mules from before dawn to long past dark, threatening our jobs if we so much as made a complaint, attaching our wages—why, by the time many a man picked up his pay, there was often so much held out for 'payment of accounts' that *he* owed the *company*. After all that backbreaking work, he would go home to his family empty-handed!"

There was no mistaking the anger, the outrage in the youth as he went on. "But when the men began to protest, the priests would have none of it. Labeled those who spoke out as 'troublemakers'; gave them a thorough tongue-lashing in front of the entire parish."

"Would I be right in assuming that not all of these protests were of a peaceful nature?" Jack put in.

Sheridan delayed his answer, but when it came Jack felt it was truthful. "Well, some of the men did get a bit more . . . physical with their objections, pulling rough stuff on the property, the mine offices. No one got hurt, mind, but it made the priests wild. They called the men out at mass, made spectacles of them, thoroughly denounced them."

"You could hardly expect a priest to condone violence," Jack pointed out.

"Aye, that's true. Nor do I. But it wasn't right, the way the priests went after those men. They did their best to demoralize their own people." He paused. "At least, that's how it seemed to me."

"So you broke with the church," Jack prompted.

"I did. As I said, I'm not for violence, Mr. Kane; truly I'm not. But I was in the mines long enough to see why the men are desperate, why they feel forced to fight for their rights. You can't imagine what it's like, breaking your back underground day in, day out, the dank air, the dust, never seeing the light of day—I think that must be what hell is like."

He stopped, releasing a shaky breath as if the memory had choked off his words. When he finally went on, his voice was so low that Jack had to lean forward to hear him. "I didn't leave *God,* you understand, sir, though sure the priests would say I did just that. But it seems to me that God is not the one to blame for the deplorable conditions of the mines and the suffering of the men and their families. 'Tis men, not God, who must bear the shame of that injustice. But I simply couldn't continue to sit and listen to the priests blathering about the slavery of sin while turning a blind eye to another kind of slavery. Most of the miners did what they did in hopes of gaining better conditions for their wives and children. It did seem to me that the priests should have been trying to help the men, not humiliating them or condemning them.''

Jack continued to study the boy for a moment more, then pushed away from the desk. When he stood, Sheridan also drew quickly to his feet. "There's nothing else, then?" Jack said. "Just this business with the church?"

"There's nothing else, sir, and that's the truth."

"Well, what you do with your religion is your own business, Sheridan. As I'm sure anyone would tell you, I'd be a most unlikely man to give you spiritual counsel.'' He came around the desk. "We'll try you for a month to see how it works out. I warn you, my schedule is often erratic—I'll expect you to be ready at a moment's notice and with no complaining.''

"You'll hear no grumbling from me, I promise you, sir.'' The lad seemed to be debating with himself over something. Finally, he said, "Mr. Kane? There is one other thing perhaps I ought to mention."

So the boy was in trouble after all. The disappointment that rose in Jack was probably unreasonable, but he had responded to Sheridan's unmistakable intelligence, his eagerness, and his straightforwardness. Clenching his jaw, he waited.

"I feel I ought to be honest with you, sir.'' The youth stood wadding his cap between his big hands. "Grateful as I am for the job, it's not the sort of position I'll be wanting forever.''

"And what exactly does that mean?" Jack growled around the cheroot.

"It means, sir, that in time I hope to gain a place for myself at the newspaper. *Your* paper, that is,'' he added quickly. "Once I'm better prepared, of course.''

Jack frowned. "I think you'd best explain yourself. If you wanted a job on the paper, why didn't you apply at the *Vanguard*'s office to begin with?"

Sheridan's features tightened. "I did, sir. But I was told there was no place for the likes of me, my not having the book learning or experience required. Your manager wouldn't even let me into his office, you see. Said I was too young, too shabby, and too ignorant.''

Jack suppressed a smile. Walter Goff had never been a man to mince words. "No doubt he was right," he quipped. "So, you thought you'd work your way into my good graces by hiring on as my driver and then wangle a place for yourself on the newspaper?'' Though he deliberately roughened his voice, he regarded the youth with growing interest. "And what makes you think you'd want to work on a newspaper in any event?"

"Not just any newspaper, sir," Sheridan corrected. "Your newspaper. The *Vanguard*. 'Tis the best of the lot."

"Well, thank you very much for the vote of confidence, Mr. Sheridan," Jack said, his tone dry. "But that doesn't quite answer my question."

The young man—for by now Jack found it strangely difficult to think of Sheridan as a boy—appeared to frame his reply with great care. Once again, his answer was surprising—and obviously fired by a deep-seated conviction.

"Most men seem to believe there's power in guns or in great wealth—or in politics," Sheridan said. His tone was studied, his expression thoughtful, yet Jack could sense the passion behind his words. "It seems to me, though, that the real power of a people—of an entire country, if you will—is in what they read. Books. The press. These are the things that change people's minds . . . even their lives. You of all people must know what I mean, Mr. Kane. You and your newspaper, you can make people look at things the way you want them to, make them believe what you want them to believe—even move them to act the way you think they should act. *That's* real power, it seems to me, and the only kind worth having."

Jack expelled a long breath. What Sheridan said was the truth, and he couldn't have stated it better himself, though he had never thought of it in quite that way. For some reason, Sheridan's insight made him both curious and somewhat uncomfortable. "And that's what you want, then, is it, Cavan Sheridan? Power? For what purpose do you want this power, if you don't mind my asking?"

The level blue gaze never wavered. "I don't actually want it for myself, sir. At least, not entirely."

No, he wouldn't, Jack thought. There was more to this one than a narrow selfish streak. Much more, he'd warrant.

"What, then?" He couldn't resist probing a bit further.

For the first time since their meeting, young Sheridan smiled. It was a peculiar smile, and though it eased the good-looking, taut features somewhat, it nevertheless seemed far too grim for a youth of Sheridan's years. It was a smile that failed to conceal the haunted look in the eyes, the hint of old, unhealed sorrows—and unless Jack was badly mistaken, a low-burning but ever present anger.

"For our people," Sheridan said quietly.

"Ah, for our people," Jack repeated, unable to keep the sarcasm from his voice as he extinguished his cigar. "On which side of the ocean in particular?"

Cavan Sheridan regarded him with a steady, oddly unsettling stare. "It seems to me," he said slowly, "that things are pretty much the same for the Irish on both sides. Wouldn't you say so, Mr. Kane?"

Jack said nothing, other than to indicate to Cavan Sheridan that he was hired and could assume his duties at once.

He reached to seal their agreement with a handshake, strangely moved when his new employee, as if out of long habit, wiped his hand quickly down the side of his leg before responding.

8

Too Long Apart

Bitter is your trouble—and I am far from you.
DORA SIGERSON SHORTER

A week later, Cavan sat in the kitchen of the Kane mansion, having his breakfast and taking in the morning prattle of Mrs. Flynn, the cook, and Nancy Lynch, the young Irish day maid.

The latter was a bold sort, plump and pretty enough with her laughing eyes, high color, and shiny chestnut curls that invariably resisted the confines of a dust cap. From Cavan's first day on the job, the girl had made it clear that she would not be averse to his attentions. Cavan, however, was not interested. Even if the girl hadn't been a bit too coarse for his liking, he had more important things on his docket than dallying with the maids.

Besides, Jack Kane made it known to all his employees that he would not tolerate such goings-on among members of the staff, and Cavan had no intention of getting off to a bad start with his employer. This job was too important to him. So while he endured the maid's coquetry with good humor, he made no pretense of encouraging her. Despite his indifference, though, the girl did not seem easily daunted. Already this morning she had been eyeing him, taking what seemed an excessive length of time to collect the previous day's soiled tea towels and napkins for the laundry.

Aware of her scrutiny, Cavan made a determined effort to avoid her gaze as he ate his oatmeal and picked at the plate of bacon Mrs. Flynn had set before him. A fine cook, Mrs. Flynn, and she seemed to have taken a liking to Cavan right away. Every morning when he entered the house he found a generous breakfast waiting for him.

"So, then, Mr. Sheridan, how are you faring in your new job with Black Jack?" Nancy Lynch asked, watching Cavan as she pressed the linens down into the basket.

"Ach, girl, hush with such talk!" Mrs. Flynn swept the kitchen with a furtive glance, as if she expected their employer to suddenly appear from one of the dim corners. "Don't be repeating that vulgar nickname. He is 'Mr. Kane' to you and all the rest of us."

"As if he doesn't know what he's called behind his back," the girl countered with a shrug. She shot Cavan a smile as she snapped another towel into the laundry basket.

"His knowing it and liking it aren't the same thing, now are they? You'd do well to keep a civil tongue, miss, if you value your position here."

The maid wrinkled her nose. "Well, I wasn't talking to you, now was I?" She angled another look at Cavan. "So, what does *Mr. Kane* have you doing when you're not squiring him about town or cleaning out the stables?"

Cavan set his spoon carefully beside his bowl. "I keep busy," he replied, "looking after the horses and doing odd jobs about the newspaper."

"From the looks of that woodpile out back," put in Mrs. Flynn, "you've been busy with the ax as well. And, sure, aren't we going to need it this day? 'Tis bitter cold out. With snow on the way again by evening, I'll wager."

"I'll bring in more wood if you like," Cavan offered, pushing away from the table. "There's time before we leave for the office."

The good-natured cook waved a hand, then reached to tuck a strand of gray hair back under her cap. Her face was flushed from the heat of the cookstove, her crisp apron beginning to wilt, even at this early hour. "No, there'll be more than enough until later this evening. See here, Cavan Sheridan, you've scarcely eaten anything. You don't take in enough to keep a wee boy fit, much less a big strapping lad like yourself." Ignoring Cavan's protests, she scooted a plate of buttered scones closer to him.

Cavan's lack of appetite was nothing new. He supposed the idea of sitting down twice a day to the bountiful fare of the Kane household should have seemed like a gift from heaven itself after so long a time of going without. Yet Cavan could never quite bring himself to enjoy the variety of dishes from Mrs. Flynn's kitchen. Too often the savory morsels brought a bitter image of his mother and sisters, turned out in the cold and dying hungry and homeless by the sea.

Those times the food sat on his tongue like so many dry, tasteless kernels of grain.

From the hallway just then, a tuneful whistle heralded the approach of their employer. As Jack Kane entered the kitchen, it seemed to Cavan that the man didn't so much walk into a room as *appear* in it. Kane moved with the silent, lithe grace of a mountain cat, often creeping up on a body with no warning except his soft, melodic whistling.

He had already donned his well-tailored black overcoat and, as always, appeared jaunty and brisk. "As soon as you've finished your breakfast, lad, we'll be leaving. I need to go in a bit early this morning."

Cavan was already on his feet. "The carriage is ready, sir."

Nancy Lynch slipped out the door behind Kane, darting one last look at Cavan. Mrs. Flynn turned around from the sink, wiping her hands on her apron. "Has there been any word from Mr. Brady yet, sir?"

Kane's features darkened. "I'm afraid not. I expect I'll be sending a man across to see what's become of him, once the weather eases."

Mrs. Flynn wrung her apron with hands red and work roughened. "Sure, he'll be perfectly fine, sir. It would take more than an old windstorm to foil Mr. Brady."

Kane's smile appeared slightly forced. "No doubt you're right, Mary. But I'd feel better if I knew where he was."

In the entryway, Cavan waited while Kane snapped a white carnation from a vase and slipped it into his lapel. On the way outside, his employer seemed inclined to conversation, which wasn't always the case; most mornings, Kane had little to say until they reached the *Vanguard*'s offices.

Today, though, he peppered Cavan with questions. "You told me you still had family in Ireland. A sister, I believe?"

Cavan nodded, his throat tightening. "Aye, sir. My sister, Terese."

"There are just the two of you?"

"That's right, sir. Terese has been staying with our aunt, but I hope to bring her across soon."

They took the walkway with care. A light coating of freezing rain had fallen during the night, leaving the grounds glazed and slippery. Cavan shrugged his aching shoulder a couple of times against the chill; the pain from the injury always seemed to worsen as temperatures dropped.

He felt his employer's eyes on him, as if the other were expecting more in the way of information. After a moment, Kane again took up the conversation. "I don't suppose you've heard how your sister fared in the storm yet?" he said, slowing his pace as they approached the carriage.

Cavan stopped, looking at him.

Kane frowned. "Sorry, I thought you knew or I'd have said something before now. There was a bad windstorm, it seems. From all accounts, I'd say it must have been nothing less than a hurricane."

"When—when exactly was this, sir?"

Kane smoothed his gloves. "Right after the first of the year, on Epiphany Sunday. Swept over most of Ireland, apparently—just about blew the country to pieces. Terrible destruction. Trees uprooted, houses leveled, fires—" He paused, then added, "I'm afraid the reports indicate great numbers of people dead or missing." He stopped. "You've had no word at all from your sister?"

Cavan shook his head. He felt suddenly chilled, and the ache in his shoulder escalated. "I wrote her with my whereabouts, but that was only a few days ago. The last letter I had from her was before I left Pennsylvania."

"How old is she, your sister?"

Cavan had to think. "She must be close on seventeen by now, I expect." He swallowed. Terese had not even been eleven years old when he and Da left Ireland. "Do you know, sir—did this storm strike the islands as well? Inishmore and the others?"

Kane nodded, his expression sympathetic. "I'm afraid so." He climbed into the carriage then, saying, "As I told Mrs. Flynn, I'll be sending a man over to see about my brother when the weather breaks. We'll have him stop at the islands to ask after your sister as well, if you like."

"That's very kind of you, sir," said Cavan. "Sure, I'd appreciate it."

"Yes, well, that may be a few weeks yet. Perhaps in the meantime you'll hear something from her."

Kane ducked his head back inside the carriage then, and Cavan climbed up to the driver's bench, trying not to think about Terese on her own in the terrible storm. He knew she was no longer a child, yet he could not think of her as anything else. The image of the way she had looked that last day in the harbor, the day he and Da had left for America, was frozen on the frame of his memory. She had not aged in his mind since then but had remained a thin, awkward little girl with slightly wild hair and eyes red and swollen from crying after himself and their father.

She had clung to him, her arms locked about him as if to physically bind him to her. "Take us with you! Please, Cavan! You mustn't leave us here! Take us, too!"

They had made promises that day, he and Da. They would send for the others soon, they vowed. In no time at all, they would all be together again. "As soon as we find jobs for us both, we'll arrange for a flat. Or perhaps even a house. The time will pass before you know it; you'll see."

Their mother had stood by, oddly silent, holding Baby Mada, while Honor, the oldest of the girls, hovered near. Terese would not let go of Cavan but instead begged him not to leave without her and the others. At the end, Cavan had practically shoved her away and run for the ship, hiding his own sobs from his father.

Even now when he thought of that day, his eyes stung with unshed tears of grief—and guilt. They had failed, he and Da. Failed his mother and the little sisters . . . and the babe. They were all dead, and so was Da. No one was left except for Terese and himself.

And now, with word of this storm, who could say that he hadn't lost her as well?

He tried to console himself with the reminder that Terese had always been strong. From the time she was small, she had possessed an uncommon nerve and a will of iron. Indeed, she had always been the boldest and most resourceful of them all. Fiery, clever, and stubborn to the point of their mother's despair at times. Terese would be fine. She could take care of herself. Besides, she wasn't entirely alone after all. She had Aunt Una and Uncle Felim.

Small comfort, that. Those two had been more children themselves than a man and woman grown, he thought uneasily.

But Terese would manage, he assured himself. She would be all right.

All the same, he spent the rest of the drive praying for his sister, beseeching God to guard her until the day he could finally bring her across. Just as fervently, he implored—and not for the first time—divine forgiveness for having left her behind in the first place.

As was his custom, Jack Kane perused a number of rival newspapers during the morning ride to his office. The *Herald* presently lay open on his lap, but his attempt to read Bennett's latest splash of sensationalism was halfhearted at best. For some reason, he couldn't keep his mind off Cavan Sheridan.

Jack had seen guilt often enough in his life to recognize the signs of it in his young driver. The look on Sheridan's face when he'd learned about the storm had been one of unmistakable shock mixed with fear—and guilt.

No doubt the boy had left Ireland, like thousands of other Irish males, with the intention and expectation of bringing the rest of his family across within a few months at most. As was often the case, months had turned into years, with still no means of sending for the others.

Young Sheridan talked sparingly of himself. He had spoken but once of his parents and two younger sisters, all deceased. This morning's conversation had been only the second allusion to the surviving sister. Jack thought it highly possible that the lad blamed himself for not being able to save his family.

He put the *Herald* aside, slid his feet closer to the warming bricks, and gave the lap robe a tug against the early-morning chill. He didn't know the facts, of course, but something told him that his new driver was the sort who tended to be excessively hard on himself. He appeared to own a keen conscience and an equally keen sensitivity.

If Sheridan had a sense of humor—and Jack suspected that he did—he kept it under wraps in the presence of his employer. He seemed to look at all things soberly and seriously, which made Jack speculate as to just how much the lad might be blaming himself for something completely beyond his control.

Odd, the difference in men when they lost control of their circumstances. He had seen it more than once. Some seemed to take on a kind of fierce resolve, a strength of purpose that eventually turned out to be either the making or the breaking of them. Others allowed guilt to oppress them to the point that it completely distorted their sense of reality. The latter very often ended up believing themselves to be less than the men they actually were. Some managed to shake off the guilt completely, either through their religion or by sheer force of will. Others, however, let it eventually destroy them.

He didn't know young Sheridan well enough yet to speculate on what sort of man he might become. New York would make it difficult for him, of course; the city was no friend to the immigrant, especially the Irish immigrant. The battles he was almost certain to face would challenge him mightily. Given the predictable difficulties, combined with whatever was obviously gnawing at him, who could say whether the boy would succeed or fail in his aspirations?

Jack found himself hoping that his solemn young driver with the wounded eyes would prevail over his demons, whatever they happened to be. Cavan Sheridan had been in his employ only a week, but Jack was already coming to like the youth, even to gain a measure of respect for him. He wanted better for the lad than a life of guilt and regret.

He knew only too well what that kind of life could do to a man.

9

To Catch a Thief

The end of ages is drawing near;
As the world grows withered and old,
Charity will grow icy cold.

FROM *SAINT BRENDAN'S PROPHECY*,
EARLY SEVENTEENTH CENTURY

THE CLADDAGH, WESTERN IRELAND, MARCH

An oppressive fog shrouded the Claddagh in the early-morning hours. The mist hovered low over the district's narrow streets, its talonlike fingers creeping between the houses as if to beckon the unsuspecting to a deadly tryst.

Terese Sheridan stood shivering in a doorway, clutching a basket of stolen bread as she assessed her chances to break and run without being caught. Her stomach pitched at the smells from the river and the fish market. Her heart pounded crazily as she scanned the marketplace near the old gates.

She could not be caught! Under English law, she could swing for stealing. Somehow, she must get away!

Terese held her breath, watching for the right moment. At another time, she might have berated herself for the act she had just committed. She was no thief. Time had been, and not so long ago, that she would not have stolen a crumb from another's table, much less bread from a stranger. But the rules that once governed her behavior had succumbed to the burning misery in her belly. If she was to survive, she must eat. Her two dollars were long since gone, and she had not been able to locate even the most menial employment in the whole of Galway City. So for the past few days she had lifted a fish here, a crust there, until by the time she came upon the two house-wives gossiping in the marketplace, a basket of bread resting nearby, she did not stop to consider the deed but merely acted upon instinct.

Even when the women had begun to screech at her and give chase as she dashed across the quay, Terese had felt no real guilt. There had been only a scalding flash of anger—anger at landing in the kind of circumstances that would bring her to such a thing. Another day or more without food would find her too weak to search for work, too weak to withstand the raw March wind as it came gusting in on the abandoned door stoops or alleyways where she sought shelter at night. It had come down to stealing or begging, and Terese would die before she would beg.

The damp chill steamed her breath and stung her skin, and she reached with her free hand to tug the ends of her shawl more tightly about her. If she had any real regret at all, it was for having drifted into the Claddagh earlier that morning. She had not intended to come this far, but in the fog she had lost her bearings.

If the old city of Galway had unnerved her when she'd first arrived, the Claddagh discomfited her altogether. The people in the Claddagh were known to be reclusive and somewhat peculiar. The colony was made up mostly of fishermen and their families, who had not changed their ways for centuries. Here, the inhabitants married among them-selves and lived their lives along the narrow lanes of small but well-built houses of mud walls and thatched roofs. Outsiders were not encouraged to enter.

It was said that the people of the Claddagh were so religious—or so superstitious, depending on who happened to be giving the ac-count—that the men would not go out in their boats to fish except at certain prescribed times blessed by the priest. They believed that the presence of God was always among them and tried to live ac-cordingly, even refusing to greet one another without first invoking the name of God.

She wondered bitterly if these peculiar folk still felt so piously inclined toward their God after the monster wind he had unleashed upon them. For here in the Claddagh, as well as in Galway City, the storm's devastation was evident everywhere. Many of the small, sad houses lacked a wall or a roof, while others had been reduced to no more than a heap of thatch and mud.

As Terese's attention returned to her surroundings, she recalled with uneasiness that the Claddagh fishermen claimed complete rights and control over the bay and the entire district. It was rumored that if those rights happened to be violated, the people had been known to become so violent that there was no withstanding them.

Perhaps she might have chosen a better place in which to commit her thievery, but now was no time for such speculation. She could hear the voices of her pursuers, their shouts strangely muted by the dense fog overlying the entire district. Fear gripped her. At the same time, the heavenly aroma wafting up from the bread basket filled her senses, causing her stomach to wrench in a fiery spasm.

The angry voices were closer now. Terese knew she had no time left if she was to avoid capture, but fear and weakness threatened to buckle her legs. Only the thought of the precious, sweet bread so near at hand—and her resolve to survive—gave her the courage to bolt from the doorway and go charging down the street, intent on ducking into the nearest alley.

With her long legs and lean form, Terese was uncommonly fleet. But hunger and the bitter elements had taken their toll. Her lungs felt ablaze, her heart banging against her chest so fiercely she thought it would surely explode. Her ears roared with the thunder of her own pulse as she ran.

Behind her, the angry shouts began to close in. She felt like a fox with a pack of slavering hounds at her back. Dizziness washed over her, threatening to bring her down. An alley opened before her, and she lurched into it, gasping for breath as she sprinted over the cobbled street.

She heard the heavy tread of boots scraping the stones and knew others had joined in pursuit, turning into the alley behind her. Suddenly, at the exact instant when Terese feared she would go sprawling facedown into the street, she saw a man appear at the exit of the alley, blocking her escape.

She was trapped!

She stopped, pivoted about to see the mob of enraged pursuers closing in from behind, then whipped around to see the man at the other end of the alley coming toward her. She lowered her head and butted forward, hoping to push by him and gain her freedom. But he was upon her in two easy strides, a hand shooting out to break her flight.

Terese twisted, attempting to wrench free. The bread basket went flying out of her hand onto the street, its precious contents spilling onto the wet stones.

She threw her head back, a long wail of despair tearing from her throat. The man eased his grip on her but only for an instant before catching her by the arm and pinning her in place.

Terese's eyes burned, and she squeezed them shut, refusing to weep in front of her captor and the others. Even now, though she knew she had lost all hope of escape, she tried to shake free. But the man's grip was like an iron band about her arm.

She opened her eyes, surprised to encounter a gaze more curious than hostile. Indeed, the dark, deep-set eyes sparkled with something that almost hinted of amusement. Fury welled up inside her, and Terese found herself wanting to slap his smug face. Wasn't it enough to be starving and on the run from her own foolishness? Must she be an object of this *amadon*'s entertainment as well?

She tried again to break free of his grasp, a vain attempt, for he was strong, his hold on her unyielding. She caught an expression of impatience in the dark eyes, but nothing more. "Stop it, you little alley cat!" he grated out. "I'm only trying to save your hide."

Terese stared at him in surprise. He wasn't Irish, and he was no Britisher either, not with that accent. She thought he might be American. He was young and nice looking, his clothes casual but obviously of good quality. He had the look of a man who wanted for nothing. Who else but an American could sport such a well-fed appearance and the clothing to go with it? But what under the sky would an American be doing in the Claddagh?

A few renegade tears had spilled over in spite of her best efforts, and Terese lifted her free hand to brush them away. The man's expression seemed to change slightly as his eyes followed her movement.

Shamed as much by the tears as by her capture, Terese twisted to avoid his gaze. To her surprise, he turned to face her pursuers, bringing her gently, but firmly, around to stand at his side.

He raised a hand as if to ward off their complaints. Then, without waiting for the angry accusations and outcries to abate, he called for their attention. He spoke to them in English, his voice deep and well controlled, but with a distinct note of authority.

Terese had no choice but to face the crowd, and when she did she saw that, although their tempers were obviously still inflamed, they were at least paying heed to the man who stood before them.

To her astonishment, the American—if that's what he was— seemed to be defending her!

"Will you look at yourselves? Running down a defenseless girl like a pack of wild dogs! Why, you ought to be ashamed!"

"Defenseless in a pig's eye! She's a thief!" someone shouted from the crowd.

"Is she now? And what did she steal, this dangerous felon?"

One of the red-faced housewives who had been standing near the bread basket stepped out and jabbed a finger at Terese. "Didn't she steal me bread? The entire basket!"

Someone in the crowd muttered a dire admonition Terese took to be from Scripture, something to the effect that "bread gained by deceit tastes sweet but leaves the mouth full of gravel."

Terese was surprised that they were speaking in English. Even though many in the west knew the language of the Crown, most preferred their native tongue, especially on the islands and here in Galway. She wondered if some of these people knew the American and were speaking English out of deference to him. Yet they did not seem in the least deferential.

The American glanced at the basket in the street and its spilled contents, then turned back to Terese's accuser. "Two loaves, mother," he said, his tone laced with contempt. "What were you going to do, tear the girl to pieces for two loaves of bread?"

"We'll see her in gaol!" shouted another woman.

A collective cry swelled from the crowd. Terese's dark-haired rescuer dug his free hand into the pocket of his trousers, tossing a few coins at the housewife. "This will pay for your bread! Now go home and leave the girl alone."

From the back of the mob, a lantern-jawed man pushed forward, his eyes blazing as he confronted the American. "Who do you think you are, to be telling us our business? *You're* the one who had best be going home, Yank, if you value your neck!"

Again the crowd began to grumble among themselves, but the American shouted over them. "You've been paid for your bread! Now back off, and leave this girl alone!"

"Or you'll do what, Yank?" his challenger bellowed.

Now the grousing among the mob grew louder and more agitated. Terese saw two other men wedge their way to the front. One of them, wearing a broad-brimmed hat and a red kerchief around his neck, came to stand directly in front of her and the American.

"Claddagh men don't take kindly to meddlers, Yank," he grated out.

"Nor to desperate young girls either, it seems," countered the American.

He didn't look a bit frightened, Terese decided, wondering if he was fearless or merely foolish. At the same time, she caught a glimpse of movement, and as she watched, a dark colossus of a man stepped into the alley.

He was an intimidating giant with a head of curly black hair, an inky beard, and shoulders wide enough to block the light. Involuntarily, Terese flinched, again reviling herself for the folly that had brought the wrath of these savage people against her.

The American was standing his ground, but she felt his grasp on her arm tighten as he began to draw her slowly behind him. The man in the wide-brimmed hat took a step forward, his expression ugly. The crowd too began to press closer. The American muttered something under his breath and suddenly dropped Terese's arm.

"Run!" he cried, shoving her toward the exit of the alley.

At that moment, a shout exploded from the back of the mob. Terese whirled around. The towering figure who had entered the alley only a moment before was now parting the crowd, shoving his way through to the front.

The American uttered something that sounded like "Gabriel," then, "Just in time!"

The giant reached them, locked gazes for an instant with the American, then, ignoring Terese entirely, turned to the crowd. "Go back to your homes and your work, the lot of you!" he commanded them in the Irish.

His voice was like a low rumbling of thunder as he raised a fist the size of a dinner plate and jabbed it at them. "The girl is hungry! She's one of the islanders, can't you see? No doubt the big wind drove her out. Haven't you seen more of the same these past weeks, roaming the streets half-starved?"

At last the pandemonium subsided, and the crowd's anger and hostility began to ebb. There were a few additional murmurings, but these, too, soon faded as the giant went on. Terese could scarcely take in the fact that he seemed to be rebuking the others instead of her. More amazing still was the effect of his words. Watching the facial expressions in the crowd, it seemed to Terese that this was a man they respected, a man of great influence among them.

He called to the owner of the bread basket, whose face was still flushed. "The American paid you for your bread, Bridget O'Brien!" he roared. "Go home now, woman! Go home, and say a prayer of thanks for your blessings and one for mercy on those less fortunate."

Relief washed over Terese as the crowd began to disperse.

Not waiting until they were gone, the giant turned to face her and the American. This time he spoke in English, his tone dry as he faced the younger man. "That was a foolish thing to do, Brady Kane. The blow to your head must have been worse than I thought."

The American grinned. "You may be right, Gabriel. In any event, you are a welcome sight, I can tell you!"

So they knew each other, then! Dazed by this sudden turn of events, Terese shrank back as the giant turned a piercing blue glare upon her. "Are you slow-witted, girl, or daft entirely, to try such a stunt? You're from the islands; you must know about Claddagh law. It might have gone much harder for you."

Terese refused to let the man think he could intimidate her, though in truth he did.

Despite her own height—she was taller than most women—he was an oak, towering more than a head above her, and he looked somewhat wild, with that unruly hair and black beard.

He continued to impale her with his fierce, hard stare until Terese had to look away. " 'Twas steal or die," she muttered.

His dark brows lifted. "Some would say the one deserves the other."

Terese lifted her head to meet his gaze straight on. "I would have gotten away," she said stubbornly, "if it hadn't been for *him.*" She jerked a finger at the American.

Anger flared in her when she saw the younger man's impudent grin break even wider.

"I saved the girl from jail, and she's angry with me," he said, shaking his head as if to bemoan Terese's mental state.

"It seems to me that the both of you need to be locked away," the big man said sourly, "if for no other reason than to let you collect your wits. 'Tis obvious you've lost them somewhere along the way."

The two men proceeded to ignore Terese, speaking over her head as if she were no longer there. The giant did a great deal of mumbling and glaring, but it seemed to Terese that in truth he wasn't all that vexed.

Even so, she had had quite enough of their boorishness. Her legs were trembling, her entire body shaking from cold and exertion. Even her head seemed to be swimming, making it difficult to see, much less think.

Somehow she managed to draw herself up and stand without swaying as she looked first one, then the other, in the eye. "If the two of you will allow me a word," she said, mustering what was surely her last shred of dignity, "I will thank you both for 'rescuing' me, and then I must be on my way."

10

Angels Unawares

The luck of God is in two strangers meeting,
But the gates of Hell are in the city street
For him whose soul is not in his own keeping
And love a silver string upon his feet.

T. D. O'BOLGER

Brady had all he could do not to applaud the girl. She was absolutely *magnificent!* Even with the smudges on her face and the shadows beneath those great smoke blue eyes, she was nothing less than splendid: all fire and passion and bravado.

Nearly as tall as most men and willow slim—she stopped short of actual gauntness—she reminded him for all the world of a high-strung mare. He half expected her to toss that wild mane of russet hair over her shoulder and go bolting down the alley.

Despite her fiery pride, however, she was obviously about to fall where she stood—no doubt from hunger, given the fact that she had been caught stealing bread. If that was the case, if the girl was actually hungry, what were they to do with her? They couldn't very well set her off on her own to steal again. As Gabriel had pointed out, she could bring real trouble down on her head.

"Where will you go?" Brady blurted out.

The girl whipped around, eyes narrowed. "Wherever I please, I should think."

"But . . . do you have a place to stay?"

Her nostrils flared, and again Brady thought of a restless young mare.

A thoroughbred.

"I expect that is my affair."

She was a scrapper, this one. But somehow her brass didn't irritate him as much as it might have coming from another, perhaps because of the fear he saw lurking in those enormous eyes. He was beginning to suspect that her sauciness was mostly show—a defense. The girl was obviously hungry, more than likely homeless and on her own. She had to be frightened.

Gabriel had been silent throughout this exchange, had merely stood, quietly watching the unlikely thief as if taking her measure. Now he spoke, his voice giving no hint of what he might be thinking. "It was bad on the islands, they say."

The girl looked at him.

"The big wind," he explained.

"How would you be knowing I'm from the islands?" she challenged, her tone defiant.

The big man shrugged, his gaze flicking over her as if her clothing were explanation enough. Brady realized that he had seen similar apparel on some of the other women wandering around Galway City: the long scarlet skirt against bare legs, a tattered shawl, and that strange multicolored sash at the waist.

"The Big Island, I expect?" Gabriel said.

After a slight hesitation, the girl nodded. "Aye. Inishmore."

Unwilling to be excluded, Brady posed a question of his own. "What about your family?"

She shot a look of impatience at him, making no reply. Clearly, she found him of less importance than the mighty Gabriel.

Understandable, certainly. Even so, he couldn't resist vying for her attention one more time. "If you need a place to stay, there are rooms to let at my flat. Mrs. Hannafin's rents are fair."

The girl's look would have quenched a live coal. "And would she be letting out rooms for *free,* then?"

Out of the corner of his eye, Brady saw Gabriel begin to dig down in his pockets. But apparently he came up empty-handed, for he remained silent.

Brady had a little cash on him, but he sensed that to offer it would invite yet another rebuke. Besides, Gabriel had already succeeded in engaging her in a brusque dialogue—one that again excluded Brady.

"Are you on your own keeping, girl?"

"I am," she said, the strong chin lifting a bit.

"The storm took your home, did it?"

She looked at him, a hard look that dramatically altered her appearance, adding years to her features. "Aye," she said, the word sounding as if she'd forced it out between clenched teeth. "The storm took it all."

Brady saw with some interest that the Big Fella's expression had gentled considerably as he went on questioning the girl. "And what has brought you to Galway, then?"

"I mean to find work to pay my passage to America."

Gabriel crossed his sturdy arms over his chest. "But you have found no work, so you resort to stealing, is that so?"

Her mouth curled downward, her eyes betraying a great depth of bitterness.

There was a long silence, during which Gabriel continued to study the girl closely, as if gauging her mettle. When he finally spoke again, his words were a surprise.

"You will come home with me for a bite to eat," he said.

It was not an invitation but a command. Brady had known the cryptic giant long enough by now to have learned that the Big Fella did not ask. He spoke, and others obliged.

The girl was a stranger, however, and either she did not realize she had just been given a direct command or, if she did, she chose not to acknowledge Gabriel's authority.

"I will not, but my thanks to you all the same."

Gabriel scowled at her. Not for the first time, it occurred to Brady that nobody could scowl quite as fiercely as Gabriel, except possibly his brother, Jack.

"Then you will starve," the big fisherman said flatly, as if he cared little one way or the other.

"Perhaps I will; perhaps I won't."

"Pride goes before a fall," Gabriel said in the same even tone of voice.

She glared at him. "I do not go off with strange men to their houses."

Brady almost strangled. Good heavens, did the girl actually think Gabriel was propositioning her?

He glanced at the Big Fella, somehow finding it impossible to imagine the dour giant with a woman. Why that should be the case, he wasn't sure. Gabriel wasn't an old man, by any means—he was probably no more than forty, if that—and though some might find his size intimidating, he wasn't a homely man, not even a plain one. In fact, he might actually be considered good-looking by the women, especially if he were to smile every now and then.

Perhaps it was the presence, the bearing of the man, that seemed to place him above the needs or weaknesses of mere mortals, Brady thought, intrigued. Somehow Gabriel seemed to exist and move within his own sphere of power, drawing, even trapping, those around him in its force. So compelling was the giant's persona that Brady had seen others actually shrink back when the giant came near. At the same time, there seemed to be a fundamental decency about the man—a sense of goodness and an innate morality to which others, even Brady, invariably responded.

But even if Gabriel had been inclined to lasciviousness, Brady doubted that this half-starved runaway would entice him. She was all angles and planes, for one thing—too thin by far. The riotous mane of hair was badly tangled, her face smudged, her clothing shabby, and, splendid as she was with that fiery temper and brave show of dignity, at the moment she wasn't exactly a sight to turn a man's head. Besides, Brady sensed that she was also very young. Perhaps younger than she would want them to know.

Gabriel appeared to dismiss the girl's shaded insult. "You are to be commended for your virtue, lass," he said dryly. "But I do not fancy scrawny little girls."

Her face flamed, and she was clearly about to spit out some venomous retort, but Gabriel ignored her indignation. "I do not live alone," he said. "There are others at my house—a girl older than yourself and a wee wane—and we will take this strapping young Yank along for your protection, if you like."

The girl cut Brady a scathing glance before turning back to Gabriel. "Why would you do such a thing?" she challenged.

"Our Lord bids us feed the hungry," said the big fisherman, his tone mild. "You are hungry, I think. So come along now, before you faint here in the street. I have no wish to carry you the rest of the way." With that, he started off.

The girl watched him, and Brady watched her. He could almost see that monumental pride warring with her body's obvious privation. Then, as if conceding defeat, she gave a short nod and started off, scurrying to keep pace with Gabriel's long stride.

Brady, having received an invitation of sorts, followed after. As he hurried along behind the two, a portion of Scripture came to mind. Of course, the only Scriptures Brady knew were those his sister, Rose, a nun, was fond of quoting. This particular verse was one of her favorites—Jack accused her of pulling it out every time a stray beggar came to the door, so as to justify the lack of good sense in taking a stranger into their midst.

It had something to do with "entertaining angels unawares."

Brady grinned to himself as he watched the haughty girl with the thoroughly disreputable appearance take off after the Big Fella. No angel, that one, he would warrant. But wasn't she fascinating all the same?

11

In the House of
the Fisherman

What change has put my thoughts astray
And eyes that had so keen a sight?

W. B. YEATS

Terese Sheridan was her name. She pronounced it *T'reece,* her tongue
merely grazing the first syllable before lingering on the second. She
was seventeen years old, she said, and the only surviving member of
her family, other than an older brother who had emigrated to America
years before.

Brady listened to the girl recite the basic facts about herself as they
ate their midday meal of potatoes and buttermilk. The room was dim,
for there was only one window, too narrow to admit much light. Both
the Sheridan girl and Gabriel sat on stools pulled up to the rough-
hewn plank that served as a table, while across from them Brady
perched on a *boss*—a low seat made of straw. The child, Evie, sat
beside him, wide-eyed and for the most part ignoring her food as she
took in the conversation.

As was frequently the case, Roweena declined to share the table.
Instead, she busied herself at the fire, watching over a fresh pot of
boiling potatoes, then tossing them into the *kish*—a wicker basket—
for straining. Brady knew from experience that when she eventually
got around to eating, she would seat herself on one of the stone
benches by the hearth, her milk and potatoes set out neatly beside
her as she watched the exchange taking place around the table.

It still puzzled him—to some extent *annoyed* him—that Roweena so seldom participated in a meal but instead behaved as if she were a servant, compelled to wait table for others. He had carefully broached the subject of her odd behavior with Gabriel on one occasion, but the big man had simply shrugged and replied, "That is her way."

By now, this small, humble cottage had become comfortably familiar to Brady. After his recovery from the head injury, he had returned to help restore the roof, as a way of thanking Gabriel for taking him in. During that time, he and the Big Fella had become *almost* friendly, at least tolerant of each other. While Brady was no longer intimidated by the taciturn giant, he still had a tendency to tread with care when his host fell into one of his tight-lipped moods.

He hadn't expected that he would actually come to like, even admire, the big fisherman, especially in so brief a time. Incredibly, he found himself coveting the man's approval; the fact that that approval didn't seem to be forthcoming puzzled, even irritated, Brady more than he cared to admit.

Roweena puzzled him even more. At first he'd suspected that her subservient behavior must be Gabriel's doing, had wondered if the man had deliberately consigned her to a housemaid's role, perhaps as a way of payment for providing her a home.

It hadn't taken him long to realize that wasn't the case. Although the big fisherman made a show of sternness with both girls, he was much more a father figure to them than a master. With Evie, especially, he could be surprisingly gentle, in spite of his occasional feigned severity.

When it came to Roweena, Gabriel's conduct was somewhat more complicated. Although he was kind to her and openly protective, at the same time he seemed to maintain a certain distance between them. Whereas he would tease Evie, and even rough and tumble with the child, with Roweena he became more a patriarchal figure: watchful, often stern, though never bullying or impatient.

Now he seemed to have adopted a similar stance with the Sheridan girl. At the moment, he was studying her with that fixed gaze of his that seemed to discern everything while revealing nothing. For her part, Terese Sheridan appeared to have steeled herself against the giant's scrutiny and brusque demeanor, answering his questions succinctly, and once or twice a little sharply.

Mostly, she ate. Brady hadn't missed the eager way she eyed the food when they first pulled up to the table. But instead of digging in, as he suspected she was longing to do, she partook of the meal with an admirable measure of restraint, as if she were too proud to call attention to her hunger.

Gabriel didn't seem in the least offended by the shortness of her replies but went right on questioning her. He added little to the conversation but mostly sat listening to her replies with the poker-faced expression Brady had come to know well by now.

Although the two frequently lapsed into the Irish as they spoke, Gabriel would occasionally glance at Brady and steer the conversation back to English. Brady was able to catch the gist of their exchange well enough. Apparently, Terese Sheridan was on her own, had lost her entire family except for the brother in America, and had survived the killing windstorm with no more than the clothes on her back. It sounded to Brady as if she had made her way here from her island home by sheer spunk and her own wits.

When she calmly declared her intention to join her brother in the States, there seemed no reason to doubt that she would do just that. Despite her disheveled, half-starved appearance, the girl's iron will and strength of purpose were blazingly evident. Even so, Brady suspected she would find her course a difficult one, for by her own admission, she was penniless.

"I had my own money, you see." The reply to Gabriel's question about her circumstances was given without hesitation, though her tone was not without an edge of bitterness. "Money I'd saved from what my brother sent. But didn't my aunt Una steal it away from me? All but two dollars, which are now gone. That's why I must find work, and find it soon. Not only for my keep, but to earn my passage."

"Your *aunt* stole your money?" Brady put in. "What kind of woman steals from a member of her own family?"

The girl shot him a look that clearly questioned his knowledge of human nature. "A spiteful, greedy woman, it seems to me." Her lips curved slightly in a cold mockery of a smile. "But a *Christian* woman, you understand."

Brady stared at her. There was the same hard edge he had seen earlier. It was gone as quickly as it came, but not before the thought occurred to him that while Terese Sheridan might be only seventeen, she seemed to be more woman than girl—and one with a marked streak of cynicism, at that.

"So . . . what do you mean to do now?" he asked casually.

She looked at him but offered no reply. Instead, she turned back to Gabriel. "Is there work to be had in the Claddagh?"

He shrugged. "The work of the Claddagh is fishing. We go out in our boats, and we fish.'' He studied her. ''Still, there might be something for a strong girl who is willing to work.''

The girl leaned forward slightly on the stool. ''I *am* strong, though you may not see it in me today. I am strong, and I am not afraid of hard work.''

The big man rubbed his chin. For a moment he lapsed into the Irish, but with a quick glance at Brady, reverted to English. ''There is a woman. Not wealthy, mind, but not poor either. She's not an old woman, but her man is dead—died at sea, God rest his soul. The daughter married outside the Claddagh and moved away to Australia.''

He paused and sat stroking his heavy black beard in a reflective gesture. ''Jane has a sickness in her bones,'' he continued, ''that grows worse by the day. Her hands are drawn and knotted like old tree limbs, her legs, too—she can scarcely walk at all but must use a chair most days. She can no longer tend the house or do her own marketing. She suffers in a bad way, Jane does.''

He shook his head, then went on. ''Roweena goes and helps sometimes, but I can't be sparing her every day. She has work enough to do here, and there's the little one to look after. Besides, it makes it difficult, her not being able to hear. I expect poor Jane would pay if she could find a reliable girl to do for her.''

This was by far the longest speech Brady had ever heard from the big fisherman, and he stared at him in surprise.

''This widow woman—do you think she would hire me?'' Terese Sheridan watched Gabriel closely for his reply.

He gave a shrug. ''She will or she won't. We will take you to her and let Jane speak for herself, if you want.'' He paused. ''But the woman is in a bad way, mind. On her worst days, you would have to do for her almost as you would a babe. And then the house needs care and the cooking done. If you're shy of sickness or lowly work, don't be volunteering yourself.''

The girl pressed forward even more, her meal seemingly forgotten. ''I'm not too proud to care for a poor sick woman. And there is no work I would not do. Would you be taking me to her, please?''

Gabriel regarded her for a long moment. ''First you will finish your food and warm yourself,'' he said. ''Afterward, Roweena will help to make you more presentable.''

Brady saw the girl's face flame, but she said nothing, merely glanced down over herself with a rueful look. ''And then you will take me to this woman?'' she pressed.

Gabriel's steady gaze continued to measure her. Finally, he gave a short nod. "Then I will take you to Jane."

Brady studied the big fisherman, somewhat puzzled by his ready acceptance of the intriguing young thief. But then, Gabriel was a constant enigma to him. One minute the man seemed little more than a sour-tempered hermit, the next, a kindly benefactor. The Big Fella had myriad facets to his nature, all of them unpredictable.

Despite his many peculiarities, however, he had been decent enough to the "bothersome Yank," as he sometimes was wont to call Brady. So long as Brady did not annoy him with too many questions—or pay Roweena excessive attention—the Big Fella seemed tolerant of his presence. In fact, Brady suspected that the only reason he and his sketchbook were allowed to roam at will among the Claddagh community was because Gabriel had first accepted him at his hearth fire.

That the big fisherman wielded that sort of influence among the colony's inhabitants had become obvious to Brady early on. Gabriel might not be the "king," as they referred to their official governor, but he clearly held a great deal of power in his own right.

It hadn't taken long to discover that Gabriel—if the man had a last name, it was his secret—was a man of great importance in the Claddagh. There was his formidable physical presence, of course; it was difficult not to be awed by the giant. But there was much more to this man than mere brawn. For one thing, the people of the settlement seemed to view him as a sort of healer. They brought him their ill children, the occasional accident victim, and even sought his advice on ailing animals. Apparently, the big fisherman had a way with such things, for more often than not his "patients" went away much improved.

Brady had noticed an abundant supply of dried herbs and tins of medicine stored on shelves above the painted dresser. He had also seen the Big Fella, with Roweena's assistance, set a broken arm or foot. Less frequently, Roweena might be summoned to help with a birthing. At those times, Gabriel would sign some hurried instructions, then send her off with a small valise that looked like a physician's case.

Brady was roused from his thoughts when Terese Sheridan stood and made an oddly formal statement of appreciation to her host. "I am grateful for your hospitality, sir. I will repay you as soon as I find a position."

Gabriel took a long sip of tea, then said mildly, "You will not speak of payment for an open door and a plate of potatoes, lass, unless you mean to insult me.''

The girl blanched, then tried to stammer a protest, but Gabriel ignored her. Getting to his feet, he summoned Roweena to him and began to instruct her, voicing his words slowly and emphatically as he always did, much like an accompaniment to the fluid hand movements by which he ''spoke'' to her.

Roweena cast a quick glance at Brady, then made a gesture that the other girl should follow her. Struck by the contrast between the two, Brady could not help staring. The dark-haired Roweena, slight and delicate in appearance—and clearly awed by this stranger in their midst—was like a timid fawn in contrast to the taller, oddly regal Terese Sheridan. The latter, with eyes of blue smoke and a tumultuous, wild beauty, might have been one of the mythic warrior queens readying herself for battle as she accompanied the diminutive Roweena behind the curtain. Queen Maeve on a rout.

Abruptly, Brady tried to force his thoughts away from the two girls—especially from Roweena, who he sensed might, if he did not take care, represent the first serious threat to his emotions in a very long time. Roweena was no mere girl, as he had thought upon their initial encounter during the storm. He had come to realize that she was probably in her early twenties at least—not all that much younger than himself, at twenty-seven.

Even so, he had found her to be nothing like he would have expected from that first encounter during the storm. That night, in her frenzy to get the child, Evie, to safety, she had appeared impetuous, brave—even impassioned. But inside these snug walls, she was scarcely more than a shadow of that fleet-footed sprite. At times, she seemed almost childish, less womanly than the subtle curves of her body might indicate. To Gabriel, she was submissive, scurrying to do his bidding and see to his comforts. With others she maintained a shy, deferential demeanor that almost made her appear slow-witted.

Even with Evie, she seemed more a big sister than a maternal figure. And her pretty blushes each time Brady caught her eye only confirmed his suspicion that Gabriel had kept her thoroughly sheltered from the outside world—particularly from men.

As for the strange relationship between Gabriel and the two girls, Brady had learned nothing more than what Evie had expressed the night of the storm. The child, apparently abandoned when she was little more than an infant, had been rescued and taken in by the big fisherman. Similarly, Gabriel had provided Roweena a home from the time she was a small girl. There had been something about a fire, but he hadn't been able to figure out much else from Evie's chatter.

So far as Brady knew, there was no blood tie between Gabriel and either of the girls, but both were obviously devoted to their guardian. On numerous occasions, he had wanted to ask about the girls' backgrounds, but Gabriel had a way about him that discouraged too many questions.

As for Roweena, the appeal she held for him had come as a total surprise to Brady, and a distinctly unsettling one. He had never been attracted to the shy, "nice girls" at home. No doubt it spoke volumes about his character that his tastes had always run to the more flamboyant sort of women, often older than himself, whose morals— according to Jack, at least—were as questionable as Brady's own. It wasn't typical that a girl like Roweena—lovely as she was—would capture his interest.

Yet he couldn't deny his response to her. She aroused something akin to tenderness in him—an instinct to protect, to cherish—that up until now he hadn't known he possessed. He found himself uncharacteristically considerate of her feelings, careful of his behavior toward her. At the same time, he fervently wished he could somehow breach her defenses, draw her out of her shyness so he might get to know her better.

Not that he would allow himself a serious attachment. He had made a practice of shunning commitment. To even consider some sort of involvement with a backward deaf girl in this remote, primitive place would border on sheer lunacy.

He blamed his temporary fascination on the fact that Roweena was so dramatically different from the other women he'd known. Brady adored women. He had made an art of pursuing them, flirting with them, enjoying them. And *leaving* them, more often than not with little rancor on either side.

He had no interest in the domestic life. There was too much he wanted to do, too many places he wanted to see. Jack sometimes accused him of having "the Gypsy in his soul," and Brady wasn't so sure that his brother might not be right. In truth, he was restless by nature, seldom satisfied for very long at a time. Something inside him continually urged him on to new faces, new experiences, new relationships.

That being the case, he would be the worst kind of fool to let his emotions run out of control. To take up with a girl like Roweena would jeopardize the freedom he prized so highly.

Besides, Gabriel would almost certainly murder him.

Fortunately, it wasn't all that difficult to turn his attention else-where. The Claddagh itself had captured his interest. The place and its people had almost immediately seized him and drawn him in. Brady was convinced that some of his best portraits to date would come out of the Claddagh. Among these dusky, narrow lanes and crooked alleyways, he had found the many faces of sorrow, suffering, and despair. Yet he had also seen features chiseled of strength, en-durance, and a strange kind of peace—a serenity unlike anything he had ever before encountered. Here the past blurred with the present. An age-old faith and ancient secrets were as much a part of the people's existence as the sea that fed them and the God who they insisted dwelt among them.

The dark mystique that was the Claddagh had staked a claim on his soul. Nowadays he found himself increasingly reluctant to leave the place and return to his flat and even more loath to think of leaving Galway for good.

Later, when Terese Sheridan reappeared from behind the curtain—now scrubbed clean, her riot of russet hair brushed to a blaze of copper—it occurred to Brady that perhaps here was yet another at-traction to heighten the Claddagh's appeal.

Gabriel watched the young American rascal—for if his instincts did not serve him false, this Brady Kane was just that, a *rascal*—as Roweena and the island girl returned. At first he thought the spark of interest in the lad's eye was for Roweena, and his jaw tightened. But upon closer appraisal, he realized that the object of the Yank's scrutiny was the girl from Inishmore.

He almost smiled. That one would be a match for the young *jack-een,* he would warrant. She might be young, but she was no foolish girl. Trouble and hard times had hardened her; that much was plain. In her own way, she seemed years older than Roweena or the Amer-ican.

He stood, gave a nod of approval to the tall island girl, then another to Roweena for her help. The wee wane was clearly wanting to be included in their midst, so he dipped low to scoop her up. "You may go with us to see Jane. She likes your company well enough, for some unaccountable reason," he teased.

The child beamed at him and chuckled. "I like your company, Gabriel."

"Indeed? And I expect you would like to ride upon my shoulders as well, eh? Come on, then,'' he said, swinging the child around to piggyback him. "We will be on our way."

He turned to Roweena, then Brady Kane. "It is time for you to be getting along, too, Yank," he said pointedly. "Roweena will go with us to see Jane Connolly."

The young American looked at him, then glanced at Roweena, not quite concealing his disappointment. But he made no protest. Instead, he cracked his roguish grin and, with a courtly bow for the girls and a wide sweep of his hand, made a jaunty exit.

With wee Eveleen still hugging his neck, Gabriel stood watching the American leave. He was disquieted to realize that Roweena's gaze also followed the bothersome Yank until he was completely out of sight.

12

Jane Connolly

For who can say by what strange way
Christ brings His will to light. . . .
OSCAR WILDE

Terese hurried along the cobbled streets, close behind the others. With her belly satisfied for the first time in weeks and the chance for a position as well, she could almost allow herself to feel hopeful. But fast on the heels of this flicker of optimism came the reminder that she must not dare to hope too much, lest the devil should resent her light heart and cast a weight on it.

For all she knew, this Jane Connolly person might turn out to be an evil old shrew who would shriek and squawk and make life wretched altogether. But sure, wouldn't she plug her ears and tend to the woman in spite of her hatefulness if it meant paying her passage to America?

Not to mention a reprieve from the workhouse . . .

People died in the workhouse, and from the tales Terese had heard, they died from worse things than starvation. For her part, she would rather drop in the street from hunger than die of some filthy disease or at the hands of a raving lunatic.

The little girl—Evie, they called her—glanced back over her shoulder and smiled. An imp, that one. But the child's ingenuous, cheerful nature was somehow heartening after the hostile stares to which Terese had grown accustomed.

These seemed to be good people, if somewhat peculiar. She had always heard that the Claddagh fishermen were a wild lot, but the giant, Gabriel, and the two girls certainly appeared civilized enough.

At least they had been kind to her—kinder than she had any right to expect, she conceded grudgingly.

Even the American had seemed genuinely concerned for her safety, although Terese didn't quite know what to make of him. There had been something disturbing in those dark eyes, something too bold, too inquisitive—and something too much like amusement, as if he found her curiously entertaining. Terese didn't trust him, but it was clear that he had some sort of connection to these Claddagh folk— and she *was* inclined to trust them. She had never met an American before, of course. For all she knew, they might all be as insolent and peculiar as this Brady Kane.

Ahead of her, the big man, Gabriel, and the two girls now came to a halt in front of a stoutly built thatched house. The place was set off to itself, not squeezed in among others, as were the majority of dwellings Terese had noticed on the way. Although the house appeared sturdy enough, there was a forlorn air of abandonment about it. Rotted netting and other debris had been strewn across the yard. On one side of the front door was propped an eel spear, on the other, a splintered barrel. The thatch of the roof also showed signs of neglect.

Terese suppressed a shudder at the gloom and pall of dejection that seemed to hover over the place. But when the big fisherman gestured for her to accompany them to the door, she didn't hesitate. She had already decided that a leaking roof over her head would be better than no roof at all.

Inside, the afternoon gloom bathed the room in deep shadows, but here, too, the same sense of neglect was unmistakable. A stale odor of dust and mold hung over the room. Terese took in the unswept floor, the dingy furniture, and the unwashed dishes with the eye of one who had not so long ago labored over such things in her aunt Una's household.

Despite Gabriel's description of Jane Connolly, Terese had to make a concentrated effort to conceal the blast of pity that shot through her at the sight of the woman. She had expected to be greeted by a hunched, misshapen figure whose temperament would no doubt be as dismal as her physical state. But the widow Connolly was something of a surprise. The woman seated in the wheelchair by the turf fire was so small that she could have easily been mistaken for a child. Her head was bent low, and she appeared to be dozing. But when

Gabriel called out a greeting of "God bless all here," she looked up with eyes that were bright and welcoming.

Gabriel had said the woman was neither young nor old, and Terese could see what he meant. Jane Connolly had the kind of pinched and wizened features that might have been drawn by pain just as easily as by the passing of time. Her hands on the wooden arms of the chair were almost deformed; the wrists were swollen and red, and her right hand in particular was painful to look upon, with its thumb bent toward the palm and the other fingers toward the wrist. The body beneath the lap blanket was clearly twisted. But the hair coiled at the back of her neck was more brown than gray, and the hazel eyes were alert and knowing.

Terese didn't miss the way the woman's features softened at the sight of Roweena and the child, who immediately ran to her and, at the instruction of Gabriel, handed over a small pouch. The woman gave the fisherman a nod as if to thank him, then turned a narrowed gaze on Terese.

When Gabriel began to explain in the Irish, Jane Connolly seemed more intent on studying Terese than on hearing what the big fisherman had to say. The woman's scrutiny was bold and somehow unnerving, and Terese found herself wanting to look away from those searching eyes. Instead, Roweena caught her hand to bring her up close to the crippled woman as Gabriel set about making an introduction.

There was no acknowledgment by the widow, no effort to make a civil greeting. Only that sharp-eyed, measuring stare. After another moment, she turned to Gabriel, and a quick, barbed exchange ensued in the Irish.

"What are you thinking, man? I am not a wealthy woman. I can't afford a hired girl."

"We've talked of this before, Jane. You need a girl. You know you do." The big fisherman spoke evenly and quietly but with a firmness that brooked no argument. "This girl will work for a reasonable wage."

"Ha." The small face creased even more as she shot a skeptical glance at Terese.

Ignoring the woman's surliness, Gabriel continued. "The girl needs a place to stay. And you need help. Look at her—she's strong and fit and will be of much use to you."

The widow glared at him. "She's not one of us. She might be a lunatic or a murderer, for all we're knowing."

"Jane, Jane, I thought you trusted me," the fisherman countered reasonably. "Would I bring you a dangerous girl?"

The woman sniffed. "She might steal me blind, a wild girl like that."

Terese clenched her hands at her sides. The big fisherman's eyes sparked with something that might have been amusement, but his tone was offhand and agreeable as he replied. "Now, Jane, you say you are but a poor widow woman, with nothing to steal."

Jane Connolly rolled her eyes toward heaven and gave an exaggerated sigh. " 'Tis true," she said. "But she might murder me in my bed, even so."

The woman was daft entirely, Terese decided. The dread disease that had twisted her body must have also afflicted her brain.

Gabriel shook his head. "Now, Jane, haven't you told me that most nights you cannot get yourself *into* your bed at all but must sleep in your chair?"

Ah, now the eyes *really* narrowed, and the square little chin jutted out a bit more. Terese felt an irrational urge to laugh. This poor crippled woman was such a wee thing, yet she obviously considered herself a force to be reckoned with. Something told her that the widow Connolly was actually warming to the idea of hiring her on, but for some fatuous reason of her own was bent on making the fisherman first prove his case.

The giant was nothing if not even natured—Terese would give him that—allowing this sour-tempered woman to rant at him so.

"You surprise me, man, truly you do, putting me at the mercy of an outsider."

Gabriel crossed his sturdy arms over his chest. "Why don't you just speak with the girl, Jane? Have you no word of welcome for a stranger?"

She curled her lip at him, then turned to rake Terese with a hawk-eyed stare. "Well, girl? You're from the Big Island, says Gabriel."

"I am."

The woman curled her lip. "My husband never did trust an islander."

Terese clasped her hands behind her back, drew a long breath, then let it out.

"My man always said the islanders were a bunch of savages."

Only the thought of another cold night in the alleys enabled Terese to hold her tongue.

Jane Connolly lifted a gnarled hand, and Terese couldn't help but notice the way she flinched with the movement. "Well, come here, then, girl," the woman demanded. "Come closer."

Terese stepped up to her, hands still behind her back.

"Show me your hands," the little woman demanded. "Let's see how well acquainted you are with work."

Grinding her teeth, Terese extended both hands palms up and stood unmoving as the woman examined them. The widow's eyes gleamed almost spitefully as she looked up. "Ach, and don't those nails need a good scrubbing? I'll not have a slatternly girl working for me."

With an effort, Terese clamped down on her anger. She was familiar with humiliation, but that did not mean she would tolerate it gladly. Still, the woman was in a pathetic condition. Sure, her pain must be fierce.

"What of your family?" the widow probed. "Why would a young girl like yourself be on your own keeping?"

Terese looked at her. Reluctantly, she gave a brief account of her father and brother's emigration, the subsequent deaths of her family members, and the destruction of her aunt's house in the storm.

She was aware of the widow's scrutiny as she spoke, the knowing expression, the curt nod. "So, then, your menfolk abandoned you," the woman put in, "and now you've run off from your aunt in her time of need, is that it?"

Something in Terese snapped. She yanked her hands back and whipped about as if to go. "You are a batty old woman, do you know that?" she shot over her shoulder as she started for the door. "I will not work for a mad woman."

"Get yourself back here, girl," the big fisherman rumbled. "And mind your manners. Jane isn't through with you yet."

Terese whirled around, facing him. "But I am through with *her!*"

She was amazed when the widow woman cackled. "Didn't I tell you, man? She is a wild island girl."

"And you," Terese repeated through bared teeth, "are a rude old woman!"

Again Jane Connolly laughed. The child, Evie, laughed, too, obviously delighted by the exchange taking place.

These people were more than strange, Terese decided. They were demented.

"Ach, enough now, enough." The widow Connolly attempted to wave a hand, but the twisted, swollen appendage made the gesture seem almost grotesque. In spite of herself, Terese felt another quick stab of pity. Even so, she had no intention of suffering the woman's abuse.

Jane Connolly's next words surprised her, however. "It seems to me that you will do well enough, girl. They do say the island girls aren't afraid of hard work."

Gabriel nodded now in apparent satisfaction, while Roweena smiled at Terese as if to encourage her. And from the corner where she had perched herself on a stool, the peculiar Evie chuckled.

"I will give you a bed and food," said the widow in a brisk, no-nonsense tone. "You don't look as if you eat all that much in any event. You will cook for us and tend to the house, inside and out." Her tone now turned grudging. "And you will tend to me as well. It's little enough I can do for myself these days."

"That sounds to me like a great deal of work," Terese pointed out.

The woman gave her a fierce glare. "Was I looking for you when you came, girl? You can go out the door just as easily as you came in, it seems to me."

"*Jane—*"

The stern word of rebuke from Gabriel merely earned him a terrible scowl.

"What will you pay me?" Terese broke in before the two could take up again.

"Didn't I just offer you a bed and potatoes?"

"A bed and potatoes are not enough. You are requiring a full-time girl. I will work for wages or not at all."

The woman turned to Gabriel. "Impudent. You see? She's a very lowbred girl."

The fisherman lifted his dark eyebrows. "'Tis true for her, though, Jane. You are expecting a great deal of work for no wages. I doubt that you'll find another girl as strong and willing to work as this one."

The shrunken widow woman glowered at him, then turned an even blacker look on Terese. "One shilling a week," she finally said, the words sounding as if she might choke on them.

Hands on hips, Terese glared down at her. "Two."

"Ach, girl, do you think I am the goose laying eggs of gold?"

Terese didn't so much as blink an eye. "Two," she repeated.

Jane Connolly muttered something to the effect that she would "die in the workhouse and all for a greedy girl," but after a moment more gave a grudging nod. "You will begin today."

"If you wish," Terese said just as shortly.

The widow woman wheeled around to Gabriel once more and gave a semblance of shaking a finger at him. The finger, Terese noted, was swollen at the knuckle to almost twice the normal size and was badly inflamed. "And you, man, will bear the burden if she steals from me or murders me altogether."

The big fisherman appeared to be suppressing a smile as he dipped his head in a gesture of agreement. " 'Tis as you say, Jane." He straightened then and beckoned to Roweena and the child. "We will be away now and let you and your new girl get acquainted."

At their departure, Terese braced herself. As cantankerous as her new employer had been in the presence of others, she hated to think what her temperament might be once they were alone. She consoled herself, however, with the thought that she finally had found a position—a position that included two shillings a week and a roof and hearth fire, not to mention "a bed and potatoes."

With that in mind, she actually managed to force a tight little smile for the woman in the wheelchair. "And what shall I be doing first, Mrs. Connolly?" she asked politely.

Jane Connolly regarded her with the same narrow-eyed scrutiny. "I don't suppose an island girl knows much at all about hanging out a proper wash."

"This island girl does," Terese said evenly. "My people were clean and civilized."

"Ha. We will see about that, now won't we? Well, then, get on with your work, girl. Behind the curtain there's a basket of clothes needing to be laundered. All this blather with you and that thick-headed fisherman has exhausted me entirely. I will need to rest now."

"Would you be wanting me to help you to bed, then?"

Slowly, Jane Connolly shook her head. "I can no longer find any comfort in my bed," she said, averting her gaze. The woman appeared drawn and deathly pale. "I spend most of my hours in this infernal chair. That great oaf, Gabriel, doesn't he nag at me to get up more, never mind the pain? 'Get up, Jane, and uncoil yourself,' " she said in a sneering imitation, " 'or you will surely turn to stone.' "

Her head dropped even lower. "He doesn't know," she said bitterly. "He can't know what it's like for me. I *am* turning to stone, and there is nothing anyone can do about it."

She glanced up at Terese then. "I am not an old woman, you know. You think I am old, and our dear Lord knows I feel it. But in truth I've no more than ten years or so on Gabriel."

Terese evidently failed to conceal her astonishment, for the woman gave a rueful smile and nodded. " 'Tis true." As if she suddenly decided she had said too much, she clamped her jaw. "Well, all right, then. Go and see to your work now. Make no mistake about it, miss, you will earn your two shillings a week.''

Not doubting for a moment that she would do just that, Terese gave a resigned sigh and went in search of the clothes basket.

13

Regarding Women

One had a lovely face,
And two or three had charm,
But charm and face were in vain. . . .
W . B . Y E A T S

NEW YORK CITY

Jack Kane looked idly around the ballroom of the Harrington mansion. It was unlikely that a Russian palace would have boasted more opulence or excess. White fire danced back and forth from the crystal chandeliers to diamond-bedecked socialites, only to be swept up in the flames of what must have been two hundred or more flickering candles placed all about the room. The place was so brightly lit it might have set the entire city ablaze.

Not the typical Irish *ceili,* that was certain. The thought brought a wry grin. For once, being Irish hadn't prevented Jack from receiving an invitation, indeed had actually helped to guarantee it. Had he been shanty Irish, however, that wouldn't have been the case. Only the very rich Irish would be showing their gobs at this affair, a benefit ball put on to aid the work of some of the immigrant societies.

There was never enough money, of course, to keep up with the increasing waves of immigrants flooding the harbors these days. So when Richard Harrington and a select few among the city's elite circle—those who had not lost their fortunes in the crash last year— agreed to host a benefit for "the destitute and the despairing," every Irishman with a bank account and a tailcoat got himself an invitation.

For most of the evening, Jack had been preoccupied with his own thoughts, primarily of his brother's whereabouts. The young rogue's unaccountable silence had gone on long enough. Foul weather or not, Tom West was set to go across and have a look if there was no word from Brady in the next couple of weeks.

At the moment, there was another source of irritation, this one closer at hand: the annoying Miss Patricia Woodstock. It wasn't that his dinner companion lacked appeal. To the contrary, Miss Woodstock was quite fetching. Blonde and elegant, she had the kind of patrician features and form that never failed to turn heads. But to Jack's thinking, her looks were just about all she could boast of. In fact, in one of his more fanciful moments, he had decided that the fair Miss Woodstock rather resembled one of those French cream puffs that Addy was forever bringing home from Cree's Bakery—a kind of powdery confection that made the mouth water but turned out to be little more than sugar-sprinkled air.

All frosting and no filling, as it were.

The girl had been like a leech throughout the entire evening, fixing her attention on his every word, rolling her china-doll eyes and chiding him with a dainty shake of the head at each hint of what she referred to as his "outrageous wit." Even when Jack had deliberately taken up flirting with *Mrs.* Woodstock, Patricia's widowed mother—who was actually far more interesting than her daughter—the vacant young woman had continued to fawn on him in the most foolish fashion, as if she hadn't noticed his boorishness.

Jack had toyed briefly with the idea of deliberately insulting the girl, then decided against it. He supposed she was only trying to help her family, after all. Perhaps she should even be commended for her willingness to sacrifice herself by consorting with an Irishman. As for her dear, departed father, poor old Woodstock would almost certainly turn in his grave at the idea of a Paddy for a son-in-law.

Still, if Miss Patricia was to be successful in her campaign to restore the family fortunes, he thought nastily, she would have to learn not to patronize the candidates. Even an Irishman had his pride, after all.

Jack held no illusions about the girl's interest in him, and he wasn't about to underrate what he suspected might be some very highly developed predatory instincts. She would retract her claws for only so long. She might tolerate him well enough at a banquet table; since she, no doubt, believed him to be filthy rich, perhaps she didn't find him altogether offensive—for an Irishman. But if he were to fall for her ploys and take her to the altar, things would change quickly enough, he'd warrant. Once she got her mitts on his money, she would more than likely bar him from the bedroom and find a way to boot him out of the rest of her life as well.

Too bad for Patricia Woodstock that he wasn't quite the dolt she apparently believed him to be. As a widower for nearly eight years now—and a *wealthy* widower, at that—he had been targeted several times by most of the empty-headed fortune hunters about town. For a time he had actually considered the possibility of making a marriage of convenience. He would have liked children and a home. Although Addy kept his household running as efficiently as any wife would have, perhaps more so, it wasn't the same as having a family.

But he had never given any real credence to the idea. He knew himself too well, knew he could never be satisfied with anything less than a real marriage. He would always end up comparing another woman—a woman he didn't love, at least—to Martha.

She had been no beauty, his Martha, but she had had a certain charm, a quiet graciousness, and a fundamental goodness that, combined with her quick, incisive mind, had not only made her desirable to Jack but won his respect as well. Martha had been his lover, his sweetheart, and his best friend, and every woman he had known since seemed to pale in comparison.

Unfortunately, they had had less than two brief years together before she died from cancer. That had been almost eight years ago, and Jack still missed her.

But not so much that he would make an ill-fated match with a silly little schemer like Patricia Woodstock. He had been nearly thirty when he married Martha, was close on forty now, and he would spend the rest of his life alone if he must. He had the newspaper, enough money to live the way he wished, and, of course, he had Brady and Rose.

His mouth turned sour as he reminded himself that his brother was missing somewhere in Ireland, and his sister, Rose, was *Sister* Rose, a nun in a New Jersey convent.

But even though Rose might never make her home with him, Brady would eventually come back. Though at times he worried himself to desperation about his brother, somehow Jack could not imagine anything really disastrous happening to the careless young rascal. Brady always seemed to come out with a winning hand.

Please, God, let that be the case this time. . . .

A rather insistent tug on his arm reminded Jack that he had been too long disengaged from the philistine ritual taking place around him. He gave a discreet sigh, then turned back to his dinner companion, forcing a show of interest that served to brighten still more the calculating glint in her eye.

※❦❧❀

Cavan Sheridan was having trouble concentrating on the grammar text in front of him. His difficulty had nothing to do with the lesson itself, however, but rather with the instructor, who at the moment stood beside his desk, watching his progress as he attempted to rearrange the parts of a sentence.

Samantha Harte was like no other woman Cavan had ever met. Certainly, she defied every preconceived idea he might have had about schoolteachers before he enrolled in this night class.

The classroom itself, which was in the basement of the parish hall, had turned out to be predictably gloomy, cold, and musty. Cavan had expected the teacher to be equally drab.

As it turned out, the slender Miss Harte, though quiet and seemingly possessed of great dignity and reserve, was anything but drab. By tonight's session—the fourth so far—Cavan was half in love with the woman. It concerned him not in the least that she might be a few years older than he. Indeed, it only made her that much more intriguing. Nor did it bother him that Samantha Harte was obviously an educated, refined woman whose genteel demeanor and graceful manners clearly marked her as a lady. From the first night, she had dazzled him, until by now he was thoroughly smitten.

Everything about the woman fascinated Cavan: the thick knot of glossy chestnut hair from which one or two pins were invariably escaping; the delicate oval face; the enormous brown eyes in which flecks of amber caught the light; the faint scent of soap and rose water that accompanied her every move; the beautiful, rich voice and the shy smile that seemed strangely at odds with her air of quiet confidence. With such a splendid distraction, he told himself throughout the evening, was it any wonder he had to make an extraordinary effort to keep his mind on his studies?

When he had finally finished the assignment, Cavan deliberately lagged behind the other students, the last to approach the teacher's desk. She gave him that quick little smile he had come to look for, then scanned the paper he handed her.

"This would appear to be very good, Mr. Sheridan," she said, glancing up. "Your usual fine work. You do seem to have an excellent grasp of grammar. I almost think you could have omitted this session and gone on to the more advanced class."

Cavan shook his head, at the same time trying to ignore the skip of his heart at her approval. "I'll be needing all the grammar and such I can get," he said, "for the job I'm wanting."

She folded her hands on top of the desk. "What job would that be?"

"I mean to work for the *Vanguard*—the newspaper—you see. So I'll be needing a great deal more education."

She smiled at him. "You plan to be a printer, do you?"

"No, ma'am," Cavan said firmly. "It's a reporter's job I'm after."

Her dark brows lifted slightly. "A reporter? Well, that's certainly an ambitious goal for—" She broke off, as if embarrassed by what she had almost said.

"For an Irisher?" Cavan finished for her, managing a tight smile. She blushed, and he hurried to ease her awkwardness. "You're right, of course. But I already have one foot in the door, you see, and I'm hoping to get myself the rest of the way in before long. I mean to be ready when the time comes."

At her questioning look, Cavan went on to explain. "I'm presently employed by Mr. Jack Kane as his driver. But that's only temporary. I won't be driving his buggy forever."

"I see." Again she smiled, then stood. "Well, I can see you have ambition, Mr. Sheridan," she said, looking up at him. "And you're a very good student. I should think your chances for success are excellent."

Was he imagining it, or did she seem slightly flustered? Had he said something wrong? Or perhaps he had said too much. Perhaps he'd embarrassed her with his crack about the "Irisher."

"Miss Harte?" he ventured, her name on his lips threatening to choke him.

She gave him another quick smile.

"I—" he had to swallow before finishing—"I want to thank you. You're a fine teacher. You've helped me more than you can know."

"Oh . . . well, I meant what I said, Mr. Sheridan. You're an excellent student. A pleasure to teach, actually." She put a hand to her throat, where a small black bow was tied, and Cavan couldn't help but admire the long, slender fingers. Her skin was like rich cream, he thought. Wouldn't it be grand to hold that fine-boned hand in his?

He realized with a start that she had apparently said something and he'd missed it. "Ma'am?"

"I . . . before . . . I wasn't referring to your . . . being Irish. I was about to say that you're ambitious for a young man." She paused. "And also, it's . . . *Mrs.* Harte."

The bottom drained out of Cavan's heart, and he glanced away, unable to meet her gaze. Suddenly, he felt very much the oafish schoolboy.

When he made no reply, she went on, her voice low. "I'm . . . a widow, actually. My husband passed away four years ago."

May God forgive him, he had all he could do to conceal his relief. Instantly guilt ridden, Cavan mumbled, "I'm—sorry to hear that."

He felt like the most wretchedly selfish lout under the sun, to be grateful that she had suffered such a loss. Yet grateful is what he was, or at the least relieved, and there was no denying it.

Abruptly, her mood turned brisk as they started for the door. "Well, it's getting late. The custodian will want to lock up."

Cavan followed her from the room, then up the steps and down the dim, deserted corridor. In the silence between them, he found himself wondering what her life was like. Since she was a widow, would she live alone, or had she gone back to her family after her husband's death? It struck him then that she might even have children. The thought caught him up short. Somehow, he could not imagine Samantha Harte as a mother. She seemed so youthful herself, so delicate and vulnerable.

There were many questions he would have liked to ask, so much he wanted to know about her. But he didn't want to pry, didn't want her thinking he was too bold.

As it happened, she had questions of her own. "What is it like working for Mr. Kane?"

They were at the front of the building now, and Cavan held the door for her, then followed her out before replying. "Jack Kane is a fair man, I suppose. Some might find him demanding, but it seems to me he asks no more of his people than he does of himself. He treats me fine, I'd have to say."

"Really? He has a, ah . . . rather *questionable* reputation, doesn't he? I would have thought—" She broke off. "I'm sorry. I shouldn't have said that. Mr. Kane is your employer, and his reputation is certainly none of my business, after all."

There was just enough light from the streetlamp across the way that Cavan could see the golden flecks in her eyes, and for a moment he couldn't seem to find his tongue. "I've heard the stories," he finally managed. "And I expect Jack Kane is no saint. But I've seen nothing to indicate he's the blackguard some claim he is. In fact, I would say I have it pretty good—" he grinned—"for an Irisher."

It was too dark to tell if she was blushing again, but she smiled up at him somewhat ruefully. "Haven't I heard that Mr. Kane is Irish himself?"

Cavan nodded. "He is. And he makes no apology for it."

"I should hope not." She stood there a moment, regarding Cavan as if she couldn't quite decide whether to go on. When she did, her words surprised him. "I must say, I think it's a disgrace, the way the Irish are treated in this city. I want you to know, Mr. Sheridan, that not everyone feels unkindly toward them." She blinked. "That is . . . toward you . . . and your people."

She was obviously finding it difficult to express herself. Sensing her hesitancy, her awkwardness, Cavan warmed to her that much more.

"Well," she said, turning to go, "thank you for seeing me out, Mr. Sheridan."

On impulse, Cavan put a hand to her arm. "You're not walking, sure?"

Her glance went to his hand before she again met his gaze. "I always walk. I really don't live that far away."

"Still, you ought not to be walking alone in this neighborhood, Mrs. Harte, a lady like yourself." He dropped his hand away. "I'll be happy to drive you home."

Cavan thought she was about to agree, but instead she shook her head. "No, really, that's not necessary, Mr. Sheridan. It's only a short walk, and I don't mind it at all."

"Please?" he insisted. "It would be my pleasure. I have the small buggy, you see. Mr. Kane lets me use it most nights I have class."

"Well, I don't know—" Still she hesitated. "You're quite certain you wouldn't mind? But what about Mr. Kane? Are you sure he wouldn't object to your using the carriage for someone else?"

Cavan again took her arm, starting toward the street. "Jack Kane would never allow a lady to go home unescorted if he could help it. Why, if he were here, he would insist on driving you home himself."

She raised one eyebrow in a skeptical glance. "I must say, I can't quite see myself getting into a carriage with your notorious employer, Mr. Sheridan."

"Ah, well, I'm a very *un*notorious fellow myself, so you can feel entirely safe with me," Cavan said as he helped her into the carriage, then draped the lap robe over her. She leaned forward, settling herself, and for a moment her face was very close to his, making it nearly impossible for him to catch his breath. "If you'll just tell me where you live?" he finally managed to choke out.

"Oh, it's not far. Bleecker Street, near Thompson. Do you know it?"

Cavan nodded, vaguely aware of the district.

"It's a brick four-story," she said, adding, "I have a flat on the second floor."

Living in such an area of decent but modest brick fronts, she would not be well-to-do, Cavan reasoned as he climbed onto the driver's seat and took up the reins. A comforting thought, that. Her being an educated woman was obstacle enough. He would not have had any chance whatsoever with her had she been a wealthy woman as well.

※❦※

Later that night, Samantha Harte sat at the small painted table in the kitchen of her apartment. Her intention had been to grade papers. Instead, she found herself drifting back in time, an exercise she would normally have avoided because of the pain that inevitably accompanied it. Tonight, however, she seemed unable to stop the memories.

And all, she thought with a sad smile, because of a carriage ride.

The carriage had felt strange to her, almost unnatural. For a long time now, she had availed herself of that sort of luxury only on rare occasions, for special events—holiday dinners or the rare wedding or funeral. Tonight, it seemed as if each bump of the wheels had jarred her back to another time, a time when she had taken things like carriage rides and fur lap robes and handsome, high-stepping horses for granted.

It wasn't that she minded walking; to the contrary, she thrived on it. During that awful time after Bronson died, the long, solitary walks had helped to bring about a kind of healing in her. She had actually sneaked out of the house numerous times, just to extricate herself from the smothering solicitude of her family, sometimes walking for hours before returning home.

She smiled at the irony, to think that a habit initially born of willful desperation had turned into one of sheer necessity. The reality was that she simply could not afford a carriage, not on the meager wages she earned as a textbook proofreader and a part-time teacher for some of the immigrant societies.

She knew that her family and few remaining friends thought her a little mad. She could almost hear them whispering among themselves, speculating as to whether Bronson's death might have unhinged her mind. What else could possibly account for her decision to leave the fellowship *and* seek independence from her family?

There were times in the dead of night when Samantha wasn't at all sure that they weren't right. Even she would be hard-pressed to cite a sensible reason for the direction she had taken.

Although Samantha *did* feel a sense of purpose in her life these days, if she were to be altogether honest she would have to admit that she had gained far more from her new lifestyle than she had given. There was never any real thought of any kind of "sacrifice."

So even though some might view her behavior as a reaction to grief, others as an act of foolishness, Samantha knew it was more an act of self-preservation. She did hope that the Lord approved. Whether anyone else recognized the truth or not, she could not escape it: her decision to break with her past, and by doing so reject all the comforts it would have offered, had been an almost desperate attempt to finally make something meaningful and worthwhile of her life.

For a long time after Bronson's death, she had been unable to focus on anything more demanding than getting through one day at a time. It had been months before she was able to grasp the reality that, even if her marriage had produced nothing else of any lasting value, it had at least enabled her to grow to the point where she could no longer return to the shallow, self-centered creature she had once been.

She knew now that if she *had* gone back to her former useless mode of existence, she might well have perished, might never have come to believe that her life could have some real value after all.

Her thoughts went to the awkward young Irishman who had driven her home earlier that evening. Perhaps her prize student wasn't the best example of why her work mattered—Samantha suspected that Cavan Sheridan would attain his goals with or without her help—but she *was* helping him, and others like him, to improve their lives, even as she enriched her own. That was worth something, surely.

With a rueful smile, she admitted it had also been nice to have a handsome young man like Cavan Sheridan pay her a measure of attention. He had been so sweet in his insistence on seeing her safely home. His thoughtfulness had almost made her feel young . . . even attractive . . . again.

She had almost forgotten what it was like to feel that way. . . .

Immediately, the memory of Bronson's voice forged a stern rebuke in her spirit for such frivolous, worldly thoughts. With an effort, Samantha shook off both her girlish musings and the echo of her husband's denunciation. Then, straightening, she raised the wick on the lamp and returned to her students' papers.

14

A Letter of Opportunity

All for the good comes an unexpected word,
God opens a window, a door,
And hope comes in.

CAVAN SHERIDAN,
FROM *WAYSIDE NOTES*

A week later, a letter from Brady finally arrived. Jack stood by the fire as he read the first few words, breathing a deep sigh of relief once he learned the young pup was safe.

He scanned his brother's account of the devastating windstorm, giving most of it little more than a quick glance, since he had already read much of the same information in some of the city's rival newspapers. Another sore subject, and one he meant to raise with Brady as soon as he returned. The *Vanguard* was usually first to report European news of any significance, not last!

As he continued to read, his initial relief gave way to exasperation, then anger as he realized Brady's intentions:

> I KNOW I AGREED TO STAY NO LONGER THAN TWO MONTHS, BUT I'M
> SURE YOU'LL UNDERSTAND THAT, IN THE WAKE OF THE STORM AND ALL
> THAT'S HAPPENED, I CAN'T POSSIBLY COMPLETE THE JOB IN SUCH A
> SHORT TIME.
>
> THERE'S SO MUCH TO TELL, JACK! SURELY THERE NEVER WAS A
> COUNTRY LIKE IRELAND, SO RIFE WITH POVERTY, SO OPPRESSED BY
> INVADERS. WHY, WHAT THE BRITISH CROWN HAS DONE TO OUR PEOPLE
> IS NOTHING SHORT OF AN ABOMINATION!

So, it was "our people" now, was it? And this from the same little brother who was always so quick to rib Jack about his "insufferable

Irishness." A grim smile played about his mouth as he went on reading:

THE IRISH ARE MAGNIFICENT, JACK—SO BOLD AND FEARLESS. THEY
MAY BE HELD CAPTIVE TO THE BRITISH, BUT YOU WON'T HEAR THEM
CRYING "UNCLE!" FOR THE FIRST TIME I'M BEGINNING TO UNDER-
STAND THE "CELTIC SOUL" YOU USED TO SPEAK OF. I ALWAYS KNEW
I'D LOVE THIS LAND, JACK, AND I'VE NOT BEEN DISAPPOINTED A BIT.
I'VE ALREADY MADE DOZENS OF WONDERFUL SKETCHES, SOME FROM
MY MEMORIES OF THE STORM, OTHERS OF THE LANDSCAPE AND THE
PEOPLE. I THINK YOU'LL BE PLEASED WHEN YOU SEE THEM.

WHAT I WANT TO PROPOSE, JACK—AND I FERVENTLY HOPE YOU
WILL AGREE, FOR THERE IS A FAR BIGGER, MORE IMPORTANT STORY
HERE THAN EITHER OF US COULD HAVE IMAGINED—IS THIS: EVERY TWO
OR THREE WEEKS, I'LL POST TO YOU A SERIES OF ARTICLES, ALONG
WITH THE APPROPRIATE SKETCHES, FOR YOUR USE IN A KIND OF
SERIALIZATION OF THE IRISH CONDITION. MY IDEA IS TO FIRST PRESENT
IRELAND AS IT WAS BEFORE THE WINDSTORM—IN ALL HER AGONY AND
GLORY—AND THEN COVER THE STORM ITSELF AND SHOW WHAT
TERRIBLE DEVASTATION IT WROUGHT UPON AN ALREADY DESPERATE
LAND.

THINK OF IT, JACK. THERE ARE THOUSANDS AND THOUSANDS OF
IRISH IN NEW YORK ALONE, NOT TO MENTION THE COUNTLESS
NUMBERS WITHIN THE CIRCULATION AREA OF THE VANGUARD. ADD TO
THAT THE BENEVOLENT SOCIETIES SPRINGING UP ALL OVER THE PLACE,
AND THE INTEREST IN THIS KIND OF STORY SHOULD BE
EXTRAORDINARY! JUST IMAGINE WHAT IT CAN DO TO GENERATE
FINANCIAL AID FOR IRELAND. AND WASN'T THAT ONE OF THE PRIMARY
REASONS YOU SENT ME ACROSS IN THE FIRST PLACE?

Jack's scowl deepened as he read on. Brady knew him too well,
knew exactly how to work him. Any newspaperman worth his salt
would not miss a story like this, especially an *Irish* newspaperman.
Not only would it make a banner serialization—if he agreed to run
it Brady's way—but it might actually help the Irish, both here and
across. And while this wasn't exactly the kind of information the
Committee was looking for, it was a start. Certainly, it should help
to increase the contributions. He dared not hope it would put an end
to the rank prejudice and hostility leveled against the Irish, but at the
same time it couldn't hurt.

Jack had little faith in the "basic decency of man" some of the
do-gooders in the benevolent societies were always blathering about.

He was far more familiar with man's basic *depravity*. Even so, he was willing to concede that the first step in gaining acceptance for those who were "different"—*foreign*—might be to foster understanding of them. Perhaps a measure of compassion would eventually follow.

Certainly, he would be the last to underestimate the power of the press. Cavan Sheridan had simply echoed Jack's own conviction with his remark that "the press can change people's minds . . . even their lives."

He had seen it happen. Look at the way Horace Greeley, though little more than a pawn in the hands of Thurlow Weed and his bunch in Albany, had all but guaranteed their man Seward's election as governor—the first New York governor in forty years who wasn't a Democrat.

Jack shook his head. Ah, yes, his clever little brother knew just how to get his attention—and get his own way in the process.

He almost smiled at the rascal's cunning. As he read on, however, he quickly sobered. Apparently, Brady had rented a flat for himself in Galway City and meant to stay "for a time." He had even taken up with some strange Claddagh fisherman and his brood.

Jack drew a sharp breath. His hands shook as he stared at the letter. Of all the rotten luck! The one place in Ireland he had hoped to keep Brady out of, and he had landed right in the heart of it!

Galway. There was no telling what he might come upon there. Not in the Claddagh; he was unlikely to stumble onto anything of any real importance there. In fact, Jack was surprised to learn that Brady had found his way into the place. Odd folk, the Claddagh people.

But in the Old City itself—in Galway—there was always a chance the lad would unearth something that was best left buried. He thought for a moment, searching his memory. So far as he knew, they had no close kin left in Ireland. Both uncles were gone, along with their father. That left only Aunt Selia, and she had remarried and gone with her new husband to live somewhere near Killaloe. Their mother had been an orphan herself, so there was no immediate family there.

But Jack had spent his boyhood in Galway, and Brady had been born there. Da and his brothers had been well known in the district. Wasn't there a possibility of a distant relative or acquaintance . . . someone who might remember?

By the time he reached the end of the letter, Jack was grinding his teeth:

I HOPE YOU APPROVE OF MY PLAN, JACK. NOW, I KNOW THAT WITH MY PAST HISTORY, YOU MIGHT BE THINKING THAT I'M JUST LOAFING

AROUND, LOOKING FOR EXCUSES TO AVOID ANY REAL WORK. BUT I SWEAR TO YOU THAT I *AM* WORKING, AND THAT'S THE TRUTH! I'M WRITING AND SKETCHING LIKE A MADMAN—I'VE NEVER BEEN SO INSPIRED—AND I THINK YOU'LL BE PLEASED WITH WHAT YOU SEE. SO WHAT DO YOU SAY, JACK—CAN WE TRY IT MY WAY FOR A COUPLE OF MONTHS MORE? THEN IF YOU'RE NOT SATISFIED I'LL COME HOME AT ONCE, MY WORD ON IT.

IN THE MEANTIME, GIVE MY BEST TO EVERYONE. TELL MRS. FLYNN THAT I MISS HER COOKING IN THE WORST WAY. AS I TOLD YOU, THE FOOD SITUATION HERE IS A DISGRACE. ONCE I GET BACK TO THE STATES, I DOUBT THAT I'LL EVER WANT TO SEE ANOTHER POTATO AGAIN!

WRITE SOON, BIG BROTHER. JUST POST ANY LETTERS TO THE GALWAY ADDRESS. I'LL BE HERE FOR AT LEAST A FEW MORE WEEKS.

MY BEST TO ADDY, OF COURSE, THAT TERRIBLE, FIERCE WOMAN!

GOD BLESS US ALL . . . YOUR BROTHER, BRADY

A few more weeks, was it? Slowly, Jack folded the letter and stuck it in his pocket before going to stand at the window. It was a bitterly cold evening, already dark, with nothing to be seen but the shadows cast by barren tree limbs quaking in the wind. Much as he tried to shake off the infernal Irish darkness that sometimes overcame his spirit, on nights like this it was as thick and heavy as a grave shroud.

Brady's letter hadn't helped the melancholy that had plagued Jack for years, even as a boy. In truth, it had been on him that first day off the ship, his first day in America. . . .

❧❧❧

He had been fourteen at the time and doing his best to act as both father and mother to his baby brother and little sister, though he was little more than a frightened child himself.

With Brady in his arms and his sister, Rose—no more than seven or eight at the time—clinging to his free hand, Jack had taken his first long look at the city of New York. They trudged along the docks, pressed on all sides by countless other immigrants—all of whom seemed to be carrying babes in their arms and shouting at one another in foreign tongues.

Rose was squeezing his hand hard enough to send pain shooting up his arm. "I don't like it here, Jack! Please, take us home." Her curly black hair was wet from sea water and perspiration, her tiny face streaked with sweat and dust. She looked like a street urchin, and Jack was ashamed he hadn't been able to clean the children up better before they got off the ship. But their bunks had been squalid, their water foul, and their clothing long ruined from weeks in the dark, wet steerage.

Rose began to cry then, and wee Brady took up the chorus, wailing against Jack's shoulder. For one interminable black moment, a flood of fear and despair overwhelmed Jack, and he almost turned and ran.

The noisy, teeming city terrified him, and he wanted nothing so much as to rest his head on his mother's bosom and weep. But his mother was dead, had died in childbirth with Brady, and their father was in the ground as well. The wee ones had no one to look after them, no one but Jack. And the truth was that they could not go home to Ireland. There was nothing to go back to, and even if there had been, there was no money to take them. They were poor—poor as beggars.

But Jack would not beg, nor would he allow his siblings to demean themselves in such a manner. So somehow, instead of giving in to his own terror, he found the courage to calm the children and go on walking. They made their way past the docks and merged onto the stinking, filthy streets of New York, where at some point, Jack realized that he would conquer his fear of the city only by conquering the city itself.

⁂

Sometimes Jack deluded himself into thinking he had accomplished that boyish resolve. But a deeper, saner part of him knew that that sort of thinking was only illusion. The truth was that New York would not, could not, be conquered, not by any man. She was a terrible, mean woman who ate princes as easily as paupers and spit them out of her mouth without a thought, showing no pity for those who allowed themselves to be swallowed up. Anyone who believed otherwise was a fool, and he was no fool.

At a light rap just then, he swung around to see Cavan Sheridan standing in the doorway, scrunching his cap against his chest and watching Jack.

"Begging your pardon, sir, but I was wondering if I might leave now?"

For a moment the youth's request didn't register.

" 'Tis Thursday, sir. I have the night class—"

"Ah, yes," Jack said, nodding. "Of course. That's fine, lad. Go along to your Miss Harte."

" 'Tis *Mrs.* Harte, sir. She is a widow."

Again Jack gave a nod, not really interested in the teacher Sheridan

had so obviously enshrined. The lad clearly had himself a case of
puppy love, but Jack suspected it would not really take much of a
woman to turn the head of a *gorsoon* like his driver. The boy had a
strange and uncommon admiration for knowledge and those who
owned it. His Mrs. Harte might be squat and middle-aged with a row
of warts hanging from her lip, but if she was even half the scholar
Sheridan apparently believed her to be, no doubt she had the means
to dazzle him.

Jack's mood had brightened somewhat, and he detained young
Sheridan long enough to share the news about Brady. "I've heard
from my brother at last," he said, patting his coat pocket. "It seems
he is alive and well after all."

Sheridan smiled and stepped into the room. "I'm glad for you, sir.
You must be relieved."

"Yes, well, I'm relieved, all right, but no less annoyed with him
for taking so long to let me know his whereabouts. Still, he's had an
idea for the paper that might help him wangle his way back into my
good graces." Jack paused. "And I expect he knows it."

Briefly, he explained Brady's suggestion, then added, "Serializa-
tions seem to work nicely, if the reader cares enough about the subject."

He was surprised at Sheridan's response. "And you think they will
care enough?" he said quietly. "About Ireland?"

Again Jack caught a glimpse of a certain cynicism in the lad that
chanced to appear at odd moments, when least expected. "You disagree?" he asked, going to sit down at his desk.

Sheridan shrugged. "I confess I've not seen much sign of any real
interest in Ireland." As if he sensed he might have overstepped, he
added, "But it's not for me to be saying, of course. You and Mr.
Brady would know better what to expect from your readers."

Drumming his fingers on the desk, Jack shook his head. "Not
necessarily. There's no predicting human nature, Sheridan, at least
not consistently. It's folly for any man to think otherwise."

He studied the tall youth, who had filled out a bit on Mrs. Flynn's
cooking. Sheridan was anything but brawny, but he no longer had
the hollow-eyed look of the starving immigrant about him. "What's
on your mind? You might just as well spit it out."

Of late, it wasn't unusual for Jack to bounce an occasional idea
off the lad. He had caught a glimpse every now and then of a fine
mind, with exceptionally keen instincts. "But perhaps you need to be
going—"

"No, sir, I have time." Sheridan hesitated only a second or two, and Jack had the impression he hadn't far to search before forming his reply. "I agree with what you said, sir, about giving readers a subject they can care about."

Jack leaned back in his chair, waiting.

"It's just that . . . I'm not certain you can make them care about an entire country," Sheridan went on. "At least not in a way that would be of any help to our people. To the Irish, that is," he quickly amended, as if perhaps he shouldn't be lumping Jack and himself together. Sheridan's gaze held steady, but the way he continued to knead his wool cap with his hands told Jack the youth was not entirely comfortable with speaking freely.

He moved to reassure him. "I never ask a man his opinion unless I want it, lad. Speak your mind."

Sheridan seemed to relax a little. "I was wondering if it might not be better to single out only a few individual stories, rather than try to give a broad view of the entire country. It might help to make the people seem more . . . *real*. If your readers could come to know the Irish as real people, on a more . . . personal basis, they might take the plight of Ireland itself more seriously. I think—"

He stopped, watching Jack as if he might have said too much. But Jack's interest was piqued now, and he gestured that Sheridan should go on.

"What I'm trying to say is that it would seem a difficult job, at best, to interest the readers in something as big and impersonal as a country, but not so difficult perhaps to interest them in a young mother whose husband has died at sea and left her with two or three hungry tykes and no money to buy food or pay the rent."

Sheridan's clear blue eyes began to sparkle as he continued. Something in Jack wrenched at the sight of this youthful enthusiasm, this excitement about something as simple and as fundamental as an idea. Had he ever been that young? he wondered almost sadly. That exuberant, that eager? Somehow it didn't seem as though he had ever been a boy—carefree, idle, with the luxury of carving a whistle or daydreaming in the sun. He had worked from the time he was old enough to run messages and make collections.

As a boy, his existence had been worry and hard work. As a young man, his existence had been less worry and more hard work. And now—well, nothing had changed much.

But as Sheridan went on, Jack felt a quickening of his own senses, the familiar skip of his pulse that almost always signaled a worthwhile idea or, back in his gambling days, an unbeatable hand.

"I'm not saying your brother's idea isn't a sound one, mind. Giv-

ing your readers a close-up view of Ireland and all her troubles—
well, with Mr. Brady's ability as an artist, no doubt a firsthand account of Ireland as he sees it will be fascinating. My idea is to add
a bit more to it—to *personalize* it, if you will, perhaps choose four
or five particularly desperate families or individuals, tell their stories—complete with Mr. Brady's sketches, of course." He stopped,
his expression, even his tone, less confident as he added, "And then
bring the subjects of those stories to America."

Jack's head snapped up. "Bring them across?" he repeated in-
credulously. "*All* of them?"

"Indeed, sir." Sheridan said nothing more for a moment, but simply stood looking at Jack.

"An expensive venture, I know, sir," he finally said, his voice
low, "but perhaps if you have the means it would eventually pay for
itself. In terms of increased readership," he hurried to explain, "not
to mention the . . . ah . . . goodwill that would be sure to accrue to
you for your generosity."

Jack looked at him in amazement, then quite suddenly threw back
his head and laughed. It took him a moment to recover, and when
he did he could still scarcely keep from laughing. "Sheridan, I expect
I ought to be grateful entirely that I didn't hire you on as my bookkeeper. Hang it all, but you're generous with my money!"

Sheridan blushed but grinned at Jack. "Sorry, sir. It just seemed
a good idea. I didn't mean to presume—"

Jack waved off his apology. "It *is* a good idea," he said, his mind
racing. "I must admit, I think you're on to something. But if you'll
permit me an observation—this being your idea but my newspaper—
it could take a bit of doing. Even if I'm willing to finance the crossing
of several good Irish souls—and mind, I'm not committing to that
particular madness just yet—but if I do, someone is going to have a
bit of work on their hands, seeing to the arrangements and getting
them settled after they arrive, wouldn't you agree?"

Sheridan nodded, his mind obviously working. "Mrs. Harte and
some of her friends could help with that."

"Who?" Jack said, his own thoughts coursing ahead.

"My teacher—Mrs. Harte. You recall my telling you that she
works with the immigrant societies—"

"Right, right," Jack said, eager to spare himself further rhapso-
dizing on the part of his infatuated driver, who no doubt would have
Mrs. Harte, too, spending the *Vanguard*'s money with unbridled enthusiasm if not held in check. "Well, perhaps that sort of thing can
be taken care of easily enough. But there's the actual reporting—the

developing of the stories, if you will. Seems to me it would take a clever fellow to carry off that sort of writing, wouldn't you say?''

Sheridan smiled a little. ''Addy—Miss O'Meara—goes on and on about Mr. Brady, how clever and bright he is.''

Jack shook his head. ''Brady is good enough with getting the facts straight, and he can draw pictures that would make a saint weep. But that's the rub. He's an artist, not a writer. He could sniff out the stories and give us a good enough rough draft, but I'd have to hire a top-notch writer to whip them into shape.''

His mind darting from one thing to another, he almost missed young Sheridan's quiet reply.

''I could do it, sir.''

15

Key to a Dream

A little love, a little trust,
A soft impulse, a sudden dream,
And life as dry as desert dust
Is fresher than a mountain stream.

STOPFORD A. BROOKE

Kane looked up, clearly distracted. "What's that?"

Cavan expelled the breath he hadn't realized he'd been holding and cleared his throat. "The writing. I could do it. I could write the stories from Mr. Brady's material."

Kane's black eyes raked him so thoroughly that Cavan's skin tightened in self-defense. "I seem to recall your admitting a need for more education, if you're to better yourself," Kane said abruptly. "That's the reason for the night classes, isn't it?"

Without giving Cavan a chance to reply, he added, "There is also the fact that I need you as my driver—which, you might recall, is the reason I hired you." Kane's expression was neutral, but Cavan knew Kane was testing him.

"I would continue as your driver, sir," Cavan hurried to assure him. "I could write the stories at night, after you no longer needed me, don't you see?"

Kane continued to study him. "What makes you think you can write, lad? Do you have some sort of experience you've kept to yourself?"

Cavan ignored his lightly mocking tone. "No experience, sir. I've written only for myself up until now. But it's something . . . I know I can do it, Mr. Kane. I wouldn't have asked for a chance to try if I didn't believe I could do it."

Kane lit a cigar. As he did so, his features drew into a hard, speculative expression that Cavan had come to recognize by now, a look that meant he was paying an idea careful consideration. There was nothing Cavan could do at the moment except to hold his tongue and wait in silence.

He could almost feel the tension that crackled from his employer. The longer he worked for him, the more he had begun to understand the city's love-hate fascination with Black Jack Kane. The man's meteoric rise from poverty to riches, his outrageous but wildly successful business dealings, his deadly black-Irish charm and even deadlier Irish temper, and his enviable attraction of some of the most beautiful women on the eastern seaboard were the stuff that legends were made of.

But Cavan had begun to question some of the more lurid tales so freely circulated by the gossipmongers. From what he could tell, Kane's spectacular success was due more to the fact that he worked harder than any two men combined than to any sort of incredible luck or corrupt business practices. Though it was true that Kane demanded a great deal from his employees, he gave even more of himself; he appeared to never run out of energy. Yet he did not seem so much a driven man as one who truly enjoyed his work and went at it with a passion.

As for his prowess with women, the tales of Kane's endless love affairs were almost certainly exaggerated. Oh, the women couldn't resist him, that much was true. Some of them made absolute fools of themselves over the man. But to the best of Cavan's knowledge, his employer seldom involved himself in any sort of liaison more entangling than a dinner engagement at one of the city's elegant restaurants or an evening at the theater—most often, the opera. He had never known Kane to bring a woman home, nor had he ever left him at a woman's residence. While Jack Kane might spend a great number of evenings out on the town, he spent his nights at home. Alone.

Cavan was beginning to suspect that at least a part of his employer's charm with the ladies was in the way he managed to elude them.

But as he faced him across the desk, he reminded himself that Kane had not attained the pinnacle on which he stood by being soft or careless. He was a hard man who, as Addy was fond of saying, "brooked no foolishness and suffered no fools."

He was also inclined to be impatient, so Cavan hurried to make his case. "I understand you're probably wondering why you should consider such a suggestion on my part," he said in as steady a voice as he could manage.

Kane stood, crossing his arms over his chest, his dark eyes glinting with mild amusement. "I must admit the question had occurred to me, yes."

Cavan considered going into a long, detailed explanation as to why he thought himself qualified for such an undertaking, but the truth was that he *wasn't* qualified, and both he and Kane knew it. So he took a deep breath and offered the only reply that seemed truthful. "My only experience is the writing I've done for myself. But you can trust me, sir. My grammar may not be expert just yet—" Kane lifted one dark brow in a wry expression as Cavan pressed on—"but Mrs. Harte is helping me a great deal, and she says I'm the best scholar she's ever taught. Besides, wouldn't one of the proofreaders be correcting me if I trip up too badly?"

Kane twisted his mouth downward. "I have only two proofreaders I can trust," he said. "My front-page reader, Hailey, can no longer see well enough to be of any real value. And Jimmy Kidder is set to retire come fall."

Something went off in Cavan's mind, but for the moment he kept his silence.

"You meant what you said that day, didn't you, Sheridan?" Kane asked abruptly.

Cavan frowned. "Sir?"

"The day I hired you on as my driver, you admitted that what you *really* wanted was to work for the newspaper."

Cavan did, of course, remember. "Aye, I meant it, sir." He held Kane's gaze. "I still do."

Jack Kane dropped his arms away from his chest and put his hands in his pockets. For a long time he made no reply but simply stood there, regarding Cavan in an unhurried, speculative manner.

Cavan felt his hands turn clammy with perspiration. Even though Kane kept the study reasonably cool compared to the rest of the house, he could feel the heat rising up the back of his neck.

"All right, then. Why not?" Kane flung out, his tone surprisingly casual. "An old gambler like myself can't resist taking a chance now and then. Here's what we'll do, Sheridan," he went on in a clipped, precise voice. "I will write to my brother and explain your idea, ask him to design his copy in such a way that he focuses on only a few specific people—and on highly interesting ones, at that."

Cavan had all he could do to suppress a shout of excitement. Instead, he balled his hands into such tight fists at his sides that he feared he might draw blood.

"When Brady's first post comes," Kane went on matter-of-factly, "you will make it into a story so compelling it will seize the city by the throat, sizably increasing the *Vanguard*'s subscription list—" he paused, his tone again turning sardonic—"and at the same time making you the most sought-after reporter in the state of New York." The dark eyebrows quirked. "You will, of course, remain wholly loyal to me, in spite of your newfound fame."

As Kane finished, a quick, challenging grin broke over his face.

Cavan didn't quite manage an answering smile. "Of course, sir." He swallowed hard. "You mean it, then—that you will let me try my hand at the stories?"

Below the black mustache, Kane's mouth thinned slightly. "I mean that I will give you a chance, but only if you do not slack off in your responsibilities as my driver. And if your aspirations to be a reporter are genuine, you will familiarize yourself with the *Vanguard*'s operations from the ground up. You will learn the presses and even a bit about keeping books—though only if you vow to control your penchant for spending my money. And you will get to know the newsboys and their trade."

Cavan nodded, scarcely able to contain his excitement. Perhaps Kane thought he was demanding much of Cavan, when in truth the man was handing him the key to a dream.

"One more thing," Kane went on. "You will do your writing on your own time, not mine. And if I decide your effort is lacking and not up to the *Vanguard*'s standards, you will accept my opinion as final in the matter. Oh, and Sheridan—you will lose most of your Irish brogue, at least enough that it doesn't destroy your credibility as a writer. Understood?"

Cavan never wavered as he looked his employer in the eye. "Understood, sir."

Another slow grin broke over Kane's dark features as he chomped on his cigar. "Do you know, Sheridan, you sometimes remind me a bit of myself at your age?"

Now Cavan did manage a smile, but in truth he wasn't at all sure whether he had just been saluted or insulted. He braced himself, wondering how far he dared press. "Mr. Kane? Do I understand that you're thinking of hiring a new proofreader for the paper?"

Kane nodded, his smile giving way to a frown. "I can't think what else to do. I'll not be kicking old Hailey out, of course. He has to

eat, and no one else is likely to hire him, the shape he's in. I expect
I can find another place for him somewhere downstairs.''

"I thought I would mention a possibility as a replacement,'' Cavan
ventured carefully, "if you're interested, that is.''

"And that would be . . . ?''

"Mrs. Harte, sir. I'm sure she would do an excellent job for you.
She's had experience, you see.''

"*Your* Mrs. Harte? The schoolteacher?'' Kane's look was altogether dubious.

"Aye, sir. She teaches the night classes, but she also works part-
time as a proofreader for a textbook company. The problem is they
don't give her enough work that she can earn a fair wage.''

"Well, now, lad, it sounds to me as if you and your Mrs. Harte
are becoming quite friendly, if she's letting you in on her financial
affairs.''

Kane's smile was somewhat snide, his tone teasing. But Cavan
didn't mind. He had observed that Jack Kane characteristically confined his teasing to those few men he favored.

"Nothing like that, Mr. Kane. But we do talk now and then. Mrs.
Harte indicated that the textbook company can't afford to employ her
more than a few hours a week, and she's looking for a more lucrative
position.''

"I could hardly bring a woman into the newsroom. Especially a
lady.''

"Yes, sir, but she works for the textbook company from her home.
Couldn't she do the same for the *Vanguard*?''

Kane flicked the ash from his cigar. "That's a possibility, I suppose. But see here, Sheridan, you've already proposed this paragon
of perfect womanhood as a coordinator for our newly conceived immigrant program—if that works out and I allow you to spend my
money as freely as you seem to think I should. I want your word that
you won't have your lady friend snatching away my position as publisher when my back is turned.''

Cavan fought madly to quell the hot blush he could feel rising up
his neck. "She's hardly a lady friend, sir—''

Kane laughed good-naturedly and came around the desk. "That's
fine, lad. Perhaps I'll just stop by the school one evening to meet
this glory of a woman, see how she strikes me. But for now, I expect
you'd best be getting along to class. Else you may find yourself in
trouble with the teacher. Besides, you've still got a bit to learn before
we turn you into the city's most illustrious reporter.''

16

Possibilities

Let nothing pass, for every hand
Must find some work to do,
Lose not a chance to waken love—
Be firm and just and true.

C H A R L E S   D I C K E N S

Jack wasted no time in getting a reply off to Brady. The next morning
in his office he hurriedly penned a brief letter, saying just enough to
let the cunning young pup know in no uncertain terms that he
wouldn't be duped:

I HAD HOPED TO SEE SOME EVIDENCE OF MATURITY FROM YOU BY NOW—
EVIDENCE LONG OVERDUE, I MIGHT ADD. AN EFFORT TO RELIEVE OUR
WORRIES ABOUT YOU WOULD HAVE DONE NICELY FOR STARTERS. IN
VIEW OF THE HORRENDOUS ACCOUNTS OF THE STORM—AND THE
UNCONSCIONABLY LONG SILENCE ON YOUR PART—PERHAPS YOU WILL
CONCEDE THAT I HAD JUST CAUSE FOR CONCERN. AT THE VERY LEAST,
YOU MIGHT HAVE SENT A QUICK NOTE ASSURING US OF YOUR SAFETY.
YOUR CUSTOMARY THOUGHTLESSNESS ALLOWED ME TO ENDURE WEEKS
OF NOT KNOWING WHETHER YOU WERE ALIVE OR DEAD. AND THEN
WHEN YOU FINALLY GOT AROUND TO DROPPING A LINE, YOU SET MY
TEETH TO GRINDING WITH THE INFORMATION THAT YOU HAVE TAKEN UP
WITH SOME WILD CLADDAGH FISHERMAN AND HIS PACK AND NOW HOPE
TO TURN WHAT WAS MEANT TO BE A BRIEF REPORTING STINT INTO AN
EXTENDED TOUR—AND ALL, I MIGHT ADD, AT THE PAPER'S EXPENSE.

I NEVER INTENDED FOR THIS TO BECOME A HOLIDAY, BOYO, AND I
RATHER RESENT YOUR TAKING ADVANTAGE, ESPECIALLY IN VIEW OF

THE FACT THAT I COULD USE YOU HERE IN THE OFFICE RIGHT NOW. I
AM IN DESPERATE NEED OF A COUPLE OF GOOD REPORTERS—MEN WHO
CAN SPOT A STORY WHEN IT BUMPS UP AGAINST THEM—NOT TO
MENTION A FRONT-PAGE PROOFREADER WHO ISN'T HALF-BLIND. I COULD
ALSO USE AN EXTRA PAIR OF HANDS ON THE PRESSES, NOT THAT I
WOULD CONSIDER ASKING YOU TO STAIN YOUR ARTIST'S MITTS WITH
NEWS INK, MIND.

He went on for a few lines more, bludgeoning his brother with
sarcasm—which he knew would merely amuse Brady even as he
ignored it. Only at the last did he indicate agreement to his brother's
proposal, and then based solely on one condition:

YOU WILL NOT GET THE SORT OF STORIES I WANT BY WASTING YOUR
TIME IN THE CLADDAGH. THAT PLACE IS A WORLD OF ITS OWN, AND A
STRANGE AND BACKWARD WORLD, AT THAT. I CAN'T IMAGINE YOUR
FINDING ANYTHING NEWSWORTHY THERE, NOR DO I INTEND TO WORRY
MYSELF WHITE-HEADED THAT SOME MAD CLADDAGH FISHERMAN WILL
GO AFTER YOU ONE NIGHT WITH A HATCHET.

IF YOU'RE SERIOUS ABOUT STAYING IN IRELAND, AND IF YOUR
REASONS ARE AS GENUINE AS YOU WOULD HAVE ME BELIEVE, THEN GET
YOURSELF OUT OF INFERNAL GALWAY AND TEND TO BUSINESS. GO
WHERE THE PEOPLE BETTER REPRESENT THE COUNTRY AND ITS
PROBLEMS.

NOW I MEAN IT, BRADY. THAT IS MY CONDITION, AND I WILL NOT BE
SWAYED. YOU HAVE YOURSELF A BARGAIN, ALBEIT A RELUCTANT ONE
ON MY PART—BUT ONLY IF I SEE A CHANGE OF ADDRESS IN THE VERY
NEAR FUTURE.

He proceeded to explain what he wanted him to do, then, in the
way of finding a select few candidates whose stories would have great
appeal for the *Vanguard*'s readers, with the idea of eventually bringing them across. He would have added more—he hadn't as yet told
Brady about Cavan Sheridan or given him any news of Rose—but
just then Sheridan ducked his head inside the door. "Begging your
pardon, Mr. Kane, but you're needed downstairs right away. Some
sort of problem with the newsboys."

Jack had taken to giving Sheridan odd jobs about the paper, at
which the ambitious young driver busied himself between his other
responsibilities. The lad had already proven himself an asset. No job
seemed too mean for him; instead, he set himself to any assignment
with a cheerful capability Jack could only wish for in Brady. Earlier

that morning he had sent Sheridan to Ben Cross in the pressroom, telling him to make himself useful however Ben directed.

"I thought you were downstairs," he said, following Sheridan down the steps.

"Aye, I was, sir, but one of the printers heard a ruckus in the alley and called for Mr. Cross. He took me along."

In the alley behind the pressroom, where the newsboys picked up their papers, Jack found the small, sharp-featured Ben Cross with two raggedy lads. He recognized only one of the boys: Willie Shanahan, a redheaded, eight-year-old little scrapper, who worked harder at his "business" than any other two newsboys combined. His companion looked a bit older—nine or ten, perhaps, but he was as scrawny and narrow faced as Willie, his clothes hanging on him like sails.

"What's the trouble here?" Jack asked outright. The words were no more than out of his mouth when Willie stepped up to him. Jack fumed as he saw the boy's swollen eye and cut lip. Apparently, the older boy had been knocked about as well, for he had a bad mouse around one eye and an angry red scrape near the other.

"What happened, Willie?" But Jack knew the answer even before he asked. "Rynders's thugs again?"

"Captain" Isaiah Rynders was a scoundrel of the roughest sort, who controlled almost every gang in the city. He and his kind had been giving the newsboys a rash of trouble for months now.

Willie shrugged, and his fine red hair lifted out in all directions. Like baby hair, Jack thought. And why not? The boy was little more than a babe, and that was the truth.

"Don't know, Mr. Jack. There was a bunch of 'em, though. They gave us a terrible pounding, and didn't they say they'd do it again tomorrow if we showed up on the corner with our papers? Said next time they'd break our legs, if we don't pay the protection money." The boy stopped, wiped a hand over his nose, and added indignantly, "They even robbed us of our shoes, Mr. Jack."

"They took your *shoes?*" Anger scalded Jack's throat.

He dropped down to one knee in front of the boy. "How bad are you hurt, Willie? Are you all right?"

The thin lower lip trembled slightly, but Willie nodded. "I got off a couple of good punches, Mr. Jack. I think I might have hurt one of 'em."

Beside him, the taller, dark-haired boy gave a nod of agreement. "We put up a fight, Willie and me did."

Jack straightened, his fists knotted hard at his sides. "I'm sure you did, lads. But we can't have you scrapping just to do your jobs.

Tomorrow morning, first thing, when you come for your papers, I'll have a couple of men at the door to go with you. You're not to go out alone, mind.'' He dug down in his trouser pocket. "Here," he said, "take this money, the two of you, and go get yourselves some shoes.''

Wide-eyed, the two stammered their thanks, then bounded off. Jack knew this was no real solution. He couldn't afford to send men from the office with the boys every day.

But what else could he do? These assaults on the newsboys were becoming routine, one gang after another harassing the boys with threats and beatings, bullying them into paying a part of their hard-earned wages simply to avoid a bruising and having their papers slashed. The police had been largely ineffective against the rampant gang violence across the city, and the newspaper owners were at a loss. What made Jack even more furious was that many of the gang members were Irishmen who thought nothing of victimizing their own people—including children.

Jack would have wagered his new printing press that Isaiah Rynders was behind it all. Whatever the crime—gambling, policy games, opium dealing, brothels, or just plain petty theft—Rynders was a part of it. The slippery snake seemed beyond the law. He ran the gangs—made up mostly of hard men, the dregs of the city—with iron control and an eerie knack for evading the jail cell he deserved.

Trying to explain the situation to Cavan Sheridan as they headed back upstairs, he was surprised when the youth offered to accompany the boys the next morning. Jack shook his head. "Your heart's in the right place, lad, but I wouldn't be putting you in that position. Besides, the boys pick up their papers well before dawn. I want you available to me in the mornings, not out on a street corner swapping punches with Rynders's bully boys.''

"Who is this Rynders fellow?''

Jack gave him an earful about the city's most notorious ruffian, leaving out the fact that he had known Isaiah Rynders personally some years back, when he still visited the gambling dens. He had left the gambling madness behind him after he and Martha were married—she had coaxed a promise from him, and he'd held to his word, even after her death. But there had been a time when he would have rather played blackjack than eat or sleep—and he had made a small fortune at it. That was the source of the nickname still used behind his back, though he suspected most assumed the epithet referred to his character. Or his soul.

In any event, he knew "Captain" Rynders and his toughs well

enough to know they were capable of anything, including beating up defenseless little boys.

"I was surprised to learn," Cavan Sheridan said as they reached the landing, "that this sort of ugly business went on in America. Until I ran into the bully boys in the mines, I thought I'd left such trouble behind in Ireland."

Jack lifted an eyebrow. "The barbarians are everywhere, lad, especially in the city."

They stopped outside the pressroom. "Every place has its no-accounts. They're just called by different names. Here in New York we call them Bowery B'hoys and Dead Rabbits and Slaughter-Housers."

Sheridan's smile was thin. "And in Ireland they're called the Sassenach."

"Aye, that's true, the British have given us our share of grief. But don't make the mistake of casting an entire people into one great lump, lad. Some of the blackest scoundrels in New York have names that start with a *Mac* or an *O*. On the other hand, I've known a number of Brits who were decent enough fellows."

At his driver's openly skeptical expression, Jack grinned and added, "Well, perhaps not all *that* many. But two or three, I should think. You take my point."

⚜

Jack's day didn't get any better. After the exchange with the newsboys, he went back to his office to resume work on the financial article he'd begun the day before, only to discover that he'd left his notes at home. Later, his meeting with key staff members deteriorated into an argument about the advisability of employing European correspondents.

Their arch rival, the *Herald,* had set the precedent, and Brady's trip to Ireland had been Jack's first move to establish a similar system of his own—a move wildly disputed by Clark, his head bookkeeper, and Kaiser, his general manager. As was often the case, any talk of the *Herald* led to an even more heated discussion about the reasons for its phenomenal success. The paper's owner, James Gordon Bennett, had been the target of a great deal of spiteful speculation ever since he'd launched the *Herald.* Jack had his own ideas about why the *Herald* had been so hugely successful and had, in fact, incorporated some of Bennett's ideas into the *Vanguard*'s operation with almost immediate dividends.

There was no denying that the *Herald* thrived on scandalous crimes and shock effect. Bennett was said to have no morals at all—some of the upstanding citizenry referred to him as a "serpent." But there was also no disputing the fact that the dour, sardonic Scot's revolutionary ideas had worked well. Part of the *Herald*'s success, Jack was convinced, could be directly attributed to the fact that Bennett had found a way to reach directly to the servant girl as well as her master. The shiploads of immigrants landing at the Battery, as well as the business owners who employed them, needed information—and entertainment. Bennett had managed to provide both, and consequently the *Herald* sold like wildfire.

A great deal of jealousy had been stirred up by the squinty-eyed Bennett's penny daily among other newspapermen in the city. Even Jack occasionally winced at the *Herald*'s unprincipled dredging up of scandal for the sake of sheer sensationalism. But at the same time he had made a thorough study of Bennett's success and would be the first to admit that he had learned a great deal from the effort.

There was still a question in his mind, however, about what accounted for the loyalty of the *Herald*'s readers. He had not been able to identify exactly what he was missing until Cavan Sheridan had made his observation the night before about the difficulty in interesting readers in something big and impersonal, as opposed to attracting them with the story of an unfortunate widow unable to pay her rent.

At that instant something had clicked in Jack. Later, he had mulled over Sheridan's idea, finally seizing on the one element he thought he could use to far better advantage than Bennett ever had: the personal-interest story.

And as for young Sheridan, he thought he might just give the lad a raise.

But in the meantime, he was still grinding his teeth from the disgruntled staff meeting as he spread out his copy of the *Vanguard*'s morning edition on his desk. In only seconds, bile hot enough to choke him rose in his throat. His eye went relentlessly down the copy, stopping at every error. Even before he reached the end of the front page, he was seething. Two generalizations that Jack knew to be wholly unsupported, four wrong-font letters, two spelling mistakes, and at least half a dozen style faults.

His stomach knotted hard enough to make him flinch, and when Cavan Sheridan appeared in the open doorway to drive him home, Jack shot him a killer glare that made the lad step back.

"You're not ready. . . . I'll come back later," Sheridan said, turning to leave.

"I'll be ready in a shake!" Jack snapped. "But first you go and fetch Bob Hailey for me."

A few minutes later, on the way out to the carriage, Cavan, mindful of his employer's mood, remained studiously silent. By now he had seen Kane in a temper on occasion. He recognized the unyielding set of his back, the tight line of his mouth, the granite-hard jaw beneath the black mustache. He knew from experience that Kane would most likely not say a word the rest of the way home and on throughout the evening.

But to give the man his due, Jack Kane never inflicted his wrath on the members of his household. His anger was more a rigidly contained heat, boiling just beneath the surface of his composure, perceptible but under control.

Kane surprised Cavan this evening, however, by not keeping his silence. Instead, after muttering a stream of disjointed complaints about certain members of his staff, he stopped beside the carriage and said, "I believe I would like to meet your Mrs. Harte. I'm going to have to find someone rather quickly to help with the proofreading. Have you mentioned the idea to her at all?"

As a matter of fact, Cavan had, after Tuesday evening's class. He had driven Samantha Harte home again that night and had lingered for a few minutes in front of her flat, talking. At that time, he had carefully raised the possibility of an opening at the *Vanguard* for someone with her qualifications.

At first she had seemed flustered, protesting that she wasn't qualified. But she also conceded that her job with the textbook company was tenuous at best and she wouldn't mind finding something more dependable. Cavan was sure she was interested but suspected that her misgivings regarding Kane's reputation were at least in part responsible for her resistance to the idea. Even so, he had determined to pursue the subject with his employer, should the opportunity present itself.

Now it seemed that it had. "I raised the possibility," he admitted.

Kane seemed preoccupied as he climbed into the carriage. "I'm moving Bob Hailey to the pressroom tomorrow. They'll find something for him there. I'll handle the front page myself until I can find someone."

Cavan waited until Kane pulled the lap robe over him, then said, "The class meets again tonight. Would you like me to talk to Mrs. Harte about the proofreading position?"

Kane gave a short nod. "Why don't you? If she's interested, tell her to come round to the paper tomorrow afternoon. I'll see her then."

Cavan hesitated, and Kane noticed. "What, you don't think she'll be interested?"

Cavan shook his head. " 'Tis not that, sir. It's just that Mrs. Harte strikes me as being a very . . . reserved lady. Shy, if you will. I don't know that she would be all that comfortable coming to the offices alone, you see."

Kane frowned and made a dismissing gesture with his hand. "All right, then; if that's the case, tell her you'll come for her with the carriage. Perhaps that would put her more at ease."

"Aye, sir, I think that might be best," Cavan said. He would have gone on with more questions, but Kane had clearly turned his thoughts elsewhere.

※◆◆◆◆

Later that evening, Cavan stood at the doorway after class, striving to conceal his disappointment as he heard Samantha Harte's response to the news about the proofreader's position. He had thought she would at least be willing to talk with Kane, despite her apparent skepticism about the man. He hadn't counted on the level of her resistance, however. Her refusal was polite but immediate. And unmistakably firm.

"You understand that I would be driving you to the office?" he said, hoping to convince her. "It's not as if you'd be going on your own."

Again she shook her head. "Cavan, I really do appreciate your confidence in me, but it's as I told you: I don't consider myself qualified for a position of this nature." She paused, then added, "And to be perfectly frank, I don't know that I would be comfortable working . . . for the *Vanguard.*"

"You mean you wouldn't be comfortable working for Jack Kane," he said, making it a statement rather than a question.

She flushed slightly. "Please. I don't want to offend you. You enjoy your job, and you seem to like Mr. Kane—and that's just fine. And as I told you, I'll be only too happy to help you in any way I can with the articles you're assigned. But as for the job—it simply wouldn't be right for me."

Still reluctant to give up, Cavan pressed. "He's not what they say, you know. He's not anything at all like what they say." He was making a poor effort of this, was botching it badly, and he knew it.

The thing was, he really thought she would be improving her situation by accepting a position with Kane, and he wanted to help her.

The rest of it, of course, was that it would be a way to see her more often. He tried once more. "He's not a bad man, Mr. Kane," he said lamely. "You'd see for yourself, once you got to know him a bit. This is going to be an important responsibility, you know, if he actually brings some of the people across. I thought—I'd hoped you'd agree to coordinate things, in addition to the proofreader's position."

She regarded him with a questioning frown. "Cavan . . . why are you so intent on this? I don't think I understand."

Cavan felt the heat rise up his neck. He tried to look away from those searching brown eyes, but her gaze refused to release him. He swallowed, clenching his hands at his sides. "I only meant to help," he said, hearing the unnatural thinness of his own voice. "You indicated that your job with the textbook company might be phasing out soon, and I thought—" He stopped, shrugged, and looked away from her. "I wouldn't mind seeing you more often," he said miserably. "There's that."

A prolonged silence met his admission, and when he met her eyes again, he saw that she wore a positively stricken look. She put a hand to her crisp white collar. "Oh, Cavan, no. You can't mean . . . you mustn't . . . *think* about me . . . that way! Why, I'm . . . your teacher, Cavan. I'm years older than you, you must know that. . . ."

He shook his head. "I'm sorry, Mrs. Harte. I don't mean to embarrass you. But I doubt that you're *years* older than me, and even if you were, it wouldn't make a bit of difference, don't you see? I . . . think you're a wonderful lady, and I enjoy being with you, and I expect I can't apologize for that."

Still pale, she studied him. "How old are you, Cavan?"

He hesitated. "Almost twenty," he finally said, grudgingly.

"I'm twenty-nine years old, Cavan. A widow. You're—"

"A man," Cavan said, his tone hard. "I'm no *gorsoon,* if that's what you're thinking. And I told you, I don't care a whit about your age. Or the fact that you're a widow woman." He stopped, groping for words. "Well, I care about your loss, of course. But as for the years between us—" he looked directly at her, and his impatience fled—"you mustn't mind that at all. It's of no importance."

She moved as if to speak, then stopped and glanced away. After another moment, she murmured something unintelligible, her voice low. Cavan caught only the last few words, delivered more firmly: "Your admiration is very gratifying, but undeserved, I'm afraid. And

I must ask you not to raise the subject of this position with the *Vanguard* again. Please."

She had turned cold all of a sudden, had withdrawn from him even as he stood there wanting nothing so much as to take her hand or touch her hair. Cavan felt a door close against him with a finality that sent a cold blast of wind sweeping over his heart.

17

The Woman
Is a Puzzle

There is something here I do not get,
Some menace I do not comprehend.

VALENTIN IREMONGER

Samantha Harte might not have held Jack's interest for more than a moment had she not balked as she did at meeting him. Unaccustomed as he was to rejection from a woman, however, he found the very act of her refusal enough to pique his curiosity.

Further, Cavan Sheridan's somewhat stilted account of the conversation that had transpired between himself and Mrs. Harte on Thursday night only served to intrigue Jack that much more. He was fairly certain his eager young driver was keeping something back, but when Jack pressed him for details, none were forthcoming.

Jack probably would have dismissed the elusive Mrs. Harte from his mind entirely had Monday not been such a devilish day. He had his hands full on any day, but on Monday he added to his normal routine an exhaustive line-by-line proofing of the late edition's front page. Consequently, he didn't leave the office until almost nine, arriving home tired, hungry, and decidedly out of sorts. He gulped down his supper without really tasting it, skipped his nightly walk, and retired to a restless sleep fraught with bizarre dreams.

Tuesday didn't start off much better. He got out of bed with a thunderous headache and a bad temper, neither of which improved as the day went on. To save himself some time, he brought Donny Sullivan up from typesetting and charged him with proofing the front of the daily edition. The end result was another disaster. Jack's own quick check of the front page later that day fired his already throbbing skull with another shot of pain. The entire page was riddled with misspellings and other editorial flaws. When he confronted the perspiring Sullivan, it was painfully clear that the lad was either severely nearsighted or too dull entirely to grasp what he had neglected. And that was the end of the raw young cub's short-lived stint as a proofreader.

A little before five, Jack called Cavan Sheridan up from the pressroom. "Tell me again exactly what your Mrs. Harte had to say last week," he said from behind his desk, "about the proofreading position."

It had occurred to Jack that, as charming and clever a fellow as Cavan Sheridan might be, he was still wet behind the ears—and royally smitten with the schoolteacher. There was always a chance he might have bungled things in his approach.

The lad proceeded to recap the exchange between himself and the schoolteacher, revealing nothing he hadn't already told Jack.

"Didn't you say you thought you detected some interest on her part when you first raised the subject?"

Sheridan stood just inside Jack's office, hovering near the door. "It seems I was mistaken," he said stiffly.

"You're quite certain she understood that she could work from her home?"

Sheridan nodded. "I explained that, sir. I told her what you said about using a messenger to pick up copy and deliver it."

"Well, then, what do you think her reason is for holding out? More money?"

An angry red flush spread over Sheridan's features. "Indeed not, sir! She's not that sort of woman."

"Don't be so sure," Jack muttered, unconvinced. He looked up. Something about Sheridan's demeanor seemed a bit odd, he thought. It was unlike the boy to be evasive, yet at the moment he had an almost furtive look about him. "Too quick to judge, too quick to trust—either is folly," he said, ignoring the spark of defiance that leaped in the other's eyes.

Drumming his fingers on the desk, he tried to think. "The woman is a puzzle. What exactly do you know about her?"

"Sir?" Sheridan's strong chin lifted a fraction more, and Jack saw his hands knot at his sides, as if he were nervous or a bit riled.

Too bad. At the moment, Jack hadn't the patience to smooth the lad's feathers. "Aside from the fact that she's incredibly brilliant and bonny, what do you know about your Mrs. Harte?" Not waiting for a reply, Jack continued to speculate. "Apparently her late husband didn't leave her in such good straits," he said, "or she wouldn't be working two jobs. What was his name, this husband of hers, do you know?"

Sheridan shook his head. "She talks about herself very little. Hardly at all. The only comment I recall her making about her husband had to do with his being a clergyman."

"Ah, then there wouldn't have been much money," said Jack, his thoughts darting ahead, only to skid to a stop as an elusive bit of memory skirted the edge of his mind. *A clergyman . . . a clergyman named Harte . . .*

"Good heavens!" he burst out. "She's not Bronson Harte's widow, is she?"

Sheridan looked startled. "I . . . don't know, sir. I can't recall ever hearing her husband's given name. Why, did you know the man?"

Momentarily distracted, Jack shook his head. No, he hadn't known Bronson Harte, but the man and his wild-eyed followers had captured more than their share of space in the *Vanguard* and the other leading newspapers around the state.

Some called them "Reformists" or "Utopians," among other high-minded epithets. Jack called them "socialists" when he was inclined to be generous, "madmen" when he happened to learn of some new, particularly daft behavior by one or more of the pack.

He'd heard it rumored that Horace Greeley had fallen in with a similar pack, although Jack couldn't imagine even the gullible Horace being bamboozled by that bunch of pompous fools. Still, Greeley was known to have taken up with stranger company. There was that showman P. T. Barnum, for example, who exhibited such sensations as embalmed mermaids and dancing midgets. No, in truth one never quite knew what to expect of Horace.

In any event, he knew of Bronson Harte, all right, and now found himself fascinated by the possibility that Sheridan's *inamorata* might be Harte's widow.

His need for a competent proofreader suddenly took a backseat to his pillaging curiosity.

He realized that Sheridan was watching him with a puzzled frown, but Jack said nothing more. Instead, he reined in his errant thoughts and went on with his own questions. "You told her about our discussion—that there would be a need for someone to help settle any immigrants we decide to bring across?''

Sheridan nodded.

''And you offered to drive her here, to my office, for an interview?''

Again Sheridan gave a nod, shifting from one foot to the other. He seemed unable to make eye contact with Jack, who wondered anew at the lad's peculiar conduct. ''Aye, sir, I did. But it made no difference. She couldn't be swayed.''

''And you have no idea why she's being so stubborn?''

Sheridan glared at him. ''I don't, sir. And I must say I don't believe it's a case of her being stubborn. I'm sure she has her reasons.''

Jack sensed the lad was about to add something else, but after a slight pause Sheridan's features took on the same strange, ill-at-ease expression as before.

It suddenly occurred to Jack that perhaps the almost certainly pious Mrs. Harte objected to the idea of working for a known reprobate like himself.

Ordinarily, he might have been mildly amused at the thought. At the moment, he was simply annoyed. He needed a capable proofreader, but up until now he hadn't been inclined to waste any more time on Samantha Harte. He had to admit that he was intrigued, however, by her unwillingness to even discuss the position—even though it sounded as if she could use the money. But even more intriguing was the possibility that she might have been married to a highly controversial figure, a figure whose death had left a number of still-unanswered questions.

In the midst of his musings, Jack remembered that Sheridan's evening class would be meeting tonight. He glanced at his driver, who was watching him closely. Saying nothing, Jack stood and went to the closet to get his topcoat. With his back turned to Sheridan, Jack shrugged into his coat, still thinking. If he left now, he would have time to stop by the barber for a shave, make himself a bit more presentable. He could have dinner later.

His decision made, he smiled a little to himself. That's what he would do, then: if the cagey Mrs. Harte would not come to him, he would go to *her.*

Still smiling, he turned back to Sheridan. ''We'll be leaving early today,'' he said, ignoring the other's questioning stare. ''Bring the carriage round.''

That night, after the other students had gone, Cavan lingered near the classroom door, watching Samantha Harte. She was making a great show of straightening her desk, then filing the evening's assignment papers into her case. Clearly, she was avoiding him. Indeed, she had scarcely looked in his direction the entire evening, glancing away whenever her gaze chanced to meet his.

Only when the silence became awkward did she finally look up. Her smile appeared forced, her expression impersonal as she continued to shove papers into her carrying case.

"I wanted to apologize," Cavan said without preamble. "For last week. I—perhaps I shouldn't have spoken as I did."

She seemed to be looking at some nonexistent object past his shoulder. "There's no need to apologize. Let's just . . . forget it, shall we?"

Cavan shook his head. "I believe I offended you, and I'm deeply sorry for that."

Her gaze darted to the door. She looked as if she wanted to flee the room, Cavan thought miserably. Humiliation, combined with impatience at his own rash behavior the week before, rushed through him. He was tempted to bolt and run himself. Instead, he stood, feeling very much the bumbling schoolboy, watching her as she renewed her absorption in tidying the desk.

"Really, it's all right, Cavan—Mr. Sheridan—we won't speak of it again. That would be best, don't you—?" She broke off, turning sharply toward the doorway at the sound of approaching footsteps. Footsteps accompanied by a soft, melodic whistling.

Cavan recognized the buoyant step and the familiar low whistle at once. Stunned, he stood staring at the doorway as Jack Kane appeared.

18

The Princess and
the Pirate

*The most desperate place for the proud to stand
is upon the scorching coals of need.*
ANONYMOUS

Still bending over the desk, Samantha froze at the sight of the tall
man silhouetted in the doorway. A dim light from the lamp in the
hall haloed a broad expanse of shoulders, a head of glossy raven hair,
and a black topcoat. Around his throat was tucked a snowy white
scarf, and a single white carnation rested on his lapel.

"Mr. Kane!"

Even before Cavan Sheridan blurted out his name, Samantha recognized the man who stood watching them. Actually, she had seen
Black Jack Kane once before tonight, several months ago at the
opera, during one of her rare evenings out with her parents. Her
mother had pointed out the notorious newspaper baron between acts,
giving his name a distinct edge to identify him as thoroughly *disreputable*. With a stunningly beautiful woman on his arm and others
ogling him from the sidelines, Kane had towered above the retinue
surrounding him. Even at a distance, everything about him exuded a
striking, dark elegance—and an unmistakable arrogance.

He was a man not easily forgotten: imposingly tall and lean but
with a powerfully set frame and features that were strangely foreign.
Samantha had heard it said that every Irishman considered himself a
"son of kings," and for a moment she had the foolish thought that
the man framed in the doorway might just lend credence to such a

claim. Yet, with his snapping black eyes and bronzed skin, she decided that Jack Kane more closely resembled a Spanish pirate than an Irish prince.

He stepped inside the room, and Samantha was instantly suffused with a sense of menace, almost as if she had been physically threatened. She straightened with a jerk, facing him. Kane smiled, his white teeth flashing beneath that dangerous, dark mustache, and Samantha was seized by the mortifying sensation that the man knew he had unnerved her. She gave herself a mental shake. Obviously, she was reacting to what she had heard about Kane rather than to the man himself.

Without ever taking his eyes from her, Kane acknowledged Cavan Sheridan in short order. Then, with an almost courtly gesture, he inclined his head to Samantha in a mockery of a bow. "Mrs. Harte, I presume? Allow me to introduce myself: Jack Kane." His voice, startlingly deep and resonant, held a marked lilt that clearly identified his Irishness.

He straightened, his dark brows lifting a fraction. "I hope you'll forgive me for intruding like this, Mrs. Harte, but as Cavan may have explained, I'm very anxious to talk with you."

Samantha looked at him, then at Cavan Sheridan, who was staring at Kane with an expression of bafflement that she was certain mirrored her own. When she turned back to Kane, she found him studying her with the same self-assured smile. "I'm sorry," she said, wincing at the uncommon shrillness of her voice. "I'm afraid I don't understand—"

"Ah, I apologize," Kane said. "I was referring to the position at the *Vanguard* that I believe Cavan here discussed with you. I'm in rather desperate need of a qualified proofreader, you see. Cavan conveyed your reluctance to meet with me—so I took the liberty of coming to you."

Again the quick gleam of a smile. "Actually, I was hoping I could change your mind. Perhaps I should explain that, for the right person, the job would be as much that of a copy editor as a proofreader. I'm needing an individual with some editorial sense in addition to a keen eye." He paused. "Naturally, I would offer a salary commensurate with the demands of the job. If you'd be kind enough to give me just a few minutes of your time, I'd like to explain in more detail."

Samantha glanced from Kane to Cavan Sheridan, vaguely aware of the similarity in height between the two. But whereas the latter's was as yet the undeveloped lankiness of youth, Jack Kane's stature was that of a mature man—and a supremely confident one.

Cavan was watching her intently, his expression a plea for her to hear Kane out. But after his awkward confession of the previous week, Samantha was only too well aware of his reasons for wanting her to accept the position. She had already decided she would be foolish to even consider the idea.

Turning back to Kane, she said, "I'm sorry you've gone to so much trouble, Mr. Kane, but as I explained to Cavan—Mr. Sheridan—I'm really not qualified for this sort of position."

"Nonsense," Kane said dismissively. "Cavan here believes otherwise, and I've come to trust his judgment." He darted a quick look at his driver, then turned again to Samantha. "Fifteen minutes?" he said, his brows lifting a fraction in appeal.

Samantha felt herself being drawn into the field of those compelling dark eyes. With an irrational sense of panic, she stepped back from him. "I—no, I'm sorry, but I'm . . . simply not interested."

His gaze narrowed, and Samantha felt herself examined with a bold directness that somehow stopped just short of being offensive. After the slightest hesitation, Kane again turned to Cavan Sheridan. "I summoned Ransom out of retirement to drive me here this evening. Why don't you take the buggy and go on along? I'll see Mrs. Harte safely home after we talk."

Samantha tensed, suddenly angry. Kane was obviously accustomed to bullying his way past anything and anyone, but she was having none of it. There had been a time when she might have been intimidated by his bravado, but after enduring Bronson's tyranny, it would take more than a swaggering Irishman to cow her.

A quick glance at Cavan Sheridan only served to fuel her resolve. The boy was looking from Kane to her with a gaze that held both confusion and disappointment. Samantha thought there might also be a spark of anger in his eyes, anger at his employer.

"Perhaps I didn't make myself clear," she said, speaking directly to Jack Kane. "I have other plans for this evening, so I really need to be leaving. As for seeing me home, that won't be necessary."

Kane was regarding her with a wry expression. "*Five* minutes?" he said. His tone was deceptively meek, not at all in keeping with the intensity of his gaze. "Surely you won't refuse me five minutes, Mrs. Harte?"

Disgusted with herself, Samantha felt her resistance slip a notch. Years of her mother's coaching in "good manners and proper behavior" now threatened to overcome her common sense.

As if he had seen her waver, Kane moved to seize the advantage. Once again he turned to Cavan Sheridan with a word of instruction.

"You might as well be getting along now, lad. And mind the streets—you'll find a lot of ice on the way."

Cavan's face flamed, and for a moment Samantha thought he might challenge his employer. But at last, clearly demoralized, he bade them a hasty good-night and left the room.

Anger surfaced anew in Samantha—anger at Kane for his insufferable arrogance, and at herself for faltering even momentarily in the face of this presumptuous barbarian.

"Why don't you sit down, Mrs. Harte?" Kane said. Samantha didn't miss the fact that, when issued by Jack Kane, even a simple suggestion seemed more a demand.

She hesitated, and he grinned at her, his dark eyes warming with amusement. The man was so infuriatingly *insolent*. "May I?" he asked, shrugging out of his topcoat before Samantha could reply.

Dismayed, she realized that he almost certainly had no intention of limiting himself to the five minutes he'd requested. Her exasperation with the man boiled higher, and in an attempt to make her own statement, she went to the coat closet, retrieved her wrap, and draped it very carefully and deliberately over the back of the chair.

She took her time in lifting her gaze to meet his. When she did, she found him grinning at her as if he found her incredibly entertaining. "Point taken," he said with another low travesty of a bow. "I'll be brief, my word on it. But won't you at least sit down? And if at all possible, Mrs. Harte, stop watching for me to sprout horns. Despite what you may have been told, I'm not all that dangerous—certainly not to a respectable lady like yourself."

Samantha caught her breath. His insight into her thoughts seemed almost uncanny. It had struck her only a moment earlier that Kane *didn't* seem quite as outrageous as the myriad rumors purported him to be. Oh, he was brash, certainly, his bearing impossibly arrogant, even imperial; probably he could be ruthless and autocratic, and she sensed a coarseness in him somewhat at odds with his darkly urbane good looks.

Nevertheless, he was almost certainly not the dragon she would have expected, based on his reputation. Once or twice she even thought she might have glimpsed a hint of something behind those hooded dark eyes—some fleeting glimmer of a lingering sorrow, an old, not yet healed pain—that belied the mocking air of amusement from which he appeared to view his surroundings. She might have been mistaken, of course. She had only just met the man, after all.

In the end, it was that totally unexpected perception of his humanity, that vague sense of a basic decency in the man, that—combined with her own ingrained code of conduct—caused Samantha to relent. Even then she might have hesitated had she not caught a glimpse of his hands when he removed his gloves. There was no explanation for the peculiar feeling that swept over her at the sight of those large, callused hands with the sturdy, blunt fingers—not carefully manicured as she would have expected, but instead stained with traces of news ink.

Why it should move her so, she couldn't say. But something about the possibility that Jack Kane might actually dirty his hands by working at his own trade struck a chord in her that was still resonating when she sank down into the chair behind her desk, waiting for him to begin.

Jack's instincts about Samantha Harte had proved sound. Within minutes of first meeting her, he had sensed a fundamental spirit of fairness and the innate good manners of one who had grown up in a gracious, civilized environment. As he watched her sit down, then lift her face to him with a cool stare, he was struck by the woman's almost regal bearing.

She was a princess in a dusty schoolroom, a patrician in a city of Philistines. Blast it all, he almost felt as if he should bend his knee and call her *milady!*

Confronted by her slender elegance, her quiet composure, Jack felt himself very much the rough-edged lout and infidel she probably believed him to be. For the first time in years, he found himself at a loss in the presence of a woman.

And what a woman she was! She was nothing like what he had expected, that much was certain. Despite the smitten Cavan Sheridan's accolades to her shrine, Jack would have been surprised if Samantha Harte had been anything more than pleasant looking—perhaps even attractive in a mousy sort of way, but hardly memorable.

He realized what he had done, of course. Because she had been married to one of the more recognizable clergymen of the day, and because she apparently gave much of her time and effort to the impoverished immigrants of the city, he had fostered an image of her as virtuous but rather drab.

So much for supposition. The woman was anything but drab. She was absolutely exquisite. Jack suddenly found himself wondering to what length that lustrous chestnut hair would fall if released from the fussy little knot in which it was trapped or how it might feel to have those magnificent amber-flecked eyes turned on him in something other than suspicion or distaste.

He was completely unprepared for the sudden stab of shame that ripped through him, as if by merely speculating about her—however innocently—he might somehow sully the cloak of decency she seemed to wear.

She was sitting on the edge of her chair, regarding him with that same dignified calm that was beginning to rankle Jack for some reason. He had seen her poise slip, ever so slightly, when he'd first come into the room, but it hadn't taken her long to recover it. Now it was his turn to grope for control. What was it about the woman that put him at a disadvantage and made him feel like such a great, ponderous dolt?

But he had started this, hadn't he? He had no choice but to get on with it, though he had been a fool to come here, he knew that now. He felt a sudden sting of resentment at Samantha Harte's ability to evoke such an uncommon defensiveness in him. Peevishly, he reminded himself of why he had come. Wasn't she the one who stood to benefit most from this meeting, after all?

"Let me get right to the point, Mrs. Harte," he said, his tone sharper than he'd intended. "I came here for one reason, that being to offer you a job." When she would have interrupted, he stopped her with an upraised hand, crossed his arms over his chest, and went on. "Our lad Cavan has a great admiration for you—but no doubt you're already aware of that." Jack watched her closely, saw a faint flush creep over her features, and smiled to himself.

"He tells me that in addition to your teaching in the settlements—a most admirable vocation, for which you're to be commended, I'm sure—you also work part-time as a proofreader. You're employed by a local textbook publisher, I believe?"

She nodded, her gaze still fixed steadily upon him.

Jack hesitated only a second or two. "That publisher wouldn't happen to be Josef Stein, would it?"

The change in her expression was dramatic. It had been no lucky guess on his part, of course. Jack had made it his business to learn the place—and the status—of her employment before ever coming down here tonight.

He gave her no chance to reply. "I expect you know they're about to close their doors."

He saw the slender throat tighten as she made an effort to swallow. "How—how would you know that?"

"You haven't heard?"

She frowned, then shook her head. "No, I try to ignore rumors."

"It's no rumor, Mrs. Harte," Jack said, softening his tone.

"You can't—how could you know something like that?"

Jack dropped his arms away from his chest, putting his hands in his pockets. "Stein came to me not long ago with the idea that I might want to buy the company. He knew I'd bought out Perriman and Ware last year and thought he might interest me in acquiring his house as well."

Jack had deliberately given her no warning, meaning to catch her off guard. Clearly, he had. What he hadn't expected was the regret that coiled through him as he watched her composure seem to slip beyond her grasp.

"And . . . are you—buying him out, that is?" Her voice was so low Jack had to step closer to make out her words. When he did, he saw that she had gone deathly pale.

"No," he said with a shake of his head. "Nor, I suspect, will anyone else. Stein's son has run the company to ruin. They're desperately overextended, thanks to young Joey's excesses. There's nothing for them to do but sell off what they can and close the doors. Quite frankly, there's not enough there to make it worth my while."

Her expression was more than confused. It seemed to border on despair.

Self-disgust whipped through Jack, and he almost wished now he'd let her learn of the situation for herself, rather than from him. "I'm sorry you had to hear this so . . . abruptly," he said, meaning it, even though he knew the situation might work to his favor. "I thought you should know before you summarily turned down my offer."

He pretended not to notice the slight trembling of her hand, which now gripped the leather case on her desk. "You're . . . quite certain?" she said, her voice sounding strangled. "I don't suppose you could be mistaken?"

"Mrs. Harte," Jack said softly, "it's no mistake." He waited only a second or two, then said, "In light of this situation, am I correct in assuming that you'll be needing a new position?"

He saw her stiffen, watched the play of conflicting emotions dart across her features. The bitter look she turned on him made Jack feel as if he had ripped the job away from her himself. "Mrs. Harte, I don't mean to take advantage—"

"Of course you do," she said icily, the challenge catching Jack completely off guard.

He blinked, not quite managing to stop a smile at this blunt assessment of his motives. "Yes . . . well, perhaps you're right. But before you sling that book bag at me, won't you at least allow me to tell you a bit about the job I have in mind? I think you might be interested, if you'll just hear me out.''

Her expression never wavered, but she inclined her head ever so slightly to indicate that she would listen. *The princess grants an audience to the pirate,* Jack thought with some amusement.

In that moment, he wanted more than anything to convince her to take the job. He liked this woman, he realized—not merely because she was exceedingly attractive, though she was that, all right—but it was more than that. He sensed that Samantha Harte was an admirable woman, probably an exceptional woman—a woman he suddenly wanted to know better, even have her know him, although the very idea would probably send her running from the room.

"May I sit down?" Not waiting for a reply, Jack lowered himself into one of the student chairs closest to her desk. "First off, I want to assure you that you could work from your home. If you have any concern at all about that, let me put your mind at ease."

Pretending not to notice the way her eyes lighted with interest ever so slightly, Jack went on. "I believe I can also promise you that I'd be offering you a considerable increase in wages. And," he added, leaning forward, "a much more interesting variety of duties as well."

Yes, he definitely had her attention now, he thought, watching her. Contempt, at least for the moment, seemed to have given way to curiosity.

Even so, she voiced a protest. "Mr. Kane—what makes you think I'm the right person for this position? Or for any other position with your newspaper, for that matter. You haven't the faintest idea of my qualifications or—"

"You're absolutely right," Jack interrupted, brusquely professional as he acted to convince her of his sincerity. "Would you mind if I asked you a few questions?"

She frowned as if she hadn't expected this. "I . . . well, I suppose not, but—"

"Good," Jack said, not letting her finish before firing a rapid barrage of questions at her, all very businesslike and timed so as not to give her a chance to do more than catch her breath between replies. He resisted the temptation to toss in a few queries of a more personal nature, knowing instinctively that Samantha Harte would be offended and more than likely driven away by even the slightest attempt to breach that carefully erected bastion of self-defense.

Even so, he was intensely curious about this woman with the steel backbone and soft eyes. For starters, Jack wondered what might account for the apparently precarious state of her finances. Her distress at the prospect of losing her job with Stein had been almost palpable, and unless he was sorely mistaken, she was now leaning toward serious consideration of his offer.

He was also fascinated by a certain duality of nature he thought he perceived in her. The face she presented to him—and to the world, he suspected—was that of a quiet, almost rigidly composed, virtuous widow. Yet in the flinty edge of anger that had earlier sparked in those magnificent eyes, as well as in the sudden, unexpected glint of challenge that had shone out at him for just an instant, Jack had caught a glimpse of something else—an intensity, a vitality, carefully banked but glowing somewhere behind the wall of her control.

Increasingly, he found himself wanting to know more about the woman behind that wall.

He would warrant that Samantha Harte came from a good family, perhaps a privileged family. By her own admission, she had received a better-than-average education for a woman. Clearly, she had been a young bride, for she didn't look as if she could be much past her early or midtwenties.

He wondered how she had ended up needing two jobs to subsist. Even though Bronson Harte had apparently given his life to the ministry, the man shouldn't have been entirely without means. As Jack recalled, Harte had been the only son of a wealthy family—textile-mill wealthy—from somewhere in Massachusetts. A controversial, highly visible clergyman, he had also been widely published and sought after as a public lecturer. Surely he would have managed at least a comfortable living.

He turned his attention back to Bronson Harte's widow. Just as Cavan Sheridan had said, she seemed more than qualified for the proofreader's position—and unless Jack was badly mistaken, Samantha Harte would also be perfect for the additional responsibilities he had in mind.

Indeed, she seemed ideal, exactly what he needed, and Jack offered her the job on the spot.

19

Quest or Conquest

I have spun the fleecy lint and now my wheel is still. . . .

ETHNA CARBERY

"The job is yours if you want it," Kane said. "You'll want to know what's involved, of course."

"You said it was a proofreading position. I'm probably familiar with most of the requirements—"

"Ah, but I'm thinking it may likely develop into more than that for the right person," he interrupted. "Let me explain."

He leaned back in the chair—which was too small for him—stretched out his long legs, and crossed them neatly at the ankles. Samantha realized anew what a big man he was and was surprised that she no longer felt quite as . . . overwhelmed by him as she had at first.

Bronson had not been a large man, yet being in the same room with him had often given her a sense of being restricted . . . confined.

She shook off the thought and returned her full attention to the man across the desk from her. How quickly he had adopted an informal, casual stance with her. She couldn't help wondering if it might be merely a ploy to make her relax and throw her off guard.

Did he really think her that gullible?

Again Bronson came to mind. He had played that sort of game, not with her, but with others, especially those he considered inferior. He would feign a kind of camaraderie to gain their support—or their adulation—then cast them aside after they had served their purpose.

Bronson. Always Bronson. Would she never be free of him? How long would he continue to exert his influence over her—even from the grave?

Samantha looked up, suddenly aware that Jack Kane was watching her with a questioning frown. "I'm sorry," she said quickly. "I'm afraid I'm more tired than I realized. What were you saying?"

His look of concern seemed genuine. "Perhaps I should leave. You've already given me more time than I asked. I can come back later in the week—"

He half rose in the chair, but Samantha gestured that he should remain. Most of her initial aversion to Kane seemed to have passed. And she *was* going to need a job, she reminded herself grimly.

"No, please go on," she told him. "You made the effort to come here, after all. The least I can do is listen. Besides, I . . . just go on. It's all right."

He looked pleased, which puzzled Samantha. For the life of her, she couldn't imagine why a man like Kane would care one way or the other whether she accepted his offer. But as he went on to give her what seemed to be a carefully thought-out, concise description of the position he had in mind, her bewilderment only increased— as did her interest in the job.

Watching him, listening to him speak in that distinctive, rich rumble of a voice, she realized with some surprise that this was a man who obviously loved his work—thrived on it, perhaps even lived for it. His hard, sardonic features underwent a dramatic transformation as he spoke. The almost black eyes danced with boyish enthusiasm as he told her a little about his plans for the *Vanguard,* in particular his desire to broaden the scope of the paper and heighten its appeal for the entire city—including the immigrant population.

"Actually," Kane said, smiling, "I have young Sheridan to thank for reminding me that readers are far more eager to learn about people than politics, that they're likely to care more about a poor mother in the workhouse than a meeting at the White House." He paused, leaning forward to clasp his large hands on his knees. "I could use your instincts in that regard, Mrs. Harte."

Still uncertain as to what he wanted from her, Samantha reserved her questions for the time being. She was intrigued by Kane's account of his brother's assignment to Ireland and why he thought that assignment would benefit the newspaper. She noticed that he was careful to give Cavan Sheridan full credit for the novel idea of crafting individual stories and even eventually bringing the subjects of those stories to America. Would other men in Kane's position be so generous, she wondered?

"What a splendid idea!" she finally blurted out, unable to mask her own enthusiasm.

Kane nodded. "It is, isn't it? I ragged the lad a bit about spending my money, but in truth I think he's on to something."

He explained then that they would need someone to help the immigrants get settled, should the plan become feasible. "Preferably someone who already has some experience in that area," he said. "I think we could work that in with your other responsibilities nicely. And as I told you," he added, "your wages would reflect the additional work."

In spite of the excitement that seemed to fairly crackle about Kane as he discussed his ideas with her—and her somewhat revised impression of the man—Samantha couldn't help but question where his real motives might lie. *Altruistic* was not a word she had heard used in relation to Black Jack Kane.

"I thought you might have particular interest in this part of the job, Mrs. Harte," he was saying, "assuming that your work with the immigrants stems from a genuine desire to bring about better conditions for them."

"I can't think of any other reason," Samantha said dryly. "Obviously, the financial compensation wouldn't be much of an incentive."

"Yet you don't quite strike me as just another ordinary Polly-Do-Good."

If the remark was meant to provoke her, it didn't. Samantha thought she had a fairly clear idea as to his opinion of her. No doubt in his eyes she was just another bored, discontented widow who used benevolence work as a means of adding purpose to an otherwise uneventful life.

It didn't matter what he thought, of course. Besides, she could hardly expect him to understand her situation when her own family remained baffled by her choices.

She found his silent scrutiny increasingly unsettling, almost . . . invasive. She deliberately looked away as she framed her reply. "There really aren't that many positions available to women, Mr. Kane. I do what I must to make a living, that's all. My needs are fairly simple. I do what I do, at least so far as my work in the immigrant settlements is concerned, because it supplements my income and because I enjoy it. I like the people."

When she turned back to him, he was regarding her with something akin to approval. He gave a small nod then, almost as if he had made a judgment about her, which only unnerved Samantha even more.

To deflect his discomfiting stare, she decided to ask a question of her own. "I'm curious about *your* interest in the immigrants, Mr.

Kane," she ventured. "Oh, I understand that if you can make the *Vanguard* more accessible to the immigrant population—give it more appeal for them—you can expect to sell more newspapers. But mightn't there be a simpler way to add to your readership?" She paused. "Frankly, I can't help but wonder why a man like yourself would be . . . concerned about these people."

His eyes suddenly hardened to cold black marble, and she saw his hands tighten on his knees. "But I am *one* of those people, Mrs. Harte."

His words came slowly and deliberately, laced with a distinct Irish overtone. Of course, she had known that Kane was an immigrant himself—an Irish immigrant, though hardly a typical one. But, then, she doubted there was much of *anything* typical about the man who sat staring at her with such fierce intensity.

Unexpectedly, his dark brows lifted with a sardonic smile. "To answer your question, Mrs. Harte, I definitely expect to sell more newspapers. Aside from that, however, I doubt that you'd understand the full extent of my interest, even if I tried to explain."

Samantha felt her face heat with embarrassment, but he continued on as smoothly as if he'd already forgotten her blunder. "If you'll indulge me for another moment," he said, "I'll explain that, what with breaking in Cavan Sheridan and perhaps another new reporter or two, I expect I'm going to need a more experienced editorial eye for a time. That being the case, the position will be a higher-salaried one than that of a proofreader. And there's one more thing: I'd be offering you a bit extra if you would be willing to keep a close eye on young Sheridan's education."

Samantha frowned. "I don't understand. I'm already working with Cavan here at the night school twice a week."

With a nod, he drew himself up from the chair and went to stand at the only window in the classroom. "The lad fancies himself a reporter," he said, his back to her, "and I'm inclined to believe he just may have the makings of a good one." He swung around to face her. "I don't actually have enough top-notch reporters, you see, especially with my brother, Brady, out of the country. Now Cavan's instincts are keen, that's certain. And it seems to me the lad has a fine mind, wouldn't you say?"

Samantha nodded. She was intrigued by Kane's intention to test Cavan Sheridan by allowing him to work with some of the copy his brother would be sending from Ireland.

"Depending on how well he does with Brady's material," he went on, "I'll eventually let him try his hand at some local news, see how he manages."

He paused. "No doubt you know better than I that Sheridan's grammar is still a bit too—Irish," Kane said with a grin. "And he also has an excessive amount of idealism for a reporter—he's still very young, after all. But he's sharp—sharp as they come, I'll wager, and he's absolutely desperate for knowledge. The lad gobbles up books like a starving man at a banquet. He doesn't think I know it, of course, but many's the time he drives the carriage with one hand and holds a book in the other."

Samantha couldn't help but smile at the image. She could almost see Cavan Sheridan doing just that.

"He really can't afford anything more in the way of schooling— the lad has no extra funds, as you may have gathered," Kane continued. "I pay him a decent enough wage, but I think he socks away every penny in hopes of bringing his younger sister across."

Samantha wasn't aware that Cavan Sheridan even *had* a sister, but she could easily imagine him being that conscientious.

"Sheridan needn't know that I'm paying the bills," Kane said. "What I want you to do is give him the finest education you can manage in as short a time as possible—without making him suspicious as to what—or who—is behind it."

Had Samantha not been so intrigued by Kane's obvious desire to help Cavan Sheridan, she might have taken offense at the way he seemed to be ordering her around, as if she had already accepted the position. As it was, she dismissed a prickle of irritation at his presumption.

"The lad is quick," Kane said. "He'll soak up your teaching in a flash. I doubt that it will require all that much extra effort on your part, but whatever it takes—within reason, of course—I'll see that you're compensated." He paused, then added, almost defensively, Samantha thought, "I happen to believe Sheridan is worth it."

It was all too much for Samantha to take in—Kane's showing up as he had, completely without warning, not to mention the fact that he was nothing—*nothing*—like what she would have expected him to be. She had imagined a dragon but had instead encountered a rogue knight. Instead of flaunting his wealth and power, he seemed more concerned about an immigrant employee's future. And as to the job he was offering her, she thought she could not have custom designed a more suitable position—or a more desirable one—for herself.

Her head was already spinning with confusion and a host of conflicting emotions when Kane named a salary figure that literally stunned her. "Oh . . . no, I couldn't possibly—"

"I wouldn't hire you for less," he said, his tone making it clear he meant it.

"But you don't even know me—"

"And you don't know *me,* Mrs. Harte. Obviously, I'd be taking a risk. But I'm sure your family and friends would feel that you're taking a much bigger one."

Samantha squirmed a little at the meaning implicit in his statement. Obviously, he had recognized her suspicions, her initial hostility. But how could he know that she was already speculating on the reaction of her few friends—Bronson's friends, really—and her family? What would they make of her working for the infamous Jack Kane? Oh, dear heavens, her mother would be *livid!*

"However, you wouldn't regret the risk, Mrs. Harte. I think I can promise you that."

Samantha was struck by an irrational urge to laugh. The idea of placing any value at all in a promise from a man like Kane should have seemed outrageous. Yet as she stood, debating over whether or not she was mad to even consider his proposition, something told her she could trust his word.

But wouldn't it only make things worse for Cavan Sheridan, what with his . . . infatuation with her?

"Even if I were inclined to accept—and I'm not saying I am— I'm not sure I ought to spend any . . . additional time with Cavan— Mr. Sheridan."

Kane made a dismissing motion with one hand. "Young men often fancy themselves in love with the schoolteacher. Especially such an attractive one," he said lightly with a smile. "It will pass in time, I expect. He'll recover."

Samantha was fairly certain that Kane was right, though she felt a trifle miffed at the offhanded way he relegated the problem to a place of no importance. She was also determined not to respond too hastily.

"I won't deny that I find your offer . . . appealing, Mr. Kane. But I would have to take a few days to think it over."

"No," he said, astonishing her with his abruptness. "If you wait, you'll talk yourself out of it. I'll need your answer tonight."

"Really—" Even as Samantha drew herself up in protest, she recognized the possible truth behind his statement. The longer she delayed, the more likely it was that she would reject his offer, if for no other reason than Kane himself. But how could *he* possibly know that?

"You can think it over while I drive you home," he said smoothly, shrugging into his coat, then reaching for hers.

"Oh, no, I told you, that won't be necessary—"

"I gave young Sheridan my word," he said, holding her coat, waiting for her to slip into it. "Surely you'll not be responsible for my disappointing your protégé, now will you?"

Once into her coat, Samantha turned to face him, intending to meet his barb with a firm objection that Cavan Sheridan was not—at least as yet—her "protégé."

The quick smile that broke over his dark features made it clear he had anticipated her. "And if you're concerned about my seeing you home," he said with mocking gravity, "you'll be quite safe, I assure you. My driver, Ransom, is very respectable." He paused. "Even if I am not."

≈≈❦≈≈

To Samantha's great surprise, Kane remained silent during the entire drive to her flat. Even so, she found it nearly impossible to think. She stared out the window of the carriage into the night, trying to ignore his dark presence at her side. More than once she was aware of his gaze on her, but she kept her face turned resolutely toward the window, making at least a pretense of concentration.

Finally, she did manage to think through Kane's offer in some detail, weighing the merits of the job with the possible pitfalls—the most obvious of which was, of course, Kane himself. Yet despite his dubious reputation and her own conflicting emotions about the man, Samantha thought she would be wise to base her decision not on her prospective employer but on the opportunities presented by the position.

If she really were to lose the part-time job with Stein—and she had no reason to doubt Kane's story—she would be reduced to living on her teaching salary until she could locate something else. That or accept help from her parents, an option she didn't even like to consider.

The increase in wages would afford her more security. It might mean a few extras in her life—perhaps even her own buggy eventually, the only real convenience she could honestly say she missed. Oddly enough, though, the money wasn't the greater appeal. It was the work itself, as Kane envisioned it, that excited her.

The two things she thought she could accept unequivocally from Kane's discourse were his desire to help Cavan Sheridan attain his goals and his interest in appealing to a wider segment of the immigrant population. While she understood how she might be helpful in the former, Samantha wasn't at all certain she would be of any real assistance in the latter—though Kane obviously thought otherwise.

It disturbed her to think that by working more closely with Cavan she might only make things more difficult for him. Yet here, too, she suspected that Jack Kane was right. Cavan was a bright, good-looking young man. Whatever appeal she held for him would likely pass with the first pretty girl who came along to turn his head.

All things considered, it seemed to Samantha that the positives greatly outweighed the negatives. Except for the most obvious hindrance of all—the man for whom she would be working. There was no getting around the fact that she would have a most difficult time of it, convincing her parents and acquaintances that she had not sold her soul to the devil himself by accepting a salary from such a notorious infidel.

She reminded herself that after Bronson's death, once she had resolved to establish a life of her own independent of her family's standards and strangleholds, she had faced an overwhelming amount of criticism, even censure, from all sides. Even now she endured her share of subtle—and some not-so-subtle—allusions to the sins of pride and willfulness. But she had weathered the denunciation and reproach, had managed to care less about the disapproval than about finding God's place for her, and she had never been sorry. It occurred to her now that if she must, she could do the same thing all over again. The realization surprised her and at the same time strangely comforted her.

In the end, she was able to retreat into the quiet place where even Jack Kane's probing gaze could not intrude. Silently, she closed her eyes and offered up the entire decision to the only One whose opinion really mattered.

By the time the carriage pulled up to her apartment building, Samantha had her answer.

Kane was watching her, his dark features taut with speculation, when Samantha turned to him. "Here is what I will do, Mr. Kane," she said quietly, "and I will commit to nothing else. I will try the position for three months, with the understanding that if I'm not comfortable with it by the end of that time—for any reason—you will pay me one month's severance pay and make no protest to my resignation."

He regarded her with a steady, measuring stare, his black eyes snapping in the faint light from the street lamp. He had removed his gloves and now sat tapping one against the palm of his hand. His tone was as solemn as Samantha's as he stated his reply. ''Agreed. So long as your work is satisfactory, of course,'' he added wryly.

One of his gloves slipped out of his hands, and he bent to retrieve it. When his dark head snapped up, he was wearing a wickedly smug smile, much like that of a pirate raising his colors aboard a conquered vessel.

PART TWO

In the Crucible

The crucible for silver and the furnace for gold,

but the Lord tests the heart.

PROVERBS 17:3, NIV

20

Different Kinds of Men

I turned my back on the dream I had shaped,
And to this road before me
My face I turned.

P A D R A I C   P E A R S E

THE CLADDAGH, IRELAND, LATE APRIL

It was springtime in Ireland, and Brady Kane was half in love. Half in love with one girl, and half in love with another. With a rueful smile, he wondered if that made him in love entirely.

As he hoofed it down the Claddagh lane toward Gabriel's house, his sketch pad under one arm, a bag of sweets dangling from the fingers of his free hand, he acknowledged that his affection for the one girl could hardly be counted, since she bolted like a frightened rabbit every time he came near her.

He slowed his pace a little at the thought of Roweena, giving a sigh completely out of keeping with his jaunty mood. He had begun to despair of ever winning more than a furtive smile from the girl. If he so much as tried to coax her out for a walk—hoping to escape Gabriel's ever watchful glare—she would quickly shake her head and scurry off to her corner near the hearth, as if he had suggested running off to the North with him. And even though, in spite of her deafness, she could speak, the only words she ever directed to Brady in that strange, strangled-sounding voice were a simple greeting of welcome or a shy farewell. Even these weren't always spoken but just as often indicated by a few quick movements of her hands and a dip of her head.

At first he'd blamed Gabriel—an unspoken accusation, of course—
for the way the girl continued to dodge his attentions. The Big Fella
directed a singular scowl at Brady whenever he chanced to eke out
a few moments alone with Roweena in the yard before she darted
back inside. And if he happened to follow her into the cottage, he
was sure to be met with the sort of murderous look that only a man
of Gabriel's impressive size and fierce features could affect. Except
for Jack, of course; Jack had a look that could set titans to trembling.

But Brady had finally come to accept, however grudgingly, that
Roweena's reluctance to walk out with him apparently had nothing
to do with Gabriel.

" 'Tis her way," the child, Evie, had informed him with a look
that clearly said he ought to know as much by now. "Her's shy,
Roweena is."

It was more than shyness, Brady was convinced. Other than Gabriel and Evie, Roweena appeared to be almost frightened of anyone
who came round. Even Terese seemed to intimidate her.

But then Terese could intimidate most anyone, he thought, grinning. She could be a real banshee, his Terese. The fire in her would
scald even the toughest fellow. Only Gabriel and that harridan Jane
Connolly seemed capable of dousing her smoke.

As he approached the walk to Gabriel's house, Brady reminded
himself that he would have to watch it with this "his Terese" stuff.
He fancied the girl, that was true, and he had no doubt but what she
was sweet on him as well. But he had no intention of leading her to
expect anything from him in the way of love everlasting. He wasn't
about to fall into *that* trap.

As keen as Terese was for him, she was even wilder to go to
America, he knew. Lately, she'd begun to drop thinly veiled hints
that perhaps Brady could help advance her aspirations. He had said
nothing to encourage her hopes, but she continued to hint.

He had deliberately kept his silence regarding Jack's idea to introduce a few specific individuals—or even entire families—to the *Vanguard*'s readers, with the possibility of later sponsoring their passage
to America. It still amazed him that his brother had dreamed up such
a scheme. Jack had never been tightfisted with his money. In fact,
Brady would have to say that he had always been generous, at least
with himself and Rose. But neither had Jack ever been unnecessarily
extravagant, and Brady couldn't help but wonder if there was something more behind this sudden idea than his big brother was letting
on.

In any event, he wasn't ready to let Terese in on the plan. She would hound him to death if she thought there was any possibility he could help her get to the States. Actually, he had every intention of making sure she got onto the list of prospective candidates, but later.

Terese's story was just what Jack was after, a real tearjerker, complete with suffering, deprivation, and struggle. But Brady wasn't ready to make a break with her, not yet. Even though he would soon be leaving Galway for a time, he planned on coming back. And when he did, he wanted Terese here, waiting for him.

At the thought of leaving, he gave another sigh and slowed his pace a bit. He had delayed his departure as long as he dared, had even deceived Jack into thinking he *had* moved on, paying a coach driver to post his letters outside the county. In one of those letters, he had given Jack a spiel about having to look around a bit for prospective subjects, then interview them and make some sketches before putting together the accompanying stories. The truth was he hadn't even begun looking as yet, but at least he'd bought himself a longer stay in Galway.

On Wednesday of next week, though, he was leaving for Limerick. He hadn't told Terese yet. He had a hunch she might take on, even though she liked to feign indifference to him. He smiled at the thought. She wasn't indifferent, and he knew it. Over the past few weeks, they'd gotten pretty cozy. He even thought it wouldn't take much at this point to coax her up to his flat, if she could just sneak away from old Jane long enough. It was a tempting possibility, but he wasn't at all certain he wanted to deepen the relationship just yet.

Sometimes he thought he was crackers about the girl, but other times she worried him a little. Terese had this . . . *intensity* about her that was almost threatening. She had grit, that much was certain, a kind of dogged determination and stubbornness he hadn't encountered in any of his other girls. She could be downright fierce sometimes.

Brady was used to being the one in control of a relationship, never the one being controlled. And he had no intention of changing roles, not with Terese or any other girl. He was in no hurry to get further involved with her, not until he knew just what he wanted from such a liaison.

In any event, he would have to say his good-byes over the next few days. When he came back from Limerick, he would let her in on the business with the *Vanguard* and the rest of it. For now, though, he would tell her nothing.

Actually, he hadn't told Terese much of anything about himself.

The only thing she really knew about him was that he worked for a New York newspaper and had a brother named Jack.

As it happened, it was Jack who had cautioned him never to reveal too much about himself, especially to women: *"A woman may take up with you for your dandy looks and your devilish charm, boyo. But make no mistake about it, if she learns you've got a bit of money, she'll be harder to shake than a bad case of the grippe. She may adore you as a pauper, but won't she love you to death if she learns that you're a prince?"*

Was that what he was—a prince? He supposed that's how it looked: Brady Kane, heir apparent to the Kane dynasty, pretender to the throne. Brady laughed aloud at the thought, but the sound had an empty ring to it. He could never fill Jack's shoes, should it ever become necessary for him to try. He had no illusions about that. He was a different kind of man altogether than his brother—perhaps no less a man, but certainly not so *big* a man either. Jack had the stuff of greatness, whatever it was, and Brady not only didn't aspire to those heights but he found the whole idea somewhat distasteful. He was more than content with his life as it was. He had the traveling, his painting, and almost always a pretty girl nearby wherever he went. What else could a man want?

He looked around the yard—the best kept of any in the Claddagh—and saw no sign of Gabriel or the girls. But the front door was standing open, so after rapping on the door frame once, he walked inside, where he was greeted by a smile from Roweena, a childish trill from the precocious Evie, and a look that clearly said, "You again, Yank?" from Gabriel.

Brady sought Roweena's smile again, and in that instant it struck him that he was going to be saying good-bye to her soon as well. The awareness was like a knife in his heart, much more painful than the thought of leaving Terese.

But he wouldn't think about that at the moment.

※

Gabriel turned, though he didn't need to look; he recognized the brisk tapping on the doorframe.

Brady Kane. For as often as the Yank visited, Gabriel wondered that he still bothered to knock.

The American was a welcome enough guest, for the most part, though Gabriel had full measure of mixed feelings about the young rascal. The lad was clever with words, well read, and amusing in a brash sort of way. He was generous natured as well, though Gabriel sometimes wondered where the money came from to finance his generosity.

He watched as the child, spotting the bag of sweets in the American's hand, sprinted across the room toward him. Rare was the day that the Yank appeared on their threshold without something for the wee girl, and Roweena as well. Today it was candy, enough for them all, though Gabriel had no taste for sweets.

Kane did spoil Evie, but Gabriel considered the occasional indulgence harmless enough. It was Roweena who worried him most when it came to the American. He had seen the way she looked for him those days he did not come, had also seen the way her eyes lighted when he did.

So far, he didn't think Kane had noticed. Roweena was too timid to pay a man any obvious interest, too shy to encourage his. But Brady Kane wasn't shy, not in the least. And Gabriel had seen the way those deep-set eyes followed the girl's every movement about the room.

He went on with the net he was mending, keeping an eye out as the child coaxed the Yank and Roweena to the hearth for a game of jackstraws. Watching them, he decided it wasn't a lascivious kind of interest he sensed from the young monkey. Had Kane shown designs of that nature, Gabriel would have banished him long ago. In truth, the lad appeared to be more taken with Roweena's shy sweetness, her fragility, than her looks—lovely though she was. Yet, only the fact that the American had exhibited no salacious intentions—so far, at least—gave sanction to his presence. One wrong move—one wrong *look*—and he would find himself a stranger in this part of Galway. And a mortally unwelcome one, at that.

Gabriel suspected that Kane's intentions toward the Sheridan girl might not be quite so innocent. He had seen the two of them any number of times on the quay, so close together that daylight couldn't squeeze between them, the girl hanging onto the Yank's arm as if she owned him.

The lass would do better to set her sights elsewhere, Gabriel suspected. He couldn't imagine anyone staking a claim to the young *jackeen* across the room. Brady Kane had the look about him of a wild stallion roaming the hills, kicking up dust, then shaking it from his feet as he ran into the wind.

But better the island girl for him than Roweena. That one could take care of herself, no doubt, though at times Gabriel suspected she wasn't nearly as hard as she would have others believe. Even so, she would be immensely stronger than Roweena, less likely to be the victim of an unprincipled rogue—if that's what Brady Kane turned out to be.

Roweena had already endured more than her share of pain in her young life. Inasmuch as he had it in his power to protect her, Gabriel vowed that she would suffer no more.

He was realistic enough to know, however, that there was only so much he could do to shield her, only so much hurt he could spare her. Knowing this sometimes made his spirit writhe in helplessness.

But at least he could protect her from careless young Corinthians like Brady Kane. The very possibility that Roweena was fascinated with the American was enough to evoke caution on Gabriel's part. Although he sensed nothing inherently malicious or brutal about Kane, he *had* perceived a certain callousness in him that might point to an intemperate, self-indulgent nature, the sort disposed to using others, then going on his way with never so much as a backward glance.

Even so, it was not the Brady Kanes of the world that troubled Gabriel most but those who were more beast than man. The predators among them. There would always be those who, possessing neither conscience nor compassion—perhaps not even a soul—took some sort of deranged satisfaction from tormenting, even destroying, the innocent.

Didn't the Scriptures themselves warn of them, those who prowled about like dogs, filth and curses spewing from their mouths as they sought unsuspecting victims on whom to inflict their evil? These were the deadly ones, the ones who struck at random, with no thought of consequence, no concern for the lives they might devastate.

Roweena herself had been born of such mindless savagery.

And her mother had died of it.

※※※

Gabriel had been only a boy when he had first heard the story of Ena MacHugh. He hadn't always lived in the Claddagh but had grown up in Galway City until such time as his uncle Nessan—a well-to-do bachelor who had hoarded his earnings for years—decided that young Gabriel should go to France to be educated, and offered to sponsor him.

While there, a letter from his mother arrived that related, in terms too delicate to convey the real tragedy of the situation, the "MacHugh family's ordeal." Later his uncle had also written, in more explicit terms, of the brutal rape that had been perpetrated, not only on the young MacHugh girl, but upon two others as well. In three separate but related acts of terror, three Galway women had been humiliated, violated, and tortured. Apparently, the victims had all been wives or daughters of men deeply involved with one of the countless secret societies forever springing up across the country, covert organizations bent on ridding Ireland of her English oppressors. These were violent men, riding about the countryside inflicting their own cruel form of justice on landlords, magistrates, even the police. After one particularly vicious incident wherein a dozen or more officials were terrorized and injured, three men considered to be leaders in the movement were captured and jailed.

But imprisonment didn't satisfy their captors. A few nights after the men were apprehended, a gaggle of British soldiers—drunk as lords and afire with bloodlust—visited the homes of the prisoners and inflicted their own manner of "justice" on their womenfolk.

Ena MacHugh, the daughter of Seamus MacHugh, a widower and one of the imprisoned felons, was a girl of no more than fifteen years at the time. Excessively sheltered and innocent of the world's cruelties, she was both mentally and physically devastated by the savagery wreaked upon her. After the birth of the child conceived during that attack, Ena began a spiraling descent into madness.

By the time Gabriel returned from France, Ena and her child were living with the sisters at a convent in the country. Occasionally, Gabriel would catch a glimpse of Ena and the raven-haired little girl in the garden behind the convent. Though Ena herself was clearly demented by now, ranting and shrieking at all who happened by, the little girl—Roweena—had even then been a delicate, achingly lovely child.

Gabriel went away once more, and when he returned the convent was gone, burned to the ground during yet another nighttime raid by unknown marauders. Ena had died in the fire. Her child, Roweena, was living with Gabriel's parents. An elderly couple who had been unable to have any other children after Gabriel, they had volunteered to take in the orphaned MacHugh child after the fire.

Gabriel was immediately drawn to the silent, sad-eyed Roweena, doting on her and caring for her as if she were his very own little sister. In spite of his and his family's affection for her, however, Roweena's situation was a pitiful one. She was looked upon by the townspeople as "that strange, wild girl," born in shame to a mother who was mad as a brush. Her deafness—the result of a severe blow the night of the convent fire—only made things worse, for such a thing was viewed with suspicion and, by some, with outright fear.

Gabriel's parents died within a few months of each other while

Roweena was still a child, leaving him to make the decision as to her fate. He went away only long enough to settle his affairs, leaving Roweena with his uncle Nessan and a kindhearted housekeeper. Incredibly, there was another fire. No one perished this time, but Gabriel was summoned back to Galway, where he found Roweena, numb with shock and frozen in terror, hiding in an abandoned building on the quay.

She was like a wild animal when he finally found her. He had to coax her to him as he would have a badly mistreated pup. He took her home, to the house where he had grown up, but by now a number of the townspeople were in a frenzy about the "little witch on the hill," accusing Roweena of everything from setting the fires to conjuring sea storms and crop failures. A neighbor accosted Gabriel at his own front door, demanding that he "get rid of the witch" before she brought a curse down upon them all.

Finally, desperate to protect Roweena, Gabriel made the decision that was to change his life. Under cover of night, he took her from his boyhood home to a place where he thought they would be safe, a place where few ever entered unless they were born to it. He was known there, and they accepted him and the frightened little girl without questions or condemnation. In the Claddagh, Roweena was not viewed as a wild thing, as mad or accursed. A deaf child was simply "special," touched by God.

Gabriel promised her he would never leave her again, and he kept his word. Over the years, he took in others, mostly children, who had been wounded or abandoned, providing them food and shelter—and as much attention as he could manage—until he could find a home for them. Wee Evie was the most recent. She had been but a babe, put out by a mother who didn't want her. Gabriel had not even tried to find another place for Evie. From the beginning, Roweena had developed such a fierce love and devotion for the babe, he could not think of separating them.

He had made the best home he could for all those who chanced to shelter under his roof. His life was far different than the one he had planned for himself, but it was not without its satisfaction and small rewards. They were good folk, the Claddagh people—primitive and pious, yet with a wisdom the outside world could never comprehend.

And they did not even seem to find it curious that a man who had once come within a handbreadth of a foreign mission field would give up everything to live among them as a fisherman—and a surrogate father and brother to those in need.

21

A Cloak in Which to Wrap the Fire

I gave a whistle and a lie,
And you were deaf to both. . . .

A N O N Y M O U S

By four o'clock, Terese was planning a scalding speech for Brady Kane—who was late, as usual—when she finally saw him coming up the path.

Closing the door quietly behind her, she hurried out to meet him. "Jane is sleeping," she warned, putting a finger to her lips.

He grinned, pulling her up close for a hug. "Good. That's how I like Jane best."

"Will you stop now? The neighbors will be watching."

"Let them watch," he said, dipping his head for a kiss. "Won't they just think what a lucky man that worthless American is to have such a gorgeous lass after him?"

Terese gave him the elbow and pulled away. "There's no one after you except the devil himself, you conceited Yank."

He laughed at her. "Ah, now, T'reesie, why can't you just admit that you find me irresistible entirely?"

She glared at him. "Aren't you even beginning to sound like a pigheaded Irishman, you fool? And will you stop calling me that silly name? My name is *Terese*."

Brady lifted an eyebrow. "Aren't we in a state today? I thought you'd be all excited about the play tonight, not carrying on like a bad-tempered fishwife."

Terese mellowed a bit at the thought of the play. She had never in her life seen the sort of thing Brady had been telling her about, where people in bright-colored costumes got up on a stage and acted out stories. She *was* excited, and that was the truth, but it wouldn't do to have him taking her for granted. Besides, he seemed to like it when she showed a bit of spirit.

"Jane hasn't agreed as yet that I can go," she cautioned glumly.

His dark eyebrows drew together in a frown of impatience. "You shouldn't even have to ask. The old crone isn't entitled to your soul, Terese, not for a measly two shillings a week. Stand up for yourself."

Terese squared off with him in the middle of the yard. "Two shillings a week might be nothing to a rich American like yourself, Brady Kane, but 'tis the hedge between myself and the poorhouse. I have to keep my position." She paused. "And don't be calling Jane a *crone.*"

"Your *position,*" he said, his mouth turning down. "The woman treats you like a slave."

"That's not true a bit!" Terese glanced back toward the house. "Didn't she tell me right from the start what she expected? She asks nothing more than what I agreed to." She saw the tight set of his mouth, his stubborn frown, and added, "The only reason you don't like poor Jane is that you know she doesn't like *you.* She doesn't trust you."

He pulled a face, as if surprised to find her defending Jane. In truth, Terese surprised herself. Without question, the woman could still set her teeth to grinding with her cantankerous ways. But even though Jane liked to goad her at every chance, for the most part they lived together peaceably enough.

" 'Poor Jane,' " Brady mimicked, "doesn't like *anyone.* The woman's disposition would curdle new milk." He shifted his sketch pad to his other arm and withdrew an envelope from his pocket, bringing it close to Terese's face. "The tickets," he said. "Give us a smile and a kiss now, or I'll go and find myself a girl who's not so cruel."

Hands on her hips, Terese stared him down. "You didn't tell me I had to *pay* for my ticket, Brady Kane. Didn't you say it was to be a treat on you?"

He inched closer to her. "The play is your treat. The kiss is mine."

"You're a fool," Terese said, trying to keep a straight face.

He grinned at her. "Ah, but you're a lovely girl."

"Light in the head, that's what you are."

He dangled the tickets in front of her.

"And late again as well," she reminded him. "What kept you *this* time? I suppose you stopped by Gabriel's house on the way."

He shrugged. "I'm not all that late."

Terese bristled. She had nothing against Gabriel—the man had been kind to her, in his fashion—but she'd seen how Brady's eyes turned all soft when he looked at Roweena. She didn't want him looking at anyone that way except herself. Too much depended on it.

"Did I tell you how pretty you look?" he said. "Dressed up just for me, did you?" Again he tried to steal a kiss, and this time Terese allowed it but quickly turned her face so he managed only a light peck on the cheek. "I'm not dressed up, you great *amadon*. I have nothing to dress up *in*."

"Still, you're gorgeous. Go and tell Jane good-bye now. And get a wrap. It's already turning cool."

"If she's still sleeping, I'd hate to wake her. She'll be cross."

"Fine," he said, catching her hand as if to start back down the path. "We'll go without waking her."

"Indeed we will not," Terese warned. "But you'll come in."

He grimaced but let her lead him to the door. "I don't see why I can't just wait outside."

" 'Tis not proper. You'll come in and make a greeting and tell Jane you'll be very careful of my safety and have me home immediately after the play."

He bared his teeth. "She thinks I'm the wolf at the door."

"Jane is known for her discernment of character," Terese said archly, pulling him toward the front door as she went to check on her employer.

✦❧❀❦✦

Inside, they found Jane sitting in the shadows by the window, no longer dozing. Her flint-edged stare darted from one to the other as they approached.

With only a slight hesitation, Brady started in on the exchange that had become a kind of ritual between him and Terese's employer. "Good evening, Mrs. Connolly. And how are you this fine day?"

The look she turned on him would have withered a snake. "I am exactly as I was when you last inquired, which was not all that long ago, it seems to me." She glanced at Terese. "You're walking out with him again?"

"Do you mind terribly?" Terese held her breath. She would defy her, if it came down to it, but she would rather not. Jane was a fright when she got upset, those poor gnarled hands shaking and crimson splotches breaking over her skin.

Jane cast a disdainful look at Brady Kane. "Sure, and you must have something better to do, girl."

Brady merely smiled—a thoroughly unpleasant smile.

Terese hurried to take an edge off the tension between the two. Brady was convinced that Jane didn't like him, and there was no denying that's how it seemed. Terese was fairly certain, however, that her employer's behavior toward Brady wasn't born so much of dislike as simple contrariness. Jane had seen early on that she could rile Brady and from then on took pleasure in doing just that. She did the same thing with *her,* but Terese had toughened herself to the constant barbs, could actually ignore them—most of the time.

"Please, Jane," she said in a tone as ingratiating as she could manage. "Tonight's the play—you remember, don't you? I've been counting on going, if you can make do without me."

Terese couldn't understand for the life of her why she wanted this eccentric old woman's approval, yet more and more often of late she found herself striving for at least a measure of it. At the moment, she was deliberately shining up to her, of course, but even so she really did want Jane's favor.

Jane lifted a hand in a weak motion of dismissal. "Go on, then. I'll not keep you from your folly." As if she'd only then thought of something else, she turned to Brady. "What do you know about this—*play* business, Brady Kane? Is it a decent event, where you're taking the girl?"

Brady gave another tight smile. "Entirely respectable, I assure you, Mrs. Connolly. It's a play based on the legend of Grania and Dermot. One of the traveling guild wagons is performing it in Galway, just for tonight."

"There's very little respectable about that legend," Jane said, her eyes narrowing as if to challenge his opinion. "Grania was a stubborn, selfish girl bent only on having her own way. Got her man killed in the process, as I recall. But then he was a fool for taking up with such a wild, heathen girl and no doubt deserved what he got."

Terese saw the way Brady was staring at Jane, as if some unidentifiable object had just sprouted from her head.

Jane's eyes flared, and she cracked a decidedly nasty smile before turning back to Terese. "Didn't I say to go on, then? 'Tis not for me to keep you from squandering your time."

Outside, Terese linked her arm through Brady's as they started down the path. "I don't know how you put up with her; I swear I don't," he said. "That woman would drive a saint to murder."

"She's not so bad, once you get used to her," Terese insisted. "In truth, she's decent enough to me, in her own way."

He shot her a look of disbelief. "I'd be interested in knowing what 'her own way' might be. I've never heard her give you a kind word yet."

Terese shrugged, then smiled a little. "I didn't say she was kind. But she hardly ever calls me a 'wild island girl' anymore. And she now allows me two cups of tea a day, instead of only one."

They turned into the lane leading away from the house. "Oh, well, of course that makes all the difference," he quipped. "Next thing you know, she'll be offering you a raise in wages."

"And wouldn't I be glad to take it?" Terese muttered.

"You could probably find something better in the city, Terese," he remarked, as he did at least once every time they were together. "Perhaps something in one of the shops."

Terese pulled her shawl more tightly about her, already chilled from the wind off the bay.

Brady noticed. "Don't you have a coat or something heavier?" he asked.

"Wouldn't I be wearing a coat if I had one?"

"We're going to get you a coat," he said firmly.

"You're going to stir your own stew," Terese fired back at him. "I'll be buying a coat for myself when I'm inclined, you insufferable rich Yank."

"Why do you keep calling me rich? I'm not rich."

"All Americans are rich," Terese said. "Everyone knows that."

He looked at her, slowing his pace to match hers. "Is that what your brother told you in his letters?"

Terese didn't answer right away. "No," she admitted. "He told me jobs were often hard to come by. Especially for the Irish."

Brady nodded. "I'm afraid he's right. Have you heard from him yet, by the way?"

Terese shook her head, not wanting to spoil her earlier mood.

"How long has it been since you wrote to tell him where you are?"

She tensed. "I've written twice. Jane loaned me the paper, and I posted the last letter three weeks past."

"Well, Pennsylvania's a long way off," he said somewhat lamely. "But you're sure to hear something soon."

Terese knew he was only trying to reassure her, but with every passing day she grew more anxious. If something had happened to Cavan, she didn't know what she would do. He was all the family she had now.

For years she had counted on joining him in America, where the two of them would build a better life for themselves. He was her big brother, but he was little more than an obscure shadow in her memory. She could hardly recall what he looked like. Of course, he would no doubt be greatly changed by now. Even so, she wished she could remember his face more clearly.

But tonight she didn't want to think about Cavan. She wanted to make the most of every minute of this special evening, wanted to enjoy hanging onto the arm of a handsome lad, going out for an evening to a play, just like the girls in America undoubtedly did. Just for tonight, she didn't want to think of anything unpleasant, anything worrisome. She didn't want to imagine Cavan meeting with some terrible misfortune or accident, and she certainly didn't want to think about what she would do if she never heard from him again.

Tonight, she wanted to savor each moment, make the most of it, make it last as long as possible. Tonight, she didn't even want to think about America.

※✿✿✿※

They had plenty of time before the play, and on impulse Brady led her onto one of the streets fronted with small shops. True to form, Terese's mind focused solely on the event to come—the play—and the detour only made her impatient with him. When Brady tried to lead her into one of the shops, she resisted.

"We've gone too far already. Didn't you say the performance was just off the quay? We need to be turning back—"

"We're far too early. Let's have a look around," he said, tugging her along beside him.

"I'd not want to be late. You said we should watch from the front, so we can see everything that's going on."

"And so we shall. But we've plenty of time. Come on now."

"I think we should be going back," she said, glancing over her shoulder.

"*Terese,*" Brady said, at the same time pulling her the rest of the way into the shop.

Her eyes widened as she saw where he was leading her. A row of cloaks hung against one wall, while tables neatly stacked with woolens took up most of the floor space. On the opposite wall, bolts of material filled the shelves.

With the sharp eyes of the generously whiskered owner following their every move, Brady led Terese down the row of cloaks, until one caught his eye. It was a brilliant, regal green, velvet soft and meticulously sewn.

"Here," he said, "put this on."

Terese stared at him as if he'd taken leave of his senses.

"Come on, try it on," he insisted, holding out the folds for her inspection.

Still, she hesitated. The owner wedged his way between the cloaks and one of the tables and began to comment—in the Irish. At a loss, Brady asked Terese, "What's he saying?"

She looked from the owner to Brady. "He says he'll make us a generous offer, since the weather is warming. But, Brady—"

Brady whipped the cloak free and draped it about her slender shoulders, then stood back just enough to have a look. With sudden mischief in her eyes, Terese spun around, and Brady caught his breath. He had never seen her in anything but her old frayed dress and one other, equally as worn, that Jane had collected for her somewhere. At this moment, with the splendid green wrap drawn close about her throat and the fiery riot of hair haloing her face, she might have been the daughter of the High King himself.

He let out his breath in a low whistle as he studied her. "I wish I could paint you right now, at this moment," he said softly. But even as he spoke, he knew he could never capture the passion, the mercurial spirit or formidable will that lent the fire to her beauty. She was beyond depiction. She was magnificent, and so fiercely alive she almost frightened him.

"Tell him we'll take it," he said, his voice gruff.

Her smoke blue eyes grew enormous. "Brady, you can't mean to—"

"Ask him the price."

She did, then relayed what she obviously thought to be a monumental amount. " 'Tis outrageous!" she blurted out.

"We will take it," Brady interrupted. "Tell him you'll wear it from here, not to wrap it."

"Brady! No, I can't—"

Brady turned to the owner himself, gesturing his intent, and soon they were on their way out of the shop.

The entire distance to the quay, he relished the sight of her touching the soft wool, eyes shining with a smile for him at every stroke. She was light on her feet at any time, but now she virtually danced, a vision in emerald, a glory to rival the Galway sunset and the jeweled mountains. She was enough to make a man's heart go wild.

Clearly, she was overwhelmed . . . delighted. Never before tonight had Brady enjoyed giving a gift quite so much.

And never before tonight had he wanted something so much, yet hesitated to take it, for fear it might consume him.

22

Star of Destiny

The ceremony of innocence is drowned;
The best lack all conviction, while the worst
Are full of passionate intensity.

W . B . Y E A T S

Brady tried to see the performance through Terese's eyes, for it was a new experience, an exciting one for her, and she was obviously enthralled with it. But he had to stretch his imagination to the limits, for he had seen a number of stage plays in New York and Dublin, and tonight's production was without a doubt the poorest he'd ever witnessed.

The performance was given inside a rickety auditorium by a small traveling group, most of whose members looked too old for life on the road. They also looked hungry, and probably were. The costumes were shabby; the sets were inferior—and for the most part, so were the performers. The actress who played the lead was too clumsy on her feet and too jaded in appearance to make a convincing Grania, but even so, at moments she became a spirited, if not inspiring, rebel. And of course the legend itself was intriguing enough that it held even an indifferent audience captive.

Terese was anything but indifferent. It seemed to Brady that she scarcely caught a deep breath until the last line was spoken. Throughout the entire performance, her face was radiant, her eyes shining, so much so that the height of Brady's own enjoyment came from watching hers.

She was a sight in that emerald cloak, statuesque and vibrant, her hair aflame in the light from the lanterns—a vision that would steal any man's senses. He was feeling especially fond of her tonight, even tender, in light of their approaching separation—of which she as yet knew nothing. He held her hand throughout the performance, and when she reached to clutch his arm at a particularly moving scene, he found that he rued the assignment that was about to take him away from her.

Tonight, for the first time, he realized how foolish he had been, what a mistake he had made, to think he could leave her behind, even for a brief time, with no regrets.

***

Terese did not weep easily. She had struggled through too much pain, too much anguish in her life, to indulge her sorrows with tears. But when the last line of the play was spoken, the curtain drawn, she wept. Overcome by a sense of loss that the experience must come to an end, overwhelmed even more by a dawning awareness that there was something in this night more significant than the play itself . . . something waiting for her discovery . . . she found herself unable to control the storm of emotion sweeping through her.

For almost two magical hours she had stepped into a different world, drawn the breath of another person, lived in a time and place so far removed from her own life that it would have been previously unimaginable. She had *become* Grania, daughter of the High King, condemned to marry the aging hero, Finn Mac Cool . . . the princess who defied her destiny by eloping with the handsome young Dermot . . . a fugitive pursued by the Fianna warriors for sixteen years . . . a widow and mother who trained her sons to avenge the death of her husband—only to end up, years later, as the bride of the man she once fled, the elderly war chief, Finn Mac Cool.

Terese knew the ancient epic, of course—had known it since she was a child. She had always loved the story of Grania and Dermot best of all the old legends. But to see it come to life in front of her eyes—a *wonder!*

In their lively colored costumes, the stage paint bright on their faces, their voices resonating out across the crowd, the actors seemed to take on the very life and essence of the fierce, rebellious Grania and the poor, doomed Dermot, the aged and bitter Finn Mac Cool and his noble Fianna warriors.

Tonight she had walked with giants and kings, moved among chieftains and warrior queens. Tonight her heart had burned with love for a handsome hero, only to break in sorrow at his death. Tonight she had known the thunderous rage of revenge and the unexpected grace of forgiveness. Tonight she had escaped, for two precious hours, the bitter reality of her life for the excitement and drama of another.

And tonight, in the depths of her spirit, she had glimpsed, for the first time ever, the faint and distant star of her destiny.

───────

They stood side by side, looking out over the water, watching the curraghs and other small craft bob up and down in the gentle night wind. It was a heavy night, with lowering clouds and thick shadows hovering over the quay.

Brady put an arm around her shoulder and coaxed her closer to him, brushing his face over the softness of the emerald cloak. "Warm enough?" he asked.

She looked at him and smiled. "In my fine new cloak? Of course I am."

"You enjoyed the play," he said. "I'm glad."

"It was wondrous!" She paused, biting at her lower lip. "How does a person go about such a thing—becoming a stage actress?"

He shrugged. "I don't know. I suppose you're born with the ability, though I expect you'd have to take a few lessons all the same."

"You mean at a school? Where would I be finding such a school? Are there such places in America?"

"Sure," Brady said, assuming there were, though he really didn't know.

"In your city?" she pressed. "In New York?"

He laughed a little. "If it's not in New York, it doesn't exist, T'reesie."

She frowned at him.

"Sorry. *Terese,*" he amended. "What's this all about? One play, and you've decided to go on the stage?"

"Don't laugh at me, Brady!" she warned, tossing her hair. "Perhaps that's exactly what I will do, once I get to America. It's something I *can* do. I know I can."

Brady didn't laugh. He was struck by the realization that she was probably right. She had a certain . . . presence. An inner fire that sometimes seemed to set her ablaze. Tonight had been such a time, right now, at this moment. She was so . . . intense, so vibrant. Her eyes were enormous in the night, glistening with excitement and purpose. She had pulled the hood of the cloak about her face, but now the wind played at it until it slipped away, leaving her wild russet hair to blow free.

Brady smoothed a strand of hair away from her face, his hand lingering on the cool softness of her cheek. She looked at him, and he caught his breath. She was so incredibly *beautiful!* He actually tried to look away from her, to drag his gaze from hers. He told himself he couldn't afford this kind of entanglement, not now . . . he was leaving. It would be madness to become any more involved with her than he already had. There would be time enough later, when he came back to Galway. But not now.

Her face was close, and she was watching him, her expression puzzled but rapt, as if the magic of the evening still enveloped her. He reminded himself of how young she was, though in truth he had never felt the difference in the years between them. Still, he had a responsibility. . . . She was innocent; he was sure of it.

Something warred inside him . . . tried to force its way past the temptation, past the need—something not quite strong enough to overcome either. Heat scorched his face, and he lifted her hands, brushing a light kiss over the knuckles of each, making a weak attempt to cool the fire flaming up within him.

He looked at her, saw how her eyes had grown heavy, her lips full and willing. The blood thundered to his head. One last time he tried to count the cost of what he was about to do. She was no bored cosmopolitan looking for an idle, meaningless evening of pleasure. She was a seventeen-year-old girl who cared about him, even trusted him in her fashion . . . at least he thought she did. She had already known more than she ought of cruelty and loss and deprivation. She could be hurt even further if he treated her lightly. But he *did* care about her. She had become important to him, perhaps *too* important.

He released her hands, cupped her chin, and lifted her face to his. His eyes searched hers, probing, trying to see some sign of fear or hesitation or even rejection—something to make him stop, because he knew by now that he wouldn't stop himself. What he saw was something he hadn't seen before, something he couldn't comprehend, and for a moment his desire slaked.

Then the moment passed, and he knew he had only imagined it. She was too young to calculate, too naive to speculate. Besides, she was wild for him, just as he was for her. The yielding warmth of her body was proof of it, despite whatever he thought he had seen lurking behind her gaze.

"Terese . . ."

She locked her arms about his neck, and for an instant he had an unbidden thought of the foolish Dermot, beguiled—*used*—by the ruthless, cunning Grania.

Then she was in his arms, and he was leading her back the way they had come, through the night, back to the town, to his flat.

⚜

Terese knew it was wrong, knew she could have stopped it, could *still* stop it if she would. Even at the door to his flat, when he put both arms around her and coaxed her inside, she could have stopped things from going any farther.

At first she told herself it wasn't so wrong, after all, because it was Brady, and she loved him. . . . Of course she loved him. But in an instant of brutal clarity she knew that was a lie, because in truth she didn't know what love was, didn't know if she wanted any part of it, not if it meant being weak or dependent or foolish. Besides, at times she didn't even *like* Brady, so how could she love him?

Even as he led her inside the flat, her mind was flinging out questions and warnings, telling her she was doing not only a wrong thing but a foolish thing. But she shook off the caution, shook off the shrieking questions for what she *did* know—that she must get to America, must get out of Ireland, or she would wither up like poor Jane Connolly and simply die of defeat and despair. She had to get out if she was to survive, had to follow that faint beckoning star she had glimpsed for the first time tonight, had to find what was out there waiting for her.

She must not let it matter whether she loved him or that it was wrong, a terrible sin. What mattered was to make him love *her,* at least make him *need* her to the point of desperation. So she went with him, went up the steps into his flat with him. She would let him believe what he obviously wanted to believe, that she was mad for him and must be with him now, tonight.

Eventually, she knew, he would leave—leave Ireland and go back to America. Before that day, she must make absolutely certain that he would not go back without her.

23

Reverend Ruthless

Thank God for one dear friend,
With face still radiant with the light of truth.

JOHN BOYLE O'REILLY

NEW YORK CITY

Jack's lunch was already sitting heavy on his stomach when he came back to his office and found the Reverend Rufus G. Carver waiting for him.

"I'm warning you, Rufus, I've just come from Wissen's—beef and dumplings and a cherry torte. Don't you be stirring up my digestion."

With a thunderous laugh, Reverend Ruthless, as Jack had dubbed him years ago, hauled his considerable girth out of the chair and extended a mammoth hand in greeting.

"Jack, God bless you, brother!" he boomed. "How long has it been?"

"A week, as I recall," Jack said dryly. His treacherous insides clamped in protest as Rufus yanked his hand up and down several times. It was a bit, Jack imagined, like being mauled by a bear. A large, extremely well-fed bear.

When Rufus finally released him, Jack sank down in the chair at his desk to recover. "Well, Rufus—how much this time, and what for?"

Still standing, the burly black preacher feigned a hurt look. "Jack . . . Jack," he said, shaking his glistening bald head sadly, "I surely hope you don't think I only come around when I'm looking for money for the Work."

The *Work* covered a vast array of projects, mostly in the slums and tenement settlements of the city, spearheaded by Rufus and two or three other members of the clergy. Jack bared his teeth in a semblance of a smile. "Not at all, Rufus. I recollect a few times that you settled for the shirt off my back and a pint of blood."

Rufus folded his hands over his ample midsection and rolled his eyes toward heaven. The black preacher had a number of standard postures; having seen them all, Jack tended to think of this one as *The Divine Messenger Pleads for Patience.*

"Before you make your pitch, Rufus, how's Amelia? And the family?"

The other's dark, good-natured face now broke into a smile. "Why, the children are as well as can be, and my Amelia, the good Lord love her, is just fine, Jack, just fine!"

Jack nodded. "I'm glad to hear it. The woman is a saint."

"Now that's the truth, if ever the truth was told, Jack! She is a beautiful, pure-hearted, God-fearing woman, if I do say so myself."

"You forgot *long-suffering*," Jack pointed out.

"That, too," Rufus said cheerfully, ignoring the jibe. "She sends her best, by the way. And she said I shouldn't come home without a definite date from you as to when we can expect you for supper again."

Jack put a hand to his stomach, trying to ignore the fact that the dumplings had seemingly turned to lead. "I will be only too happy to plop myself down at Amelia's table any night of the week, and she knows it. Best cook in New York."

"Now that's a fact. It just so happens that the reason I came by today was to invite you to a special supper. This one's not at our house, though Amelia will be doing some of the cooking. She sent me special to ask you, and she said I shouldn't take no for an answer."

Lowering himself into the chair across from the desk, Rufus unbuttoned his black suit coat to reveal a multicolored vest, no doubt tailored by his wife. Rufus always wore a plain white shirt and a black suit—shiny enough that Jack sometimes wondered if it was the *same* black suit—but he had the finest collection of good-looking vests in New York, and today's was no exception.

Knowing he was expected to comment on it, Jack did so. "Amelia's latest creation, I suppose?" he said, inclining his head toward Rufus's middle.

Rufus smiled and opened his coat a bit wider. "You like this? I never did care for those worn-out drapes in the front room, but I do believe they made a right nice vest, don't you? Amelia said she had to patch several pieces together to get enough cloth to stretch around me, but isn't that woman a wonder?''

Jack shook his head, unable to stop a smile. ''What's this supper you're inviting me to? What are you up to now?''

''Ah, this Saturday. It's going to be a fine evening, Jack. A fine evening. The church is hosting a meal as a way of thanking some of the good folks who helped build the new schoolhouse. You being the one who made the school possible in the first place, we're counting on you to be there, maybe even say a few words to the people.''

Jack leaned back in his chair and locked his arms behind his head. ''The building's all done, is it?''

Rufus nodded. ''It is indeed. And it's a fine, sturdy building, thanks to you, brother.''

''Thank the men in your church. They did all the work.''

''Wouldn't have been any money to buy the lumber without you, Jack. They're setting in the stove first thing Monday, by the way— more thanks to you. 'Course they won't be needing it much longer now, with warm weather coming, but in the fall those children will be glad for it.'' He paused, then gave Jack a wide, beatific smile. ''You're a good man, brother. A mighty good man.''

Jack scowled at him and dropped his arms. ''What do you want, Rufus?''

''Now, Jack, I already told you. I'm here to invite you to the supper. It'll be held in the church basement, by the way. We realize you might have other things to do, you being such a busy, important man and all, but it would mean a lot to Amelia and me if you would honor us.''

''Oh, *stop* it, Rufus!'' Jack growled impatiently. ''All right, all right; I'll come. But I won't be making any speeches, and don't you dare try to trick me into it once I'm there, do you hear?''

Rufus put a hand to his heart. ''Whatever you say, brother. Far be it from me to interfere with a man's humility before the Lord. I consider it highly commendable, Jack, your insisting on giving your alms in secret. That's the Good Book's way, after all.''

Rufus was forever trying to put a religious connotation on everything Jack did. He ignored the remark and sat silently studying the man across the desk with concealed fondness.

Rufus G. Carver was the *blackest* black man Jack had ever known—a big, jovial man of indeterminate age, with a polished dome of a head and a fastidiously trimmed beard. It didn't take much stretching of the imagination to picture Rufus as an ancient African chieftain. It never failed to baffle Jack how the smiling dark monolith sitting across from him could wind him around his little finger with such a minimum of effort. After all these years, Rufus could still squeeze more money from Jack than any two con men combined and talk him into doing just about anything he or his incredible wife, Amelia, asked.

No two men could have been farther apart in terms of personality, philosophy, or perspective. Rufus, though hardworking and energetic, tended to let things roll off his solid back, never fretting about whether or not a job would get done, but simply "trusting the Good Lord" to take care of things. Jack, on the other hand, would drive himself until he was ready to drop. Something in him resisted any kind of dependence. Even today, after years in business, he still found it almost impossible to delegate responsibility. He thrived on the demanding pace he set for himself, in truth found his enjoyment far more in the work itself than in the financial gains or influence that went along with it.

In matters of the spirit, he and Rufus were drastically removed from each other. He was fairly sure that popular opinion had him at best a lapsed Catholic, at worst, a hopeless infidel. At the opposite end of the pole was Rufus, a washed-in-the-blood, filled-with-the-Holy-Ghost, pulpit-thumping PREACHER—Rufus invariably spoke the word *preacher* in capital letters—who delighted in telling Jack he was a good man at the same time he was nipping at his heels to save his soul.

They traded insults like sworn adversaries, lived in two different worlds, associated with none of the same people, and viewed life from radically diverse platforms. But when it came right down to it, Jack loved Rufus Carver like a brother, and he never doubted that the feeling was mutual.

He could hardly fail to appreciate the irony in the fact that the one man he could honestly count a friend was a zealous black evangelist who viewed money as nothing more than a tool to feed the hungry and build churches and schoolhouses—and who thought the only thing wrong with Jack Kane was that he'd never had a "face-to-face meeting with the Lord."

Jack wasn't even sure what Rufus meant by that, but he had a suspicion there was a lot more wrong with him than his friend would like to think. Even so, he appreciated Rufus's giving him the benefit of the doubt.

Their friendship had begun years ago, before Martha had taken ill. Against Jack's better judgment, she had spent a considerable amount of time helping out at some of the orphanages—perhaps because even then she was longing for the child they would never have. In any event, one of the homes had been for black children, and during that time she had struck up an acquaintance with Rufus and Amelia. One thing had led to another until Jack—despite his fierce resistance to the very idea of befriending a preacher—found himself doing just that.

During Martha's illness and the agonizing days leading up to her death, Rufus had continually stood by Jack, ignoring his embittered tirades against the God who had allowed Martha's suffering.

Perhaps it was Rufus's total lack of pretense, the fact that he made no attempt to give Jack pat answers that would have meant nothing, that had allowed their friendship to come through the ordeal intact and even stronger than ever. To this day, Jack couldn't think of that terrible time at the end without also thinking of Rufus standing by, silently weeping, quietly praying for the friend he could not help. And to this day, there was no man Jack trusted quite as completely as Rufus Carver.

He sighed now and made a resigned gesture with one hand. "What time should I be there?"

Rufus beamed. "Amelia said you should come at six-thirty." He paused, his dark gaze wandering to some unseen object across the room. "She also said that you should feel free to bring a lady friend, if you like."

Jack laughed, and Rufus looked back at him, smiling. "Amelia still thinks all I need is a good woman, eh?" Jack said, shaking his head.

"Well, now, Jack, you've said it yourself—Amelia, she is one smart woman. Could be you ought to take her more seriously."

"Oh, I take her seriously, all right. I just don't agree with her." He shot Rufus a wicked grin. "Besides," he said, "I'm not at all sure I even *know* any good women."

Ah, now it was the *Father Admonishing the Prodigal Son* stance. Rufus wagged a finger at Jack and tried to twist his features into a disapproving frown—not entirely successfully, Jack noted, probably because Rufus's face didn't lend itself to frowning. "Now I'm going to pray that's not so, brother. And I don't believe it is."

Still grinning, Jack stretched and yawned. "If you're through making a nuisance of yourself, Rufus, I have a newspaper to get out."

"Far be it from me to keep an important man from his work, brother. We each have our jobs to do, don't we?" Rufus brought himself to his feet, with some groaning at the effort. "I'm getting to be an old man, Jack. I really am."

Jack watched him. "How old are you anyway, Rufus?"

"Well, now, I don't rightly know," the other said, adjusting his suit coat. "When Dr. Sandleton took me and my mama in, I was just a little fella. Couldn't have been much more than five or six, I don't suppose. That was a lot of years ago. I must be an old man by now, sure enough."

"You're not a day over forty-five, if that, and don't give me that poor-little-slave-boy routine," Jack countered. "You were probably as much of a slyboots when you were five years old as you are now."

Rufus grinned back at him. They both knew the truth, that Rufus Carver *had* in fact been a little slave boy but had never once considered himself *poor*. By his own account, his mother had been an amazing woman—"a little crazy, maybe, but a truly remarkable woman all the same"—who, after his father had been killed by a water moccasin, still managed to escape the slave hunters and get herself and her son to safety in the North. Along the way she had almost drowned pulling another slave child out of the water. In Cincinnati she had narrowly avoided being trampled by a runaway wagon. Finally, a kindhearted Christian doctor and his blind wife had taken in the two runaways, given Rufus's mother a job, and provided both of them with a home for the ensuing years. Rufus was fond of telling anyone who would listen that "if the Good Lord can get a poor little slave boy out of Mississippi with his head still fastened on his shoulders, then he can surely get the devil out of any man's soul."

He left Jack with a hearty reminder not to be late come Saturday, that "the family" was counting on him.

An evening with the Carvers was always a grand time for Jack. Rufus and Amelia's six children, who ranged in age from four to sixteen, were a fine, lively set. Jack was fond of each of them. Yet at times the experience turned bittersweet for him, when, after a noisy, rambunctious evening at the Carvers', he went back to his spacious, silent house, feeling his own lack of family even more keenly.

The thought of family jerked him out of his self-absorption with a reminder of something he needed to take care of, and before he started anything else he sent one of the messenger boys downstairs to fetch Cavan Sheridan.

"Two things," Jack said shortly when young Sheridan stepped into the office. "First off, I wanted to tell you that I wrote my brother a couple of days ago, and I mentioned your sister's name and last known whereabouts to him. I told him to do some checking around and see if he could locate some word of her."

The boy smiled, his ink-smudged features creasing in pleasure. "I can't thank you enough, sir!"

Jack waved off his thanks. "Yes, well, with all this business about bringing others across, it occurred to me we ought to see to your sister first off. I told Brady, if he can find her, to arrange for her passage as soon as possible."

Sheridan wiped his hands down the sides of his trousers. "I—not that I don't appreciate it, sir, you understand—but I haven't quite saved up enough to pay her way—"

Again Jack made a dismissing motion with his hand. "You needn't fret yourself about the cost. I'll take care of it."

"No, sir, I can't let you do that."

Blast, the boy was stubborn. "And why *can't* you let me do that?" Jack said with forced patience.

Sheridan looked uncomfortable—but then, he usually did. "I'd rather not be beholden, sir. As I said, I'm extremely grateful to you, but I'd really like to pay Terese's passage myself, you see."

"No, I *don't* see," Jack snapped. "It seems to me that you shouldn't be splitting hairs about your own sister's well-being. But if you're bound to be pigheaded about the issue, we'll make it a loan, which you can repay when you have the money. Will that satisfy your pride?"

Sheridan regarded him with a solemn expression. Suddenly, he smiled a little—a wonder in itself, Jack thought, gratified that the boy was actually learning to smile in his presence.

"Yes, sir. Thank you, sir. I—you'll let me know if Mr. Brady learns anything?"

"You'll be the first," Jack assured him. "But remember, it will take some time. Now, then, I wanted to see how you're doing with the story on Willie."

As yet, there had been no posts from Brady regarding the new assignment. In the meantime, to let Sheridan try his hand at some writing until the stories from Ireland began to come through, Jack had given him the job of coming up with an article about the newsboys: where and how they lived, their family situations, and especially some of the dangers and dilemmas they faced in their work.

He'd suggested to Sheridan that he use little Willie Shanahan as an example—unnamed, of course, for the boy's own protection.

It had been Jack's observation that most of the boys took their jobs very seriously—and why wouldn't they, since to most of them it meant their survival? He had the idea of exposing the worthless scum who were beating them up and stealing from them. Perhaps if he could get some of the decent citizens sufficiently aroused, they'd apply a bit of pressure to the police and the politicians to clean some of the human rubbish off the streets.

"I talked with Willie and two of his friends just yesterday," Sheridan said. "It took some explaining, but I finally convinced them they weren't in trouble. I tried to speak with Willie's mother later on, but the woman acted as if I had a tail and horns. She told me to go away and practically slammed the door in my face." He paused, then added, "Mrs. Harte offered to approach her. She knows some of the other women who live in the same building."

At the mention of Samantha Harte, Jack's interest quickened. "How would that be?"

"From her work with the society, I expect."

"Where does Willie live?"

"Well, Willie lives on the street with the other boys, sir. But his family lives in one of those belowground flats in the Bowery."

"Good heavens, you can't ask Mrs. Harte to go into the Bowery!" Jack exclaimed.

Sheridan gave him a puzzled look. "Mrs. Harte goes to the Bowery all the time, sir. And the Five Points as well."

"*Five Points?* Samantha Harte goes into the Five Points?"

"Well, not alone, naturally. The police provide protection for some of the members of the benevolent society when they need to visit the Points."

Five Points—so named because of the five streets that converged in the center of a squalid square in the infamous Sixth Ward—was the worst slum in New York City. In fact, from what Jack had been told by some who had traveled extensively, the mean streets of Five Points just might comprise the worst slum in the world. It was a vile, nightmare of a place, the terror of decent people, and a veritable blight on the city. Reeking with human waste, animal filth, and all manner of corruption, the area provided a perfect hideaway for hardened criminals and a breeding ground for unbridled evil.

It was also populated by what was probably the largest Irish settlement outside of Dublin and a fast-growing community of Negroes—two groups continually at odds with each other, which only added more friction to a place already teeming with trouble.

Even the police avoided going into the foul sinkhole unless it was absolutely necessary, and then entered only in pairs and with their weapons at the ready. The thought of Samantha Harte so much as allowing her skirts to brush the filthy stones of the streets was almost beyond Jack's comprehension.

"A remarkable woman," he muttered. "If a bit foolish."

"She *is* a remarkable woman, that's true," Sheridan agreed, his tone somewhat defiant. "But I'd hardly call her foolish."

"Neither she nor any other decent woman has any business going into Five Points. Or the Bowery either, for that matter. And I'd suggest you not encourage her to take such preposterous risks."

Giving Sheridan no time to object, Jack went on. "Mrs. Harte studiously avoids me, so perhaps you would give her a message?"

"Sir?"

"Just tell her I couldn't be more pleased with her work," Jack said, meaning it. "I haven't seen a typo since she took over the proofreading. I'd like her to know I'm impressed."

Sheridan broke into one of the brightest smiles Jack had ever seen on that thoroughly Irish face. So that's what it took, then, to lighten the boy's typically severe countenance—a bit of praise for Mrs. Harte.

"I'll be happy to tell her, sir. I'm sure she'll appreciate hearing it."

After Sheridan left, Jack pulled in a long breath and sat for a moment thinking about Samantha Harte. She really was doing an exceptional job with the editing and proofreading responsibilities. And based on what he could learn from Sheridan, she was working him like an army mule at the books—with progress already evident. Clearly, the remarkable Mrs. Harte was more than meeting the terms of their agreement.

In fact, Jack's only disappointment with his newest employee was the fact that he never caught so much as a glimpse of her. Sheridan or one of the other boys delivered the daily copy to her flat and went back to pick it up. It was a smooth, efficient system, and he could hardly complain about it, since he'd approved it at the start.

Still, he wouldn't mind seeing her again.

Indeed, he wouldn't mind at all.

24

A Moment between Memories

They never knew the carefree dust of gladness,
but only ashes scattered in the wind.

ANONYMOUS

Samantha left her apartment earlier than she'd planned Saturday afternoon. Since the Shanahan residence wasn't all that far from the church, she decided to make the visit Cavan Sheridan had asked of her before going on to the dinner.

Even though she didn't especially like walking alone on Houston Street, she'd grown used to it by now. She couldn't stop a rueful smile at the thought of her mother; Angela Pilcher would almost certainly fall over with a stroke if she knew her daughter was on foot in such a neighborhood.

But it was a lovely spring day, so warm she scarcely needed a wrap, and she'd been traipsing this area long enough that for the most part even the more disreputable types left her alone. Besides, if she wanted to get anywhere these days, she had to walk. And despite the ever present stench of New York's notorious garbage problem, she usually enjoyed the experience.

The streets were bustling, as usual, with a continual press of people. Young girls in bright-colored dresses giggled as they strolled along with their beaus. Children laughed and shouted as they whipped in and out among the pedestrians. Hard-looking women and even harder-looking men, their voices often raised in anger and in a variety of languages—mostly Irish and German—shot suspicious looks at

Samantha in passing. Others, recognizing the schoolteacher, eked out a smile. Dogs were everywhere, sniffing out their choices from the rubbish piled along the streets. As she rounded the corner onto Mott Street, Samantha met a signboard man with his advertising signs slung over his shoulders. He gave Samantha a toothless grin in greeting and went on by.

In front of the tenement house that was her destination, Samantha had to step back to avoid being run down by a pack of ragged children playing ball. The Shanahans lived in the rear of the building, and Samantha's sense of well-being fled as she took a long look at the front before going around to the back. It was a dark, leprous-looking place, three stories and a basement. Some of the windows were broken, others missing altogether. Rust-covered barrels of waste stood near the stoop, ringed by a group of poorly clad, hungry-looking men who huddled together, talking and laughing loudly.

Samantha was familiar with the neighborhood, having visited numerous families here from time to time. Even so, she felt increasingly uneasy, especially when she caught a glimpse of flasks being passed among the loiterers. It was a corner lot, so she could reach the rear of the building from the outside rather than having to navigate one of the dark hallways typical of these old structures. Keeping her gaze averted, she ignored the catcalls and smirks as she started around the building.

An almost palpable stench met her in back, and she hesitated before going any farther. Not for the first time, she questioned the wisdom of coming into such a neighborhood alone. But she was here now, and she thought it would be even more foolish to come this far and turn back.

She took in a deep, steadying breath and started down the rickety steps, surprised to note that the steps and the stoop were completely free of litter and grime, as if they'd recently been swept. At the unpainted door, she rapped and waited. When she heard no stirring from within, she knocked again, a little more firmly this time.

Finally, the door creaked on its hinges and cracked open, but only enough for someone to look out. Samantha could scarcely make out the appearance of a thin female face with frightened eyes. Shadowed as she was in the late-afternoon gloom, she might have been either woman or child, Samantha couldn't tell which.

"What d'you want?" she said, her voice hushed, as though to avoid being heard.

"Mrs. Shanahan?" Samantha ventured, for a closer study revealed that the doorkeeper was indeed a woman and not a child. "My name is Samantha Harte. I was wondering if I might speak with you for a moment.''

Immediately, the door began to close. On impulse, Samantha put her hand between the door and the frame to keep it from shutting in her face. "Please, Mrs. Shanahan—I won't take much of your time. I'd just like to talk with you, if I may. It's about Willie.''

The woman's face, already pale, turned ashen. "What about Willie? Is he hurt?''

"Oh, no," Samantha hurried to reassure her. "It's nothing like that. Willie is fine. I'm employed by the *Vanguard,* you see, and the paper is doing a story on newsboys. I'd like to ask you some questions to help our reporter write the article. Please, can't you just spare me a few minutes?''

"Willie's all right, then?" The woman seemed less than convinced, but she did finally crack the door a little wider.

"He's perfectly all right," Samantha said again. "I'm so sorry if I frightened you. I—may I come in, Mrs. Shanahan?''

Something Samantha recognized as fear leaped in the woman's gaze. "No! I mean, not now . . . the baby is sleeping. . . .''

Her accent was Irish, of course, but not terribly pronounced. Apparently, the Shanahans weren't new to the city. "I'm sorry," Samantha said, disappointed. "I suppose I *have* come at a bad time. Perhaps I can stop by one day next week.''

The woman glanced over her shoulder, then opened the door just enough to step outside onto the stoop. She was a young woman, small, not quite as tall as Samantha, who wasn't much more than three or four inches over five feet herself. Mrs. Shanahan was also painfully thin, almost to the point of emaciation. Studying her, Samantha thought she might have been pretty once, but now she simply looked worn-out and ill. Her red blonde hair needed combing and fell idly over one side of her face. But her dress, though well worn, was clean and neat.

There was something else about her, something strangely . . . familiar that Samantha couldn't identify. She suddenly realized that she must have been staring, for the woman was eyeing her suspiciously.

"Mrs. Shanahan, let me explain about the article—''

"I don't have time for that," the other said, not rudely, but more as if she was intent on getting rid of Samantha. "There's three besides Willie, don't you know." She glanced behind her at the door. "They keep me busy. Right now I have the supper to cook and—''

"Maura!"

Without warning, a man lumbered into the open doorway. He

wasn't a big man, probably only a few inches taller than his diminutive wife. But his wiry frame looked muscular, and there was a hard, mean look about him that didn't stop at his eyes. At the moment, he was scowling at his wife with undisguised anger. Then his gaze cut to Samantha, who felt his malice like a blow.

She saw two things at once: first, that the woman was trembling, shrinking from him as if she expected him to lash out at her, and second, that the man's pale gray eyes didn't quite conceal a spark of wildness that might have been either rage or lunacy.

The recognition was so unexpected, so sharp, that Samantha nearly doubled over. She actually had to wrap her arms around herself to hide her own trembling. Immediately, she took a step back, almost stumbling with the effort. She knew too well what she was witnessing, and she felt sick with the awareness.

"Who's this?" the man growled, his eyes raking first Samantha, then his wife.

"'Tis only a lady from the newspaper, Heber, asking after Willie—"

"Willie?" He glared at Samantha. "What about Willie? What's the worthless little jacksnipe done now?"

The need to defend the boy was all it took for Samantha to recover her composure. "Willie hasn't done anything wrong, Mr. Shanahan! Nothing at all. Please don't misunderstand—as I explained to your wife, the *Vanguard* is considering an article about the newsboys, and I'm just trying to gather some information for the reporter."

The man drew himself up to full height, fixing Samantha with a look that was clearly meant to be intimidating. "If Willie's in no trouble, then it seems to me you got no business coming around here, bothering us with your questions. You leave us alone now."

Obviously, he felt no urgency to see that his dismissal was carried out but turned sharply and started back inside. "Get yourself in here, woman!" he shouted over his shoulder. "You've enough to do without standing out there blathering to some busybody."

The woman darted a look at Samantha, who realized for the first time that Maura Shanahan seemed to have either an injured or perhaps a withered left arm; the entire time she'd been standing there, she had kept the arm drawn up against her side, slightly crooked at the elbow but motionless. Her mouth trembled as she started to back up toward the door. "I'm sorry," she stammered, again glancing behind her. "You'd better go now. I—have you seen my Willie?"

"No, I haven't, Mrs. Shanahan. But I'll be glad to see that he gets a message from you, if you like."

The woman lifted a hand to her hair. "Just tell him . . . that his mother said to take care of himself." She brushed the hair away from her face, and Samantha saw it then, the ugly bruise mottling her temple. Her stomach knotted, and she fought against the nausea welling up in her. There would be similar bruises on her arms, concealed by the long sleeves of her dress, and perhaps others as well over her body. And that arm, that poor thin arm the woman had been favoring throughout their exchange, was no doubt stiff or injured from being wrenched. . . .

"I'll tell him," Samantha choked out. She swayed slightly, fighting off the weakness that threatened to seize her. She had to get away from here before she was ill. On impulse, she dug down inside her bag for a pencil and paper. "Mrs. Shanahan," she said, trying to stop the shaking of her hand as she scrawled on the paper, "here's my name and an address where you can reach me if you should—" she glanced up, then handed the paper to Maura Shanahan—"if you should want to talk with me about Willie . . . or anything else. I teach a class there every Tuesday and Thursday evening until eight. And on Friday afternoons I'm at the new Negro school on Mercer Street. Please, feel free to come and see me."

Samantha gave the woman a quick, forced smile, then turned and practically ran up the steps. She knew she had to get out of there, had to get away from Maura Shanahan before she lost the last remnant of her self-control. She could not endure the woman's obvious pain, her humiliation, a moment more.

When she reached the front of the building, she scarcely noticed the same group of men who had jeered at her only minutes before. She had all she could do not to take off running. The entire distance to the church, she felt as if the dogs of her past were hot on her heels in pursuit.

⚜

The first person Jack saw when he entered the church basement was Samantha Harte. She was standing with Amelia, near one of the serving tables at the far end of the room, looking absolutely splendid in a simple frock of a dusky rose hue, her only adornment a bit of frothy lace at the throat. She was just as lovely, her bearing as coolly elegant, as he remembered.

Just inside the door, he caught Rufus by the arm to stop him from going any farther. "What's Samantha Harte doing here?"

Rufus glanced across the room, then at Jack. "You know Mrs. Harte? Isn't she a *fine* woman, though?"

Jack nodded, not taking his eyes off Samantha Harte. Three rows of long banquet-length tables stood between them, and he took advantage of the distance to study her.

"How is it that you know her, Jack?"

Jack turned to look at him. "Actually, I don't know her—at least not very well. She's an employee." At Rufus's look of surprise, he went on to explain. "Mrs. Harte proofreads for me on a part-time basis. I met her through Sheridan, my driver. She's the instructor at the night school he attends." Jack returned his attention to the woman across the room. "You didn't say what she's doing here."

"Why, Mrs. Harte is one of our volunteer teachers," Rufus said. "She donates her Friday afternoons to the school. Yes, indeed, she is a fine woman. A *good* woman," Rufus said pointedly. "Amelia thinks the world and all of her."

"Yes, I'm sure," Jack said, his attention still diverted as he watched Samantha Harte now turn to survey the room. Her gaze locked with his, and Jack smiled and gave a small bow when he saw her look of surprise.

"Rufus," he said, not taking his eyes off Samantha Harte. "A favor?"

"Why, anything for you, Jack. Anything at all."

"Seat me beside Mrs. Harte at the table, would you?"

Jack wasn't so distracted that he missed the smile in Rufus's voice when he replied. "I surely will, Jack. I surely will."

With a quick check of the carnation in his lapel, Jack started to make his way across the room.

⚜

Samantha was just beginning to put the visit to Maura Shanahan behind her and relax when she saw Jack Kane standing next to Rufus, looking directly at her. There was no accounting for the sense of panic that slammed into her at the sight of him.

He caught her eye, gave her a roguish smile, and bowed. As Samantha saw him start toward her, she whipped around to Amelia. "What is *he* doing here?"

Amelia followed the direction of Samantha's gaze. "Jack? Why, land, he and Rufus have been friends forever."

Samantha stared at her. "Jack Kane . . . and Rufus? You aren't serious?"

Amelia smiled as if she understood Samantha's surprise and was completely unoffended by it. "Not exactly what you'd expect, I reckon, but they do get on. Always have." She looked at Samantha with a puzzled frown. "I didn't realize you knew Jack."

Samantha shook her head. She could almost feel Kane closing in on her and tried to ignore the frantic clamoring of her heart, the sudden dryness of her mouth. "I—I've been working part-time for Mr. Kane from my home, proofreading. His driver—one of my night-school students—introduced us."

"You're working for Jack?" Amelia beamed. "Well, now, isn't that nice, Samantha! He is such a *fine* man!"

Samantha stared at her. "Jack Kane?"

Amelia laughed and ran a hand over her perspiring brow before bending over the table to rearrange a few of the dishes that had been moved too close to the edge. "Oh, I know all the stories about Jack, but I don't pay them any heed. This town don't know all there is to know about Jack Kane—nor half of what it owes him, and that's the truth!"

Samantha's eyes widened still more in disbelief. "Are you *serious*, Amelia?"

"I reckon no one knows Jack Kane any better than Rufus and me, and I can tell you that man is not the devil he's made out to be. No, sir," Amelia said emphatically, straightening. "Not at all. He's just a man who made some mistakes when he was young. Don't we all?" She shook her head. "Some folks can't seem to get past the man he *used* to be long enough to get to know the man he is today. Jack, he's just a lonely man who's got nothing much in his life except money—and maybe too much of that."

"Lonely?" Samantha parroted. Out of the corner of her eye she saw Kane and Rufus stop to speak to one of the deacons in the church. "Are you sure we're talking about the same man, Amelia?"

Amelia nodded, the satin sheen of her black hair catching the light from the lamps flickering around the room. She, too, was watching Rufus and Kane as they stood talking. "Oh, Jack's lonely, all right—not that he'd admit it." She looked at Samantha. "He was married once, you know."

Samantha hadn't known.

Amelia gave a long sigh. "They weren't married all that long before Martha took sick and passed away. Jack did love that woman. I think he still misses her, though she's been gone a long time now."

Samantha swallowed against the thickness in her throat. Somehow the thought of Jack Kane as a loving husband or a lonely widower was almost impossible to grasp. "But what is he doing *here?*" she asked again.

A head taller than Samantha, Amelia smiled down at her. "Why, Samantha, honey," she said, "if it weren't for Jack Kane, we wouldn't be *havin'* this supper tonight! There wouldn't be a *school.* Jack, he put up almost all the money for it, don't you know?"

She stopped, eyeing Samantha with a peculiar expression before slowly turning to Jack Kane with a big smile as he reached the two of them.

"Jack! I knew you'd show up!" Amelia said, laughing. "And won't you be glad you did, once you see the dessert table!"

Stunned, Samantha watched Jack Kane draw Amelia's ample frame into a brisk hug and kiss her lightly on the cheek. "How are you, my beauty?" he said, grinning as he set her at arm's length to admire her. "How did an old dog like Rufus ever win such a woman?"

Then he turned to Samantha. "Mrs. Harte," he said, his voice low as he gave that quick, mocking bow again. "My elusive employee. I'm delighted to see you again."

Samantha swallowed with difficulty. For one insane moment she half feared he was going to embrace her as he had Amelia, and she took an involuntary step backward.

One corner of his mouth quirked, and his dark eyes danced as if he knew exactly what she was thinking. Embarrassed, Samantha felt the heat rise to her face and, for the second time that day, knew the urge to run.

25

A Meeting
on Mercer Street

And I knew what it meant
Not to be at all.

RHODA COGHILL

Seated at the table to Jack Kane's left, directly across from Rufus and Amelia, Samantha struggled to swallow another bite of chicken. She knew her anger toward the man at her side was irrational, but at the moment she didn't much care. Had it not been for Kane, she would have been able to enjoy Amelia's succulent chicken and dumplings. As it was, every morsel she took into her mouth tasted as bitter as old coffee grounds and seemed to bond with her throat all the way down.

It was evident that Jack Kane was having no such problem. Out of the corner of her eye, Samantha saw Kane attack his third helping of dumplings as eagerly as if it were his first. Between mouthfuls, he and Rufus had been trading stories about some of the more colorful city officials, regaling each other like a couple of schoolboys. Obviously, they found themselves highly amusing.

It was a noisy gathering, partly because most of the families were large, with several children, a number of whom had finished eating and were scampering in and out among the tables, laughing and poking at each other. Rufus had more than once ordered them back to their places, but they obviously knew their good-natured preacher too well. For the most part, they simply waved and went on.

Samantha had actually been looking forward to this evening, and she resented Jack Kane's showing up to spoil it. She thought she might even resent Rufus for inviting him—and that *was* irrational. Most of all, she resented herself for letting a man like Kane get under her skin to the point that she couldn't even enjoy a church supper. She might have found him easier to ignore if Amelia hadn't confused her with all that talk about Kane's reputation not being entirely deserved, planting just enough doubt in Samantha's mind that she now found it somewhat more difficult to dislike him.

But why was she so set on disliking Kane in the first place?

The question unsettled Samantha more than she cared to admit. Up until now, she had found it fairly easy to rationalize her feelings about her employer. He represented everything she had been taught to abhor, everything any decent Christian woman would find anathema. Jack Kane was a known libertine. A gambler, a mercenary, a womanizer. A *shark*. Before tonight, aversion would have been a perfectly natural response—indeed the only acceptable response—to a man of his reputation.

But now, if the rumors *had* been exaggerated as Amelia seemed to believe, Samantha supposed she had to consider the possibility that her own judgment of him might have been unfair. After all, she *had* formed her opinion of Kane on little more than hearsay. Even so, she wasn't entirely convinced of Amelia's defense of the man. Wasn't it just possible that Rufus's friendship with Kane might have clouded the Carvers' perception?

On the other hand, she had always known Amelia to be remarkably objective about everything and everyone, even Rufus and the children. That made it difficult to simply disregard her remarks about Jack Kane.

In light of that, why was she still so set on disliking him?

The unsettling reply came roaring in on her like a tidal wave. The truth was that her dislike of Kane amounted to little more than self-deception—because in some perverse way she was actually *attracted* to him.

The admission stunned her. Samantha had never thought to feel even a vague attraction to any man after Bronson. In fact, she would have thought the very idea impossible. The realization that she had deceived herself, that a man like Jack Kane could actually hold some sort of appeal for her, shook her to the point that she froze with a momentary sense of panic.

Suddenly, Samantha was keenly aware of the shoulders that were too wide to comfortably fit the space between her and Dr. Younger without brushing against her, as well as the faint scent of cinnamon and tobacco she'd noticed the night she had met Jack Kane for the first time. She couldn't seem to drag her gaze away from the movement of those large, sturdy hands every time he lifted his water glass or his silverware. And when he laughed, the deep, rich rumble struck a chord that resonated somewhere inside her.

Instinctively, she edged to the other side of her chair as much as possible. As if sensing her movement, Kane turned to her, his dark eyes glinting with something unreadable. *Amusement,* Samantha thought, resenting him anew for the fact that he seemed to find her so entertaining.

"You're not enjoying your supper, Mrs. Harte?" he said. "I hope you're not unwell."

"I'm fine, thank you," she replied formally, keeping her eyes focused on her plate. Her food was virtually untouched, and she made a quick, almost involuntary stab at a piece of chicken. She could feel him watching her as she lifted the fork to her mouth. Her hand jerked with the motion, causing her to gouge her lower lip. She suppressed a wince and resolutely began to chew the chicken, trying not to choke as she swallowed it.

"I hope Cavan Sheridan gave you my message," Kane said, matching the formality of her tone.

Samantha glanced at him, not comprehending.

"I asked him to convey to you how impressed I am with your work."

"Oh—yes, he told me. I—yes, thank you. I'm glad you're pleased. I'm . . . enjoying the work, actually."

"Good, I was hoping you would."

This line of banal chatter seemed harmless enough, and Samantha tried to cooperate. "Cavan is doing extraordinarily well in his studies," she volunteered.

He took a sip of water before replying. "I should hope so. I seldom see the lad without a grammar or a dictionary, and I notice the midnight oil is often burning in his room."

"He's very dedicated."

Kane seemed intent on finding at least one more bite of chicken. He managed and, after finishing it off, said offhandedly, "Still sweet on you, is he?"

"I beg your pardon," Samantha fairly snapped at him. She glanced across the table to see if Rufus or Amelia had heard, but the two of them were engrossed in conversation with their oldest son, Gideon.

"I asked if Sheridan is still sweet on you, or has he recovered?"

"You needn't make it sound like a *disease,*" Samantha said caustically. While she wouldn't want him to think she had encouraged Cavan—she would never have done so—she didn't particularly like the idea that he considered her something to "recover" from. He grinned at her but, to Samantha's annoyance, made no apology.

Dessert was a fairly lengthy process, involving a long stroll down the aisle to choose one's favorites from among the countless varieties lining the table. Jack followed Samantha back to their places, holding her chair for her as she sat down. As he seated himself, he glanced from his own plate, with its two samplings of cake and generous slice of apple pie, to her dainty serving of custard.

"Do you always eat so little?" he said, so absorbed in the way her dark lashes brushed the delicate curve of her cheek that he suddenly lost interest in his own food.

She looked at him, blinked, then turned her gaze back to the custard in front of her. "I . . . must have eaten too much dinner. I'm really not all that hungry."

In truth she had eaten hardly any dinner at all, but Jack let the remark pass. "I confess that I'd make room for Amelia's apple pie, no matter what," he said amiably. "That woman is the best cook in New York City."

Samantha smiled and nodded. "Rufus says that's why he's always outgrowing those wonderful vests she sews for him."

Jack looked around, saw Amelia gathering her choir members together on the other side of the room, and smiled. "I believe we are to be treated to some music."

"Have you heard them? They're a superb choir."

Jack nodded. "A performance by the Mercer Street Tabernacle Choir is quite an event, even for a sinner like myself."

Samantha Harte turned and looked directly at him. Much to his surprise, Jack found himself slightly unnerved by that searching, amber-flecked gaze.

"According to Amelia," she said gravely, "you're really not such a sinner at all. Should I believe her . . . or you?"

The instant the words were out, she flushed slightly. No doubt Samantha Harte was not one given to impulsive remarks. Jack studied her, intrigued and at the same time somewhat amused. "Ah, well, I'd advise you not to pay any heed to Amelia," he said lightly. "She knows very well I'm a terrible man, but, softhearted soul that she is, she pities me all the same."

Not quite comfortable with the way she was studying him, he

moved to change the subject. "I wanted to tell you that I've seen a great deal of improvement in young Sheridan already. Your tutoring is obviously successful."

She regarded him for another moment, then returned her attention to the custard in front of her. "He's extremely bright, you already know that. I don't so much tutor Cavan as make the material available to him and monitor his progress. If you don't mind my saying so, it's almost a waste to employ him as a driver. He's far too capable for that sort of position."

Jack pushed a morsel of cake around idly on his plate. "I couldn't agree with you more, but don't concern yourself. I'll be replacing him soon in any event, I expect."

"You *wouldn't!*"

Jack lifted an eyebrow. She had misunderstood him completely, but her indignation only heightened her attractiveness. "Eat your custard, why don't you?" he said, gesturing toward her plate. "I didn't mean that I'm going to *fire* him," he explained. "To the contrary, if he comes through on this story about the newsboys the way I suspect he will, I plan to put him on the *Vanguard*'s payroll. I'm fairly certain I can find an adequate driver. Finding a capable reporter is another matter entirely."

"Oh," she said softly. "I see."

"Sheridan says you're helping him with the article," Jack said. He'd lost interest in stuffing himself any further and put down his fork. "He told me about Willie's mother shutting the door on him, said you were going to try your hand at speaking with her."

She paled slightly. "I—yes, as a matter of fact, I stopped by this afternoon, before I came here."

"Ah. And how did it go?"

She replaced her silverware, not looking at him. Jack saw that her hand was trembling slightly. As though sensing his scrutiny, she kept her back straight, her gaze fixed on the table in front of her. "Not very well, I'm afraid."

"She wouldn't talk with you either?"

She shook her head, still avoiding his gaze. "Only for a moment. Not long enough to really learn anything helpful." She paused, then added, "Willie doesn't live at home, you know."

Jack nodded. "A number of the boys don't. They band together, stay on the streets or in one of the shelters. Usually, they're either not wanted at home, or things are so hard for them there that they prefer the streets."

She offered nothing further. Jack sensed that mention of the visit had disturbed her in some way and wondered why that should be. As far as he knew, she had never even met the boy. "What's she like, Willie's mother?"

She turned to look at him, but her reply was slow in coming. It was almost as though she found it painful to answer. "She's . . . a very sad woman, I think."

"Sad?"

Samantha nodded. "Sad. And frightened." Her hands went to her lap, and Jack didn't miss the way she began to twist her napkin.

"Frightened of what?" he probed. He leaned toward her, for her voice had become so soft he could scarcely make out her words. But when he saw her flinch, he quickly withdrew. There was no accounting for the hurt that shot through him at this evidence of her dislike, though he forced himself to pretend he hadn't noticed.

"Frightened of *what?*" he asked again.

Still avoiding his gaze, she continued to wring the napkin. "Her husband," she said, her voice sounding strained and unnatural.

"Oh, *that* type," Jack said, making no effort to conceal his disgust. "Small wonder Willie prefers the streets, then. Well, don't worry about getting any more information. Sheridan will just have to manage on his own."

He was puzzled by the peculiar tension that seemed to have gripped her all of a sudden and wondered at the reason for it. But just then chairs began to scrape the floor as people pushed away from the tables, their hands clapping in rhythm with the choir, which now broke into its first number.

Amelia was the primary soloist for the group, and there was nothing Jack enjoyed so much as that strong, soulful voice and the lively, swaying rhythms of the huge choir as together they filled the room and shook the walls with their songs of praise.

Jack loved music, always had. It probably would have surprised even those who thought they knew him reasonably well to learn that he attended the opera regularly, not with any thought of elevating his social status, but rather because he simply could not resist the music. No doubt it would have astonished his contemporaries even more to discover that the music of this wholly unprofessional black church choir affected him in much the same way. Sitting here tonight beside the lovely Samantha Harte, tapping his foot along with the rest of the people in the room, he would have found it difficult, if not impossible, to name his preference—*Don Giovanni* or the rousing rhythms of the Mercer Street Tabernacle Choir.

As it happened, his enjoyment was short-lived. When they were almost at the end of the evening, Amelia stepped forward. As soon as she began singing, Jack recognized the selection and felt a familiar, uneasy stirring deep within, followed by a creeping heaviness, like a stone slowly being rolled over his spirit. It was so intense he wanted to bolt from the room, but it would have been decidedly awkward to do so at that particular moment.

This had happened to him before. On each occasion his mood had been one of contentment, even lightheartedness, so no preexisting melancholy could be blamed for the experience. He had simply been assailed without warning, without reason. It took only the first few words, the first notes of that plaintive, wrenching hymn, and suddenly it was as if a kind of bleak bereavement had seized his soul and held him captive. . . .

> *Amazing grace! how sweet the sound,*
> *That saved a wretch like me!*

Wretched was an apt enough description for the enormous emptiness that now engulfed him. Chilled, Jack crossed his arms over his chest and hugged them to himself to prevent any outward show of his inner trembling. His surroundings seemed to recede and fade from view. The longer the song went on, the greater his feeling of utter desolation. As was usually the case, he heard few of the words past the first line or two, for he was pressed into immobility by the weight of this wintry isolation and despair.

When the music ended and the assault on his emotions had lifted, the sense of loneliness remained. Jack looked about the room, almost painfully aware of a separation that had nothing to do with his surroundings or skin color or social station. It was a far more profound schism between himself and these people. No matter that he sat among them, had been invited into their midst, was even held in a certain measure of respect and, at least by Rufus and Amelia, affection. He was not a part of them and what Rufus referred to as their "holy joy." The faith they professed somehow made them what they were and at the same time served to separate Jack from them as effectively as a towering wall. He was an alien, a stranger among them, and somehow he knew that at the heart of the enervating oppression from which he had just emerged lurked a yearning, an agonizing to be like them.

He shook it off, this inexplicable strangeness that always left him feeling restless and somehow deprived, as if he lacked something in the very essence of his being. He reminded himself that within the hour, the gloom would likely pass and he would undoubtedly be mocking the infernal black Irish depression that could enshroud even a church supper in crepe.

***

At the end of the evening, as the fellowship hall began to empty, Amelia cornered Samantha and insisted that since Samantha had been foolish enough to walk to the church alone, she and Gideon would see her safely back to her apartment. Samantha saw Jack Kane watching this exchange and half feared he would insist on taking her home, as he had the first night they met. That would have been unthinkably awkward for her, what with Cavan Sheridan being Kane's driver.

She need not have worried, however. Kane made no offer of his carriage, even though once outside Samantha saw that he had come alone, without a driver. In parting, he merely gave her a distracted nod and indicated that it was nice to have seen her again. Then, springing up to the driver's bench of his carriage, he drove away as if in a terrible rush.

Samantha stood watching him for a moment. When she realized that the relief she would have expected to feel at his departure was minimized somewhat by a faint sense of disappointment, she turned and hurried back inside in search of Amelia and Gideon.

***

When Jack heard Amelia scolding Samantha Harte about walking to the church alone, his first instinct was to interrupt and insist on driving her home. He had given Cavan Sheridan the evening off, driving himself to the supper with the intention of spending some time with Rufus and Amelia afterward. He could just as easily have used the opportunity to spend some time alone with the elusive Mrs. Harte. In fact, he had even considered asking her if he might take her to the theater or to supper one night soon.

By the end of the evening, however, he was feeling too raw, too edgy and restless, to be with anyone—especially Samantha Harte, who so clearly did not want to be anywhere near *him*. He was still smarting from the way she had drawn back from him at the table, as if she had somehow caught the stench of corruption about his person.

Well, perhaps she had, he thought angrily. *And what of it?*

Feeling as he did, he could not get away fast enough. Without giving Rufus or Amelia time to question him—and with little more than a curt acknowledgment to Samantha Harte—he took his leave.

He was aware of Rufus's searching look and Amelia's surprise at his hasty departure but made no explanation.

As for Samantha Harte, no doubt she was relieved to see him go. Again came the sting of wounded pride. That and a sudden breach of self-assurance—an uncommon ailment for him, to say the least— had quickly escalated to an impatience with himself that now threatened to burst out of control and turn to rage.

As he pulled away from the church, his eyes were smarting, his skin virtually crawling with agitation. Had he not given up the whiskey years ago, he would have gone straight home and gotten blind drunk, just to dull his senses. As it was, he drove the carriage like a madman through the streets for close to an hour, slowing the horses and turning toward home only after the night air had finally cooled his fevered skin and quelled his fury.

26

A Day of Surprises

And the gray, chill day
Slips away with a frown.

JAMES STEPHENS

Samantha's mother showed up at her door at half past ten on Monday morning. It occurred to Samantha that a visit from one's mother, even so early on a Monday morning, was probably not all that unusual among ordinary families. But her family had never been ordinary, and since this marked only the second time her mother had deigned to visit since Samantha had taken the apartment, it was practically a historic event.

"Mother!" Samantha blurted out, unable to mask her surprise.

"Well, you might invite me in, Samantha," her mother said with unconcealed impatience. No word of greeting, no "How have you been, dear? I've missed you," not even a smile.

"Oh, of course! I'm sorry!" Samantha stammered, moving aside as her mother made a sweeping entrance into the narrow hallway.

It had been raining since dawn, and even in the short walk from the carriage to Samantha's second-floor apartment, Angela Pilcher had gotten her hat feathers doused and her skirts stained with mud.

"Here, Mother, let me help you with your wrap." But her mother had already removed her rain cloak. Pressing it into Samantha's arms, she started off to the kitchen.

"I'll fix us a cup of tea," Samantha said, hurriedly hanging up the wrap before following her mother into the kitchen. "You must be chilled through from the rain. It's such a miserable morning."

In the kitchen, her mother stood surveying the room with obvious distaste. "Really, Samantha, this apartment is deplorable. If you insist on living like a pauper, couldn't you at least brighten the place up a bit?"

Samantha suddenly saw the tiny room through her mother's eyes, and a heaviness settled over her. It was no longer the cozy haven of a quiet, reasonably contented life. Instead, she now saw the walls that needed new paper, the small cookstove that would have been more appropriate for a child's playhouse, the ironing board propped in the corner, and the towels she had just folded and stacked at one side of the table.

"I've been planning to redecorate soon," she said, irritated at the note of defensiveness she heard in her voice. "Please, sit down, Mother, while I start the kettle."

"I don't want tea, Samantha. I didn't come here to visit."

She made no move to sit down but simply stood, statuesque and thoroughly aristocratic in her elegant gray morning dress trimmed in rose. Samantha realized anew what a striking figure of a woman her mother really was. Even in the midst of their worst disagreements, it was impossible not to admire her.

Samantha had never been able to find a trace of her mother in her own appearance; she had taken the dark hair and deeper skin tones of her father rather than the Saxon fairness and blue eyes of her mother. Angela Pilcher possessed an almost Junoesque figure—rigidly corseted, of course—and the clear, virtually unlined skin of a much younger woman. With her imposing height and extraordinary good looks, she still turned heads when she walked into a room.

And she could still make Samantha want to run from the room when she turned that chilling blue stare on her in disapproval. Samantha hated herself for the way she suddenly felt like a child—like a nasty little girl who has once again disappointed her mama. It took a concentrated effort not to squirm where she stood, for she was fairly certain she knew why her mother had come.

"I have heard a most disturbing rumor, Samantha, and I felt the only thing to do was to confront you with it. I can only hope you will have a reasonable explanation."

Samantha said nothing. She had to look up to meet her mother's gaze, but she steeled herself not to glance away.

"I hope you can tell me it's all a mistake, that you're not really associated in any way with that *disgusting* man!"

Samantha swallowed. "What man is that, Mother?"

"*Jack Kane!*" Her mother sounded as if she might strangle on the

very words. "I have been told that you are—*working* for him." She
stopped. "Well?"

Samantha drew a deep breath. "As a matter of fact, I am, Mother.
But only part-time."

Her mother actually paled. Her mouth thinned and pulled downward. "Why in heaven's name would you do such an outrageous
thing? Have you taken complete leave of your senses?"

Samantha braced one hand on the back of a chair. "My job with
Stein was about to end, Mother. They're closing their doors. Mr.
Kane offered me a position, and I accepted. I might add that it's a
much better-paying position."

"Oh, Samantha, how could you degrade yourself like this? Have
you no pride?"

Samantha tensed. She actually considered telling her mother that
this was none of her business. She was a grown woman, had not
lived at home for years, was self-supporting, and did not need to
submit her actions to anyone for approval.

Instead, she swallowed down her anger and said, "Mother, it's a
perfectly honest position, and it pays well. I don't see what possible
difference it could make who pays my salary."

"Oh, *really,* Samantha! Of course, it makes a difference! That
man, Kane, is so disreputable that decent women won't even mention
his name in public. And you think it doesn't matter that you're *employed* by him?"

Samantha recalled some of the "decent women" she'd seen fawn-
ing over Kane in the theater some months ago and had to suppress
a rueful smile. "No, Mother, I don't think it matters in the least. But
if you don't mind telling me, how did you learn of this?"

Angela's eyes could have sharpened knives. "From your friend
Marjorie Fletcher. And I might add that she and Gordon are as appalled by your behavior as your father and I are."

"The Fletchers were never *my* friends, Mother. They were Bronson's friends."

"Yes, well, perhaps that's why they're concerned that you might
degrade Bronson's memory with your behavior." She paused, raking
Samantha with a look of abject disapproval. "There's something I
feel I should say in that regard, Samantha. I'll confess that your father
and I had misgivings about your marrying Bronson Harte. There was
the matter of his being so much older than you, and all those . . .
religious fanatics that flocked around the man. But I think you'll
admit that, once we got to know your husband, we accepted the
marriage and made the best of it."

From experience, Samantha knew where this was going, and she had to fight the surge of nausea that boiled up in her. "Mother, please, I'd rather not discuss Bronson."

"Samantha, I simply do not understand you." Finally, Angela sat down. She sat the way she stood—straight backed, rigid, and uncompromising, her hands clasped tightly together at her waist. "How could you possibly be married as long as you were to a decent, God-fearing man like Bronson and then do something so foolish as to involve yourself with a total reprobate like Jack Kane?"

Something in Samantha threatened to snap. She clenched her teeth together with such force that a sharp stab of pain shot up her jaw. "Mother, for goodness' sake, I'm *working* for the man, not having an affair with him!"

"*Samantha!*"

She had genuinely shocked her mother. Unrepentant, Samantha reminded herself that her mother was easily shocked. Or at least pretended to be.

"I'm sorry, Mother, but you really are making altogether too much of this. I needed a job. This one came to my attention through one of the students in my night classes—" she ignored the look of contempt that creased Angela's features at the mention of the night school—"and I accepted it. I work right here, at my own kitchen table. The copy is delivered and picked up by a messenger. I've never even been inside the *Vanguard*'s offices. I have virtually no contact whatsoever with Mr. Kane."

"*Mister* Kane." Angela spat the words out of her mouth as if they were tainted. "Really, Samantha, what will people think? What would *Bronson* think? That poor man—even your father and I came to realize he was a saint—cared so deeply for you. Your behavior would horrify him, I really believe it would. Moving into a dismal little pesthole, in this awful neighborhood—and now ... *this.*"

Everything in Samantha screamed to lash out at her, to finally tell her the truth about Bronson, the *God-fearing* man, the ... *saint* she had married. Tears, not of sadness but of rage, scalded her eyes, and she actually had to turn away from her mother, else she knew she would lose the last thin shred of control left to her.

With her back still turned, she choked out, "Bronson is dead, Mother. I can't live my life based on what he might think."

"Well, your father and I *aren't* dead, though heaven knows your willfulness may well drive us to early graves!"

Samantha heard the chair scrape the floor and turned to see Angela draw to her feet. Her face was no longer attractive but rather waxen and taut with anger. Samantha knew, however, that her mother would not lose any more of her composure than she already had. Angela Pilcher was far too genteel for vulgar displays of emotion. No, she would simply issue a final pronouncement and take her leave.

"I can see that I've made a mistake by coming here, Samantha. You obviously have no self-respect, no shame. I suppose that comes from associating with those immigrant people in the slums, not to mention your new employer. I would simply remind you that, ultimately, you are known by the company you keep."

She rejected Samantha's attempt to help her into her cloak. "You ought to know, Samantha, that you have broken your father's heart. All he ever wanted for you was a good marriage to a decent man, with a home and children. It isn't as if you couldn't have married again, after all."

Samantha cringed at the thought, but she kept her silence. At this point, it was best to let her mother believe what she wanted, have her final say, and leave the apartment.

At the door, Angela turned and said, "I cannot for the life of me understand why you've chosen to live your life among the dregs of the city. Your father and I don't deserve this from you, Samantha. You do have a responsibility, whether you realize it or not—to your family and friends and to the members of Bronson's congregation. Those people looked to you to continue in his work after he passed away, and instead, you not only abandon their fellowship but you defile your husband's memory as well." She paused, then fired her parting shot. "You should be ashamed, Samantha. Truly ashamed."

Samantha waited until her mother had reached her waiting carriage. She suddenly felt feverish and closed the door, leaning against it with her cheek pressed to the cool wood.

After a moment, she went to the window and looked out on the street below. She stood, one hand against the windowpane, watching her mother leave. *I am ashamed, Mother,* she cried out in her spirit as she watched the carriage clatter off down the street. *You'll never know how ashamed. But not for the reason you think. Not because I've defiled Bronson's memory . . . but because I allowed him to defile me. . . .*

⁂

Bronson Harte had been forty-seven when Samantha, then twenty-three, married him. At first her parents had attempted to dissuade her, in part because of the difference in their ages, but even more because they hadn't realized right away that Bronson was from a "fine old family''—indeed, a very wealthy family. Later, after learning that his background was impeccable and that he wasn't quite the zealot that some of his followers were, both Angela and Samuel Pilcher affected a real fondness for their renowned son-in-law, treating him with parental pride and affection even though Bronson was more nearly *their* age than Samantha's.

The difference in years between her and her husband, though considerable, was of no importance whatsoever to Samantha. Nor did she care about the Harte family's reputation or fortune. She loved Bronson for what he was, loved him deeply when she married him— at least she thought she did.

He had come into her life unexpectedly—and suddenly. One day Bronson Harte had been a cloud on the horizon, a name with increasing recognition about the city, but to Samantha still only a name. In a heartbeat, he became real to her, sweeping into her life . . . and sweeping her off her feet.

She met him through some friends, young adults who, like herself, had grown disenchanted with the lukewarm formality of their own congregation and, unlike Samantha, had left their home church to go seeking after something more dynamic, something more "spiritually challenging.'' At first Samantha stayed put, unwilling to disappoint her parents, outwardly resigned but inwardly resentful. As time passed and her friends began to rhapsodize over the exciting new "fellowship'' they had discovered—and its compelling, visionary leader—she finally gave in to their coaxing and accompanied them to a midweek meeting.

Although she went more out of curiosity than from any real intention to effect a change, after that night Samantha never went back to her former congregation.

The fast-growing new fellowship was made up of a wide spectrum of individuals. Many were members of the academic community— educators and intellectuals—but there were also a significant number from among the laboring classes. They were an outgoing, energetic group: friendly, warm, and seemingly hungry for a deeper experience with God.

As for Bronson Harte, he seemed unimpressed by his personal magnetism, if not entirely unaware of it. A vigorous, attractive man whose silvering hair marked him more with dignity than with aging, Harte had never married but instead had apparently led a life of quiet devotion and self-sacrifice, dedicating himself to his God, to the members of the fellowship, and to the work of the movement.

He was a man with great presence, yet a man who seemed pos-

sessed of a genuine humility and gentle nature. At the podium, he
was nothing short of mesmerizing. Unlike the soft-spoken Pastor
Chapman at Samantha's family church, Bronson Harte wore no
stately robes, used no notes when he spoke. In his rich, well-
modulated voice, he addressed his listeners as if he were speaking to
each one on an individual basis.

His messages were universal ones; he spoke about suffering and
peace, death and eternity, the slavery of sin—and the enslavement of
men. He neither thundered nor raved, yet his words about the depravity of man and the wrath of God caused many to squirm where
they sat. For the first time, Samantha was convicted of a sense of her
own worthlessness, a degradation of spirit so intense that she, who
had never once breathed even the most frivolous of confidences to
anyone else, was soon seeking out the counsel of Bronson Harte for
her soul's miasma.

He was not easy on her that day but instead instructed her about
the weakness and corruption of the flesh to the point that she might
have given in to total despair, had he not placed a firm but gentle
hand upon her head as if to administer the healing of forgiveness.
Through a veil of tears, Samantha looked up into his face, and from
that moment she was never the same again.

Soon, despite the protests of her parents, she was spending more
and more time with the fellowship—and with Bronson Harte. She
devoted her days and most of her strength to following the example
of other members, teaching and working among the immigrant settlements, even going into the vile streets of the Bowery and the hideous tenements of Five Points.

She was young and idealistic, and the beliefs of the fellowship
appealed to that part of her that had always yearned to change the
conditions of those less fortunate—indeed, to help change the world.
Bronson Harte taught, and his congregation eagerly accepted, a doctrine of social reform—a type of "social Christianity" that began
with self-examination and criticism, a continual purging of individual
sin.

As the movement grew, it was often likened to the Utopians and
other similar reformation groups, but in reality it shared little in common with any of them. It was, Samantha came to realize later, first
and foremost Bronson Harte's movement. Yet, in spite of the adulation of his followers and the phenomenal growth of the fellowship—they never referred to themselves as a "church"—Bronson
never seemed to hold himself above the other members. He worked

as tirelessly as anyone else, giving away most of his personal wealth to fund the work they carried on.

It was a fact that Bronson had a great deal to do with the reputation and effectiveness of the fellowship. The Hartes were an extremely wealthy New England family, known for the fair labor practices in their textile mills and their charitable efforts among the underprivileged. Bronson had shortened an intellectual tour of Europe, during which he had studied under some of the great reform leaders of other countries, to return to the States and begin his own organization. His unceasing efforts, his compelling personality and riveting appeal as a speaker—combined with his family's money—had brought a rapid, exceptional growth to the fellowship, which he soon moved from New England to upstate New York, then to the city.

The movement wasn't without controversy and criticism. Some of the more traditional churches in the city had branded Harte's followers as extremists, dangerous radicals, or socialists. Their reformist doctrine seemed threatening to many among the more conservative congregations, while other advocates of class equality and equal rights considered the fellowship's work a distraction from the more critical problems facing the country. For the most part, however, the fellowship enjoyed a healthy measure of respectability, even admiration. It didn't hurt that they counted among their members several esteemed leaders of the city: politicians, businessmen, and academics.

Samantha married Bronson six months after becoming a member of the fellowship. Her parents fought her, as she had known they would. But she had the support of her friends in the fellowship and Bronson's dizzying devotion to buoy her resolve. Besides, by then she was so much in love—and so in awe of Bronson Harte—that she would have braved the gates of hell if he had demanded it of her.

To her near destruction, he did just that.

27

Among the Shadows

*A pity beyond all telling
Is hid in the heart of love.*

W . B . Y E A T S

Samantha's second surprise of the day arrived with Cavan Sheridan,
only minutes after her mother had left.

As was his practice, Cavan took the news copy to the kitchen for
her and laid it out on the table. Today, however, he also handed
Samantha an envelope. "From Mr. Kane," he said.

Samantha looked at him as she took the envelope and placed it,
unopened, with the news copy. They had fallen into a daily routine
by now, she and Cavan, whereby he would bring the copy in and
exchange pleasantries for a moment or two, then leave until it was
time to return for the work. Samantha always offered him a drink of
water or a cup of tea—which he always refused.

He never seemed quite as comfortable around her during these
brief daily encounters as he did in class. Samantha thought she understood. Even though they were often alone in the school building
on those evenings when they stayed over to drill on a particular
assignment, it was a more impersonal setting than her apartment.

He had been the soul of propriety ever since that night when he
had blurted out his interest in her. Samantha had hoped the infatuation
would have ebbed by now, but she was sometimes aware of him
watching her at odd moments, his gaze following her about the
schoolroom. Occasionally, if by chance their eyes met, he would flush
slightly and look away.

Cavan Sheridan was by far the most exceptional student she had ever taught. Samantha admired his intellect, his energy, and his eagerness to learn. Because she also liked him as a person, she hated the awkwardness between them. However, nothing she did seemed to ease the tension.

On his way out, Cavan turned. "I almost forgot—Mr. Kane said you could send your reply by me if you would," he said, gesturing toward the envelope. "This morning or when I come back this afternoon would be fine." He seemed to delay for a moment, but when Samantha merely nodded and smiled, he turned and started for the door.

After he left, Samantha raised the wick on the lamp. She was still shaken from her mother's unpleasant visit, and her hand trembled as she slit the envelope and withdrew a thin sheet of paper. As she deciphered the broad scrawl of Jack Kane's handwriting, she could feel the hammering of her pulse in her throat:

DEAR MRS. HARTE,

IT OCCURS TO ME THAT I MIGHT HAVE APPEARED RUDE SATURDAY NIGHT WHEN I LEFT THE CHURCH SO ABRUPTLY. MY ONLY DEFENSE IS THAT I WAS SOMEWHAT PREOCCUPIED THAT EVENING AND NEEDED TO GET AWAY. I WOULD VERY MUCH LIKE TO APOLOGIZE IN PERSON IF YOU WOULD EXTEND ME THE OPPORTUNITY. MOREOVER, I'D LIKE TO FURTHER DISCUSS YOUR IDEAS ON OUR YOUNG CAVAN SHERIDAN'S PROPOSITION REGARDING THE STORIES AND POSSIBLE RESETTLEMENT OF SOME SELECTED IRISH IMMIGRANTS.

I WAS WONDERING IF YOU MIGHT ALLOW ME TO TAKE YOU TO DINNER ONE EVENING THIS WEEK. LET ME BE VERY DIRECT—SINCE I SENSE THAT YOU WOULD BE TOO KIND TO ADDRESS THE SUBJECT: I UNDERSTAND IF YOU'RE RELUCTANT TO BE SEEN IN MY COMPANY. THAT BEING THE CASE, I HAVE IN MIND A SMALL, OUT-OF-THE-WAY—BUT PERFECTLY RESPECTABLE—CLUB WHERE WE WOULD BE WELL-CHAPERONED BUT AFFORDED THE SORT OF PRIVACY I IMAGINE YOU'D PREFER.

I CONFESS THAT I AM MOST EAGER TO SEE YOU AGAIN, NOT ONLY TO MAKE AMENDS FOR MY BOORISHNESS SATURDAY NIGHT, BUT IN HOPES OF GETTING TO KNOW YOU BETTER. YOU'VE ONLY TO NAME YOUR CHOICE OF EVENINGS AND CAN DO SO BY SENDING A REPLY WITH CAVAN SHERIDAN TODAY.

I AM MOST SINCERELY YOURS,

JACK KANE

Samantha stared at the note in her hand as if it were a snake. Heat rushed to her face. Her emotions began to riot, anger and indignation colliding with an unbidden tingling of excitement, which she instantly shook off.

As the full impact of the note struck her, she expelled a sharp breath. Her first thought was that he had an outrageous nerve, a man of his notoriety asking her out for an evening. Did it demean her somehow in his eyes that she had to work to make a living? Or did he think that just because he employed her she would feel an obligation to accept an invitation from him? Did he seriously believe she was that weak?

Her heart raced so crazily that she had to sit down at the table to steady herself. Her feelings were still warring against each other as she sat there, staring at the note, trying to fathom the intent behind it. A man like Jack Kane would hardly care if he'd been rude to an employee, would he? Certainly not enough to feel the need for an apology. And even if, by some stretch of the imagination, he *did* care, it wouldn't require a dinner invitation to set things right. A simple note like the one he'd sent today would be more than adequate.

Could Kane have possibly sensed the pull she had felt toward him, the reluctant—but undeniable—attraction? Did he think she was the same as all the other women who reputedly threw themselves at him?

Samantha closed her eyes and fought down a wave of humiliation as she tried not to consider too closely the initial flush of excitement she had felt upon reading the note. Unexpectedly, it occurred to her that her feelings of "righteous indignation" might be just as misplaced as the forbidden sense of attraction. Surely it was insufferable snobbery on her part to consider his dinner invitation a kind of insult.

As Samantha reread his blunt assessment of her supposed unwillingness to be seen with him, something tugged at her heart. Even though she couldn't deny the truth of his statement, she found herself mortified that he would have anticipated her so well.

The truth was that, for an instant, she had known a genuine desire to accept his invitation. She wouldn't, of course, but not entirely because of his questionable character. There was the fact that whatever else Jack Kane might or might not be, depending on whose account she believed, he was by his own admission a "sinner"—an unbeliever. The very fact that he rejected everything on which Samantha had staked her life and her future made him forbidden.

She refused to delude herself for a moment that she could influence a man like Kane or change him. Her attraction to him had nothing to do with wanting to "win him for the Lord," although she would certainly be willing to try just that if the opportunity presented itself.

But her feelings were not godly, and she would not compound the sin by pretending they were.

For too long she had existed in the shadows of deception, and the darkness had almost sucked the very life from her. The worst of it had been *self*-deception. She had deceived herself—or attempted to— as well as her family and friends. It had taken her months—no, years—to grope her way out of those shadows and find the truth. Once she found it, she promised herself that she would never live in darkness again.

She began each day by praying for the light of discernment, that she might recognize truth and find the strength to live by it. But she sensed that Jack Kane, and the conflicting feelings he evoked in her, held the potential to draw her back into the shadows.

She wasn't at all certain she could escape the darkness a second time.

Finally, Samantha drew in a deep breath, then very deliberately and precisely shredded the note, as if by tearing it into pieces she could remove the temptation from her path.

It took her only a moment to pen a polite, but unmistakably firm, refusal.

<hr />

Jack wasn't surprised when he read Samantha Harte's reply to his note later that afternoon. Her rejection, while courteous, could not have been more final. Whatever had possessed him anyway, to think she might have accepted? He had acted on impulse, and this was the humiliating result.

And it *was* humiliating, he realized. He wasn't used to women turning him down. Some of them might be interested in him for their own mercenary reasons, that was true—but at least they were *interested!*

Samantha Harte was a cool one, all right. Not the sort he usually went for, as it happened. For the most part, he had little use for the "ice maidens," those paragons of virtue and good breeding. If they weren't altogether boring, they were often the worst sort of snobs.

So why couldn't he get Samantha Harte out of his head? Oh, she was attractive, all right, an uncommonly lovely woman, and with an understated elegance about her that both intrigued and annoyed him. She was smart, too—not just book smart, but sensible as well, he'd wager. And he was almost certain she wasn't entirely indifferent to him. He had sensed . . . something . . . at the church the other night— a look in her eyes, some pull between them that hadn't really surprised him. He had felt it the first time he met her, and again the other night at the church. He suspected she had felt it too, though she would probably never admit it, not even to herself.

But what of it? It wasn't the first time he'd been attracted to a pretty woman, hang it all! He wasn't looking for anything special, no lifetime commitment, just a pleasant evening. He hadn't asked the woman to *marry* him, after all, just to have dinner with him!

He couldn't stop the image of her that suddenly filled his mind, any more than he could deny the fact that he was lying to himself—a practice he rarely indulged in. He might just as well face the truth: He had seen something extraordinary in Samantha Harte, had seen it right from the beginning—something rare and fine and unsullied. He already knew that she was no ordinary woman, knew that he would eventually want something more of her than a casual evening or a brief, tawdry affair. But apparently she thought having anything at all to do with him would be just that—*tawdry*.

He crushed her terse note in his hand, as if by doing so he could destroy the reality of her rejection. He had wanted to somehow touch the goodness in her, that unspoiled, unstained part of her that put him to shame even as it seemed to hold out to him some hope of re-demption. He had thought if he could know her, be with her, per-haps—

Perhaps *what?*

Suddenly furious with himself, he shoved away from the desk. He tore out of his office, slamming the door with such force that those employees nearby froze.

Outside, Jack charged down the alley. He walked for an hour in the rain, going almost at a run, taking the slick streets like a dark bull in a rage, seeing nothing and hearing only the sound of his own blood pounding in his ears and the driving roar of his own self-disgust.

28

Sad and
Unexpected News

The Lord God judges "crime" above,
But not as man has weighed it.

MARY KELLY

Samantha met the newsboy Willie Shanahan for the first time on the day Willie's mother shot and killed his father.

The night before it happened, Samantha had stayed late after the evening class to help Cavan Sheridan with the article he was writing about the city's newsboys. He was doing a splendid job, indeed had required little editorial guidance from her, other than in some of the finer points of grammar. Another day or so and he would have the copy completed.

On Wednesday afternoon, when Cavan returned for the day's proofing, he arrived out of breath and visibly distraught. His face was crimson, and although the day wasn't particularly warm, he was perspiring.

The instant he was inside the apartment, he burst out, "Mrs. Harte—have you heard? Mrs. Shanahan has shot her husband! She's killed Willie's father!"

Stunned, Samantha struggled to take in what he was saying. Even as he spoke, the image of Maura Shanahan's forlorn countenance flashed across her mind. She saw again the ugly bruise, the frightened eyes. She shivered in apprehension as all the warmth seemed to leave the room.

"What happened?" she choked out.

Cavan shook his head. "I don't think anyone knows yet. One of Willie's sisters came to the office, looking for him. They hadn't found him yet when I left."

Samantha was already regretting that she had not gone back to the Shanahans' after Saturday's failed visit. She had known even then, seeing that poor, careworn woman, her fear and despair so starkly evident . . . she had *known*. And she had done nothing.

She reminded herself that there was nothing she *could* have done, at least not then. And there had been no time since to go back. But would she have gone in any event? She recalled with disgust how she had practically run away from Maura Shanahan, her own emotions rioting in sick turmoil at the memories the woman's distress had called to mind.

Cavan Sheridan's rush of words jerked her back to the present. "Mr. Kane has sent two of the other newsboys out to fetch Willie. He'll be needed to help with the younger children now, with his mother in jail."

Samantha stared at him in horror. "Maura Shanahan is . . . in *jail?*"

He looked at her strangely. "Why . . . yes, of course she is. The police took her away right after it happened."

"Dear heavens," Samantha murmured. "What will become of her?"

"Are you all right, Mrs. Harte? Wouldn't you like to sit down?"

He was watching her closely, his expression fraught with concern. Samantha made an attempt to shake off the sick weakness that had seized her. "No, I'm all right." She looked at him. "Cavan, I wonder . . . would you take me to the jail on your way back to the office?"

He frowned. "The jail?"

Samantha was already heading toward the closet to get a wrap, although she knew the chill that had gripped her had little to do with the weather. "Perhaps I can help," she said. "Would you bring the copy off the table, please?"

Cavan hesitated only a moment before going to the kitchen, but when he returned he stopped in the foyer. "Mrs. Harte, if you'll excuse my saying so, I don't think it's a good idea for you to be going to the jail. From all accounts, it's a terrible place, even for the criminals who end up there. 'Tis not a fit place for a woman."

Samantha looked up as she shrugged into her wrap. "Maura Shanahan is a woman, too, Cavan. Besides, I've been there before."

He stared at her. "You've been to the jail?"

Samantha nodded and gave a grim smile as she locked the door behind them. "Several times."

It occurred to her that he would be altogether dismayed to learn of the places her work among the immigrants had taken her over the years. She wasn't the fragile hothouse flower Cavan seemed to think her. Most of what her mother called her "delicate sensibilities" had been stripped away long before now. She had grown all too familiar with the more squalid features of the city—she knew the slums, most of the hospitals, the foundling homes—and the jails. She had witnessed more than her share of filth, disease, and debauchery.

The city of the poor was an entirely different place from the city of the privileged. By now Samantha was well acquainted with both worlds, enough to know that each bred its own share of secrets and horrors.

                ✦✦✦✦

Cavan was reluctant to leave her at the jail, but Samantha Harte insisted. "You have to get the copy back to the office," she told him. "I'll be fine. I know most of the guards and the policemen. I'll be well protected; you needn't worry."

Even so, he insisted on escorting her into the building. Just inside, a young, red-faced policeman was haranguing a small boy hunkered down near the door. Cavan hadn't seen Willie Shanahan since the swelling had gone from around his eye, but he recognized him immediately.

"Willie? Whatever are you doing here? Your sister has been looking for you."

"You know this boy?" said the policeman.

Cavan nodded.

"Then make him understand that he's to leave. He's been skulking about since early morning. If he doesn't go along, I'm going to lock him up!"

"You will do no such thing, Officer Malloy."

Cavan stared as Samantha Harte stepped up to the policeman. He wouldn't have guessed that those delicate features could turn so severe. Crossing his arms over his chest, he watched the exchange with interest.

Only then did the policeman seem to notice her presence, stammering out her name and muttering an apology. "Sorry, Mrs. Harte— I didn't see you. But this boy here is making a nuisance of himself, hanging about as he is. This is no place for the lad."

"I can't disagree with that, but I hardly think you need to threaten him."

"Yes, ma'am—I mean, no ma'am. But—"

"You're Willie Shanahan?" Samantha Harte said kindly as she turned to the boy.

Willie unwound himself and stood up, crushing his tattered cap to his chest as he nodded. "Yes'm."

"Well, I'm afraid Officer Malloy is right. This is not a good place for you. Wouldn't you be better off at home with your brothers and sisters?"

"Buster—that's me brother—is looking out for them," the boy said. "I mean to stay nearby, should Mum need anything."

"And that's just the thing, Mrs. Harte," Officer Malloy put in. "He'll not be allowed to see his mother anyway. He's only in the way here."

Samantha Harte studied Willie for another second or two, then turned back to the policeman. "I find it hard to believe that one small boy would be that much in the way," she said. "Surely he could see his mother for just a moment?"

The policeman shook off the suggestion like a dog throwing off cold water. "The sergeant said absolutely not, ma'am!"

"That would be Sergeant Garvey?" she said coolly.

"That's right, ma'am."

"Would you tell the sergeant that I'd like to speak with him, please?"

Officer Malloy looked at her for only an instant before hoofing it down the hall. In the meantime, Samantha Harte turned back to the boy. "Willie, if they let *me* speak with your mother, will you do the right thing and go home until I can arrange for you to visit?"

The boy studied her, his thin face utterly solemn. "You can do that? You'll get me in to see Mum?"

"I'll do my best, Willie. I believe I can arrange something for you by tomorrow. But you must cooperate. Do you understand?"

Finally, Willie ducked his head and, with obvious reluctance, nodded agreement.

"Good," Mrs. Harte said softly. "You're obviously a very good boy, Willie."

Willie Shanahan brightened considerably. It occurred to Cavan that the boy was probably not accustomed to that sort of kindness or affirmation.

Officer Malloy reappeared just then, followed by a big hulk of a fellow with small, watchful eyes and an astoundingly large belly—Sergeant Garvey, he presumed.

It was clear from their greetings that he and Samantha Harte knew each other. She wasted no time in stating her request. "I realize you don't have to allow it, Sergeant, but I'd like to ask that you let Willie here visit his mother, just for a moment."

The sergeant frowned. "You know the Shanahan woman, Mrs. Harte?"

Samantha Harte nodded. "I do."

The sergeant glanced from Willie to Mrs. Harte. "Then you know she's a murderer," he said, dropping his voice. "I can't be letting the boy into a cell with a murderer."

"She's his *mother,* Sergeant Garvey." Samantha Harte's voice was like a splash of icy water.

"Even so," the policeman muttered. "Sorry, Mrs. Harte. But if the captain found out, wouldn't he have my badge? No visitors for the felons. That includes family. Besides, Mrs. Harte, you know what it's like in the back. You wouldn't want the boy to see his mother like that."

Cavan looked at Samantha Harte. Her face could have been sculpted of marble, so taut were her features. "You may have a point, Sergeant. In that case, I must insist that you let *me* see Mrs. Shanahan. And afterward, I will speak to Captain Ryan about arranging some sort of a visit for Willie, perhaps outside the . . . cell."

The sergeant was visibly flustered. "Now, Mrs. Harte—no visitors means just that—*no visitors.*"

"You've been kind enough to bend the rules for me before, Sergeant," she said quietly. "Besides, I'm here not as a visitor but as a representative for Immigrant Aid. In that regard, may I ask you if Maura Shanahan has been charged yet?"

"She's to be charged with murder." This came from Officer Malloy, who received a sour look from his sergeant.

"If I let you see her—just for a moment, mind—will you send the boy home?" asked Sergeant Garvey.

Samantha Harte looked from him to Willie. "Willie? You remember our agreement?"

Willie Shanahan hesitated only a moment before replying. "Yes, ma'am." He plopped his cap down over his ears, and, after a slight delay, during which he made eye contact with Samantha Harte one last time, he turned and went out the door.

"All right, Mrs. Harte," said the sergeant. "Officer Malloy will take you back. But he's to stay with you. And you'll have to leave in ten minutes." He paused. "You won't be telling the captain about this, will you?"

"Of course not, Sergeant." Samantha Harte smiled sweetly at him, then turned to Cavan. "You really should get that copy back to the office now, Cavan."

He nodded. "I'll do that. But I'll be back to drive you home."

She hesitated, but only for a second. "That would be very kind of you. I am feeling a little tired."

Cavan dropped his arms away from his chest, waiting until Samantha Harte and the police officer had disappeared at the end of the corridor before he opened the door and stepped outside. On the way to the buggy, he shook his head, almost smiling as he made a mental note to tell Mr. Kane about the way Mrs. Harte had handled the policemen.

29

The Familiar Face
of Despair

A prison wall was round us both.

OSCAR WILDE

"You took her *where?*"

Kane's look was murderous. Cavan tensed but didn't cower in the face of his employer's fury. He had only done what Samantha Harte had asked of him, after all. Besides, he couldn't see that it was any of Kane's affair *where* he had taken her, other than the fact that he had used the office wagon.

"To the jail, sir," he repeated evenly, hands clasped behind his back. "She insisted on seeing Mrs. Shanahan, once she learned of the shooting."

Kane stared at him, cigar clamped between his teeth, his face a thundercloud. "Which jail?"

Cavan didn't relish the idea of his employer's wrath. Although he had never as yet felt the brunt of Kane's temper, he had worked for the man long enough to know that he could get ugly when riled. "Eldridge Street, sir."

"What in blazes were you thinking of, Sheridan? I haven't been inside the place, but no doubt it's as bad as all the other city jails. Do you have any idea what those places are like?"

Irked at being treated like a recalcitrant child, Cavan forced himself to maintain an even tone of voice. "'Tis what she wanted, sir. As I said, she insisted."

Kane bared his teeth, his cigar wedged between them. He got up from his desk with such force that the chair banged against the wall. "And if the woman is fool-headed enough to stand in front of a runaway coach, will you oblige her by driving the team?" He shook his head, muttering something Cavan couldn't make out but assumed to be an oath.

"Mrs. Harte assured me that she's familiar with the jail, sir," he said in his own defense.

Kane's head snapped up. "What? How would that be?"

"Because of her work with the Immigrant Aid Society, I believe. She seemed well acquainted with two of the policemen."

"So you did go in with her, then?" Kane still looked like a storm rolling in, but his voice had dropped a bit, and he was no longer chomping down on the cigar quite as fiercely.

"Aye, I did, sir. She talked with a Sergeant Garvey and an Officer Malloy, and I can tell you, neither was any match for Mrs. Harte."

Kane frowned, his dark eyes hard as marble. "What do you mean?"

"'Tis my impression that once Mrs. Harte sets her head to something, she won't be easily dissuaded. She may not look the part, but I suspect she is a very strong-willed woman."

Kane regarded him with a studying expression, then muttered a grudging sound of agreement. "You may be right. Even so, she's got no business inside a jailhouse—" He broke off, glancing sharply at Cavan. "Well—I suppose it could have been worse, if she was that set on the idea. At least you were there to drive her. Otherwise she might have walked, and that's hardly a neighborhood for a lady."

"Exactly, sir. That's why I told her I'd come back to drive her home." Cavan paused. "If you've no objection, that is."

Kane looked at him as he stubbed his cigar out in the copper bowl he used as an ashtray. "That won't be necessary," he said.

"Oh, but, sir, I as much as told Mrs. Harte I'd be back."

Kane cracked a testy smile. "I admire the way you volunteer yourself on my time, Sheridan—as well as the office wagon."

Heat burned Cavan's face, and he started to explain, but Kane waved him off.

"No harm done. I only meant that you needn't bother. I'll see to Mrs. Harte myself."

Cavan stared at him in bewilderment. "Sir?"

Kane was already shrugging into his suit jacket. "You take the wagon home, and I'll drive the carriage. We can drive in separately tomorrow."

"Yes, sir, but—"

Kane didn't give him time to finish. With a wave of his hand, he swept out the door. "Lock up the office for me, if you would."

Cavan watched him leave, his first sting of disappointment giving way to apprehension and even a kind of resentment. He told himself he was surely wrong. What interest could Kane possibly have in a fine lady like Mrs. Harte? She was a good Christian woman, virtuous entirely. And while she was exceedingly lovely, she wasn't any of the things he would have expected to interest Jack Kane.

On the other hand, he hadn't actually seen Kane with a woman often enough to *know* his interests. But wouldn't he be more likely to favor the flamboyant, perhaps even vulgar, sort of woman, rather than the subtle, refined beauty of Samantha Harte?

Uneasily, he realized he might be deluding himself. In all fairness to the man, Kane's tastes seemed anything but ostentatious. His few excesses appeared limited to expensive cigars, fine food, and quality tailoring. No, he might as well admit it—there was every possibility that Kane would find Samantha Harte highly appealing.

What man wouldn't?

Anxiety rose up in Cavan, an acid bile that threatened to steal his breath. Most of the time, he liked his employer, even admired him. But there was a darkness, a ruthlessness about Kane—and at times, an almost feral shrewdness—that was unsettling, even somewhat frightening. He found even the thought that Kane might actually pursue Samantha Harte nothing less than revolting.

His hands shook as he locked the office door and started down the steps. He wished he had protested, but what possible good would it have done? Kane might treat him decently enough most of the time, but he was still the man's lackey. Any objection on his part would have been futile. He would have either angered Kane or amused him; it was hard to say which.

Black Jack Kane did what he wanted and, from all accounts, almost always *got* what he wanted.

That being the case, Cavan could only hope Kane wouldn't decide he wanted Samantha Harte.

❧

Inside the cell, Samantha sat motionlessly, looking into the face of utter hopelessness and despair.

It was a dank, cold, squalid place. Several women—some raucous, others bitterly silent—milled about, but for the most part, they took no notice of Samantha and Maura Shanahan.

Although she wouldn't have expected the other to welcome her visit, Samantha was still taken aback at Maura Shanahan's air of remoteness. Her eyes, glazed and seemingly without focus, had not met Samantha's once. Her white, taut face registered no emotion—only a number of dark, ugly bruises. One eye was red and crusted—probably not from tears, Samantha speculated, but with blood.

It took every shred of self-control she possessed to sit there, confronting the wretchedness of the woman across from her. Every glance at the other's face made Samantha wince in pain, and the awareness of the woman's misery caused her insides to virtually writhe in anguish. Upon entering the cell and seeing Maura Shanahan, she had wanted to turn and run. Even after the initial rush of panic, it still took a deliberate act of will to stay.

"Mrs. Shanahan? Do you remember me?" she asked softly. "I'm Samantha Harte. I came to see you last Saturday about Willie."

Maura Shanahan made no response but simply looked at Samantha, her eyes dull and clouded.

Samantha drew in a steadying breath and tried again. "Maura—may I call you Maura? I . . . came to see if there's anything I can do for you. Any way I can help you."

Something flickered in the lusterless eyes, then quickly died.

"I wanted to tell you how sorry I am . . . about everything." Samantha cringed at the inanity of her own words. "This is awful for you, I know. Would it help to talk about it?"

Finally, there was a flicker of recognition. "I shot him." She might just as well have stated the time of day, for all the emotion the words held.

"So . . . you did it, then?" Samantha asked gently. "You shot your husband?"

Maura Shanahan nodded, a gesture that appeared fraught with numb exhaustion. "He's dead."

Samantha swallowed. She was almost certain she knew the answer to her next question, yet she felt compelled to ask. "Why, Maura? Why would you do such a thing?"

The other looked at her with an expression so devoid of feeling that Samantha felt suddenly chilled. "Because he was going to kill me," she said flatly. "This time he meant to murder me entirely."

Samantha gripped her hands in her lap to still their trembling. She swallowed, her throat so swollen she almost choked. "This time?" she said thickly.

Maura Shanahan's red blonde hair had fallen over the encrusted eye, giving her the forlorn appearance of a battered child. "'Twas different this time. He beat me with the gun. He hadn't never done that before.''

She lifted a thin, unsteady hand to brush the hair out of her eye. Her gaze was level, but Samantha suspected she wasn't really seeing her, was instead recalling the terror—and the pain.

"This time he said he would murder us all. Me and the children as well.'' As she spoke, Maura began to rub a hand up and down her injured arm, which she hugged tightly to her side.

The words came as little more than a whisper, but they struck horror into Samantha's heart. "Oh, Maura . . . I'm so sorry . . . so sorry.'' It was all she could say. She didn't trust her own emotions.

"I might not have tried to take the gun away from him if he hadn't threatened to hurt the children,'' Maura Shanahan went on in the same wooden tone of voice, almost as if retelling the incident by rote. "But I could see he meant it, and something came over me.'' She glanced at Samantha. "A terrible feeling, like my head would explode. A devilish rage, it was. I got the gun away from him, and when he came at me I just—I shot him. I shot Heber.''

Samantha had not known she could feel another's misery as keenly as she felt Maura Shanahan's right now, at this moment. It was almost as if she had taken upon herself the pain and the rage and the desperation of the tiny, worn woman sitting across from her.

"You did what you had to do, Maura, to save your own life—and perhaps the lives of your children as well.''

"He wasn't always like that,'' the other went on, her voice a low drone. "When we was first married and came across, he had such dreams. We both did. We was going to have us a house and a bit of land somewhere. But he couldn't get a job, you see—no one wanted him. There was no work for the Irish.''

There still wasn't, Samantha thought. She had seen the signs. They were legion. On storefronts, factory warehouses—all over the city: No Irish Need Apply.

"After a time,'' Maura continued, "he got on doing jobs for Captain Rynders. That's when he took to the drink—Heber had never been one for the drink back home, don't you know, not until we came across—and he got mean when he drank. He just kept getting meaner and meaner, and when he was in a state, it was as if he blamed me for it all. For not being able to get a decent job, for not having money to feed the children or buy a house—''

Yes, he would have . . . He would have had to blame someone for his own misery and twisted mind. . . .

Maura lifted her eyes to Samantha's, and there was so much pain, so much regret and hopelessness in that look that Samantha felt as if she had been physically struck.

"I can't help thinking it might have been different had he found a proper job," said Maura Shanahan. It seemed to Samantha that there was an entire world of desolation in those few words.

"Maura," she said, reaching across the rickety table for the other's hand, "I must go—they've allowed me only a few minutes with you. But I'll be back. In the meantime, I'm going to try to find someone to help you. Do you understand? You're not alone in this. I know some people—perhaps I can locate an attorney for you, someone who will know what to do."

Maura Shanahan looked at her with unmistakable distrust and confusion. "Why would you do that? Why would you be wanting to help *me?*"

Samantha held her gaze as she again pressed the woman's hand. "Because . . . I think I understand why you did it. Perhaps I understand more than you could imagine. I only want to help you, Maura."

Maura Shanahan stared at her with an expression of incredulity, and what Samantha recognized to be no small measure of bitterness. "Begging your pardon, Mrs. Harte—you're a good woman, I'm sure, but you couldn't possibly understand."

"Oh, but I do, Maura," Samantha said quietly, ignoring the tremor in her voice. "Believe me, I do."

When she left Maura Shanahan, Samantha refused Officer Malloy's offer to accompany her to the door. Instead she walked halfway down the long corridor alone, then stopped. Badly shaken and depleted, she leaned against the wall to support herself. In spite of her efforts to restrain them, the tears now came. She turned her face toward the wall as if to hide—from her surroundings and from Maura Shanahan's despair.

And from her own.

When she finally regained control and turned to leave, she uttered a gasp of surprise. Jack Kane was standing little more than a handbreadth away, so close he could have reached out and touched her. Indeed, he did lift a hand as if to do just that, but after an instant dropped it away.

His face was a dark mask that revealed nothing. But when he spoke, the deep rumble of his voice was incredibly low and gentle. "I've come to take you home, Mrs. Harte. If you'll allow me, that is."

Samantha began to shake her head slowly, uncertainly. Her legs were unsteady, and she even felt somewhat faint, but she knew it was because of the emotional drain she had just experienced. When Kane offered his arm she was tempted to take it. "I thought—Cavan said he would come back—"

Kane smiled at her, and there was as much kindness in his smile as in his voice. "I confess to usurping my driver's job. I wanted to see if there was anything I could do to help. I'm fond of Willie." He paused. "Mrs. Harte—Samantha—please, let me drive you home."

Watching him closely, Samantha could detect no sign of insincerity. She hesitated only a moment more before drawing in a deep breath and taking his arm. It was all she could do not to lean on his strength as they started down the corridor and toward the door.

30

A Parting without Good-Byes

For the vision of hope is decayed,
Though the shadows still linger behind.

THOMAS DERMODY

GALWAY, IRELAND

Terese's heart pounded with a mixture of excitement and apprehension as she mounted the steps to Brady's flat. He had warned her about his landlady—the "starched and stuffy" Mrs. Hannafin—who without exception forbade any of her gentleman tenants to have "lasses above the stairs." If she should happen to catch Terese sneaking in, there would be the very devil to pay.

But later today, Brady would be leaving. And although it galled Terese something fierce to swallow her pride, she knew she couldn't let him go with things as they were. The bad feelings from last night's quarrel still stood like a pool of tainted water between them. Pride to the wind, she had known since early dawn what she must do.

She had spent most of the night trying to convince herself that she hated him, that she never wanted to see him again, and that she certainly did not need his help to get to America. Even if she *never* got out of Ireland, she assured herself, she would not look to Brady Kane for assistance.

Her bitter resolve had lasted only so long. In truth, she would have let herself be keelhauled all the way across the Atlantic if it meant getting to the States, and getting there with Brady at her side. Her feelings for him had deepened far beyond what she had intended in the beginning. All her sensible plans to go her own way and avoid any attachment that would not advance her goals suddenly seemed unimportant. Ever since the night of the play, she had found it more and more difficult to think of Brady as simply a means to an end, an instrument by which she might further her dreams. To her great consternation, he seemed to have become a part of those dreams.

It was the last thing she would have wanted, to become so involved with him—with anyone—that she would consider subjugating her own needs and desires to his. Yet by allowing herself to care for Brady so deeply, she had done exactly that.

Even in his embrace, she had deluded herself, trying to pretend that she was simply using him to achieve her own ends. Perhaps that had been her design in the beginning, but everything had changed. If she had thought that by giving in to his passion she would somehow gain greater control over him, she had been sorely mistaken. To the contrary, she was beginning to fear that she was losing whatever advantage she might have held. Last night she had realized that there was as much need on her part as on his—and the realization had shaken her to the core.

As she stole down the hallway to his flat, her mind was awash with confusion and impatience—impatience with her own foolishness. She should never have allowed herself to become so entangled with any man, but especially with one like Brady, who made no pretense of being anything but what he was—a sweet-talking rover with no apparent purpose or ambitions. More than likely he would be content to spend the rest of his days trekking from one place to another, his infernal sketch pad tucked under one arm and a pretty girl on the other. He would never put down roots or own more than a pocketful of change to pay the fiddler.

Yet even knowing that, here she was, creeping down the hall like a common slattern, intent on making amends and setting things right between them.

Madness.

The argument had been folly itself, but it had taken Terese most of the night to grudgingly acknowledge that the fault was entirely her own. She was altogether careless to push Brady as she did. It was too soon—much too soon—to make any sort of demands. They had been together the night before, and the night before that, and on impulse she had suggested they could be together every night if he would but take her with him on his travels.

He was clearly taken aback by her boldness, but once into it, Terese didn't know how to extricate herself. "If you've meant all the things you've been saying to me, I can't think why you'd want to leave me behind. You said yourself there's no telling how long you'll be away."

"Terese, I can't take you with me," he said, holding her at arm's length. He looked uncomfortable but not actually dismissive. "I'm not here on holiday—I've work to do." He smiled teasingly at her. "And you, my beauty, make it nearly impossible for me to concentrate on work."

Unable to conceal her disappointment, Terese tried again. "It doesn't seem to me that you've been all that concerned about your work of late."

"That's my point exactly," he said, still smiling. He tried to pull her into his arms, but Terese resisted. "Oh, come on now," he urged. "I'll be back before you've even had time to miss me. It's not like I'm leaving forever. I'm only going to Limerick."

"And who knows where else?" Terese said petulantly. "Didn't you tell me yourself that you've all number of places to visit before you go back to New York?"

"And didn't I also tell you I'd be coming back to Galway in a few weeks, before going on?"

"You've been playing loose with me entirely, haven't you? I'm nothing at all to you, no more than any of your other women."

Gripping her shoulders, he forced her to look at him. "That's not so, and you know it. I've never been with any girl I care for as much as you. Come on now, T'reesie, let's go upstairs. Don't you want to be alone with me on our last night?"

Aching with disillusionment and at the same time infuriated that he could treat her so casually, Terese wrenched away from him. "I don't want to be *anywhere* with you tonight! You've been dallying with me all along, and I'll not cheapen myself for you again! And you needn't think I'll be here waiting for you when you get around to looking me up again."

"You knew I was leaving, Terese," he fired back at her. "I never told you anything else but what I'd be going, come tomorrow. I also told you I'd be back, didn't I?"

"And wouldn't you promise me anything I wanted to hear, to get what you wanted?"

She was completely unprepared for his sudden transformation. His eyes went hard, his mouth even harder, as he stepped back from her. "I don't recall taking anything you weren't eager to give," he bit out. "Now do you want to be with me tonight or not? I'm not going to coax you. If you'd rather go back to Crazy Jane, then go on. It's getting late."

Oh, he was cold! Those dark eyes of his were like polished marbles, registering not a hint of feeling as he made his challenge.

Dumbstruck by this uncharacteristic display of indifference, Terese whipped around as if to go. But he caught her, yanking her around and forcing a hard, bruising kiss on her as if she were nothing more to him than a common strumpet.

Furious, Terese drew back a hand as if to slap his insolent face, but he caught her, trapping her against him. "That temper of yours is going to be your downfall one day, you little alley cat. I swear, sometimes I think you might be a bit mad. What do you expect of a man, Terese? You spend the entire evening playing the cozy kitten, stringing me along—and then you fly into a rage just because I won't destroy your reputation by making a scandal of you. You can't just go rambling around the country with me, you foolish girl—you'd be ruined!"

"Not if I were your wife!"

Her comeback was born strictly of impulse. The instant the words were out of her mouth, Terese knew she had made a mistake. And the worst part was that she didn't even mean them.

Did she?

He stared at her, then drew back. "Whoa, my beauty. I never said anything about marriage. That is one subject I religiously avoid, as you might have noticed."

"I'm good enough to bed, just not good enough to wed, is that it?"

His jaw tightened, and his eyes again went cold. "Don't do this, Terese," he said, his tone a warning in itself.

Regret surged through Terese. Miserable in the growing awareness of her mistake, stung by his coldness, she allowed anger to cover her distress. Turning her back on him, she tried to think what to say, what to do.

"Did I ever once mention marriage to you, Terese?" he asked quietly behind her. Not trusting herself to speak, she shook her head.

"That's not what I'm about, Terese. It has nothing to do with you—I'm wild for you, surely you know that by now. But marriage isn't for me. Not now, maybe not ever." He paused. "It's up to you, Terese. What's it to be?"

In the end her humiliation and self-disgust fueled her earlier rage, and she turned on him. "It's to be *nothing* with you, Brady Kane! Go on to Limerick, then. Go tonight for all I care! You'll not be seeing me again before you go—and I'll not be caring if you ever come back!''

She hurled the words at him blindly, scarcely spitting the last of them out before taking off down the lane at a near run without looking back.

It had been a lie, of course. She *did* care. He *had* to come back! It was no good trying to convince herself that he was important to her only inasmuch as he could make a difference in her future. Even as her mind insisted, her heart cried out in denial.

Perhaps the real truth was hidden somewhere between what she needed to believe and what was actually so. In any event, here she was, skulking down the hall toward his flat like any cheap girl of the streets, set on making things right, whatever it took.

But not for a moment would she allow him to think that she needed him. She realized now that her only hope of binding Brady to her was to make him believe that none of the need was hers—but his alone.

✦

The door to his room was ajar. Terese rapped softly once. When there was no response, she walked in.

"Brady?"

There was still no reply. Terese's gaze swept the small sitting room, and the first prickle of apprehension skated down her spine. The room looked dusty and unexpectedly vacant. No books or papers lay strewn about; there was not so much as a teacup on the table, and the drapes had not been opened.

Her mouth dry, she went on to the bedroom. "Brady?" she said again, her voice echoing in the silence of the flat.

Her earlier uneasiness intensified to a wave of dismay as she saw the evidence of his departure. The bedding had been randomly tossed, and the clothes press stood gaping and empty. No luggage rested near the door, no toiletries lined the dressing table.

There was no sign of him, no indication that he had ever inhabited the premises. The room had suddenly turned into a hollow shell, devoid of anything to give it warmth and life. The light that issued from the window was weak and gray, for in here, too, the drapes remained closed.

The morning suddenly seemed to take on a chill. Dazed, Terese tried to swallow against the tightness of her throat, but instead nearly gagged on a knot of despair.

She should have come earlier. . . . She shouldn't have left him last night, should never have flung the angry words at him. Now he was gone, and even though he had insisted he would return in mere weeks, that had been before the bitterness of their parting. She couldn't count on his promise now, couldn't count on anything.

Devastated, she stood there in the gloom, scarcely breathing. After a moment, a violent torrent of shivering gripped her, and she began to quake as if a giant claw had plucked her off her feet and was shaking her in a rage.

When the seizure had finally passed, she stood there, looking about the bedroom where only two nights past she had lain with him. Loneliness fell over her like a shroud. Once again she knew herself to be left behind. Not for the first time, someone who was supposed to care about her had instead forsaken her. It made no difference at all that she had brought this latest abandonment on herself. All she could think of was that Brady had left her, and she was alone.

Again.

PART THREE

The Storm's Edge

He calmed the storm to a whisper
and stilled the waves.
What a blessing was that stillness
as he brought them safely into harbor!

PSALM 107:29-30

31

Price of Dreams,
Penance of Folly

I am worn out with dreams.

W . B . Y E A T S

IRELAND, JULY 1839

Brady Kane stood looking east, across the river, to the turrets and towers of King John's Castle. The setting was both splendid and bleak. Limerick itself was laid out on an extensive plain, watered by the majestic Shannon—the "King" of Ireland's rivers. The old city was divided into an "English Town" and an "Irish Town," with a more recent third division called Newton Pery. Brady preferred the old districts and had grown especially fond of the castle that stood frowning down on the main approach to "English Town."

This warm summer's evening would be his last in Limerick, at least for a time, as well as his last opportunity to finish his painting of the castle.

He had quickly come to appreciate Limerick's charm and particular advantages. He had purchased several pairs—some for gifts—of fine Limerick gloves, supposedly unrivaled in quality anywhere in the world. He had also studied and sketched a variety of Limerick laces, famed even in the States for their delicate perfection. And, of course, he had given careful attention to Limerick's lasses. The women of Limerick, after all, were said to be among the most beautiful in Ireland, if not the world. Comely as they were, however, Brady had been frustrated to find that they couldn't seem to distract his thoughts from Terese's fire or Roweena's gentle loveliness—at least not for long.

There he went again. He shook his head, as if by the mere physical gesture he could dismiss the two sylphs who had staked a claim on far too many of his waking hours—and more than a few of his dreams.

As his return to Galway neared, he found himself often brooding over what sort of reception he might expect from Terese. Surely she would have gotten over her pique by now, although the fact that she hadn't answered his letter did not bode well.

He had written to her a month ago. His intention had been not to take back anything he'd said that last night they were together, but to try to explain that his resistance to a permanent sort of commitment had nothing to do with the way he felt about her.

He *did* care about Terese, Brady told himself as he put the finishing touches on the painting. She was beautiful, passionate, sharp-witted, and, although she could be something of a shrew when in a temper, most of the time she was great fun to be with.

But he also cared about Roweena, though in a different way. Whereas Terese was fire and fury, Roweena was like a fine piece of Limerick lace—exquisitely lovely, but perhaps dangerously fragile. His feelings toward her were puzzling, ranging from protectiveness to a sweet, aching kind of desire—not the tempestuous, raging need he felt for Terese, but more a tender yearning for something as elusive as the morning mist.

Of course, he thought ruefully, there was also the fact that the mighty Gabriel stood as solidly as a mountain between Roweena and any man who dared approach. No insignificant barrier, that, by any means. Brady couldn't stop himself from conjecturing what it would mean if by some unimaginable circumstance the Big Fella were to step aside, leaving Roweena more . . . accessible. Would he still be so averse to a permanent commitment?

Brush suspended in midair, he paused, then shook his head again. Best not to go down that road. As appealing as the prospect might be, it was about as likely as the fall of the British empire.

In any event, he had a few other things to do yet tonight besides indulging in boyish fantasies. For one thing, he had to finish packing. But before that he needed to make a last brief visit to the orphanage, just to make certain all the details regarding the Madden children were in order.

As he packed away his brushes and paints, his thoughts went to young Shona and Tully Madden. Finally, he had set in motion Jack's plan. After receiving his brother's scrawl of approval for the first story, Brady had moved quickly to draft what he deemed a passably adequate article on the two Madden orphans, at the same time initiating preliminary arrangements for their passage to the States.

As per Jack's instructions, he had gone in search of only those stories with "irresistible" appeal—stories that would "wring tears out of the Cliffs of Moher," as Jack so colorfully put it. Thanks to the local Orphan Friends Society, Brady was fairly certain he had found just the story for his first effort.

Shona and Tully Madden had been orphaned three years ago in an occurrence that was apparently all too common in Ireland. A landlord had set a consumptive widow and her two children out of the house in the dead of winter—for rent in arrears or some such offense. Within a month the mother was dead, leaving the children entirely on their own.

By the grace of God and the intervention of the Orphan Friends Society, the two had managed to stay alive. Shona was now a frail ten-year-old with the sorrows of the world looking out from behind her haunted eyes. Her brother, Tully, was a surprisingly good-natured child with a quick, ingenuous smile that inspired thoughts of the angels.

Poor little tykes, Brady thought, closing his paint case. Tully had lost most of his toes to frostbite and would always be lame, while Shona seemed to live in constant fear of the cold, quaking like a palsied old woman every time a door was opened and she felt a draft. Still, they had survived—no small feat, given all they had endured.

The two made Brady ashamed of every luxury he had ever enjoyed, every indulgence he had granted himself, and he sincerely longed to better their circumstances. Thanks to Jack, it would seem that he could do just that. As it stood now, Shona and Tully Madden would be the first two beneficiaries of his brother's recent, and to Brady's thinking, somewhat uncharacteristic, magnanimity.

He left the bridge, mentally ticking off the tasks remaining before he could grab some sleep. It was going to be a long night, but he felt no hint of fatigue. To the contrary, the thought that he would soon see Terese—and Roweena—infused him with energy and a rush of eagerness to be on his way. He quickened his step, not even taking the time to enjoy one last glorious sunset over the Shannon.

Gabriel waited until the Sheridan girl left the cottage to feed the chickens before turning back to Jane Connolly, who sat in her chair by the window, looking out. He drew an arm over his forehead to blot the perspiration. The day had been uncommonly warm, even for July, and there was still no breeze to relieve the sultry evening.

Jane seemed more uncomfortable than usual. Hot, humid days like this always aggravated her painful joints. Gabriel deliberated over whether or not to even ask the question on his mind, but he wouldn't want Jane unaware of what he suspected.

"Does she know, do you think?" he said bluntly, watching Jane closely to gauge her reaction.

She turned to look at him. He took in the exaggerated puffiness about her eyes, the angry red flush across her cheeks. As he had countless times before, he wished he could find a way to relieve her misery.

"Know *what?*" she said irritably.

Gabriel drew a long breath. So she hadn't noticed.

"I believe the girl is with child, Jane. Has she said nothing about it, then?"

For a moment she simply stared at him, her hands like claws on the chair arms. She glanced once to the door, still standing open. When she turned back to Gabriel, her features were drawn in a taut mask, as if she was making an effort to conceal her pain. "Are you sure?"

"I can't be certain, of course. But she's not nearly so lean, and she has the look about her."

Jane's shoulders slumped, and she looked away. "Aye, you would know," she said simply. "And since you mention it, I've seen it, too." She paused. "I doubt that she's even aware, though she's clever enough about everything else."

Again she raised her eyes to Gabriel. "Will you speak to her, then?"

Gabriel shook his head. "'Tis for you to do that, it seems to me."

Jane's face creased to a sour look. "She'll not be thanking me for it."

Gabriel lifted an eyebrow. "Nor will she be thanking Brady Kane, I expect. But she needs to know her condition, if she doesn't as yet."

"You believe it's him, then?"

"Who else would it be? Of course it's him. We should have seen it coming." He paused. "And so should she."

"She's very young. And raised without a mother, for the most part."

The softness of her tone surprised Gabriel. "All the more reason for you to speak to her," he said carefully. "She will hear it better from you than from anyone else, I'm thinking."

He started for the door, then turned back. "It would be best not to wait too long, Jane."

She gave a nod, a weary gesture. "I'll see to it."

Gabriel studied her for another moment. She looked sad, he realized. Like a mother who has been given sorrowful news and can't quite take it in.

He turned then and left the cottage. Poor Jane. For some time now, he had seen her growing fondness for the girl, had seen as well her attempts to conceal it. This would be a hard thing for Jane, and the Lord knew she had already endured more than her share of troubles. She had cared deeply for her husband, but he had died. She had doted on her only daughter, who had gone to live in a far country.

No doubt she had tried to guard her heart against caring for yet another, but Jane's heart was not the stone she would have others believe it to be. Still, she had to have known that Terese Sheridan would not stay. The island girl had made no secret of her intentions, telling anyone who would listen that she was bound for America as soon as she could pay her passage.

And where would she be bound for now? Gabriel wondered. Brady Kane had left Galway insisting that he would return in only a few weeks, but two months had come and gone, and there was still no sign of him. There had been a letter, Jane said. But only one.

Gabriel sighed, and a heaviness settled over his heart like lowering clouds. It seemed that a part of Jane's sadness had attached itself to him. His own dolor was not for Jane alone, however, not even for the foolish, impetuous girl, although his concern for both was deep. Somewhere in his spirit he also grieved for the child—the unborn, unwanted child who would almost certainly prove to be a burden.

The thought brought wee Evie and Roweena to mind, and his heart wrenched in silent protest. In such cases as this, it was always the child who suffered most. The innocent paid the price for the sins of others, and more often than not it was a dear price indeed.

As he reached the lane that turned home, the Galway sun slipped down behind the horizon, leaving the Claddagh in near total darkness. But in the window of his cottage, a light flickered. Roweena and the little one had instituted the custom, which by now Gabriel had come to count on. No matter where he went, or how late the hour of his return, he knew a candle would be burning in the window until he reached safe home.

He started up the walk, smiling a little as the glow reached out to light his spirit even as it rent the shadows of the night.

※◎※

Alone with Jane in the dimly lighted cottage later that night, Terese silently massaged her employer's hands with the new supply of oil that Gabriel had brought. Next she would do Jane's ankles and feet, a task that some might find demeaning. Terese, however, didn't really mind; she viewed it as merely a part of her job.

Of late, she thought she had seen some slight improvement in Jane and wondered if the massage sessions might be providing a bit of relief, albeit temporary, from the pain. Terese had even suggested that they increase the frequency of the ministrations, but Jane insisted she could not afford the additional purchases of oil.

She glanced at the older woman and saw that her eyes were closed, the lines of her face smoothed in a rare look of peace. Terese was caught off guard by the quick warmth that poured over her. That she could help to ease her pain-ridden employer's distress gave her an unaccountable feeling of satisfaction.

She had been with Jane some months now, long enough to witness firsthand the extent of the woman's misery. So far as Terese could tell, Jane Connolly was never without pain or, even at her better moments, acute discomfort.

There seemed to be little in the way of any real relief for her suffering. Gabriel often brought herbs in addition to the oil Jane sent for, but many times he left the cottage with a look of utter frustration on his face. His desire to help was obvious; his disappointment that he could not, just as evident.

Terese hadn't realized that she had ceased her movements until Jane's sharp rebuke jerked her out of her thoughts. "You might just as well stop mooning about the Yank. He will be back when he's good and ready and not a day before."

Terese looked at her. "What? Oh—I wasn't thinking about Brady at all, as it happens."

Jane sniffed and rolled her eyes.

"I wasn't, I tell you."

Terese refused to let herself be goaded. Jane dearly loved a match of wits, and Terese was usually quick to oblige. But it was getting late, and she was bone tired. "Here, now," she said briskly, standing to adjust the wheelchair. "Let's have your feet."

She snapped the footrest up too sharply, and Jane cried out.

"I'm sorry, Jane! The rod slipped! I *am* sorry. Are you all right, then?"

Jane glared at her but said nothing.

"I need to be greasing your chair, I'm thinking," Terese offered. "Your right wheel is sticking, and so is that pesky rod. I'll see to it tomorrow."

"You'll have to be getting some grease first. Gabriel used the last of it a week ago when he fixed the gate."

Terese was careful to keep her touch firm but not too heavy as she began to knead the swollen ankles. "Gabriel's very good to you, isn't he? Were he and your husband friends?"

Jane nodded. "As much as Gabriel would be a friend to any man, I suppose."

Terese glanced up. It was an uncommon thing for Jane to respond to even a casual question without a sharp-tongued remark or an attempt at mocking humor. "He's a peculiar sort of man, Gabriel is. Wouldn't you say?"

"Some might think so. But there's not much strangeness about Gabriel except his habit of minding his own business. There are those who don't understand the practice and so might think him odd." She fixed Terese with a pointed look.

Terese still refused to rise to the bait. "I'm not meaning to pry," she said lightly. "'Tis just that he seems such a . . . different sort of man. He's obviously had a grand education—he speaks like a scholar at times. And doesn't he seem to know something about almost everything—even doctoring?" She glanced up. "And why is it I've never heard his last name? He does *have* a family name, now doesn't he?"

Jane lifted an eyebrow. "You've an itchy nose this evening, it seems. But since you've asked, of course he has a family name, and a fine one, at that. He is a Vaughan. Gabriel Vaughan, son of Martin. An old family and a much esteemed one."

"Are you related, the two of you?" Terese asked.

Jane looked down her nose and frowned. "Related? No, not a bit. Why would you ask?"

Terese shrugged. "He's very kind to you," she said, continuing the massage.

"Gabriel is kind to everyone," Jane said tightly. "'Tis his way. Though the Lord knows there are those who take advantage."

Terese looked at her. "You don't mean Roweena and wee Evie, do you?"

Jane waved a hand. "No, not them. Sweet Roweena would die for the man, she's that devoted. And the little one—Gabriel is the only father she has known, and hasn't he been a fine one, at that? No, those two are blessed to have such a home as he provides, and sure, they seem to be grateful entirely.''

She leaned back then, eyes closed. Thinking that all the talk might be tiring her, Terese grew silent. She had learned to let Jane doze whenever and wherever she could, for the woman managed little enough sleep as it was.

For a few minutes more, she went on with the massage, her thoughts drifting past the hushed room to Brady. She wondered if she would hear from him again soon. Miffed because he had taken a good month to write, she deliberately hadn't answered his letter. Of late, though, she was beginning to think she might be cutting off her nose to spite her face and decided that tomorrow she would pen a note to the address in Limerick.

Terese had found herself missing him more than she would have expected. She didn't like to admit that just possibly she was in love with Brady Kane. She found the very idea almost frightening. Love was not for her, at least not yet. There was too much she had to do, too much ahead of her. She had a future. She must not allow anything to divert her from that.

Besides, if this was love, she wasn't at all sure she wanted any part of it. So far she had seen nothing of the lightheartedness, the giddy happiness others seemed to associate with the condition. More often these days, she felt glum and weary, dragging through her work almost like an old woman. And there were her moods—they seemed to swing from testiness to out-and-out rage, though she could seldom single out the object of her resentment. At times she simply did not feel well at all, and these were the times she almost wished she had never set eyes on Brady Kane's insolent face. Perhaps he wasn't directly responsible for her malaise, but if not him, then who?

Still, she *did* have feelings for him, feelings she couldn't simply dismiss. And there remained the possibility that Brady would eventually take her with him to America, even though he seemed to be in no hurry at all about going back—and even though he had made it clear enough that he wasn't even remotely interested in anything permanent between them.

She gave a long sigh, suddenly angry with this ongoing war between her thoughts and her emotions.

''What are you going to do about the child?''

The sharpness of Jane's words startled Terese out of her intro-

spection. When she looked up, Jane's eyes were wide open and probing.

"What?"

"Ach, girl, surely you've realized by now that you're carrying his
child! And what are you going to do about it?"

Terese gaped at Jane, too stunned to reply, suddenly numbed by a
sense of her own stupidity. Had she known all along but denied what
was too devastating to admit? Quickly her mind calculated the time,
the way she had been feeling—the fatigue, her treacherous stomach.
And hadn't her mother been the same when she carried baby Mada?

Terese froze. *No. No, it can't be true. . . . It mustn't be true. . . .*

But it *was* true. She knew it instinctively, felt the certainty of it
closing in on her, could almost hear the sound of the lock turning in
the gaolhouse door.

32

Lament of the Lonely

None care why the colour from my wan cheek has fled—
Lonely and bitter are the tears I shed.

LADY WILDE (SPERANZA)

"I don't suppose you know how far along you are?"

Terese blinked, then shook her head. Without warning, a searing blade of shame ripped through her. She scrambled to her feet and turned away from Jane, unable to bear the gaze of those astute hazel eyes.

Instinctively, her hands went to her belly, and she stood in the middle of the room, hunched over, clasping herself as if she might fly apart.

"Two months?" Jane prompted sharply. "Three? You must have an idea, girl!"

Terese tried to think. "I—a little more than two, perhaps," she choked out. "No more."

"Will he marry you, do you think?"

Terese whipped around, her hands dropping to her sides. "Marry me?"

Jane was watching her, her expression unreadable. "When he learns about the babe—do you think he'll marry you?"

In spite of the humid closeness of the room, a wintry cold began to seep into Terese's bones as she remembered her last night with Brady, the argument, the things he had said to her. . . . *"Marriage isn't for me. . . . Not now, maybe not ever . . ."*

But surely a child—*his* child—would change his feelings . . . would change everything. . . .

"No," she heard herself saying before she had time to build any false hope. "I think not. He's not the man for marriage."

Jane's eyes glinted with anger. "And knowing that, you lay with him anyway? How could you be so reckless, girl? Didn't you once think where it might lead?"

Terese made no reply. She hated the way Jane was looking at her, with a mixture of pity and something akin to contempt, as if she might as well try to reason with a fool.

And at that moment, a fool is what Terese felt herself to be.

"No doubt you're right," Jane rambled on. "The Yank does not seem inclined to tie himself down to home and hearth fire. So, then— how will you manage?"

Terese thought she would surely scream if Jane hurled another question at her. She shook her head. "I don't know yet. I will have to think."

Even as she said the words, a part of her recoiled at the very idea of her circumstances. She would have to make plans, of course—but what sort of plans?

"Perhaps you should speak to Gabriel," Jane offered. "He might be able to advise you."

Terese twisted her mouth. "You mean *condemn* me."

Jane was immediately defensive. "Gabriel would never condemn you, nor anyone else. He lives his life and allows others to live theirs."

"He makes no secret of the fact that he doesn't approve of me," Terese pointed out. "His face turns to stone every time I walk into a room."

She found herself squirming under Jane's studying gaze.

"Perhaps your conscience makes you see things that are not there. If you're not comfortable in Gabriel's presence, I submit the fault is yours and not his. He is not a man to be deceived."

"And what does *that* mean?" Terese spat out. "Faith, Jane, if you think me such a terrible person, why do you keep me on?"

Jane made no reply but instead regarded Terese with an expression that was not unkind, in spite of her brusque words. "I keep you on because I need a girl, as Gabriel himself was so quick to point out. Don't forget that it's him you have to thank for having a roof over your head at all, no matter how much you may begrudge the fact. Gabriel seemed to think I should take you in, and I did so because I trust his judgment. You might consider doing the same."

Resentment built in Terese, and she tried to hold a steady gaze. At last, though, she had to look away. She could not shake off the humiliation, the burden of shame. As difficult as she found Jane's obvious censure, she could not imagine having to endure the big fisherman's. And no matter what Jane said, Terese was certain he would be openly disapproving.

Jane's next suggestion absolutely appalled Terese. "I expect Gabriel could convince your worthless Yank to marry you, if that's what you want." Her expression was strangely conspiratorial as she added, "In any event, you'd best be sending a letter off to Limerick to tell him of your condition."

The idea of Gabriel strong-arming Brady to the altar made Terese cringe in shame, but Jane was probably right about the letter. She nodded and began to gather up the towels and oil to put them away. That done, she then helped Jane into her nightclothes and braided her hair. Neither of them spoke until they had finished with the nightly routine.

"Will you be wanting the chair tonight," Terese asked, "or shall I help you into bed?"

Jane waved her off. "Just leave me here for now."

Terese was reaching to set a cup of water on the table next to her when Jane caught her arm. "Listen, girl," she said, not quite meeting Terese's gaze, "you can stay here as long as you want. You needn't worry that I'll be putting you out because of the child."

Surprised, Terese had to blink back the quick tears that filled her eyes. Immediately, Jane withdrew her hand and looked away. "You'll have to tend to your work all the same, mind. I can't afford to feed an idle girl, and won't you be eating more than ever now?"

It suddenly dawned on Terese, and she could have wept at the realization, that Jane's gruffness was all a sham. That hard-edged exterior hid a heart that was far more tender than she would allow the world to know.

Overwhelmed for a moment, Terese fought to keep her voice level as she replied. "Thank you, Jane. I'm . . . obliged. And you needn't fret about the work. I'll not be slacking off on you."

Later that night Terese lay in her bed wide awake, trying to decide what to do. Thoughts swarmed in her mind like angry bees, yet she could focus on none of them. From time to time she put a hand to her middle as if to give substance to the fact that she was indeed carrying a child. Brady's child.

But Brady wasn't here, and only God knew when he would be. For a moment Terese nearly crumpled under the fear and shame sweeping through her. She choked on the unshed tears burning her throat, but instead of weeping—or screaming—she bit down on her pillow until she could finally breathe again without sobbing.

She had to think, make plans. But first she must write to Brady.

Why? She did not dare to hope that a baby would really make a difference. Brady was a wanderer by nature, a sweet-talking love whisperer. She knew that by now. He seemed to fancy himself without roots, without responsibilities—and perhaps without a conscience as well, came the bitter thought.

No, that wasn't true. Brady was simply . . . Brady. Terese even allowed herself the tenuous hope that once he learned of her dilemma he wouldn't merely cast her aside. First thing in the morning—no, yet tonight, for who could sleep?—she would write to him. He would come as soon as he learned, she was sure of it. He would come back, and together they would decide what to do. He would not leave her to face this alone.

It occurred to her that he might even be happy about the child. Proud, perhaps. The idea of fatherhood changed some men, didn't it? Perhaps this was the very thing that would give Brady roots, give him purpose and make him stop his foolish roaming.

And perhaps the bay will turn to wine before sunup, came the hateful whisper at the edge of her mind as she pressed her mouth against the pillow and wept.

⁂

That night, for the first time in a very long time, Terese dreamed of Cavan. They were standing on opposite sides of what seemed to be an immense, yawning canyon. Far below, a great waterfall roared over yet another cliff, its raging current flinging uprooted trees and pitiful, bleating animals into a dark abyss where its waters could no longer be seen.

Behind her, snarling and pawing the ground, a pack of slavering wild dogs circled, waiting to close in on Terese. Cavan was shouting at her, motioning that she should jump across the chasm to him, while Terese shrieked that she would surely fall to her death, that she couldn't possibly make such a leap.

"But you *must* jump!" Cavan pleaded with her. "The dogs will be on you any minute! Jump, Terese! *Jump!*"

Whether he was deafened by the thunder of the water or simply chose to ignore her protests, he continued to urge her to jump. Terrified, her heart hammering savagely, Terese shot a look over her shoulder to see the dogs leering and drooling, inching their way toward her. When she looked back to Cavan, he had moved as close to the edge of the cliff as he dared, arms outstretched as if to catch her.

Behind her she could hear the dogs snapping their teeth and growling, edging in on her. They were so close now that she could smell their wildness, hear their excited panting. She stepped dangerously close to the edge of the cliff, and Cavan cried out to warn her. She looked over her shoulder to see the leader of the pack—a great, red-eyed beast—charging toward her at a full run. She screamed, over and over again, but still could not find the courage to jump—

"Are you all right, girl?"

Jane's voice cut across the room, startling Terese out of the nightmare. She sat bolt upright, her body drenched in perspiration. In the clammy darkness, she heard only her own labored breathing and the squeak of Jane's chair as she stirred in it.

"I'm fine, Jane, thank you. 'Twas only a bad dream. I'll be all right now."

The other made a small sound of acknowledgment but said nothing else.

Terese lay awake the rest of the night, unable to sleep, thinking about the dream—thinking about Cavan, wishing he were with her. What would it be like to have someone—an older brother, someone who cared—to look after her, advise her, help her make the hard decisions? At the same time, she supposed she ought to be grateful that Cavan *wasn't* here to see her disgrace.

By dawn she was thoroughly exhausted, yet too tense and anxious to even doze. At last she forced herself to consider the one possibility she had been avoiding throughout the long night. She had heard that there were women in the city who would rid one of an unwanted child, for a price. She had the money she had been saving from her wages—money for her passage to America—though she doubted it would be enough. And there would be no time to save more. Even with the little she knew about such things, she was certain that the sort of procedure she was contemplating would have to be done soon.

Without warning, Terese began to tremble almost violently. The blood pounded in her head as she stared into the darkness. Such a thing was surely evil. *The devil's doing,* her mother would say. *A thought from the pit of hell itself.* How could she allow the dread idea to even enter her mind? Yet how could she allow herself to be chained to this desolate place by a child she had never thought of—a child she didn't want? And chained she would be as she grew large and unwieldy. Then, when the child was finally born, there would be no escape for her. She might just as well be in prison. She would raise a child of shame, both of them shunned, viewed with disgust and condemnation by their neighbors. By then, her only escape would be death itself.

Jane had been kind to allow that she could stay as long as need be. But bile rose up in Terese's throat as she tried to imagine living out her life in the Claddagh, with its suffocating rules and strange customs, while she went on working for the poor, twisted Jane—who had more than enough of her own troubles.

She stopped trembling and drew a ragged breath. She could not, would not, consign herself to such a life! And what about the babe growing inside her? Would it thank her for giving it life under such circumstances? Better for it to never see the light of day than to be chained to a life of utter hopelessness.

But the question remained, could she do such a thing? Could she actually do away with her own child?

Over and over she argued the same thoughts until she finally convinced herself that she had found the solution, the best solution—the *only* solution—both for herself and for the child. She would go into Galway day after tomorrow. Tomorrow Jane would give her her week's wages, and she would have a bit extra to take with her. The thought of using her hard-earned money for anything besides passage to America made her stomach wrench, but there would *never* be a passage to America if she did not take care of the unborn child.

Terese went on planning. It occurred to her that if she could find a place in the city where women entertained men for money, she would almost certainly be able to find someone who knew how to take care of such things.

Best to get it over and done with right away, before anyone else learned of her situation and tongues began to wag. Before Brady came back . . . if indeed he *did* come back. Somehow Terese knew he would not take such news cheerfully. It might change everything between them. He might even think she had done it deliberately, in hopes of binding him to her.

She almost managed a bitter smile at the thought. Small chance of that. If anything, a babe might serve to drive him away forever!

Then she thought of Jane and wondered if she could possibly accomplish the act without her knowing. Later, she could pretend that she had lost the child, and Jane would never need to know the truth.

For a moment, Terese realized the route her thoughts had taken, the web of deception that was already drawing her in, deeper and deeper. Scalding rage and self-disgust at her own stupidity almost choked her. She felt sick and even a little frightened. Sick of herself, of the folly—her mother would have called it *sin,* but it was not Terese's word—that had led her to the untenable place in which she found herself. And she was frightened that whatever she did, she would have to go through it alone.

But then she remembered her choices, the life she would lead if she did *not* get rid of the child—and she made her decision.

It *was* her decision to make, after all. It was her life, and no one else could tell her what was wrong or right. No one.

She squeezed her eyes closed, as if to shut out the image of her mother's hollow-eyed, mournful face.

"I'm sorry," she whispered into the darkness, thinking of her mother but bringing a hand to her belly.

I'm sorry. . . .

33

Storm in the Heart

The conscience still speaks,
But the heart has grown deaf.

AUTHOR UNKNOWN

The next day, a horrendous rainstorm broke the heat wave's stranglehold on the countryside. Thunder, lightning, and torrential rain hounded Brady all across Limerick, on through Clare, and the rest of the way into Galway. The coach got stuck in mud outside Athenry, and Brady—the only passenger left after two merchants got off at Ennis—had to help the driver dislodge the wheels so they could continue.

He spent the rest of the journey huddled inside the coach, chilled and growing increasingly irritable. He had hoped to reach Galway while it was still early enough to visit the Claddagh, but that seemed unlikely now. At least he had thought to arrange rooms with Mrs. Hannafin in advance. He could go right to his lodgings, have a hot bath, and then have some supper. If not this evening, then tomorrow he would get up early and go straight to the Claddagh, first thing.

He was looking forward to seeing Terese, though he hoped her welcome would be warmer than her farewell. He thought of Roweena. His pulse quickened, and he realized that he was even more anxious to see her than to see Terese.

Best not to analyze the implications of *that*, he decided.

He almost wished the intimacy with Terese had never happened. He suspected that if the relationship continued, she would begin to press him more and more for some sort of commitment—a commitment he was unwilling to give, especially in light of his conflicting feelings for both her and Roweena.

He had also begun to feel increasingly guilty that he hadn't told Terese the whole truth about himself and what he was doing in Ireland. Knowing what he did about her almost obsessive desire to go to America, he supposed he ought to be thoroughly ashamed of himself. Her dream of leaving Ireland for a new life in the States was the most important thing in the world to her, yet by her own admission, she still had a ways to go before she'd be able to pay her passage. He had the power to make her dream a reality but had deliberately withheld any hint of that fact.

By doing so, he might just as well have been lying to her all along. His deception had been deliberate, calculated for the most selfish of reasons.

He was using her.

Brady shivered inside his wet clothes, then leaned his head against the seat in an attempt to doze. But if he thought that by closing his eyes he could shut out the wave of self-reproach rising in him, he was wrong. Lately he found himself unable to think of Terese without an accompanying slam of shame. He was beginning to wonder if he should just come clean with her. Tell her the whole truth, and let her choose—stay in Ireland *with* him, or go to the States *without* him.

Brady was of no mind to go back to New York. Certainly not yet, possibly not for a long time. In a few short months, Ireland had become home to him. He had never expected to fall in love with an entire land and its people, but that was exactly what had happened. Every time he seriously contemplated his return to the States, he ended up rejecting the idea altogether.

He thought he could drag out Jack's assignment for quite an extended period yet. Eventually, of course, it would end, and at that point Jack would insist that he come home. But that was a distant tomorrow, and he refused to worry about it now.

He *did* worry about Terese, though. He had no illusions about the future of their relationship. With her uncommon beauty, her passion, and her mercurial spirit, Terese was more desirable than many of the more mature women he had known. Certainly, she was never boring. He found her fascinating, exciting, and he held a deep affection for her. But he wasn't in love with her, at least not in the way he thought he would have to be before he could consider a more serious commitment—like marriage.

The truth was that Brady didn't always trust his own emotions. As Jack was fond of pointing out, he could be deplorably irresponsible where women were concerned. Try as he might, he couldn't imagine himself married. Even if his wanderlust—and his other lusts—should one day wane, he still couldn't envision himself loving any one woman enough to spend the rest of his life with her.

A fleeting, luminous thought of Roweena suddenly impressed itself on his mind, and he started, catching his breath. Just then an explosion of thunder rocked the coach, and the storm renewed itself with a furious downpour and a frenzied dance of lightning. The noise was deafening, the wild display outside the coach almost frightening, but Brady was virtually numb to everything except the memory of another wild storm and the dark-haired fawn of a girl he had met that night.

Roweena . . .

In that moment, he decided that he *could* let Terese go, that indeed it would probably be best to do just that, for both their sakes. He drew in a long breath, almost smiling as he felt his guilt start to break up and give way to a more familiar, comfortable sense of well-being.

That behind him, he dug down in his leather satchel for the most recent letter from Jack. It had arrived yesterday, but in the flurry of activity before leaving, he hadn't taken time to read it. He slit it open now with his pocketknife, squinting in the dim light to make out his brother's scrawl.

There was mention of the Madden children and a reminder to Brady that he should advise Jack as to the date of their departure. Apparently, a Mrs. Samantha Harte would be directing the children's settlement once they arrived in the States. It seemed that Mrs. Harte, in addition to being employed as a part-time proofreader with the *Vanguard,* also worked with one of the city's immigrant societies. Jack went on about the woman for two or three more lines, and Brady smiled at the thought of Jack combining forces with some long-nosed charity worker. Not exactly his brother's usual taste in women.

He went on reading, bringing the pages closer to his face as the road wound through a stretch of low-hanging trees, blocking even more light from the coach's interior. Jack had penned his usual admonishments regarding "responsibilities," "extravagance," and "self-discipline," but Brady gave these only a cursory glance along with the next few lines, which had to do with circulation figures and news about the city.

He was on the last page, scanning it quickly, when a name suddenly seemed to leap out at him. He stared at the words, frowned, then went back to the beginning of the paragraph.

I CAN'T RECALL WHETHER I'VE TOLD YOU ABOUT MY NEW DRIVER, CAVAN SHERIDAN, OR NOT. ACTUALLY, HE'S NOT GOING TO BE MY

DRIVER FOR LONG. I'VE FOUND HIM TO HAVE A NOSE FOR THE NEWS
AND MORE THAN HIS SHARE OF GOOD WRITING INSTINCTS—AS WELL AS
AMBITION. THAT BEING THE CASE, I WILL PROBABLY BE PUTTING HIM
ON THE PAPER AS A CUB REPORTER SOON.

Cavan Sheridan. For a long moment, Brady's gaze locked on the
words, his frown deepening. It couldn't be. It would be too much of
a coincidence by far. But he distinctly remembered Terese calling
her brother . . . *Cavan.*

He dragged his gaze away from the name and, holding his breath,
went on, his eyes racing over the words that followed.

SHERIDAN IS ACTUALLY THE BRIGHT YOUNG FELLOW WHO THOUGHT UP
THE IDEA OF "PERSONALIZING" THE STORIES BY FEATURING A NUMBER
OF INDIVIDUALS AND BRINGING THEM TO THE STATES. HE'S AS CLEVER
AS A LOAN SHARK, THOUGH OF VASTLY HIGHER PRINCIPLES, I'M HAPPY
TO SAY. GIVEN THE LAD'S NATURAL ABILITY AND AMBITION, YOU'D
BEST NOT STAY TOO LONG OVER THERE, LITTLE BROTHER, OR I MAY
END UP GIVING SHERIDAN *YOUR* JOB AS WELL.

Brady was not amused as he read on:

SHERIDAN HAS A SISTER OVER THERE, BY THE WAY, AND I PROMISED
HIM I WOULD MENTION HER TO YOU. HE THINKS THE GIRL MIGHT HAVE
BEEN CAUGHT UP IN THE BIG WINDSTORM BACK IN JANUARY AND IS
GREATLY CONCERNED ABOUT HER. THEY'RE ISLAND PEOPLE—
INISHMORE, TO BE EXACT—SO IT'S NOT LIKELY YOU'D BE RUNNING
ACROSS HER NOW, TRAVELING AS YOU ARE IN A DIFFERENT DIRECTION.
BUT I DID TELL HIM I WOULD WRITE YOU ABOUT HER. THE GIRL'S
NAME IS TERESE, AND SHE WOULD BE ABOUT SEVENTEEN. SHERIDAN
HASN'T SEEN HER SINCE HE LEFT FOR THE STATES SEVERAL YEARS AGO,
SO ANYTHING COULD HAVE HAPPENED TO HER BY NOW. IT WOULD BE
GRAND IF BY SOME STROKE OF LUCK WE COULD LOCATE HER, THOUGH,
FOR THE LAD'S LOST HIS ENTIRE FAMILY EXCEPT FOR THE GIRL.

Brady went no farther, other than to retrace what he had already
read. *Terese's brother—working for Jack?* How such a thing could
be was beyond all understanding, but there it was, in black and white,
so to speak. He sagged back against the seat, the letter still dangling
from his hand. His mind was spinning. He felt almost as if a stone
had grazed his head and stunned him badly.

Terese would be wild once she heard. He would have all he could do to stop her from jumping onto the next ship bound for the States.

Not that she need learn of this right away, of course. Certainly, he would tell her, but first there were a few other things that must be taken into account.

It occurred to him that if he *were* to make Terese the subject of one of his articles and arrange for her passage to the States, it wouldn't do for her brother to know of their relationship—just in case he happened to be the vengeful sort.

And under no circumstances should Jack know. Jack was no saint, that much was certain, but he could be surprisingly old-world when it came to women. Given the fact that Terese was only seventeen—and the sister of one of his employees—he would be absolutely livid at the thought that Brady had been involved with her. No doubt he would accuse Brady of taking advantage.

No, he would have to give this considerable thought before breaking it to Terese. He wanted to make absolutely certain that he had his own plans clearly in mind before making any plans for her.

※

When Jane handed her her weekly wages, Terese drew a deep breath and said, "Could you be doing without me for the afternoon tomorrow, Jane? I'll be going into the city, if you can spare me."

Jane's eyes were sharp and searching, her reply a long time in coming. "I suppose you've earned an afternoon for yourself. Though sure you won't be wanting to go if this storm doesn't let up, I expect."

Terese had half expected a fuss, for Jane was not inclined to grant her time away. Her employer's easy assent caught her off guard and only increased her nagging guilt. "No . . . no, I'll not be going in such weather as this. But I'm needing some things . . . some items for myself . . . and I thought I might . . . see a performance or the like, if any of the players are about." She paused, then added, "I might be gone until late evening, you see. You're certain you don't mind?"

She shrank inwardly as Jane went on regarding her with that peculiar look, her eyes like glistening stones in the dim afternoon light.

Again, Jane delayed her reply. At last she looked away, toward the window. Her tone was dull and neutral when she finally spoke. "Do what you must, girl."

Still, Terese hesitated. Something inside her seemed to be waiting for Jane to voice an objection, a more typically sour refusal. When it did not happen, she could think of nothing else to say and went to stand in the open doorway to watch the storm.

The rain blowing in felt cool and welcome after the closeness of the past few days. Water overran the ditch beyond the cottage, splashing and gurgling as it flowed into the lane. The wind was coming heavier now, the thunder stronger, too, and the ground seemed to shake beneath the cottage. The noise was fierce, blasting at Terese like an angry assault.

She hugged her arms tightly to her as she stood staring outside. Her sense of approaching doom had not dissipated since last night. To the contrary, she felt more anxious and apprehensive now than ever. Yet, when a jagged bolt of lightning slashed the front yard as if to set the grounds ablaze, she scarcely flinched, for the storm taking place around her was no more violent than the tempest raging within.

34

An Unexpected
Welcome

I looked for the lamp which, she told me,
Should shine when her pilgrim returned,
But though darkness began to enfold me,
No lamp from the battlements burned!

THOMAS MOORE

Brady had never been a particularly late sleeper, but, exhausted from his journey, he slept until after ten the next morning. By the time he'd shaved and had breakfast, it was nearly noon.

He took the cobbled streets at a brisk pace, reaching the quay in minutes. The rainstorm had cleared and freshened the air, and the morning was bright and sharp, if somewhat cool for this time of day.

The unmistakable smell of the fisheries permeated the quay, along with the pungent aromas of salt and burning kelp. Some fishermen—large men for the most part—in their work shirts and coarse trousers, milled about the boats moored at the quay. They were a quiet lot, their cavernous eyes watchful as they worked and talked in low voices.

Two black-cassocked priests invoked the name of God in greeting and smiled as they passed, and Brady responded. A number of women in the familiar blue mantles and red skirts, bright kerchiefs bound around their heads, hurried to and from the markets. He saw half a dozen or more boys casting stones from rough-hewn slings—a sport for boys and men, but, in this remote quarter, also a mode of warfare known to be particularly treacherous.

Brady never entered the Claddagh without feeling as if he had stepped back into the Middle Ages. In most ways it was a pleasant, even an oddly comforting, sensation. The isolated colony was a place of bright colors and dark mysteries, a place steeped in superstition and religious ceremony. He had grown fond of it all, including the handsome, taciturn people. In the beginning they had eyed him with suspicious glances, but eventually some had begun to offer an occasional gesture of friendship.

Brady never forgot that he was an outsider here. Yet there had been times when he felt an inexplicable sense of belonging. There was an almost mystical quality that seemed to permeate the narrow lanes of the Claddagh, giving him the sensation of being able to step in and out of an entirely different way of life as if it were the most natural thing in the world.

He hesitated for a moment when he realized that he had turned not onto the lane leading to Jane Connolly's house and Terese but instead onto Gabriel's street. He thought about it, then went on, promising himself that he would stay only a few minutes. Just long enough to say hello and let them know he was back. Then he would go on to see Terese.

The decision made, his steps quickened even more in anticipation.

⚜

Gabriel saw him first. The door was standing open, and he had just finished his bowl of potatoes and was pushing away from the table when he looked out to see Brady Kane at the far end of the yard, turning onto the walk.

He darted a glance at Roweena, but she was washing dishes from the midday meal and had her back to him. Quickly, Gabriel started for the door, meaning to stop the American before he reached the house.

But wee Evie had spotted Brady, too. She came scurrying around the table, flapping her arms and crying his name. Roweena, apparently sensing the little one's movement, turned with a questioning look.

Gabriel blocked the child with his body and a stern word of warning, at the same time rapidly signing his words to Roweena. "I must speak with him alone today. I want the two of you to stay inside."

The child's face crumpled in disappointment. Roweena, too, who had already taken a step toward the door, stared at Gabriel in unconcealed bewilderment.

But Gabriel merely shook his head and lifted a restraining hand. "Stay inside, I said. I will explain later."

With that, he stepped outside into the yard, closing the door firmly behind him. The girls' disappointment weighed heavily upon him, but he would not relent. Better that they should be disappointed now than later, he told himself.

⁂

At the look on Gabriel's face, Brady lost his smile of anticipation. The big fisherman stood in the middle of the yard, legs astride, his brawny arms crossed over his chest

Puzzled, Brady looked beyond the big man's rigid posture to the house. But the door was closed, with no sign of either Roweena or Evie anywhere.

By now, Brady suspected that something was going on, and whatever it might be, it wasn't good. The big man's eyes were chips of blue ice, his expression stony and unreadable. Brady suddenly felt about as welcome as a leper.

"Gabriel . . . ," he said uncertainly, extending his hand.

If the other noticed the outstretched hand, he ignored it.

"So, you are back." It sounded less a statement than an accusation.

Thoroughly baffled, Brady slowly dropped his hand back to his side. "I am. And I couldn't be happier about it. I've missed . . . everyone." He made a weak attempt at small talk, but Gabriel seemed not in the least inclined to reciprocate.

"And Roweena and Evie—how are they?" Brady finally asked.

"They are both well. Have you been to Jane's yet?" Gabriel was watching him as if he already knew the answer.

"Jane's? No, not yet," Brady said, hating the fact that he felt like a schoolboy caught in some offense. "I was on my way there, as it happens, but I thought I'd just stop by and say hello." He paused long enough to take a breath. "Something wrong, Gabriel?"

The big fisherman's expression remained fixed. "I'll not be keeping you, then," he said, as if he hadn't heard the question. "You will want to be on your way."

Brady's puzzlement gave way to irritation. "You're not even going to ask me in, Gabriel? I had hoped to say hello to the girls."

"Not today, I think. You should go on to Jane's first."

It struck Brady then that something had happened to Terese. "What is it? Terese—"

Gabriel's eyes sparked blue fire. "You need to go to her. Your place is there with her, not here." He turned and started walking back to the house.

For a moment, Brady could only stand and stare at the broad expanse of Gabriel's back as he walked away. Then, heart pounding, he swung around and took off down the yard, now intent on finding out for himself what exactly was going on.

⚜

"Are you sure?" he asked her again, feeling sicker by the minute. "You couldn't be mistaken?"

"It's been over two months now." Terese's tone was laced with accusation, as though he knew as well as she that her condition was indisputable.

She was watching him with a keen closeness, a kind of urgency, as if the entire direction of her life would be determined by his next words.

Had he not been so overwhelmed by the shock she had just handed him, Brady might have laughed at the idea that he could possibly utter anything even remotely meaningful at a time like this. He had all he could do not to turn and run.

He couldn't do that, of course. Instead he stood there, in the middle of Jane Connolly's yard, his mind reeling, his pulse pounding, as he tried to think of what to say. He had to say *something,* after all. Terese was clearly waiting.

He had begun to perspire, though the day was comfortably cool. His shirt clung to his back, and his collar felt wet and sticky around his neck. "Well—," he said, and then again, "well—this is quite . . . a surprise, isn't it?"

She stared at him, still waiting.

"I—I may need some time to take this in, T'reesie." He laughed, a harsh, dry sound that even to him sounded like the croak of an injured blackbird. "A man doesn't hear this sort of thing every day, you know. Why didn't you write? You might have warned me."

He suddenly felt defensive, meeting her accusing gaze with one of his own.

"'Tis not the sort of thing you put in a letter," she countered. "Besides . . . I wasn't certain . . . until recently."

Brady looked away, trying to think. He had known from the moment he walked into the house and saw Jane watching him like an ill-tempered gnome that trouble was afoot. And when Terese made no gesture of welcome but insisted that they go outside "to talk," the stone of dread sitting on his chest had grown heavier still.

She had provided him with no hint of what was to come, but once outside, simply turned to face him with the blunt pronouncement that she was going to have a child. *His* child. Had she pulled a gun on him and squeezed the trigger, she could not have shocked Brady more effectively.

He was still dazed, still fumbling to collect his wits. Somehow he had to deal with this. Not only for himself, but for Terese as well. She was looking to him for a solution. But where was he to find it?

"I—ah, you won't like my asking this, but I think I must," he ventured, his disgust with himself building even as he formed the words. "You're quite sure that it—that the child is mine? I mean—"

She hesitated only a second before rearing back and slapping him hard across the face. Stunned, Brady touched his hand to his burning cheek, suddenly wanting to strike back at her—to hurt her for the way she had complicated his life. Why couldn't she have been sensible and taken precautions?

His resentment cooled as quickly as it had flamed. He was being unfair, and he knew it. Terese was seventeen years old. She had spent her entire life on a remote island that, to hear her tell of it, must surely be even more primitive and backward than the Claddagh. He could hardly expect her to be sophisticated in such matters. The responsibility had been his, and he had been careless.

And this, then, was the consequence.

"I'm sorry," he said, meaning it. "That was uncalled for. I know you haven't been with anyone else." He went on, ignoring the murderous look she had turned on him. "Terese . . . I *am* sorry. Don't let's quarrel. That's not going to accomplish anything. We have to go somewhere private."

"Why?" she spat out. "So you can accuse me of being a harlot?"

Groping for patience, Brady reached for her hand. She backed away, her eyes still blazing.

"This won't accomplish anything," he repeated firmly. "Go inside and tell Jane that you're going with me to have a bite to eat. Make her understand that you are coming with me and she needn't argue matters."

He saw her uncertainty, saw the anger and pain she was obviously trying so hard to hide, and he felt like the worst kind of bounder. How had he forgotten how young she was? In the midst of his self-disgust, he suddenly wondered if she was well. The high color so common to her complexion had faded to an unhealthy pallor, and her eyes were deeply shadowed. She had gained a bit of weight—he supposed that was only to be expected—but the extra pounds did nothing to soften the sharpness of her features. Indeed, she seemed even more tightly strung than he remembered, with a look in her eyes that appeared almost feverish.

Finally she spoke. "I already have the afternoon off," she said grudgingly.

At his questioning look, she said, her tone still sullen, "I was going into the city anyway to make some purchases." She paused, studying him. "You're right. We must talk. I will go and tell Jane we are leaving."

Brady stood where he was, waiting for her to return. He rubbed a hand over the back of his neck, feeling for all the world as if he had stepped into someone else's bad dream. He hadn't the vaguest idea what he was going to say to her. Somehow he had to reassure her without making any sort of foolish commitment. No doubt she was hoping for marriage, but as far as he was concerned, marriage wasn't even an option. He would help her, even support her and the child if it came to that. But he wouldn't marry her, and he wasn't about to give her any false hopes to that effect.

He remembered then what he had been planning to do before Terese had stunned him with the news of the child. It struck him now that her condition needn't change anything. In fact, it might even prove the deciding factor in her decision. The *Vanguard* article—and the subsequent offer of immigration—would give her a chance at a whole new life. Surely she would see it for the opportunity it was.

The more he thought about it, the more sense it made. He would arrange her passage and set up a bank account for her in the States. Once there, no doubt this Mrs. Harte that Jack had mentioned would make any arrangements necessary to get her settled. She might even see to having the baby adopted, if that's what Terese wanted—and he had no doubt that she would. She could then get on with her life. As could he.

It would all work out, he told himself. She would listen to him—he would make her listen—and she would do the sensible thing.

35

A Plan for
the Future

One heart,
wounded and weary,
searches for the remnant of a dream.

CAVAN SHERIDAN,
FROM *WAYSIDE NOTES*

The small, out-of-the-way tavern where Brady had taken Terese was empty except for two elderly men seated at a corner table. The midday trade was gone by now, and it was too early as yet for the shopkeepers to be filing in.

Brady had ordered meat pies and tea for both of them, but Terese had scarcely touched hers. Although they had been talking for over an hour, she was only now beginning to grasp the full significance of what she'd heard. "Why didn't you tell me the truth about yourself before now?" she asked him, not for the first time.

He sighed and swiped a hand through his hair. Terese knew him well enough by now to know he was growing impatient with her. She didn't care in the least. He had deceived her from the beginning. He owed her an explanation, no matter how long it took, and she meant to have it.

"I've already explained that, Terese. Jack has drilled it into me over the years that I shouldn't tell anyone *anything*. Especially women. You have to understand that my brother is the consummate cynic," he said with a thin smile. "Jack is convinced that every woman who gives him a second look—or gives *me* a second look, for that matter—is only interested in his money. And to tell you the truth, he's had a few experiences that would seem to prove his point.'' He paused. ''Let's just say that he's impressed it upon me to keep my mouth shut about who I am—and who *he* is. Jack . . . is a very wealthy, powerful man, and it's probably not in my best interest to go around boasting that I'm his brother.''

Terese twisted her mouth. ''So that's the way of it, then? You think if a woman knows about your family's money, she'll try to trap you into marriage?''

He gave her a dark look, and she knew she had made him angry. Again, she didn't care.

''It's not as if I actually *lied* to you,'' he said, his tone defensive.

Terese laughed, a harsh, ugly sound even to her. ''Oh, indeed not. You simply neglected to tell me the truth. How could you have deceived me like that, Brady? Knowing as you do how desperate I am to get out of Ireland, to go across—yet you kept your brother's entire scheme to yourself? How *could* you?''

He leaned back, watching her. ''I really was going to tell you everything when I came back from Limerick, Terese. If you don't believe me, I'll show you the notes I've already made for the next article—the article about *you*. And I had every intention of arranging for your passage to the States as soon as possible—if that's what you want, that is. Now that's the truth, whether you believe me or not.''

''Why *should* I believe you?'' Terese shot back, forgetting herself and raising her voice to the point that the men in the corner slanted curious looks in their direction. She leaned toward Brady, still fiercely angry but lowering her voice. ''How do I know you're not lying to me *now?*''

He frowned. ''What would be the point, Terese? Be reasonable. I'm trying to help you—in case you haven't noticed.''

''So you're going to post my shame in a newspaper for an entire city to read? Ship me to America like a useless piece of baggage and pass me off to some . . . immigrant society as a charity case so *you* can get on with your life?''

The quick look he gave her told Terese she'd hit a nerve. She realized then that he had worked all this out in his mind before he'd even talked with her. She wanted to slap him again. Had they been alone, she probably would have.

''You are *despicable!*'' She hurled the words at him, pushing away from the table so violently that she almost knocked the chair to the floor.

He reached across the table and caught her wrist. "Terese, listen to me!"

She tried to pull free of him, but he held her. *"Listen* to me, I said! Neither of us counted on this happening, but it *did.* I'm trying to take responsibility for it, but you're going to have to meet me halfway. Just don't expect me to act as if I'm happy about it—that would only be more pretense."

Again Terese tried to yank her hand away, but he refused to let her go. Finally, grudgingly, she sank back into the chair.

"Terese," he said, still holding onto her wrist, "I didn't mislead you about my feelings for you—I *do* care about you. And if you want to stay in Ireland, I'll look after you—and the child. You won't lack for anything. But I'm not going to marry you." He stopped, regarding her with a speculative look. "Besides, I was under the impression that the most important thing to you was getting to the States. If that's still what you want, I can make it possible. The baby is . . . a complication," he said, not meeting her eyes. "But it's not the end of the world."

"A *complication?*" she hissed, incredulity surging within her. Again she half rose from her chair. Inflamed now, she began to harangue him in the Irish, not caring that he would understand nothing of what she said.

"Stop it!" His voice rang in the room. The tavern keeper and the two men across the way paused to stare.

Terese, trembling with anger and disillusionment, was too upset to be embarrassed. Brady glanced around, as if only then mindful of his outburst. A shock of hair had fallen over one eye, and his face had turned a deep, dark crimson, but this time when he spoke he dropped the tone of his voice so that only Terese could hear him.

"Sit down and listen to me." He groped at her forearm, and the strength of his grasp burned her skin. "I haven't told you everything yet. There's more, and it's something you need to know. Now stop acting like a spoiled child—I think you'll want to hear this."

Terese glared at him, wanting to strike out at him again, hard— hard enough to make his head ring. She wanted to scream at him, punish him.

More than anything else, she wanted to weep.

Refusing to look at him, she slid dejectedly down onto the chair, wondering what more he could possibly tell her. She felt the pain of his deceit—his betrayal—bitterly, like a knife in her heart. She did not think he could hurt her any more than he already had. Certainly, he could not help her.

Finally, he released her arm, gesturing with one hand that she should wait. As Terese watched, he withdrew an envelope from his shirt pocket, unfolded what appeared to be a letter, and, after a slight hesitation, slid it across the table to her.

※※◎※◆

"I didn't know about this, Terese," he said. "I swear to you, I only learned about it yesterday."

She looked at him, then at the letter, but made no move to touch it.

Brady inclined his head toward the letter. "It's from Jack—my brother. It seems that *your* brother, Cavan, has been working for him—for some time now, apparently. Read it."

Her head snapped up, and Brady could see that his words hadn't registered. She stared at him in bewilderment.

"Read it," he repeated, again gesturing toward the letter. "Apparently, Jack hired your brother some time ago as his driver. Now he's talking about putting him on staff at the newspaper."

She frowned. "What are you talking about? Cavan is in Pennsylvania with our uncle Tibbot. He's not in New York."

Brady shook his head. "I don't know how long it's been since you've heard from him, but if you'll just read the letter, you'll see what I'm talking about."

He watched her closely as she picked up the letter and began to read. After a moment, she uttered a choked sound of astonishment, bringing one hand to her mouth. She looked at Brady, her eyes wide, before returning to the letter.

He could tell that she was reading the same words over and over again. Once she opened her mouth as if to cry out, but no sound escaped her. She must have spent a good five minutes or more going over the same page before finally meeting Brady's eyes across the table. "It *is* Cavan," she said. Her voice sounded as if she were strangling. "It *must* be! Your brother—how else could he know my name? You never told him . . . about us?"

Brady shook his head. "No. Jack could have learned your name only from your brother." He saw the pages of the letter trembling in her hand, the tears glistening in her eyes. His heart wrenched, and self-loathing poured through him like a poison.

"*Cavan.*" The name was like a prayer on her lips, and Brady feared she might dissolve into a fit of weeping.

Her hand, still shaking, went to her throat. "You truly didn't know?"

"I didn't, Terese—honestly, I didn't. Jack has never mentioned your brother's name until now. I would have told you if he had. I wouldn't have kept something like that from you."

They stared at each other in silence. Her look was openly skeptical, her eyes smoking, and Brady could almost see the war of emotions going on in her.

She swallowed with obvious difficulty. When she finally spoke, her voice was thick and unnatural. "To think that all this time, Cavan has been . . . there, with your brother. And I didn't even know. . . ." She shook her head slowly, as if to clear her mind. "He wouldn't know where I am . . . or what has happened. . . . He doesn't know anything about me—"

She broke off, looking positively stricken. Brady reached across the table to take her hand, and she made no attempt to pull away. "Terese . . . do you see what this means? If you want to go—if you want to leave Ireland and go to New York, your brother will be there. You'll have family waiting."

Slowly, deliberately, she withdrew her hand from his, staring at her fingers as if they might have become diseased. When she looked up at Brady, her eyes appeared almost feverish. "Do you think I could face him now? That I could allow him to find out—what I've done?" Her hand dropped to her stomach. "Cavan will still remember me as a child! A little girl running after him. I couldn't face him after what I've—"

She stopped, an anguished cry exploding from her as she hurled the letter across the table at Brady. She stumbled to her feet, wild-eyed, her face splotched with color.

Brady jumped up, reaching for her. She turned on him, shrieking, "Leave me alone!"

Indifferent now to the curious looks of the others in the room, Brady lurched around the table and caught her by the shoulders. "He's your brother, Terese! He's not going to condemn you—"

She brought her arm up in an arc, violently shoving him away. "Shut up! You don't know! You don't know *anything!* And you don't care!" She put her face in her hands. "Oh, God in heaven, how could I have been so blind, so foolish? I've let you ruin me! You've ruined everything! Now I'll never get away from this infernal place! I'll never be able to face Cavan, not after this! I'll rot here on this ugly old island, me and the child—*your* child!"

Brady finally managed to grasp her shoulders and bring her about to face him. She was on the edge of hysteria, and he shook her, trying to bring her to her senses. "Terese! Stop it! Listen to me! Sit down and just *listen* to me. I have a plan. Everything is going to be all right, but you have to do what I tell you.''

She had gone pale, staring at him mutely, as limp and lifeless under his hands as a rag doll. Brady coaxed her back to the chair and pulled up beside her. "All right," he said, careful to keep his tone soothing, "here's what you'll do."

❧❦❧

Over an hour later, they parted, Brady promising to arrange her passage the next day. "You'll need to go soon, if you're going," he said, not quite meeting her eyes. "While you're able to travel."

Terese merely nodded.

"You're sure you don't want me to walk you back to Jane's?" he asked.

Terese shook her head. The familiar tenderness in his gaze no longer moved her. She was exhausted, drained. She wanted nothing more than to be alone, so she could think. She had decisions to make, no matter how loath she was to make them.

She had listened to him, had agreed with him because there seemed to be no alternative. But as she watched him walk away, toward the bridge, she wondered if she could really go through with this. Brady had been insistent that it would work, that indeed it was the best way, perhaps the only way.

She had to hand it to him—he was clever. Smart. Quick-witted. A great schemer, Brady was. He had made it all sound so reasonable, so easy, back there in the tavern. . . .

"Your brother needn't know about us. In fact, he *can't* know," he had insisted. "If Cavan finds out, then he'll be sure to tell Jack. And I'm afraid my brother won't take it too kindly. Jack's a hard man. He can be as mean as a snake when he's riled. Oddly enough, he tends to be a bit old-fashioned about things like this. If he were to find out that you and I—that the child is mine—"

He broke off, searching her face. "Promise me you won't tell anyone that the child is mine, Terese. For both our sakes. Jack may be my brother, but he also pays my salary. I can't afford to have him cutting me loose in a fit of temper, especially if I'm going to help you and the child."

Disgust washed over Terese in that moment as she realized what she was seeing in his eyes. He was *afraid*. If not actually afraid of his brother, then afraid of the power the man held over him—afraid that he might sever the purse strings. And Brady, she thought grimly, would not enjoy being poor. Not at all.

"He might even fire your brother as well," Brady went on to warn her. "You must understand the importance of this."

Terese thought she understood much more than Brady would have guessed.

He laid it out before her then, the plan he'd concocted. She would say she had been attacked, he explained, and that her pregnancy was the result of that attack. He would set everything in place with the news article. The attack, he assured her, would evoke even more sympathy from Jack and the *Vanguard*'s readers.

Terese sat there, saying nothing as she listened to him arranging her life for her—fashioning her *lies* for her. The peculiar thing was that she felt nothing the entire time he was coaching her.

Strange, in light of what he had meant to her—and not so long ago—that she could feel so little for him now. Only contempt.

At the end, he tried to encourage her. "You know, you've come through an unbelievable succession of tragedies, Terese. Most people, if they'd gone through everything that you have, would be sitting around whining and feeling sorry for themselves. But not you. You're a survivor." He paused. "Whether you believe this or not, Terese, I've always admired you for your pluck. You're stronger than you know."

His flattering words had given Terese no sense of satisfaction. Perhaps when the shock of this day had worn thin, she would again come to care about what he thought of her. But at this moment, it meant nothing.

Moreover, in spite of the neatly arranged plan he had devised for her, Terese wasn't convinced that she ought to go through with it. There might be an alternative.

The thoughts she'd had during the night now resurfaced. The prospect of going to America had seemed far more desirable when there had been no child to consider. She could have gone unencumbered. There would have been no need for subterfuge and secrets. She wouldn't have had to lie to Cavan just to face him. Now everything was so complicated.

She shuddered, remembering how angry she had been with Brady for calling the baby a *complication*. But how could she possibly make such a drastic change in her life while carrying a child? And she must not forget that she would have to raise that child. Brady might make all sorts of promises to help, but she knew she couldn't trust him. And as for his rich and powerful brother, if Jack Kane was truly the hard man Brady made him out to be, it would be folly itself to rely on *him*.

Was she really willing to gamble her entire future on a wastrel like Brady or, more foolish still, a complete stranger like his brother? Hadn't she learned by now that she dared not trust anyone but herself?

Even Cavan, once he learned of her condition, might turn his back on her. He had abandoned her once, when she had been only a child. Who was to say he wouldn't do it again?

Without realizing it, she had begun to walk. She glanced around once, then quickened her pace. An urgency had begun to build in her, a need to act now, before she lost her nerve.

She had already decided that she would let the Kanes pay her passage to America. That seemed only fair, after the way Brady had deceived her. That meant she would be able to keep her meager savings either to give her a start in the States . . . or to do something about the child.

Surely the latter made more sense. Without the burden of the child, she would be free to live life *her* way. She would not have to depend on the Kanes or anyone else—not even Cavan. She would be responsible only for herself. She could make her own way.

Just as she always had.

36

Confrontation with Evil

I see black dragons mount the sky,
I see earth yawn beneath my feet—
JAMES CLARENCE MANGAN

Terese had taken care to make herself as inconspicuous as possible
for her excursion into this shameful, secret district of Galway, knot-
ting her hair at the nape of her neck and then tying a kerchief over
her head. Even though she was not known in the city, she would hate
to have anyone recognize her in this infamous place.

The afternoon had turned gloomy, with lowering clouds threatening another downpour like that of the previous day; consequently,
the narrow streets were not as crowded as they might have been
otherwise. She found the area she was looking for with little difficulty, but it was another matter entirely to locate the specific place
she needed to go. Once inside the district, she began to ask questions,
which only invited the attentions of some of the rough sailors and
other men lurking about. One great, filthy ape put his hands on her,
but Terese turned on him with such viciousness that he backed off
with a sneer and a shrug. Slatternly women stared at her with open
resentment. Some jeered or hurled coarse epithets as she passed by,
and one even stopped her with the abhorrent suggestion that she
should join their ranks.

Finally, she gained a civil answer without mockery, this from a
weary-looking harlot who appeared to be well past the years when a
man would be likely to pay for her favors. The woman—who called

herself Letty—appeared brittle and even fragile beneath the layers of face paint and tinted hair. She looked at Terese with a knowing sadness and told her of a place on the fringes of this sinful sector where she might find the solution to her problem.

"Ask for Gypsy Sorcha," she said, giving a reassuring pat to the stained red bodice of her dress. "Be sure to tell her Letty sent you. And never mind her face, love. Most get used to it after a time." Her faded blue eyes studied Terese for a moment. "You know you'll need money."

Terese nodded. She had her money pouch with her, as she always did, ever since her aunt had robbed her of her meager savings.

"Use your wits next time, love," Letty warned her, her powdered face cracking with weblike wrinkles as she sent Terese on her way. "You'll not be wanting to do this more than once, I'll wager."

It had begun to sprinkle rain by the time Terese came upon the garishly painted wagon squatting in the rear of a V-shaped pocket of dilapidated buildings.

She was shaking all over. As she approached, she felt the hair at the back of her neck rising. The street reeked with the smell of animal dung and garbage. From the front of the buildings came the sound of bottles breaking and loud, raucous laughter. But here in the back, there was no one to be seen.

The door to the wagon was standing open, but she knocked on the frame anyway, then stepped back. After a moment, the ugliest old woman Terese had ever seen appeared in the doorway. She was encased in what appeared to be several layers of multicolored fabrics, the topmost soiled and faded in several places. Some sort of headdress—a kind of turban—framed her jowly face. Strands of wet-looking gray hair tangled across her forehead. Terese tried not to stare at the sizable warts protruding from the old woman's chin or the angry red scar that trailed the right side of her face, from her forehead to her jawbone.

"Well, what is it, then?"

Terese was shaking even more treacherously now and felt almost lightheaded. "I—I am here to see Gypsy Sorcha."

"And now that you've seen me?" snapped the hideous old woman. "What d'you want, girl?"

Before Terese could answer, the other twisted her lip, saying, "So, it's *that* business, is it? Have you money?"

Terese's mouth tasted like seawater. "I—yes, I have money."

"Get yourself in here, then, and let's get on with it." The woman turned and went back inside without waiting to see if Terese would follow.

The first thing Terese saw when she stepped into the gloom-veiled interior was the soiled bed on the opposite wall of the wagon. She did not want to think what the dark stains might be or how the randomly tossed blanket might smell.

"Get out of your clothes and lie down over there," ordered the old crone, pointing to the bed and taking several sharp-looking utensils out of a basket.

Terese turned her gaze to the sagging bed, taking in the table nearby, which held an assortment of empty liquor bottles and a stack of unfolded rags. Again she looked at the old woman, who was still bent over the basket, muttering to herself as she rifled through its contents and came up empty-handed.

The stink of waste and the squalor of her surroundings suddenly struck Terese like a wall of floodwater. She felt the floor of the wagon tilt beneath her. Her legs threatened to buckle. She uttered a moan of despair, then went stumbling from the wagon into the street, looking for a place to be sick.

Behind her, the old gypsy woman shrieked an oath, then after a moment went back inside.

Terese fell to her knees on the cobbled street, heaving. It was raining hard by now, and as she huddled there, sick, her body racked with violent weeping, she welcomed the drenching rain like a blessing. She was desperate to rid herself of the sights and smells of this sordid place. She felt as if the stench of evil was all over her, and she willed the rain to wash away the filth from her body . . . and from her soul.

After a long time, she finally raised her head. Still on her knees, hunched over the street, she found herself looking down into a pool of water. She stared for a long time at the reflection of her face. She still felt dirty . . . contaminated . . . as if the filth, the wickedness of this place and the old gypsy woman had somehow mired her. In that instant, the terrible reality of where she was . . . and what she had been about to do . . . stared back at her, and she saw with dreadful clarity her own debasement.

She had no idea how long she stayed there, hunched and soaking, looking into the pool of rainwater as if it were the mirror of her soul, until at last she found the strength to get to her feet and start toward home. She staggered, stumbling over the rain-slicked streets, fighting her way past the gauntlet of questions pressing in on her, driving herself to leave the horror and the pain of the past behind her.

For the first time in what seemed an *endless* time, she prayed. She prayed to a God who, for all she knew, might not condescend to hear the prayers of a sinful girl like herself. She prayed out of the depths of fear and desperation and disbelief. She prayed for a forgiveness she was no longer sure she even believed in, a mercy that would wash away the stains from her soul even as the drenching rain washed away the reek of corruption still clinging to her body.

And for the first time since she had learned of the child she carried, she sensed—even in the frenzied confusion of her thoughts and the black uncertainty of her future—a purpose, a reason to look forward and not turn back.

37

Of Lawyers
and Lawsuits

The Pharisee's cant goes up for peace,
But the cries of his victims never cease.

JOHN BOYLE O'REILLY

NEW YORK CITY

New York City sweltered in August. No air moved between the buildings. No rain fell to ease the blistering heat. The days ended with no relief from the same hot stickiness with which they had begun.

Jack Kane, on his way to the first of two calls, slung his suit coat over his shoulder, making a face at the vicious stench given off by the garbage heaped in the streets and gutters. Even the dogs seemed loath to forage on a day like this. The rubbish piles in the street didn't bother Jack so much in the winter; frozen, they didn't stink. But in the summer he felt that the stuff was a veritable affront to a city that considered itself one of the leading commerce centers of the world.

Some commerce center, that couldn't even manage its own garbage removal.

Jack had decided against taking a cab, thinking the heat would be more tolerable if he walked. But after only a few minutes of winding his way between clattering carriages, brewery drays, and freight wagons—and the foul clods of droppings deposited by the countless horses drawing these vehicles—he was already questioning his judgment. He was drenched with perspiration, his shirt glued to his back and his hair as wet as if he'd just stepped out of the bath. By the time he reached the offices of Foxworth & McCann, he would have traded his gold watch for a jug of cold water. But at least he'd arrived free of horse dung on his shoes and had managed to avoid being run over—neither of which came easily in New York these days.

There was nothing pretentious about the painted sign in front of the building where Foxworth & McCann maintained one of the most profitable law offices in the city. They occupied only the ground floor of a four-story building in one of the seedier parts of Broadway. Supposedly, a couple of rooms on the second floor were used for storage, but Jack suspected that this "storage area" offered refuge to some of the firm's more unsavory clients until their attorneys could persuade them to turn themselves in to the authorities.

Jack stopped inside the vestibule to mop his face and hair with a handkerchief before entering the waiting room. It was late enough that there were no other clients around, and Harry Ogg, the firm's fussy, pompous clerk, wasn't at his usual place of command at the front desk.

Of course, this wasn't exactly the type of office in which respectable clients sat around waiting to keep appointments. In reality, *respectable* clients were probably at a minimum at Foxworth & McCann. The firm was known to deal with any number of individuals whom the more prestigious law firms declined to represent—the criminal underworld, crooked politicos, husbands of straying wives, and the occasional "gentleman" who compromised his reputation by the inability to control his passions.

No doubt it was this flourishing, corrupt clientele that largely accounted for the firm's prosperity. Not that Foxworth & McCann limited themselves entirely to the disreputable element. They also looked out for the interests of selected theater performers, artists, and other members of the less illustrious professions.

Since journalists were usually considered suspect—if not actually vulgar, at least common—by the old guard, Foxworth & McCann also attracted more than their share of newspapermen, Jack Kane among them.

It never failed to amuse Jack that some of the wealthiest, most influential men in the city—in the state, for that matter—were summarily rejected by the upper classes. Without a distinguished genealogy, either through his own family or his wife's, a man could acquire one fortune after another and still be held in contempt.

To be descended from an affluent, upper-crust family—an *old* family—automatically stamped a man as a person of breeding, character, and unquestionable morality. That was another source of amusement for Jack, since he had unearthed substantial evidence to the contrary. He knew for a fact that some of the most sordid and outright criminal establishments in New York were owned by a number of the city's more eminent natives.

Being Irish, of course—even if obscenely wealthy—automatically disqualified one from any sort of estimable position in society. Unlike some, however, Jack had never coveted such standing, nor did he resent the inequity. To the contrary, he took a certain perverse satisfaction in the knowledge that he could rankle most of the uptown swells simply by being what he was: an Irishman who had a great deal more money than they did—and considerably more power in city and state affairs. When the occasion warranted, he didn't hesitate to flaunt his Irishness or his influence. He was equally comfortable with both and rather enjoyed the awareness that others weren't.

The door to Avery Foxworth's office was open, and Jack wasn't surprised to find the attorney waiting for him. Foxworth stood when Jack entered, not from any sense of deference, certainly—Avery Foxworth deferred to no man—but more from the courtesy that so often seemed at odds with the rest of his character.

"I got your message, Jack. It's good to see you." Foxworth came halfway round his desk, smiling, hand extended. There was still a trace of Britain in the attorney's speech, though he claimed to be twenty years removed from his native land. As always, the man was impeccably barbered and impressively tailored. Jack had never seen Foxworth in anything but solemn gray or sober black, yet he invariably managed to give his somber apparel a certain enviable elegance.

Jack took the chair offered to him, settling himself across the desk from Foxworth, who reached to adjust an iron paperweight until it was exactly square with the edge of the desk. Jack watched him, as always curious about the enigmatic attorney. Everything about Avery Foxworth reeked of breeding. He wasn't tall but somehow managed to give a sense of height. Slender and fine-boned, he nevertheless appeared anything but delicate. His hair was the color of dark sand and showed very little gray. Overall, Foxworth projected a quiet dignity that stopped just short of being severe. Only those deep-set, slate eyes gave away the man's intensity and keen intelligence.

How Foxworth had ever ended up in his present situation was anyone's guess. His partner, Charlie McCann, was one of the most flamboyant, ostentatious Irishmen around town—and one of the most corrupt. Charlie was as ample in girth and as jolly in nature as Avery was slight and serious. Yet here in the heart of one of the city's shadiest districts, these two, wildly opposite in every respect, had made a veritable fortune defending all manner of degenerates and reprobates—at the same time disproving the almost universal assumption that an Irishman and an Englishman could not possibly coexist in any atmosphere other than that of murderous loathing.

Jack got along with both men but tended to trust Foxworth more and dealt with him almost exclusively. This puzzled him to some extent, because at times he had a sense that Avery could be brutally ruthless and utterly lacking in compassion.

But then, perhaps that was what made him such a formidable foe in the courtroom.

"You've roused my interest, Jack. Your message sounded almost urgent. Now, you're much too smart for a breach-of-promise suit, and no one in his right mind would try to cheat a mad Irishman. So what's the problem?"

"*Problems*," Jack corrected with a rueful smile. "I think I'm about to be sued, for starters."

Foxworth merely nodded. "I can't believe it hasn't happened long before now. And?"

"There's a woman I want you to help. You can start by getting her out of jail."

It was Foxworth's turn to smile. "If the woman is suing you, why would you want her released?"

Jack waved a hand. "Two different cases, Avery. The woman first. She killed her husband, and I'm hoping you'll defend her."

Foxworth lifted an eyebrow. "Perhaps I was wrong about you after all. I thought you had more sense than to play around when there's a jealous husband on the scene."

"Shut up and listen, Avery," Jack said with no real asperity. "I don't even know the woman. There's a . . . friend who's concerned enough to want to help, that's all. Apparently this woman's husband was a drunk, a mean one. You know the sort, forever beating up his wife and terrorizing his children."

"Irish, was he?" Foxworth's expression was perfectly bland.

"As it happens, he was," Jack said agreeably.

"So uncivilized, your people."

"Don't start. I know a bit about British history, as it happens."

The attorney's expression sobered. "So you think the wife acted in self-defense?"

Jack shrugged. "I can't see how a woman could tolerate such abuse indefinitely. It seems to me that sooner or later she would fly apart—perhaps do something desperate."

Foxworth nodded. "Would you care to enlighten me as to your interest in this particular case?"

Again Jack gave a wave of his hand. "I promised an employee—a friend—I'd look into it, see if I could help." He studied Foxworth. "There's not much I can do, but you've managed to free a lot worse rascals than a poor battered woman."

"A poor battered woman who by the law's definition is also a murderess," Foxworth pointed out.

"I still think it sounds more like self-defense, Avery."

Foxworth gave another nod. "I won't dispute the point. But the court might."

"You'll take her case, then? Her name is Shanahan, by the way. Maura Shanahan."

Foxworth regarded Jack with a thin smile. "Who will be paying my bill, if I might ask?"

"Mrs. Harte seems to think the immigrant society will help as much as they can."

Again Foxworth arched an eyebrow. "Mrs. Harte?"

"She works for me," Jack explained. "Part-time. She's also associated with one of the immigrant organizations. She's taken an interest in helping this Maura Shanahan."

"Are you talking about Samantha Harte? Bronson Harte's widow?"

Jack's head snapped up. "You know her?"

Foxworth gave a nod. "Yes, I know the lady. Not well, of course. I've represented a few clients for Immigrant Aid, in which Mrs. Harte is apparently very active. She would seem to be an . . . interesting woman."

Jack said nothing.

"And an uncommonly attractive one as well," Foxworth added, watching Jack closely. "So, Samantha Harte works for you?"

"For the paper." Although the Irish had never been known for being tight-lipped, Jack was determined to reveal no hint of his interest in Samantha Harte. He had the unsettling sensation, however, that Avery Foxworth missed very little.

"Odd that she would be working at all," said the attorney. "Her family is quite well-to-do, I believe."

"She's actually very efficient at her job," Jack said. "I haven't caught an error on the front page or in any of my editorials since she started proofing the copy." Not altogether comfortable with the conversation, he deftly moved to change the subject. "As to your fee, Avery—"

The attorney laced his fingers together under his chin, waiting.

"You'll be paid, never fear," Jack assured him. "I'll pick up whatever the immigrant association doesn't pay. I rather doubt that they'll pay anything at all, though Sa—Mrs. Harte seems to think otherwise."

"Good of you, I must say." Foxworth continued to study Jack with an increasingly annoying smirk. "You know, Jack, you occasionally display an alarming tendency toward being a Christian gentleman."

"For an Irisher, you mean."

Foxworth shrugged. Then, opening an elaborately engraved wooden box, he passed it across the desk to Jack.

"Now I remember why I admire you, Avery," Jack said, "in spite of the fact that you're a lawyer. You're one of the few men I know who can tell a good cigar from a bad one."

He helped himself to a slim cheroot, then, at Foxworth's insistence, another, before passing the chest back across the desk. They lit up almost simultaneously.

"What's this about a lawsuit?" the attorney prompted after a moment.

"My series on prostitution hasn't been all that popular in some quarters, it seems."

Foxworth made a grimace of distaste and nodded slowly. "Ah, yes, the 'Harlots and Hypocrites' piece. Not one of your more sensible efforts, Jack. I must admit, I've wondered why you couldn't simply be content with antagonizing City Hall. Heaven knows you'd have a virtual storehouse of scandals to choose from, and lawsuits shouldn't be a problem with that gang." He paused, then added, "Death threats, perhaps, but not lawsuits."

"I've had a few of those, too," Jack said before he thought.

Foxworth's expression sobered. "Death threats? You're not serious?"

"It happens," Jack said, not willing to pursue the subject. "A man makes a lot of enemies in my business. I can't afford to pay much heed to every crackpot with an ax to grind."

The attorney leaned back in his chair. "If you make someone angry enough to threaten your life, Jack, you might do well to take that threat seriously." When Jack made no reply, he went on. "What form did these threats take? Are you saying there's been something recent?"

Jack shrugged. He truly did consider this sort of thing little more than a pesky aggravation. "A couple of random notes," he replied. "Nothing of any importance."

The truth was that one of those notes, received at the office only the past week, had been rabid enough that at first reading he'd actually felt a slight chill. The insults had been particularly vicious, with an unmistakable depth of hatred lacing the entire letter. The writer had left nothing to the imagination about how he viewed the Irish in general and Jack in particular. He was clearly of the popular persuasion that all Irish were subhuman and blights on the land.

But Jack hadn't come here to discuss lunatics. "So, then—you'll take the Shanahan woman's case, I hope?"

Foxworth shrugged. "If you want. Where are they holding her; do you know?"

"Eldridge Street."

Foxworth nodded, adding something to the notes he had been making throughout their meeting. "Now," he said, looking up, "are you going to tell me about this lawsuit or not?"

"Turner Julian," Jack said without preamble. "He seems to think that I've defamed his sterling reputation, caused him unwarranted embarrassment, and maligned his family name. Come to think of it, if you believe the people he's been talking to, I'm responsible for just about every unpleasant thing that's ever happened to him. Why, more than likely he even blames me for his ugly daughters."

"He'd best look to his wife for that," said Foxworth, straight-faced. "Does he have grounds for these accusations?"

Jack gave him a level look. "Some, I expect. Though I'll not take the blame for his poor daughters."

"Julian wasn't the only individual you identified by name, was he?"

"Indeed not. Although I may have paid him special attention. I did apply a few appropriate epithets."

Avery Foxworth gave a dark smile and nodded. "Such as the 'crown prince of physicians'?"

"'Scion of the arts and charitable endeavors,'" Jack added. "And, ah, 'Fifth Avenue medicine man.'"

Foxworth expelled a long breath. "You questioned his professional competency, among other things, if I remember correctly. In fact, I seem to recall your calling him a 'charlatan.'"

"He is," Jack bit out. "He overdoses most of his patients with laudanum so they'll not catch on to how incompetent he really is. As for his 'charitable endeavors,' he owns no less than three high-class bawdy houses and an entire block of some of the most squalid tenement buildings—death traps is what they are—in Five Points.'' He paused. ''The pesthole that burned down on Mulberry last month, the one in which the Negro children died? Julian owned it.''

Foxworth regarded Jack with a curious look. ''And because Julian thinks your series defamed him, he is now threatening to sue the pants off you, is that it?''

''I expect he would phrase it in rather more high-minded terms than that.''

''No doubt.'' Foxworth let out another long breath. ''You don't think Julian has anything to do with these threats you've received?''

Jack shook his head. ''Not his style. Too crude for a man of his situation.''

''Mm. You're probably right. I assume you have proof of your allegations against him and the others, seeing that you emblazoned them all over the front page for a week.''

''I'm not a fool, Avery. Of course I have proof.''

''What kind of proof?''

Jack shrugged. ''A couple of the newsboys also work as bagmen for Julian and the rabble he employs.''

Foxworth frowned and gave a short shake of his head. ''No one is going to pay any attention to your newsboys. You'll have to do better than that.''

''I have signed statements from two of his former landlords.'' Jack twisted his mouth. ''And a fourteen-year-old prostitute who not only worked in one of his more prosperous establishments but was also one of the good doctor's favorites.'' Jack paused. ''Until he all but beat her to death on his last visit.''

Foxworth studied Jack, his expression speculative. ''All right, Jack. The truth: why are you so intent on exposing Turner Julian? I sense something a little more personal in all this than a right-minded desire for reform.''

Jack met the attorney's scrutiny with a direct look. ''Part of it's personal, part of it's news. I'll not be discussing the personal aspects of it. Not even with you.''

''I don't like nasty surprises, Jack. I can't provide you with the best representation if you're not forthright with me.''

''I'm no more inclined to air my personal linen than you are, Avery. You'll just have to accept that.''

After a long silence, Foxworth inclined his head in a gesture of agreement.

The truth was that the esteemed Dr. Turner Julian had made Martha's last days of life a virtual hell, and Jack simply could not bring himself to rake all that up again. After all these years, he still found the memories of her final two weeks almost unbearable. He had never told anyone but Rufus what he suspected—no, what he *knew*—and he saw no reason to do so now.

※⊛〰

Turner Julian's disdain for Martha's Irishness—and for Jack's, of course—had been almost palpable throughout the course of her treatment. Julian made no secret of his contempt for Jack or his resentment of the fact that a vulgar Irishman could afford his high-priced medical "skills." He was unforgivably callous to Martha's pain, seemingly indifferent to the savagery with which the cancer had stripped every last vestige of dignity from her.

Finally, Jack, enraged and half out of his mind with grief, confronted the physician about his failure to act. "There must be *something* you can do! I'm not asking for a cure—I know she's almost gone. But surely there's a way to ease her suffering."

Julian's Nordic features grew taut. "I told you days ago, I've done everything I can. If you want miracles, call a priest."

It occurred to Jack that a priest might know more medicine than the arrogant Julian, but lest he make things worse for Martha, he held his tongue.

The next day, Julian attempted—and botched—a hasty surgical procedure that only added to Martha's agony and final humiliation. Unable to control his fury any longer, Jack stalked the hospital corridor for nearly a full day before finally managing to confront Julian.

"You made her worse! She's in more agony than ever!"

When Julian tried to push past him, Jack caught his skinny neck with one hand, tightening his grip until the physician's eyes bulged. "You worthless piece of garbage! You call yourself a doctor? You're nothing but a quack!"

He completely snapped then, choking off Julian's air with one hand while pushing him hard against the corridor wall with the other. Had Rufus not come out of Martha's room and physically pulled Jack off the terrified physician, he probably would have killed the man.

He never saw Turner Julian again. By the next morning, he had retained another doctor, but early that afternoon Martha died, screaming in mindless anguish right up to the end. Jack thought he would go mad before it was over for her.

He would never believe anything else but that Julian's refusal to prescribe some sort of opiate or other painkiller for Martha during those torturous last days had been deliberate, born out of the physician's contempt for Martha—and Jack himself—because of who they were.

To the British aristocracy, the Irish weren't quite human, and so they let them die, cold and hungry. To New York's aristocracy, they were also not quite human, and so they let them die in despair and agony.

Nothing much had really changed for the Irish here in America. They still lived in squalid dwellings, still lived with hunger and deprivation, still faced the contempt and oppression of the upper classes. They were good enough to sweep the streets and haul the manure wagons, build the canals and mine the coal, shoe the horses and work the factories. But they were not to dirty the linens of the better boarding houses or marry the daughters of decent men or even presume to die with the same dignity as their betters.

Simply because they were Irish.

Jack had wondered then, and still wondered, how long it would take—*what* it would take—before the Irish were accepted instead of despised, respected instead of condemned.

Sometimes he thought it would take an eternity to right the wrongs that had been done to his people.

As for Turner Julian, at the time, Jack hadn't yet accumulated enough money or enough power to touch the fraudulent physician. But that was no longer the case. He had waited for years to expose the man for the charlatan he was. Information on the shameful financial dealings and shadowy, secret lives of Julian and his pharisaical counterparts had fallen into his hands during an exhaustive investigation he'd conducted on the slum areas of the city. Once he'd been able to substantiate the facts, he hadn't hesitated to print them.

※◎≈※

Avery Foxworth's low voice brought him back to the present. "You have a right to keep your silence, Jack. But I warn you, if a man like Turner Julian takes you to court, you'll have few champions. His family pedigree is bloated with famous ancestors, and between his wife's and his own resources, Julian has enough money to take ten newspapermen to trial, if he should so choose. Now tell me, has he made an actual charge against you? How do you know he's considering litigation?"

"Rumor," Jack said, giving another casual wave. "Apparently, Julian is given to rash talk when he's in his cups—which is rather often, I'm told. He's been bandying about all manner of wild threats, mostly to do with 'hauling my hide into court.' Horace Greeley, for one, let me in on some of his blather."

Jack got up. "Look, Avery, the only thing I've done is to expose Julian and his kind for what they are. I can support my story, and the lot of them know it. But if they sue, I'm going to need representation. I wanted to make certain you'll handle it for me."

Foxworth stood and came around his desk, his eyes glinting with something akin to anticipation. "Let's just say it will be my pleasure. Get in touch when you need me."

"And Maura Shanahan?"

"I'll see what I can do about getting her released yet today. You'll make bail, I assume."

Jack nodded. "Whatever it takes."

Foxworth followed him to the door. "Samantha Harte must be a very good friend indeed."

Jack kept his expression carefully impassive. "She's a fine woman. I'm happy to do her a favor."

Foxworth searched his gaze for a moment but said nothing. They shook hands once again, and after flicking his cigar into a nearby cuspidor, Jack stepped outside to head toward his second destination. A glance at his watch showed that it was nearly five. Rufus was probably home by now, so he would go directly there.

He smiled a little. Amelia would almost certainly invite him to supper, of course.

And he would almost certainly accept.

One of Amelia's delicious meals might even help take the bad taste of Turner Julian out of his mouth.

38

Cloth of Heaven

Had I the heavens' embroidered cloths,
Enwrought with golden and silver light,
The blue and the dim and the dark cloths
Of night and light and the half-light,
I would spread the cloths under your feet.
But I, being poor, have only my dreams;
I have spread my dreams under your feet;
Tread softly because you tread on my dreams.

W . B . Y E A T S

Jack had quite a walk from Broadway to Rufus's house, behind the church on Mercer. It was nearly six-thirty by the time he arrived, and it was still as hot as it had been at two. The sky was darkening, however, and off in the distance a faint, low rumbling of thunder could be heard, signifying the possibility of a rainstorm.

He'd been utterly foolish to hoof it on a day like this, but at least he wouldn't be walking home. He had instructed Sheridan to pick him up at Rufus's house by eight-thirty. Mopping his brow, he walked up onto the porch of the Carvers' white-frame house, opened the screen door, and called out. When no reply came, he stepped inside. Rufus and Amelia were used to his unexpected visits and had given him to understand that the door was open to him anytime, day or night.

The rooms were uncommonly still as he made his way down the hall. At any other time the twins would have ambushed him before he got this far, hoping he might have a licorice or some gum balls tucked away in his coat pocket. But there was no sign of them, or the older children, either.

What did assail him on his way toward the back of the house were the tempting aromas from the kitchen. If he wasn't mistaken, he detected the smell of apple dumplings. Jack smiled in anticipation. Amelia's apple dumplings were worth a trek across town, even on a hot August day.

He found Amelia at the back of the house in the small alcove off the dining room that served as her sewing nook. She was sitting by the window, her head bent over what looked to be yet another colorful vest in progress for Rufus.

He rapped lightly on the door frame to warn her of his presence.

"Jack! Land, you gave me a start!"

He walked in, motioning to the vest on her lap. "Whether he deserves it or not, that husband of yours has to be the best-dressed man about town."

"I told him just the other night that if he don't shed a few pounds around his middle before long, I'm goin' to have to stop making these vests and start workin' on a tent. So, how've you been, Jack? And what in the world are you doing down here this time of day? I'd have thought you'd be off to one of those fancy restaurants on a Friday night."

"Not when there's a chance I can wangle an invitation to your table," said Jack.

"You know very well you don't have to ask," she chided him. "I do believe you must have smelled those apple dumplings across town. Well, sit down," she said, gesturing to the only other chair in the room, a slightly sagging, overstuffed armchair. "Don't tell me you walked in this heat? Where's that nice Sheridan boy with your buggy?"

"He'll be by later," Jack said, loosening his tie and tossing his suit coat over the back of the chair before sitting down. "Where is everyone? I don't think I've ever heard this house so quiet before."

"Gideon took them over to the cake social at his girlfriend Helen's church, all except for Mary. She had to beg her daddy for two days, but he finally agreed to let her go to the band concert in the park with that nice Henry Johnson." She gave a long sigh and looked up. "They're all of them growing up, Jack. Rufus and me, we're startin' to feel old."

Jack laughed at her. "Before you know it, you'll have yourselves a houseful of grandchildren, Amelia. You and Rufus won't have time to get old."

She seemed to consider the thought, then smiled. "I expect you're right. But what about you, Jack Kane? That's what I'd like to know. A man your age ought to be thinking seriously about a good woman and a houseful of his own children. What are you doing about that?"

"A man my age doesn't have the patience for a lot of noisy children. That's why I come to visit you so often. Anytime I get the mad notion that I ought to start a family, I just stop by the Carvers' and take the cure."

"Oh, you," she said, feigning a frown and shaking her head. "I don't pay a bit of attention to you, Jack. You're full of that Irish blarney, that's what I think."

"Ah, Amelia, you know me too well. So, where's Rufus? I would have stopped by the church, but I didn't think I'd find him there this late."

"He's over at the schoolhouse, helping Samantha clean up a bit. There was a window that needed to be reset, too. She teaches at the school on Friday afternoons, you know."

Jack nodded, trying to ignore the peculiar squeeze of his heart at the sound of Samantha's name.

They sat in silence for a time, Jack watching Amelia work the thread in and out of the material, a contented smile on her face. A thought occurred to him, and he voiced it. "I don't expect you've ever thought of yourself as an artist, have you?"

She glanced up. "I reckon not," she said dryly. "Mostly I think of myself as the old woman who lived in the shoe."

Jack smiled but shook his head. "Those vests—" he motioned toward the one in her hands—"they're like Brady's paintings. The colors, the design—no two are alike. Each one is unique. And I suspect there's a lot of Amelia Carver that goes into the making of them. If that's not the work of an artist, I don't know what is."

The idea seemed to please Amelia, and she studied the vest in her lap for a moment. "I never thought of it like that. Tell you what I *do* think about sometimes when I'm sewing on something new, though. I can't help but wonder if it might not be a little bit like what the good Lord does in our lives."

Although he was curious as to her meaning, Jack deliberately refrained from asking, lest he invite some sort of religious application. Amelia wasn't usually given to sermonizing like her effusive husband, but she had been known to make a point when the situation allowed.

He suspected this might be one of those times. She held up the unfinished garment, multicolored with a satin sheen and finely stitched in dark gold. "It seems to me," she said, her tone thoughtful, "that the Lord, he takes a piece of drab old fabric—a life—and fashions it however he wants. He plans it just so, gives it its own special shape and size and color. Some people's lives seem to be all bright and glittery—and mighty flimsy, too, just like some of the fabrics I've tried to work with. Others might not be quite as showy— maybe not as elegant or fine looking. But they last longer, and they'll take a sight more launderings and rough treatment than those frilly, useless little scraps." She paused, smiled, then went on. "Even the buttons are different. Some are shiny and tarnish easy—and even break off after a while. Others have buttons that don't show up as well, but they're a whole lot sturdier and last longer."

Still smiling, she traced a finger down one seam. "Now the stitching, that's the most important part of all. That's what holds it all together, what gives the fabric its own special shape and makes it wear real good for a long time."

Again she paused, long enough to run a gentle hand over the fabric with unmistakable care and love. "Seems to me the stitching is like the Spirit's work, taking every part of our life—all the good times and the bad, the joyful times and the hurting times—and weaving them all together to make a perfect, finished garment."

On impulse, Jack voiced a question that had only then occurred to him. "But what really decides the finished product, Amelia? The one who does the sewing or the fabric itself?"

He hadn't meant it as a challenge, but as was so often the case when it came to matters of faith, he heard the faint, sardonic twist to his own words.

If Amelia noticed, however, she didn't let on but simply regarded him with a searching look for a long moment. "Well, I expect that's where the similarity ends, Jack," she said, still caressing the material in her hands. "This piece of cloth doesn't have any say-so over what I do to it. But when it comes to my life, I *do*. It's up to me whether I want my life's 'stitching' to be done by the Lord or by my own stubborn, clumsy hands. Everybody's got a choice about *that*. As for me, I decided a long time ago I didn't want my life to be some old throwaway rag. No, sir, I want my life fashioned right out of the cloth of heaven."

Her reference to the "old throwaway rag" was like a boot in the stomach to Jack. On those rare occasions when a quiet moment or two managed to squeeze between the overly busy, cluttered hours of his days and nights, when he allowed himself a singular clear thought about his existence, he might have described it just like that: an "old throwaway rag."

Jack stared at her, his emotions vacillating between admiration and disquiet. He respected Amelia Carver—and her husband—as much as, if not more than, anyone he'd ever known. For years he had been aware that there was something very special about their lives, something to which he couldn't even hope to relate, could not begin to understand. And yet if he was completely honest, he envied them whatever it was.

But at some deeper, darker level, there was a part of him—a discontented, inexplicably angry part of him—that resented Amelia's simplistic analogy. It had been his experience that nothing was that basic, that fundamental—that *simple*—in life, except possibly life's pain.

He was no fool. At the core of his being, he knew that his obsessive drive for success, for more money, for more power, had nothing to do with need. Whatever he might have felt compelled to prove years ago, as a boy and as a young man, he had proven many times over. The last thing he needed was more money, and he didn't delude himself about the value of success or power—both were as fleeting as a midnight wind.

No, the demon that rode his back, driving him to cram his every waking hour with more and more work—more busyness—wasn't so much born of need, but desperation—a desperation to fill the black, grasping hunger within him. The sick beast called misery in the pit of his soul threatened daily to swallow him whole if he allowed himself time to think . . . really *think*. About life. About the *meaning* of life. About . . . something *more* than life.

Rufus had once remarked that he found it next to impossible to comprehend what exactly Jack believed in. Understandable, since Jack himself didn't know. He believed in *something,* that much he would concede. At least he wanted to believe there was something better, something higher, something that might ultimately give value to all the suffering and despair and injustice the game of life was forever dealing its players.

Every year he seemed to sense old age—and death—hurtling faster and faster toward him. It accomplished nothing to throw his hands over his eyes in hopes of warding off the inevitable. He would give much to believe, really believe, in some divine righting of all life's wrongs—some justice for all the innocent who had been slaughtered, some eventual healing for all those who had suffered, some final

peace for those who had known nothing but fear or trouble or afflic-
tion.

There had been a time, when he was a lad—he barely remembered
it now—when his mother had taught him about a baby born in a
stable and a Savior suffering for man's sins on a cross. She had made
it all so easy to understand, so utterly real and believable—even the
part about their "blessed hope," the risen Christ, who would be
waiting at the gate of heaven, arms open wide, to welcome his children home.

But then he had been a boy, and he had known nothing of life.
Now he was a man and knew too much.

"Jack?"

Amelia's soft, questioning voice brought him back. "Sorry, Amelia. I think the heat caught up with me there for a minute."

She was watching him with undisguised concern. "Why don't I
get you a nice cold glass of milk?" she said, putting her sewing
down and pushing herself up from the chair. "Gideon went for ice
just before he left with the children, so the milk ought to be chilled
real good by now."

"Don't go to any trouble, Amelia—"

"No trouble," she assured him. "I need to be setting the table
anyhow. Rufus and Samantha will be along any minute now."

Jack had started to get up but froze at her words. "Samantha?
She's coming home with Rufus?"

Amelia turned and smiled. "Why, yes. Samantha usually has supper with us on Friday nights, after Rufus helps her tidy up the schoolroom. I'm so glad you're here, too. It'll be nice, with the children
gone. Just us grown-ups, for a change."

Jack got to his feet. Suddenly, he felt exceedingly rumpled. Wilted,
actually. He needed a shave by this time of day, and his hair was
still damp from perspiration. This wasn't the way he wanted Samantha Harte to find him. "I . . . don't believe I can stay after all, Amelia.
I've remembered something I need to do—"

What was wrong with him? Only a few days ago he would have
clicked his heels in the air at a chance to sit down to supper with
Samantha again. Now here was an incredible opportunity, and he was
acting like a backward schoolboy.

"Besides," he added, "you hadn't planned on another mouth to
feed. I don't think I ought to impose." He felt as if he were babbling,
and Amelia's expression indicated as much.

"Whatever's gotten into you, Jack Kane? Weren't you just hintin'
strong a few minutes ago for some of my apple dumplings? And if

Rufus comes home and finds that you left without having your supper, he'll fret about it all evening."

Jack glanced down over himself. "The thing is, Amelia, I didn't realize Mrs. Harte was going to be here. I'm not exactly fit company for you ladies."

She looked at him as if he'd lost his mind. "What kind of shape do you think Rufus is going to be in after working all day in this heat? Land, if I didn't know better, I'd think you were trying to avoid Samantha. I thought you *liked* her."

"Well, of course I like her," Jack said peevishly, feeling increasingly foolish. "I hired her, didn't I?"

"That's not what I meant, and you know it," Amelia drawled, her gaze sizing up his appearance—and no doubt registering his discomfort. "You look just fine, it seems to me, but if it'll make you feel any better, go on upstairs and wash up a bit. You can even tighten your necktie, if you think you must. Your shoes aren't so bad, and I don't see any gravy on your shirt, so you'll do. Go on now, and stop with this foolishness. I declare, there's no woman in the world so vain as a man, and that's the truth."

Jack felt a little better at her encouragement, but he had no chance to act on it, for at that moment they heard the sound of Rufus's booming voice in the hall. Jack only had time for a quick swipe of a hand through his hair before Rufus appeared in the doorway . . . with Samantha Harte.

Her startled expression, Jack noted, indicated that she was every bit as flustered by this unexpected encounter as he was.

39

Samantha's Smile

She smiled and that transfigured me
And left me but a lout.

W . B . Y E A T S

Samantha's first thought upon seeing Jack Kane in the doorway of
the sewing room was that she probably could not have looked worse.

The heat in the schoolroom had been almost intolerable throughout
the afternoon. By the time she sent the children home, she was already feeling wilted and cross. But that wasn't the end of her day.
Rufus had come to work on the window, then stayed to help her
clean the supply pantry. In the meantime, Samantha had dusted,
swept, cleaned the chalkboard, and tidied up the classroom.

Her hair was damp, and a few strands had slipped free to frizz
about her face. The front of her white bodice was dusty, and for all
she knew, her face might even be dirty. Instinctively, she put a hand
to her hair, brushing away an incorrigible strand that had fallen over
one eye. She was disconcerted to see the way Kane's gaze followed
her movement. Why hadn't she taken the time to freshen up before
leaving the schoolhouse?

Once she recovered from the surprise encounter, however, she observed that her employer's appearance hadn't been left entirely un-
scathed by the heat of the day. Kane wasn't quite his usual natty self.

So the titan is mortal after all, she thought with a faint touch of
grim satisfaction. Unfortunately, the man's slightly rumpled mien
seemed to take nothing away from his appeal. The thought brought
a stab of annoyance, and Samantha tensed, the familiar walls of self-
protection closing in on her.

Jack thought she had never looked lovelier, an observation that only heightened his own sense of dishevelment. Somehow he managed a civil greeting, to which Samantha Harte responded with cool composure.

Rufus saved the moment by slapping Jack soundly on the back and immediately launching into a cheerful prediction of the coming storm. "We'd better enjoy the peace and quiet while we can," he said. Already in his shirtsleeves, he whipped his necktie free and let it dangle around his neck. "Anytime now those children are gonna burst through the door. From the looks of the sky, this is going to be a bad one. Once it hits, the cake social will be over."

When Jack moved to retrieve his suit coat, Rufus stopped him. "Don't you dare put that coat on, Jack! I'm uncomfortable enough as it is. I don't reckon the ladies will mind on a night like this."

They went on to exchange meaningless small talk about the heat and the storm on the way. Jack half wished he hadn't let Amelia talk him out of leaving. For some reason, he felt uncommonly discomfited by the presence of Samantha Harte, and after a muttered remark about "getting some air," he crossed to an open window and stood looking out.

Rufus had been right about the sky. A great mass of sullen dark thunderheads had begun to boil over the city, and for the first time in days there was enough wind to stir the dry leaves. Thunder rumbled in the distance, and as he watched, quick, short bolts of lightning shot from the clouds.

The air was hot and smelled scorched, offering no real relief. Even so, he stayed by the window until he heard Amelia and Samantha Harte leave the room.

Thankfully, Rufus seemed unaware of his tension. They talked about nothing of any importance until Amelia called them to supper. By then, Jack had managed to regain at least a vestige of his composure.

The Carvers' kitchen was a large, high-ceilinged room that also served as the family's dining room. Between two long windows on one wall stood the cookstove and a sink. A rough-bricked fireplace and a large cupboard lined the opposite wall. The room was spacious enough to accommodate the entire family when they were all together, as well as any guests who might drop by. It was a friendly, comfortable room that invited laughter and conversation.

Jack normally thought of the kitchen as a kind of haven. The day's tension would usually begin to leave him almost as soon as he entered, even when the entire noisy Carver clan was gathered round the table. Tonight, however, he felt slightly less at ease. A part of his restlessness might have been due to the approaching storm or even to the unfamiliar stillness in the house without the children. More likely, though, it resulted from his futile fascination with Samantha Harte.

He was like a schoolboy with a crush. Why, he was as bad as Cavan Sheridan, though the boy seemed more or less cured of *his* infatuation these days.

Jack was seething at his own foolishness before he ever sat down to the table. Amelia's dumplings were superb, as always, but his appetite had virtually failed him. He had deliberately taken the chair directly across from Samantha, rather than pulling up alongside her—his first inclination—thinking to avoid a disturbing closeness. It turned out to be a royal mistake because he couldn't take his eyes off her.

The woman was not easy to ignore, after all.

He was, however, a bit curious as to the difference he detected in her tonight. For one thing, she seemed noticeably more relaxed around him than on previous occasions. Not that she had lost all of her reticence. She still confined her answers to his questions to quiet, succinct replies. And if she happened to catch him watching her, her eyes took on the same startled, uncertain expression he had seen all too often before. But for the most part, she appeared to find him less odious than usual, even meeting his eyes across the table once or twice instead of glancing about as if she were looking for a route of escape. And she actually smiled at him. More than once.

He blamed her smile for his undoing.

By the time they were halfway through the meal, Jack had all but forgotten his earlier chagrin about his own appearance, instead allowing himself the luxury of enjoying *her* appearance. She was absolutely delightful with that small, dusty smudge in the hollow of her cheek—of which she was almost certainly unaware—and the delicate tendrils of hair that had come undone to curl damply about her face.

Not for the first time, Jack found himself charmed by her voice. She had a wonderful voice, soft but with an unexpected intensity and an occasional winsome catch in it that somehow made him want to reach across the table and clasp her hand. With Rufus and Amelia,

Samantha laughed easily, and Jack caught himself wishing he could evoke the same spontaneous mirth from her instead of the annoying gravity with which she seemed to regard him.

Still, her sober demeanor was a decided improvement. At least she no longer seemed to suspect that he might be the devil incarnate.

The storm that had delayed itself during the meal was now building in strength and rushing in on them. The room had darkened considerably, and both Amelia and Rufus made a hurried exit to close the windows and shutters throughout the house and draw in the awnings.

Samantha got up to raise the wicks on the oil lamps placed around the room. Through the one window that remained open, the wind whipped with a sharpness that felt wonderfully cool.

When she returned to her chair, she glanced across the table to find Jack Kane watching her with the same steady intensity that never failed to unnerve her. He had seemed different somehow this evening. Perhaps because of his slightly less than perfect appearance, a marked departure for him.

But his appearance accounted for only a part of the difference. Earlier, Samantha had detected something she hadn't seen before in Kane's eyes, in the set of his shoulders—even in his speech. Oh, he was in control, as always, with the same faint arrogance she had come to associate with him. And his gaze on her held the same hint of interest and regard she found so puzzling—and so disturbing. The hard, sardonic set of his mouth, the grim amusement with which he seemed to view life in general, the easy, rumbling voice that she suspected could turn to steel in a heartbeat—all seemed as usual.

But there was something else, something less confident, some hint of vulnerability she would never have expected to see in a man like Kane.

And it drew her to him as nothing else had before tonight.

During Rufus and Amelia's absence, Jack told Samantha Harte about Avery Foxworth's agreement to defend Maura Shanahan.

The surprised—but pleased—look in her eyes warmed him, and in that instant he was shaken to realize how much he wanted her good opinion.

"I can't thank you enough for doing this!" she said, her eyes shining. Just as quickly, her expression sobered. "But is he terribly expensive? The Society has a fund for legal aid, as I told you, but I'm not sure how much we can expect from them.''

Jack waved off her concern. ''Don't worry about the expense for now. Foxworth knows he'll get paid. And by the way, he was going to see if he could arrange bail for Mrs. Shanahan yet this evening. Perhaps you can see her tomorrow at home, if you like.''

She tried to press him for more details about the financial arrangements, but Jack dismissed her questions, going on instead to tell her a little about Avery Foxworth himself. He was anxious that she understand that Maura Shanahan would be getting the best of legal defenses. At the same time, he didn't dissemble about Foxworth's somewhat unsavory reputation.

All the while, he was riveted by those incredible dark eyes watching him. The lamplight danced over her face, heightening the glow of her skin and casting golden highlights through her hair. Jack was seized by a sudden, fierce desire to reach across the table and pull her to him. He had never wanted a woman the way he wanted Samantha Harte, but it was a different kind of wanting than that to which he was accustomed. It was more than mere physical longing, more than the primitive urge to take and possess.

His blood pounded in his ears, and his pulse raced as he realized that no matter how desperately he desired this woman, what he wanted more than anything else was her approval—her respect. He wanted her to trust him.

He wanted her to need him.

Was he losing his mind? The woman was obviously more afraid of him than attracted to him. Even worse, he thought she might actually be *repelled* by him. Hardly the kind of responses he would like to kindle in her.

Just then, thunder exploded, and a powerful gust of wind came roaring through the open window. The curtains flapped, and the flames from the oil lamps flickered madly. A sudden onslaught of rain dashed against the house.

Samantha jerked and cried out. They both scrambled away from the table at the same time, rushing toward the window to close it. Jack hesitated a moment, fascinated, unable to resist the wildness of the storm. He could see nothing beyond the small patch of yard separating the Carvers' house from that of the neighbors. The huge old maple trees were writhing, bending almost double in the wind.

Another crash of thunder shook the house, and a fierce blaze of lightning froze the scene outside in eerie incandescence. Jack reached to lower the window, but before he could, a bolt of lightning streaked in front of it, startling them both. Rain blasted through the open window, and instinctively Jack caught Samantha against him with one arm as he slammed the window down with the other.

She was trembling, and it seemed the most natural thing in the world to pull her closer to steady her. The din of the wind and rain from outside was almost deafening, but it was nothing compared to the roar in his head as he stared down at her.

"Samantha?"

Her eyes were enormous, and she paled. Jack tightened his grip on her, suddenly unable to bear the thought that she might pull away. His mind . . . his heart . . . everything in him was screaming as wildly as the night around them. He thought he would suffocate in the sudden closeness of the room and in her nearness. He could not drag his gaze away from her face, from her eyes glistening in the flickering light, holding him captive. For one mad moment, he thought he saw something in those eyes besides the usual aloofness. He felt a quickening of his heart, and without warning, all his former caution and resolve dropped away. He lowered his head, brought his face close to hers, his lips—

And then he saw the change that came over her features.

What he saw was a stark, chilling terror. Not merely revulsion, which would have wounded him badly enough, but a dreadful, stricken fear—a shrinking from him that made him want to moan with despair.

No woman had ever looked at him that way. He drew back, his desire instantly gone as shame and confusion set in. He released her, but she didn't move. It was as if she were frozen where she stood. Jack took in the blank stare, the white, waxen texture of her skin, and for a moment he thought she might be ill or about to fall into some sort of seizure.

Finally her gaze cleared. As Jack watched, her shoulders sagged, and she seemed to go limp. He reached out to steady her, then dropped his hand away, remembering how she had looked at him.

Furious with himself and thrown badly off balance by the vehemence of her rejection, he could only stand and mock himself for being such a fool. He wanted to bolt from the room.

"Samantha . . . I'm sorry!" he said, his voice rough. "I . . . don't know what to say. I'm so sorry."

She stared up at him as if he had awakened her from a deep sleep. And then a wash of emotions began to play over her features—a slow, dawning awareness, mingled with something else, something

akin to dismay or even humiliation. She began to shake her head
slowly, over and over again.

Jack wanted to distance himself, wanted to be angry with her ...
wanted not to care. Instead, he couldn't seem to stop apologizing. "I
am sorry, Samantha. I didn't mean anything wrong. I've had ... feelings for you, almost since we met. I thought perhaps you knew, that
you might even—I don't know what I thought. I didn't realize you
felt so strongly ... against me...."

She lifted a hand, and for an instant Jack thought she was going
to touch him. Instead, she dropped her hand away, shaking her head.
"No. You don't understand."

Her voice sounded strangled. Jack frowned down at her, bewildered. He held his breath, wanting to seize her hand, knowing he
dare not touch her again.

"It's not you," she said in the same odd-sounding voice. "It's
me. It has nothing to do with you. Nothing." There was a strange
ferocity in her words, as if she was suddenly, unaccountably angry.

She was hugging her arms to her body as if to keep herself from
falling to pieces. She started to turn, but Jack stopped her—not by
touching her, but with the plea in his voice.

"Samantha? No, don't turn away from me! Tell me what you
mean."

Her eyes were glazed with unshed tears, and Jack ached to kiss
them away. Instead, he balled his hands into fists at his sides to keep
from touching her. "I meant no harm, Samantha. I—regardless of
what you've heard or what you may think—I would never do anything to hurt you."

She looked away. "I—I think I know that. But—," she faltered,
then went on. "I'm sorry. I know you don't understand, but I can't
explain. I can't ... talk about this."

A vicious, ugly suspicion had insinuated itself into Jack's mind, a
thought so vile he couldn't give it any real credence. Perhaps he was
only trying to rationalize her behavior, her response to him. And yet
that response had seemed too violent, too unreasonable, even if she
detested him. What he had seen in her face bordered on sheer horror.

What had been done to her that would account for such a violent
reaction to him ... to any man?

"Samantha ... are you quite sure you can't tell me ... whatever it
is?"

Still she refused to meet his gaze, but instead stood staring down
at the floor. "I can't. Please don't ask me."

Jack drew in a long, steadying breath. He had already made a colossal fool of himself, so what did it matter now if he did it again?

"All right. But, Samantha, if I may—let me say just one more thing. I've seen that you're not entirely . . . comfortable with me, and I think I understand why. And now I suppose I've gone and made things worse by my behavior—and for that I'm deeply sorry. I . . . ah—" Jack ran a hand through his hair, thoroughly annoyed with himself now. "I'm saying this badly, I know. I just want to be sure that you understand that I mean you no harm, no offense. If I've . . . upset you or embarrassed you, I couldn't be more sorry, and that's the truth."

Finally, she looked at him, searching his gaze as if she could somehow weigh his words. "It's all right. It's really . . . not your fault."

What he saw in her eyes made his heart ache. There was so much pain in her. He wanted to hold her, to somehow protect her from whatever secret torment seemed to bind her. He wanted to comfort her. He wanted to heal her.

But heal her of *what?*

"Samantha, is this about your husband?" he blurted out before he could stop himself.

Jack watched her closely as he waited for her reply. She seemed to have gone perfectly rigid. A white line tightened about her mouth, and her features were as hard and cold as marble. So still was she that she didn't appear to be breathing.

Jack sensed that she would withdraw from him, perhaps even run from him if he made the slightest move to touch her. Yet it was all he could do not to pull her into his arms.

Gradually, her features cleared. "Please," she finally said, not meeting his gaze. "No more. I can't . . . talk about this any more."

Watching her, Jack knew it would be a mistake to press any further. "Samantha?" he said finally. "Would you—please—at least consider letting me be your friend? Just—your friend?"

She looked at him and opened her mouth to reply, but just then Rufus and Amelia came sweeping back into the room, and she turned away without answering.

Almost at the same moment, the children burst through the front door and came charging down the hall. Any further opportunity to speak with her alone was lost.

A few minutes later, Cavan Sheridan arrived with the carriage. When Jack tried to convince her to let them drive her home, Samantha demurred, explaining that Gideon had already planned to do so.

Although Jack was hesitant to insist, he kept his voice firm. "Rufus's wagon is no match for this storm. I wish you'd ride with us."

"Jack's right, Samantha," Amelia put in. "You'll be absolutely drenched. You'd best go with Jack in his carriage."

At last she relented, though with obvious reluctance, and only, Jack suspected, because she might have feared a scene in front of the others.

Outside, Jack caught her arm and said, his voice low enough that Cavan Sheridan couldn't hear, "I'll ride with Sheridan. I expect you'll be more comfortable."

She turned a look of dismay on him. "No! You'll be soaked through."

Jack shrugged. "I like the rain. I often walk in it."

She studied him for a moment but said nothing.

Jack didn't reply but helped her into the carriage and, closing the door, leaned into the window. "You didn't answer me, Samantha. I'm asking you again—could you possibly allow me to be your friend?"

She regarded him with a long, searching look. Her eyes were solemn, measuring. But Jack's hopes soared when she finally answered. "Yes," she said, her voice quiet, her gaze still locked with his. "I think I'd like that, Mr. Kane."

Joy arced through Jack like a shooting star. "That's grand. And, ah, now that we're to be friends, do you think you could possibly manage to call me Jack?"

She blinked, watching him. Finally, a ghost of a smile curved her lips. "Yes, all right . . . Jack."

Jack's heart suddenly felt lighter than it had for days. Weeks. "Good! And, Samantha? We really should be going over the plans for the new immigrant resettlement program soon. Do you suppose— now that we're friends—we could get together for dinner tomorrow night and discuss some of the arrangements? I could call for you, say, about seven?"

"We just *had* dinner together," she pointed out.

"Doesn't count. It was unplanned."

She lifted an eyebrow, and Jack thought for a fraction of a second that she would shrink away from him again. Instead she nodded slowly, saying, "All right. But if you don't mind, I'll choose the restaurant."

He made a palms-up gesture to indicate his agreement. "Anywhere you say." He paused. "Anything else?"

"Yes, actually, there is," she said, pointing to the cigar in his pocket. "I'm afraid you'll have to promise not to smoke one of those smelly things anywhere near me."

Jack broke into a slow grin, slipped the cheroot from his pocket, and flicked it out into the street, in the rain.

40

Of Silence
and Shadows

And love can reach
From heaven to earth, and nobler lessons teach
Than those by mortals read.
JOHN BOYLE O'REILLY

The storm seemed to have passed, at least for the moment, leaving behind only a light, steady rain and cooler air. Jack breathed in the clean, wet scent of the night as the horse clopped along the quiet street. He didn't mind in the least sitting in the open, for he welcomed the rain.

Sheridan, however, seemed uncomfortable with the arrangement. "If you don't mind my saying so, sir, you shouldn't be sitting up here in the rain. Won't you let me pull off so you can ride inside the carriage with Mrs. Harte?"

Jack turned up the collar on his coat and hunkered down to enjoy the ride. "Don't fret yourself about me, lad. I'm fine. As I told Mrs. Harte, the rain suits me. Especially after a scorcher like today."

"Yes, sir." Sheridan didn't sound altogether convinced, but he let the subject drop. "I almost forgot, sir—Mrs. O'Meara said I should tell you that there's a letter, quite a thick one, she said, from your brother."

"Ah! About time! I'll be curious to see what Brady has to say."

Silence settled between them. It occurred to Jack that Sheridan's apparent awkwardness might not be entirely due to his employer's presence up front. On impulse, he decided to broach the subject of

Samantha Harte with the boy, partly because he felt the need to clear the air between them—and partly, he supposed, simply because he enjoyed talking about Samantha.

"Are the lessons with Mrs. Harte still going well?" Jack asked.

"Oh, yes, sir. She's a fine teacher, as I've told you."

"About Mrs. Harte, lad—are you still taken with her?"

Cavan Sheridan shot him a startled look. "Sir?"

"Oh, you know good and well what I mean, Sheridan! You were positively besotted with the woman some months back. Have you gotten past all that by now or not?"

Jack watched him. Even in the dark, he could see Sheridan color, then swallow with apparent difficulty.

He sighed, thinking he had probably insulted the lad or at least embarrassed him, though neither had been his intention. Jack knew all too well how it felt to make a fool of himself over a woman who wanted nothing to do with him.

Sheridan's reply was a long time coming, but not a surprise. "I think Mrs. Harte is the finest woman I've ever met."

Again Jack sighed.

"But in reply to your question—" Sheridan cleared his throat before going on. "I suppose I've managed to lay any other feelings to rest. Though it was a grievous disappointment."

It struck Jack that his driver's solemn statement sounded almost funereal, and at another time he might have been mildly amused by the young man's flair for the dramatic. But not tonight. He understood the lad's despondency too well to take it lightly.

"You regard her highly, do you, sir?"

Jack stared at him. He would have been perfectly within his rights had he chosen to give the boy a scathing rebuke. A man's driver was in no position to question his employer on personal matters.

Instead, he merely lifted an eyebrow in grim self-mockery. "It's that obvious, is it?"

Sheridan kept his eyes straight ahead. "Well, sir . . . it seems to me that only a blind man or a fool wouldn't be drawn to a woman like Mrs. Harte. And certainly you're neither. . . ." He let his words drift off, unfinished.

Jack tried for the proper level of indignation but couldn't quite suppress a rueful smile. "I'm not blind; that's true. As for the fool, I'm beginning to wonder." He paused. "Perhaps you wouldn't mind telling me how you managed to bury *your* unrequited affections, Sheridan."

The boy shrugged. "I suppose I finally came to realize how hopeless it was. I knew nothing could come of it. Mrs. Harte was very firm in her rejection. In truth, I think it was a case of her simply not being . . . attracted to me. She tried to make me believe it was the difference in our ages, that the years between us were too great—''

"There are as many years between her and *me,*" Jack grumbled, "as there are between the two of you. Though the difference is turned the other way around."

Sheridan glanced over at him, frowning. Clearly, he'd been about to make a reply but changed his mind.

"What?" Jack said.

A muscle at the corner of the lad's mouth jerked. "'Tis not for me to say, sir."

"It *is* for you to say, if I give you leave to say it!" Jack snapped. "You needn't always be so provokingly correct, Sheridan, at least not at the moment. Now, what were you about to say?"

Sheridan regarded Jack with a long look before turning his attention back to the street. "Only that it seems to me that Mrs. Harte might not mind the years between yourself and her, that's all."

"I don't suppose you'd care to elaborate?" Jack said through clenched teeth.

Sheridan gave a shrug, saying, "I don't know a great deal about such matters, but I'd have to say that Mrs. Harte looks at you very differently than she ever looked at me."

Jack narrowed his eyes, scrutinizing the youth for any evidence of rancor. But Sheridan's expression appeared temperate and totally without guile as he added, "At least that's how it seems to me, sir."

Completely indifferent to the rain by now, Jack crossed his arms over his chest and sat staring straight ahead. "It is, is it?"

"Yes, sir."

"And just how would you describe the way Mrs. Harte looks at me, then?"

Jack deliberately kept his gaze locked on the rain-veiled street ahead as he awaited the reply.

"Well, sir," Sheridan finally said, "I'd say she might be a bit intimidated by you." He paused, then quickly added, "But I think she also finds you . . . very interesting."

" 'Very interesting,' " Jack repeated. There was no question that Sheridan was right about the intimidating part, he thought sourly, remembering the look of horror that had crossed Samantha's features earlier.

"Actually, sir, I think it's fairly obvious that Mrs. Harte likes you."

"*Likes* me?" As a means of counteracting any false hopes raised by Sheridan's observation, Jack reminded himself of the way Samantha had visibly shrunk from his touch. Still, hadn't he himself commented on more than one occasion about the lad's keen instincts? Even so, it would be folly itself to make too much of this.

He thought for a moment. "Have you ever heard Mrs. Harte speak of her husband?" he said.

Sheridan shook his head. "Strange, isn't it, but I don't recall her ever mentioning him in any way."

It *did* seem strange, Jack thought. "Still, he must have been a good man. I can't imagine Sa—Mrs. Harte married to any other kind."

"I expect you're right," Sheridan agreed. "But I've often wondered . . . She has such a great sorrow in her eyes."

"Aye, she does," Jack said softly. "Indeed she does."

"Mr. Kane?"

"Hm?" Jack's thoughts had returned to the disturbing scene with Samantha, and he had to force his attention back to his surroundings.

"Did I speak out of turn, about Mrs. Harte's . . . 'interest' in you?"

Jack waved off his concern. "No, it's all right. Though I expect I'd be wise to discount the notion. It's not likely that Mrs. Harte will ever bear me any affection other than friendship. That much, at least, might be a possibility. But as for anything else—" Jack gave a heavy shrug, as if to throw off a burden. "Her kind of woman doesn't take up with a man like me. If she ever decides to marry again, she'll be wanting a *good* man."

"I'm thinking there's no such thing," Sheridan said quietly.

Jack looked at him. "You are far too cynical for your tender age, lad. Best to leave such jaded opinions to someone like myself."

"No, it's true," said Sheridan. "Mrs. Harte gave me a copy of the Scriptures—I had none of my own, you see—and I've been reading them straight through. What I'm coming to realize is that there's no such thing as a truly good man—except for the Savior, of course— God's Son. The rest of us—even the *best* of us—we're not good at all, not really. We don't even have the *hope* of being good unless we put on the new life offered us by the Cross of Christ."

Jack was in no mood for a theological discussion. He'd been down that road already tonight, thanks to Amelia. "If you don't mind, lad, I'd just as soon not pursue the subject."

"You don't believe in Christ's redemption, Mr. Kane?"

Jack turned a black look on him. "Do you really consider that any of your affair, Cavan Sheridan?"

The boy didn't look at him, but his reply couldn't have been more firm. "As a matter of fact, I do, sir. I'd be fearful for your soul if I thought you didn't believe."

"Well, I'd prefer that you tend to your own soul, Sheridan. And your driving as well, if you don't mind."

The boy actually smiled! "Sorry, sir. It's just what you said about Mrs. Harte's deserving only a 'good' man. It made me think that you might not even consider yourself in the running."

Jack stared at him. "Sheridan," he finally said, "has it ever occurred to you that you are occasionally downright insolent?"

"I don't mean to be, sir. Would you prefer I not mention Mrs. Harte again?"

"I didn't say that. Although I expect you resent my . . . interest in her, in any event."

"I do not, sir. Not a bit. Nor hers in you."

"She has no interest in me, Sheridan!"

"Whatever you say, Mr. Kane."

Jack brooded for another moment or two. "What did you mean back there—what you said about 'putting on the new life'? You make it sound like a wardrobe—take off the old suit and put on a new one. Is that really in the Bible?"

Jack had never liked admitting ignorance on any subject, but his knowledge of the Scriptures was sketchy at best. His mother had taught him some of the old stories, and Martha had been a great one for reading the Bible, had read it faithfully each night. But while Jack had always admired her devotion, he hadn't shared it. On those times when she read aloud to him, he hadn't liked the way the words made him feel. Uncomfortable. Uneasy. And, at times, inexplicably lonely.

Oddly enough, that hymn Amelia liked to sing—"Amazing Grace"—invariably seemed to affect him in the same way.

Jack had long ago written off religion as something for women, certainly something that children ought to be taught as well. But it wasn't for him.

Yet Sheridan had sparked his curiosity with his talk about good men and "putting on a new life." It somehow reminded him of what Amelia had said about her vests.

"It's in the Bible, all right, sir. In numerous places."

It took Jack a second or two to realize that Sheridan was answering his question of a moment before.

"Do you know the story of the Prodigal Son, Mr. Kane?"

Jack nodded guardedly.

"So perhaps you recall that after the son had squandered his inheritance, he came crawling back home, and his father put a fine new robe and sandals on him. Well," Sheridan went on, "Mrs. Harte says that the robe is like the new life we put on in Christ. She says all we have to do is turn away from our old life, and God will give us a new robe—the robe of his forgiveness and redemption."

He paused, then added, "In truth, sir, the Bible is filled with passages about that very thing—'putting off the old,' and 'putting on the new.' If you like, I'd be glad to show you sometime, Mr. Kane."

"That's all right," Jack said dryly, trying to stem the tide of unsettling emotions coursing through him. "I'll take your word for it."

"'Tis God's Word, not mine," Sheridan countered.

"Shut up and drive, boy. You're beginning to annoy me."

"Yes, sir. Sorry, sir." A silence. Then, "Mr. Kane?"

"What now, Sheridan?" Jack said wearily.

"I'd like to say that, as men go, I happen to think you're one to admire. I expect Mrs. Harte does, too, given the way she looks at you."

"Sheridan—"

"I know you might not see yourself quite in that light, but Mrs. Harte says that we ought not to pay much heed to how we see ourselves, or how others see us." The lad seemed in such a fierce rush to get his words out that they fairly spilled from him as he continued. "She says it's how God sees us that matters, and that he doesn't see us at all the way others do. Everyone else judges us by the way we act or what they've heard about us, but God looks at the heart."

It occurred to Jack that he wouldn't be comfortable with *anyone* seeing his heart—especially the Almighty—for surely by now it was as black as the coal mines in which the youth beside him had once labored.

"Mrs. Harte says," Sheridan went on, "that once we put on the robe of God's redemption, he doesn't see our old life anymore."

Something tightened in Jack. Sheridan's final words settled over him, sinking so far into the recesses of his being that they seemed to touch the very depths of his soul. He turned to study the strong, lean profile of his young driver, but Sheridan's gaze was fixed resolutely on the darkened street.

"It would seem," Jack said, still watching him, "that Mrs. Harte has been teaching you something more than grammar and history."

A slow smile broke over Sheridan's features. "I expect it would be no exaggeration to say that Mrs. Harte has changed my life, sir."

Jack studied him for a moment more, then leaned back a little and lifted his face to the cleansing rain. *And mine as well,* he thought with a touch of heaviness and solemn wonder. *And mine as well. . . .*

Inside the carriage, Samantha's thoughts were troubled.

The memory of what had happened earlier between her and Jack Kane would undoubtedly plague her the rest of the night. It had been a humiliating, shattering experience. Perhaps she should have been prepared for it, given the agonizing memories—and the fears—she still harbored. On the other hand, Jack was the first man with whom she had allowed any sort of closeness since Bronson. She couldn't have known what to expect and had been caught wildly off guard by the encounter.

Yet, the raw, undisguised hurt she had seen in Jack's eyes continued to torment her, even though to her vast relief he had shown no sign of resenting her for the experience. In fact, he had actually assumed a somewhat lighthearted tone with her there at the last.

It had taken all the control Samantha could muster not to tell him what lay behind her behavior. The plea—and the pain—in his eyes had almost been her undoing. For one of the few times since Bronson's death, she had been seized by a yearning to bare her soul, to pour out the entire hideous truth to another human being.

But what would it have accomplished? Did she really think that the simple act of confiding in someone else would free her from the curse of her marriage? Was she so naive as to hope that purging her soul would somehow bring her healing?

There was no reason to think that any purpose would be served by telling Jack about her past. If he cared for her at all . . . and she believed now that he did . . . wouldn't the truth only turn his caring to pity—or, worse still, revulsion? Samantha thought she could more easily bear his rejection than his pity or disgust.

How could she possibly reveal to Jack what she could never even bring herself to tell her own mother? How could she tell *anyone* about Bronson—the ways he had humiliated her, degraded her, *brutalized* her? How could she ever make anyone understand what she had endured as his mind became unhinged and sent him spiralling on a terrifying descent into madness?

To this day, Samantha did not understand how he had managed to deceive so many or how she could have been so pathetically naive and trusting.

No, Jack Kane could not heal her. No one could. A part of her— perhaps the very essence of her womanhood—had been defiled and ruined for any man.

And even if that were not the case, there was still the fact that she and Jack lived in two different worlds, that their differences still stood between them like an impenetrable bulwark. She lived her life based upon a faith and a code of values that she was fairly certain Jack neither accepted nor understood, any more than she could hope to accept or understand whatever it was that drove him.

And yet when he had asked if she would let him be her friend, Samantha had found herself unable to refuse, indeed had eagerly reached out for that much, at least, if nothing else. She needed a friend, and there was something in Jack that seemed to promise that she could trust him.

How long had it been since she had trusted a man ... since she had trusted *anyone?*

It had shaken her to realize that she thought she could trust Jack even with the truth about her marriage, though it was doubtful that she ever would. Out of deference to Bronson's family and the people who had trusted him and believed the best of him—and perhaps for her own self-protection as well—she would continue to keep her silence.

Besides, even if she did finally reveal the truth, no one would ever believe her. In the eyes of all who knew him, Bronson Harte had been a good man, a *godly* man. There wasn't one among them all who would ever believe anything else.

Finally, lulled by the sound of the light rain splashing against the carriage, the horse's steady clopping along the street, and an almost comforting sense of isolation, Samantha felt the turmoil, if not the pain, inside her begin to ebb.

She was only vaguely aware of the men's voices above her, was even growing slightly drowsy, when suddenly she felt the carriage skid and career sideways, tossing her hard against the door. Someone shouted. Cavan, she thought. She heard a sharp crack, followed by another, and with a stunning, dreadful clarity Samantha recognized the sound of gunfire!

Clinging to the door, she tried to see out the window. Without warning, the carriage lurched, gathering speed before finally slamming to a stop, throwing her forward.

Samantha cried out Jack's name, but there was no reply.

41

Into the Night

*What brings death to one
brings life to another.*
IRISH PROVERB

The carriage had just turned the corner at Houston and Sullivan. The streets were quiet, no doubt because of the rainstorm. Even at this hour, there would normally have been a few peddlers with their pushcarts, hoping to make an extra penny or two before calling it a night. Two or three streetwalkers—the older ones, whose slatternly features fared better in the darkness—lurked in the shadows as a small crew of factory workers trudged past on their way home. But for the most part, the street was deserted.

It was a black, bitter night. Rain was falling heavily again, as if the storm had changed its mind and turned back for yet another go at the city. The wind had taken on a definite chill, and Jack, now thoroughly drenched, shivered beneath his dripping suit coat. Sheridan fared no better in his thin jacket, and Jack made a mental note to have the lad pick up a raincoat for himself.

Not that he would be driving much longer, of course. Jack had every intention of putting him on the paper full-time soon. But even there, he would find need for a raincoat.

He was beginning to tire, his senses dulled, his thoughts rambling over nothing in particular, when he saw a figure emerge from the alley to his right, just ahead. Whoever it was came to a dead stop, as if waiting for the carriage to pass before crossing the street.

The figure was almost completely concealed in a long, flapping coat, with some sort of soft, wide hat pulled well down over his forehead. But something about the stance, the slight bend of the wide-spread legs and the rigid set to the shoulders, triggered an alarm in Jack.

Fully alert now, he put a warning hand to Sheridan's arm. "What's this?" he said, his voice low. "Have a care."

He felt the muscles tense in Sheridan's forearm, heard him click his tongue to speed up the horse. They were almost upon the figure when Jack saw an arm come up, pistol in hand.

Sheridan had seen it, too. As if by signal, he rose to a crouch, snapping the reins.

The dark figure stepped out into the street, and Jack saw that the gun was trained directly on him.

In that instant, Sheridan thrust himself almost directly in front of Jack with a shout. *"Watch yourself, sir!"*

Stunned, Jack still had the presence of mind to grasp the boy and try to shove him away. But it was too late.

Everything exploded in a rush. Sheridan took the first shot in his right shoulder, the next in his chest. He gave only a soft gasp, then pitched forward.

The mare squealed, and the carriage shot forward with a clatter. Jack caught the reins with his left hand, flinging out his other arm to block Sheridan's fall. The carriage bumped and skidded, and for a second Jack lost his balance. He righted himself, hauling hard on the reins with both hands as the carriage hurtled into the night.

When he looked back over his shoulder, the gunman was gone—just as Jack had known he would be.

He choked down his own swell of fear as he fought to rein in the panicked mare. Finally, with Sheridan slumped silently beside him, he managed to bring the horse under control and stop the carriage.

<hr />

Samantha scrambled out the door, practically falling into Jack's arms. He caught her, holding her fast.

"What happened?" She searched his face, going weak with relief when she saw that he was unharmed. "Jack?"

"I'm all right. But Sheridan's hurt."

Samantha tried to twist free, to go to Cavan, but Jack held her. "Get back in the carriage, Samantha. You don't want to see this."

She stared up at him. His face was shadowed, but she could see the rigid set of his features, the hard, angry line of his mouth.

"He's been shot, Samantha. He's bad. We need to get him to the hospital just as quickly as possible."

"Shot?" Samantha felt dazed. She couldn't think, couldn't even get her breath for a moment. "Why would anyone shoot Cavan?"

Jack looked at her. "The young fool threw himself in front of me," he said flatly.

Samantha's legs threatened to buckle.

"The bullets were meant for me," Jack said, his voice flat. "More than likely, Sheridan saved my life."

Weakness seeped through Samantha. "Is he . . . ?"

"He's alive." Jack's voice was hard, his eyes harder.

Samantha tried to push past him. "Let me see if I can help—"

"Samantha—there's no time. No time."

Samantha saw reflected in his eyes the same dread that was coursing through her. She no longer hesitated, but simply nodded and let him help her back into the carriage.

※※⊛※

They were a long way from Bellevue, but Jack was set on getting the best of care for Sheridan. He raced the carriage through the night as if the legions of darkness were at his back. From time to time, he glanced over at the still form beside him to make sure the breath hadn't left the boy's body. Once or twice he touched him, but there was no response. And all the while, the rain continued to pour down on them without mercy.

When they finally pulled up to the entrance of Bellevue, Sheridan was still alive, but only barely, Jack suspected. Jack started shouting for help even as he leaped from the carriage and flung the hospital doors open.

By the time he returned, with two attendants and a stretcher in tow, Samantha had climbed up onto the driver's seat and was holding the still-unconscious Sheridan's hand, watching him.

She was bent low over him, as if to shield him from the rain with her body. Her lips were moving, and Jack knew that she was praying.

※※⊛※

More than two hours passed before someone finally came to talk with them in the waiting room. Other than making frequent trips to the front desk to inquire, Jack and Samantha spent most of the time sitting on uncomfortable wooden chairs, side by side, mostly in silence.

Even after Jack finally managed to put down the worst of his murderous rage, his thoughts remained stormy. He forced himself not to jump to conclusions about the shooting. More than likely, the assailant had been only a hired gun. The only thing he could be certain of at this point was that the bullets had been meant for him, not Cavan Sheridan.

He knew he had enemies, knew some of them by name. But doubtless there were others who despised him in secret and harbored no end of malice toward him. Whoever was behind this, Jack vowed he would find him and make him pay.

He had already talked with the police, but tomorrow, as soon as he had the chance, he would have Avery Foxworth set his best investigator to the case. He considered offering a sizable reward but was reluctant to advertise the fact that someone had tried to shoot him; there was no telling how many additional cranks that kind of sensationalism might bring out of the woodwork. Still, if that was what it would take to find the snake behind this, that was what he would do.

His thoughts swung back to Sheridan. He still couldn't take in the enormity of what the boy had done. To risk his own life—Jack refused to think that by now Sheridan might have actually *given up* his life—what in the world had possessed him?

An unexpected chill trailed down his spine as he recalled something Sheridan had said during their first meeting, the day Jack had interviewed him for the driver's job. After assuring Jack that he was strong and "did well with the horses," the boy had gone on to remark that he would be "good to have around in the event of trouble."

Jack remembered his comeback, that he wasn't looking to hire a bodyguard. He couldn't possibly have known then that the lanky, awkward youth with the hungry eyes would end up saving his life.

Again, he puzzled over why.

Just then, a doctor entered the waiting room. Jack shot to his feet, bracing himself for what they might be about to hear.

Samantha remained seated, her hands clasped tightly in her lap. The doctor was young, too thin, and had deep shadows under his eyes. A shock of light hair fell over one eye, and his examining coat was soiled in several places.

Samantha thought he looked exceedingly weary. But his eyes held both intelligence and compassion, and she felt reassured that his expression didn't appear too terribly grim.

The physician glanced from her to Jack, saying, "You're Mr. Sheridan's family?"

Jack looked at Samantha, and after only a slight hesitation, he replied, "Yes. We're the only family he has here in New York."

The doctor nodded. "I'm sure you're anxious about him. I wish I had better news for you, but I'm afraid his condition is very serious."

"But he's going to live?" Jack prompted. His hands were knotted into tight fists at his sides. His eyes still held a trace of the same anger Samantha had seen after the shooting.

The doctor took off his glasses and slipped them into the pocket of his examining coat. "I can't say just yet. The wound to his shoulder is bad enough, of course, but my main concern is the chest wound. We were able to get the bullets out, but he's lost a dangerous amount of blood." He hesitated. "I'm sorry. It's going to be a while before we know."

"How long?" Jack said tightly.

The doctor shrugged, but it wasn't a careless gesture, merely an indication of his uncertainty. "Perhaps in a few hours, though it might be longer. I'm going to have him watched very closely, you can be sure."

He looked at Samantha, then Jack. "Why don't you and your wife go on home and get some rest? There's nothing you can do here."

Samantha felt her face grow warm when Jack did nothing to correct the doctor's assumption.

"We'll see," Jack said shortly.

After the doctor left the room, Jack sat down beside her. "I'm going to stay," he said. "But if you'd rather not, I'll see that you get home."

Samantha shook her head. "No, I'll wait with you. I couldn't possibly rest, not knowing."

Jack nodded and put a hand to her arm. "Why don't we move over there, then?" he said, gesturing across the room to a wooden bench with two thin, worn cushions. "That looks a bit more comfortable than these chairs, and I expect it's going to be a long night."

42

A Place for Memories, a Time for Secrets

For back to the Past, though the thought brings woe,
My memory ever glides.

JAMES CLARENCE MANGAN

The sounds of the hospital in the middle of the night were achingly familiar to Jack. Footsteps in the corridor, sometimes rushing, sometimes subdued. Doctors and attendants speaking in hushed voices. A chilling cry from somewhere down the hall. The jarring clatter of utensils. Someone shouting. Someone weeping.

The memories came driving in on him with a vengeance. He had thought those nights he'd spent here with Martha had finally been relegated to a place of bad dreams—not quite forgotten, but no longer real enough to torment him. Now here he was again, and the memories were back, pummeling his mind and heart in a renewed assault on an old wound.

It was past two in the morning, and they had heard nothing about Sheridan for hours now. Numerous times, Jack had gone to the door of the ward to look in, but a screen—which he knew from experience often denoted dying—had been set in place. If he so much as tiptoed in to look past the screen the matron in attendance shook her head and frowned at him as if to discourage any further intrusion.

He drew in a long breath, then stood and stretched. He glanced at Samantha and saw that her eyes were closed, but he couldn't tell whether she was sleeping . . . or praying again.

Samantha, he had learned, did not call attention to her prayers. She simply sat very quietly, eyes closed, her lips moving only slightly as she—to use one of Rufus Carver's expressions—"communed with the Lord."

He stretched again and started toward the door.

"Jack?"

He turned back. "Sorry—did I wake you?"

She shook her head. The only light was from an oil lamp on a table near the door, but the signs of fatigue engraved upon her features were clearly visible. Her eyes were deeply shadowed, her skin uncommonly pale. Even in this state of exhaustion and mild disarray, however, to Jack's eyes she was still incredibly lovely.

"I wasn't sleeping," she assured him. "Do you know what time it is?"

"A little past two. Samantha, why don't you let me get a cab to take you home? You're exhausted."

"No more than you," she pointed out. "Besides, I want to stay. Cavan may need us when he wakes up."

If he wakes up. . . . Jack kept the thought to himself.

"There is one thing, though," Samantha said. "Do you think you could somehow get word to Rufus to come? I'm sure he would, and I think Cavan would want him here. Besides, I'd feel better if I weren't the only one praying."

Jack frowned, puzzled by the request. "Of course Rufus would come. But I didn't realize he and the boy knew each other all that well."

"Cavan usually attends services at Rufus's church," Samantha explained.

Jack looked at her in surprise. "Sheridan goes to Rufus's church? But that's a Negro congregation!"

"Mostly, but not altogether." She smiled a little. "I attend there, too, as a matter of fact."

Jack studied her for a moment, then shook his head. "You never fail to surprise me, Mrs. Harte. But, yes, I'll get a message to Rufus somehow."

In the end he hailed a cab not far from the hospital entrance and paid the driver to bring Rufus to Bellevue as soon as possible. He looked at his watch. "There's an extra two dollars for you if you're back within the hour," he told the driver.

After begging a cup of water for himself and Samantha from one of the matrons, he returned to the waiting room. "There's a cab on the way," he said, handing her the water and lowering himself onto the bench beside her.

He was rewarded with a grateful smile and found himself wishing he could do something else for her. He did fancy Samantha's smile.

To help take their minds off Sheridan, Jack tried to make conversation. At first they spoke of mundane, inconsequential matters. Before long, however, Jack was surprised to find himself talking about things he had seldom, if ever, discussed with anyone else. Samantha had a way about her, he discovered, of drawing thoughts, and even feelings, from him that he would have normally found difficult, if not impossible, to verbalize.

More surprising still was that, to some extent, she responded in kind. Perhaps it was their mutual concern for Cavan Sheridan. A contributing factor might also have been the late-night quiet and the sense of somehow being cut off from reality. In any event, they talked for a long time, easily and openly, and Jack found himself more at ease with her than usual. He couldn't be certain, but he thought it might have been the same for her.

He learned that her father was Samuel Pilcher, a senior partner in one of the city's more distinguished investment firms. Her mother was apparently a moving force in New York's upper echelon of society. Samantha also revealed that, while they weren't exactly estranged, there was "tension" between herself and her family.

That her parents were old family—moneyed and highly respectable—didn't surprise Jack. He had sensed it in Samantha almost from their first meeting.

What *did* surprise him was that he found himself telling her about *his* parents: the highly unrespectable, wild, rebel father who had managed to get himself hanged as a result of a night raid with one of Ireland's countless secret societies—and his mother, who had died giving birth to Brady. He told her about his sister, Rose, "a nun and the best of the lot of us," and about Brady—his art, and even the strain of rebelliousness and selfishness Jack found so worrisome in his younger brother.

Samantha told him about growing up as a pampered, somewhat spoiled daughter. When Jack made a skeptical protest, she assured him it was true. He also learned that, having benefited from a contingent of carefully selected tutors, she probably had a finer education than most of the men he knew.

When he commented to that effect, she merely gave a small laugh, saying, "All it means is that I know a great deal about many things of no importance and not nearly enough about real life."

On the other hand, she seemed genuinely impressed by his own erratic attempts to attain an education. Jack had actually attended night classes similar to those Samantha taught. Not when he was a boy—he'd been too busy working to feed himself and the younger ones then—but later. Most of what he'd learned, however, had come about through his own continuing efforts to educate himself.

It intrigued him to learn that she had her heart set on buying her own buggy, that indeed she had been saving for some time now for just that purpose—though she evidently still had a ways to go. He was surprised to realize how much it pained him, to think of her scrimping and saving for something he could probably have purchased with the money he had in the pocket of his trousers at this very moment.

Finally, he even told her a little about Martha. He could talk about her now without much of the old hurt, could even smile a little at the good memories—and there were many. But if he had been hoping Samantha might reciprocate by speaking of her marriage, he was disappointed. In fact, she had grown silent, as if she no longer had anything to contribute to the conversation.

Acting on impulse—would he never learn?—Jack finally asked her about Bronson Harte. "I confess that I don't know how your late husband died. I don't believe I've ever heard you say."

She sat staring down at her hands for a long moment, making no reply. When she finally replied, she continued to keep her gaze carefully averted from his. "It was—very sudden."

"I see. How long has he been gone?"

"Nearly four years now."

Her voice had dropped to a near whisper. "You must have married very young," he said.

She shot a look at him. "Not really. But we were married only two years before—before he died."

Again Jack caught a sense of some undefinable tension in her, but before he could ask anything else she made what appeared to be a deliberate attempt to change the subject.

"Do you think we should check on Cavan again?" she said.

Jack knew she was genuinely concerned about Sheridan. All the same, he recognized evasiveness when he saw it, and Samantha was definitely being evasive. He had learned more about her tonight than he had in months, and he was reluctant to end the conversation.

"Why don't we wait a bit?" he replied. "The matron is starting to give me evil looks."

She nodded her assent, and after a moment of uncertainty, Jack said carefully, "Samantha? I can't help but notice—you're really not very comfortable talking about your husband, are you?"

The quick, fitful look that darted across her features confirmed Jack's instincts, but her reply still surprised him. "I—no, actually, I'm not. I'm afraid my marriage wasn't . . . as happy as yours apparently was."

Jack didn't miss the trembling of her hands or the way she had begun to press her arms against her midsection as if to hold herself together.

He wished he dared take her hand. "I'm sorry," he said softly.

"Yes . . . well, it's . . . over now."

Jack thought that was a strange way to put it. He said nothing, but the suspicion that had begun to form in his mind reasserted itself. When he thought of how concerned—how intense—she had been about the Shanahan woman and her problems, the peculiar silence she maintained in regard to her deceased husband, and most especially, the stricken look that came over her at the mention of his name, he could not help but wonder if the late Bronson Harte had really been the saint he was reputed to be.

He was seriously beginning to doubt it.

Samantha saw something in Jack's eyes she had never seen in Bronson's—a tenderness, a gentleness she could not fathom. But there was something else there as well, some unsettling dark emotion she couldn't define.

Uneasily, she wondered if she had said too much, had somehow allowed him to catch a glimpse of the sordid truth that lay buried beneath her defenses. At times his dark eyes seemed to cut through the wall of her self-protection and see far more than she wanted him, or anyone else, to see.

She hated all this evasion—always skirting the truth, hiding the pain, pretending . . . always pretending.

It was more difficult, somehow, with Jack. He had asked for her friendship, and in spite of her initial skepticism and reservations about him, Samantha was surprised to realize that she *wanted* his friendship.

Had she been less weary, less depleted, she might have found the energy to rationalize her feelings. He was her employer, after all, and since it wasn't likely she would find a more attractive position anywhere in the city that paid as well or allowed her the flexibility in hours, wouldn't she be wise to cultivate his friendship?

No. It wasn't anything like that, and she knew it. Even if ensuring her position had been at the heart of all this, she had sensed nothing in Jack Kane's character to indicate that, by rejecting his friendship, she might be endangering her job. The truth was that she had come to *like* the man, was even attracted to him, and she might just as well confront the fact instead of denying it.

Perhaps a part of his appeal for her was his kindness. Despite all the rumors about his ruthlessness and callousness, Jack *had* been kind to her—even though she had given him every reason not to be. That kindness had been a balm to her wounded spirit.

Ever since leaving the fellowship, Samantha had lived a very isolated, solitary existence. She stayed busy enough—work was never a problem. But her days revolved around her work for the newspaper, her teaching, and her other responsibilities with Immigrant Aid. Any "social life"—even the term brought a rueful smile—consisted of suppers with Amelia and Rufus and an occasional potluck at the church. As for her former "friends" among Bronson's followers, they had begun to drift away soon after his death. When Samantha finally separated from the fellowship, they made no further effort to maintain contact.

Most of the time she was able to ignore her feelings of loneliness. But once in a while, the solitude of her apartment and the lack of companionship in her life seemed to close in on her, and she found herself longing for something more.

She was loath to admit that Jack Kane might represent that something more. But if he did, how could she consider even the most innocent of friendships with him when there would always be this veil of secrecy between them?

Dear God, must I live the rest of my life in the shadows? Will there ever come a time when I'll be able to forget the past and live a normal life, when I'll find the courage to trust again . . . even to love again?

"Samantha?"

Jack's voice, hushed but laced with concern, pierced her thoughts. Samantha glanced up to find him leaning toward her, his features knit in a frown.

Again Samantha felt torn between the instinctive caution his closeness sparked in her and whatever it was that invariably drew her to him in spite of that caution.

"I'm sorry," she said, forcing a smile. "I'm afraid my mind tends to wander sometimes." She was keenly aware of his searching gaze and could almost feel him choosing his words.

"He hurt you, didn't he?"

Samantha tensed, at first thinking she'd misunderstood him. "What?"

"Your husband. He hurt you. That's why it's so difficult for you to talk about him."

An alarm went off in Samantha. What had she said . . . what had he seen that could have given it away?

The humiliation flooding over her made her want to leap to her feet and run away. From Jack . . . from the hospital . . . from the pain. Somehow he had glimpsed her secret shame.

He knew. . . .

*

So he'd been right. Jack knew it the instant her head snapped up. He saw her stiffen, saw the white-knuckled grip of her hands at her waist and the startled, almost frightened, look in her eyes.

"I don't know what you mean," she said, suddenly cool to the point of freezing him out.

"I think you do, Samantha," Jack said, as gently as possible. "And you don't have to sidestep with me. I've suspected for some time now."

She squared her shoulders and fixed her gaze on some nonexistent object across the room. "I don't know what you're talking about, but I hardly think it's any of your business, whatever it is."

This wasn't anger he was seeing in her, Jack sensed. It was an attempt to protect, to ward off. He had cut through too suddenly, too deeply, had laid open some sort of wound she'd believed to be concealed—and now she was scrambling to shield it.

He disliked himself for exposing her pain—whatever it was—at a time when she was so clearly vulnerable, but something had compelled him to voice his suspicions. Not for his sake, but for hers.

He could only hope she would forgive him.

"You can tell me about it, Samantha," he said quietly. "If you want to, that is. If not—I understand. But at least know that you don't have to pretend with me any longer."

She said nothing but merely sat there, straight-backed and unmoving, her lips pressed together as she deliberately avoided looking at him. Even now, despite the cloak of denial she had drawn about her, Jack could see the despair in her eyes, and the sight of it hit him like a blow. More than ever before, he wished he could hold her . . . hold her so closely he could somehow absorb her pain into himself so that she would feel nothing—nothing but his love for her.

His *love* for her. It was the first time he had allowed the word to identify his feelings for Samantha, even though he had feared for some time now the direction in which those feelings were headed.

So that was the way of it, then. He loved her. The admission astonished him.

It also terrified him.

To keep from touching her, he knotted his hands together. "I'm sorry if I've made you feel awkward, Samantha," he said, surprised at the hoarseness in his voice. "I thought if you realized that I knew, you might find it easier to . . . be with me, to be yourself with me. We don't have to mention this again, not ever, if you'd rather not."

Finally, she turned to look at him. Her eyes, woefully solemn now, searched his, and Jack felt himself measured as he had never been before.

"How did you know?" she whispered.

Jack shook his head. "I'm not sure. It was just . . . something in your eyes." He hesitated. "I was right, wasn't I?"

Slowly, she nodded. He saw her eyes fill with tears, and for a blinding instant of rage, he wanted to make Bronson Harte pay. "Do you want to tell me?" he prompted, dropping his voice to match her whispered tone.

She shook her head. "I can't. I've never . . . told anyone. Not even my family. I can't. . . ."

Jack thought he would strangle at the look of anguish on her face. The idea of her carrying this alone made him want to weep for her. "Samantha . . . I'm sorry. So very sorry." No longer able to stop himself, he reached out a hand to her, waiting.

She stared at his hand, then lifted her gaze to meet his. And finally, as relief and hope and love rose up in Jack, she clasped his hand. She was trembling, and Jack wished he could impart a portion of his own strength to her. "It's all right, Samantha. Perhaps someday you'll be able to tell me," he said. "I have my secrets, too, you see. But I'd like to think that one day there will be no secrets between us, none at all. That's my hope."

He drew a steadying breath. "I want to promise you something," he said, his voice soft. She was watching him closely, and he squeezed her hand. "First, I'd like you to know that if there's anything—anything at all—of any value in me, it's my word. I don't break my word, Samantha. You can believe that. And I give you my word now that I will never . . . *never* hurt you. Do you understand? I will never hurt you in any way."

Her hand trembled in his. *So small, so fragile, that hand.* She was such a small, delicate woman. And yet what incredible strength must lie within her, to endure her painful secrets in silence.

Her eyes glistened with unshed tears. He wanted to kiss them away. "I will say it again, Samantha. I will never hurt you. And neither," he promised, "will anyone else. My word on it, I intend to see to it that no one ever hurts you again. Can you believe me?"

Oh, sweetheart, please, please believe me. . . . I have never meant anything more in my life. . . .

"Yes," she finally said, her voice soft, her eyes shining. "I believe you."

Jack had all he could do not to pull her into his arms, but he checked himself. And then the moment passed, abruptly shattered by the appearance of one of the matrons in the doorway.

"Mr. and Mrs. Kane?" she said brusquely. "Doctor says you should come now."

They looked at each other, and Jack saw his own alarm and dread mirrored in Samantha's eyes.

43

Vigil at Bellevue

Now, no one is likely to die for a good person,
though someone might be willing to die
for a person who is especially good.
But God showed his great love for us
by sending Christ to die for us
while we were still sinners.

ROMANS 5:7-8

Jack was standing at the foot of Cavan Sheridan's bed, watching Samantha dab the boy's forehead with a damp cloth, when Rufus Carver arrived.

Sheridan was still unconscious, though he would occasionally moan or move his head from side to side. His eyes were closed, his face drenched with perspiration, his skin pale and waxen. The thin scar that traced the side of his face had become an angry slash against his ashen pallor. Unless the doctor was mistaken—and Jack feared he was not—any hope for recovery was slim indeed.

After giving Jack and Samantha the disheartening news, Dr. Van Curen—the same doctor who had admitted Sheridan—had left the ward, promising to return soon. Jack wondered when the young physician managed to sleep. He had seen him going up and down the corridor most of the night, and he looked absolutely exhausted.

On the opposite side of the bed from Samantha stood a new matron. This one seemed less irascible and more interested in Sheridan's condition than in keeping things quiet and undisturbed. Which was probably a good thing, Jack thought, because Rufus was not given to speaking in whispers.

The moment the big, affable preacher walked into the room, Jack felt a sense of relief, taking his first deep breath in what seemed an interminable time. Rufus had a way of easing things for others. Jack had never quite understood what it was about his old friend that should account for this rare gift, but over the years he had seen Rufus make a difference in some rather remarkable ways in some very difficult situations.

Samantha turned as Rufus entered, and Jack saw that her relief matched his own.

"How is he?" Rufus said, brushing the dampness from his coat before giving Jack's shoulder a quick squeeze.

Jack shook his head. "Bad. They called us in a few minutes ago, said he was weakening."

Rufus looked at Cavan Sheridan, then at Jack. "Your message said he'd been shot."

Jack nodded. "It was supposed to have been me," he bit out, gripped by the same angry ache that had been gnawing at him all night. "Instead, Sheridan pushed himself in front of me. He was hit twice."

"Any idea who was responsible?"

Again Jack gave a shake of his head. "I couldn't see his face. Just a man with a gun."

Rufus studied him. "But you're sure he was after you, not the boy?"

"I was practically looking down the barrel when Sheridan shoved between us. He saved my life, no doubt about it."

No matter how he tried, Jack could not seem to get past this point, that someone had deliberately taken a bullet—*two* bullets—in his place. He still found it inconceivable, and yet he was alive because of Cavan Sheridan's selfless act.

As if he could read his thoughts, Rufus again put his hand to Jack's shoulder. "It was brave of the boy, no denying it. But this isn't your fault, Jack. Don't go tryin' to make it your fault."

They stood for a moment, watching Samantha as she bent over the unconscious Sheridan, clasping his hand. Her voice was so low Jack could only barely make out what she was saying. But clearly she believed Cavan Sheridan could hear every word.

"Cavan . . . listen to me; you mustn't give up. You have so much work to do yet, so many people to reach with your writing. And your sister—you have to find Terese, remember? You have to find her and bring her here, to be with you. You still want that, don't you? You have to fight. Please, Cavan . . . fight. . . ."

Jack's throat tightened, and he turned to Rufus. "He can't die, Rufus! The boy is too young! And he's a better man than I'll ever be, certainly. He doesn't deserve to die—not for the likes of me."

Rufus searched his eyes. "Your Savior died for the likes of you, Jack," he said, his voice uncharacteristically quiet. "He didn't deserve it either, but he did it all the same. You need to realize that Jesus has a hold on this boy, brother. I expect young Cavan here was only doing what the Lord moved him to do."

Jack was as exasperated with Rufus as he was shaken by his words. This was hardly the time to start preaching at him! But when Jack would have told him so, Rufus stepped away and went to stand beside Samantha.

Jack saw him give her a reassuring nod as they both stood watching the unconscious Cavan Sheridan. "Amelia wanted me to tell you she'd be standing in for the boy, too," Rufus said to Samantha. "She'll be praying right along with us. And it appears that we'd better start doing some mighty serious praying about now."

It stung a little, being excluded in such short order, but Jack understood. There certainly wouldn't have been any point in including him in what was clearly about to become one of Rufus's prayer meetings.

Again, it was as if Rufus could read his thoughts. "Wouldn't hurt for you to put in a word, too, Jack," he said without taking his eyes off Sheridan. "The Lord knows how much you care about this boy."

Jack looked at him, then at Sheridan. He *did* care about the lad, that was true enough. But there was little chance of any prayer he might utter rising higher than the ceiling. The Almighty had turned a deaf ear on his prayers for Martha, and that had been the one and only time in his life when he had virtually besieged the gates of heaven. If his soul had been so tarnished even back then that God ignored him, He would be a lot less likely to pay him any heed now.

But Rufus was watching him as if he expected some sort of effort on his part. "Come here, brother," he said quietly, reaching out to Jack. "At least stand with us beside the boy. That would please young Cavan, I expect."

Jack tried to swallow against his swollen throat. But even as he shook his head with the futility of it all, he took his first step toward Rufus and Samantha.

Caught completely off guard by the wave of emotion that swept through him, Jack watched as Rufus clasped the unconscious Cavan Sheridan's hand and smiled gently down upon the boy as he might have gazed upon a sleeping child.

And then he lifted his face heavenward—still holding Sheridan's hand—and began to pray, his features taking on an almost transfiguring intensity and strength. "Lord . . . Lord, this is your child lying here in need of your mercy and your healing hand. Cavan Sheridan, Lord—you know him by name, and you know his heart. You know it was that good and noble heart that put him in this situation in the first place. The bullets that brought this terrible thing on him were meant for someone else, but he took the pain willingly, in love for a brother.

"Now surely it must thrill your heart, Lord, to know that one of your earthly sons was willing to lay down his life for another, just as your only beloved Son was willing to pour out his life for all of us. Yes, Lord, it must surely thrill your heart. . . ."

Jack thought his *own* heart would shatter from the pressure that had been building within him over the past few minutes. His mouth was as dry as cotton batting, and he felt about to strangle on the knot in his throat.

And yet at the same time he knew a strange, unfamiliar kind of exultation as he listened to his old friend and Samantha beseeching heaven for Cavan Sheridan's life. They had clasped hands, Rufus and Samantha, and while Rufus stood, shoulders straight, head tossed back, smiling upward as he sought divine mercy, Samantha stood quietly, eyes closed, lips barely moving, her words but a whisper.

But there was no doubt that they were both calling on the same power. And it was abundantly clear that they knew Him well and felt they had the right to address Him as a good and faithful friend.

"It's up to you, Lord," Rufus went on, "whether you take this boy home right now, tonight, or leave him here with us. That's not for us to decide, and we're purely glad we don't have that kind of fateful decision to make. But we're just asking if you might consider letting him stay. This is a good boy, Lord, who maybe can make a difference in this poor old troubled world, if you see fit to leave him here long enough.

"We trust your wisdom in this, Lord, as in all things. We trust your wisdom and your mercy, and oh, Lord, we surely do trust your Father-heart of love! Pour out that love, Lord, on Cavan Sheridan this very hour . . . and pour out your love on the one he risked his life for, your child, and our brother, Jack. Wrap your arms around them both, Lord, and hold them close, close to your heart. . . ."

Jack drew in a ragged breath. This wasn't the first time Rufus had prayed in his presence, and if Jack knew him at all, he knew it wasn't the first time Rufus had prayed for *him*. Before tonight, he had always taken his friend's efforts on behalf of his soul with nothing more than a kind of grim humor and a blatant skepticism. Tonight, however, he found himself somewhat hard-pressed to understand how the Almighty could possibly ignore the earnest praying going on in this room.

It was an unnerving thought, to say the least.

When Rufus finally concluded, Jack was suddenly seized by the disconcerting feeling that, even though he had not closed his eyes throughout the entire litany—had not uttered a word, so far as he knew—*he* had been praying too, in spite of himself.

Bewildered, badly shaken, he stepped back a little. Rufus did the same, making room for Samantha to take up her former place close to Sheridan, where she resumed her soft, strangely maternal, soothing words for Cavan's ears alone.

Cavan Sheridan was dreaming about home. He was there, back home in Ireland, with his parents, his sister, Honor, and Baby Mada. And yet there was little of the joy he would have anticipated—at least on his part—had such a thing ever come to pass. His family seemed contented enough, but the initial burst of happiness he had felt upon first sight of them was quickly fading, giving way to confusion.

They were all of them walking upon the shore, with the water splashing high upon the rocks. In his dream, Cavan *knew* he was dreaming, knew this was not real, although it was real enough that he tried to speak with each family member, even the baby.

Mostly, he was asking after Terese, her whereabouts, for he had not yet seen her. She was the only one absent, and he was growing anxious.

His family behaved in a most peculiar fashion. They spoke and laughed among themselves, but other than Baby Mada, who stared at Cavan with large, studying eyes, no one paid him the slightest heed. Cavan had thought they would be glad to see him after so long a time. Instead they virtually ignored him, even his questions about the missing Terese.

Because he knew he was caught up in a dream, he shouldn't have grown impatient with them. But he thought they might have shown a bit more sensitivity to his exhaustion, his weakness—and his need to gain some word of Terese before he could rest. Instead, they simply continued walking along the shore, not even bothering to wait for him when he fell behind.

Suddenly, he realized someone was calling out to him, and he turned, expecting to finally see Terese running up the shore to greet him. But there was no one.

The water was slamming harder and harder against the rocks now, driven by the strange wind that had blown up in the middle of the sea. Above, the sky had darkened to an ominous, dark pewter, the clouds hanging so low he could almost touch them.

His family had gone on ahead of him, not waiting, and Cavan could scarcely make them out. He could no longer keep up. His breathing was tortured, his chest pounding, and he was finding it difficult to walk, much less run, after the others.

Cavan . . .

He *had* heard someone calling his name. Again, he turned to look but could see nothing . . . nothing but a thin, dark mist where the clouds were now slipping down behind him.

Cavan . . .

The voice sounded nearer now . . . a woman's voice, sure, but not *Terese's* voice.

He turned once more to look after his parents and sisters, but they had disappeared into the distance, hidden by the clouds that now encompassed him from behind and before, hiding his family, the rocks, even the waves of the sea.

Finally, he began walking back the way he had come, away from his family, back along the shore, out of the clouds . . . out of the mist. Someone was holding his hand, and he allowed himself to be led as he followed the voice that continued to call his name. . . .

⚬⚬⚬

Over an hour later, Jack saw the boy stir slightly and moan. He tensed, fearful of the worst. But as he watched, Sheridan blinked, squeezed his eyes shut once more, then opened them again.

Jack put a fist to his mouth to suppress a gasp of relief. Samantha made a soft cry and turned to look at him and Rufus. The latter voiced an enthusiastic, "Praise God! Thank you, Lord!"

Sheridan was watching Samantha, who still had hold of his hand. She smiled at him and murmured something Jack couldn't make out. The boy seemed to be having trouble focusing his eyes, but he looked surprisingly alert, given the gravity of his condition.

"Mr. Kane?"

Jack flinched at the sound of his own name, the first words Sheridan uttered as he regained consciousness.

The matron was already rushing out to fetch the doctor, so Jack went to take her place across the bed from Samantha.

He knew as soon as he looked in Sheridan's eyes that the lad was going to be all right. He stood staring down at him, wondering at the way the boy was searching his gaze. Finally, Sheridan gave a small nod, as if to reassure himself, and said, "'Tis safe you are, then."

It was the most natural thing ever for Jack to fall into the Irish cadence they held in common, even though his throat had tightened treacherously. "Aye, 'tis safe I am, lad. All thanks to you."

The boy's smile was wobbly as with a languid motion he turned his face toward Samantha. "It was you I heard."

Samantha's expression was questioning as she leaned slightly closer to him. "What, Cavan? What did you hear?"

"It was you who called me out of the dream," he said. "I heard you, Mrs. Harte. . . . I heard you calling my name. . . ."

His eyes fluttered a little, and seeing his weakness, Jack was reluctant to risk tiring him. But the question that had raked at him throughout the night would give him no peace. He had to know.

Bending over the boy, he studied his pale, lean face for a moment. "Why did you do it, Cavan Sheridan?" he said, his voice rough with emotion. "You could have been killed, you young pup! You almost were, you know. Why would you do such a fool thing?"

The lad made no reply right away, but instead lay looking up at Jack as if uncertain as to how to answer. When his response finally came, it was so soft that Jack had to lean still closer, straining to hear.

"To give you more time, sir."

"What's that?" Jack frowned, wondering if he'd heard him correctly.

"I had . . . to give you more time, don't you see? You need . . . more time. The Father knows you, knows your heart . . . but you don't know him . . . can't choose . . . unless you know . . . his love. . . ."

Jack's breath seemed lodged in his throat. He tried to swallow but found he could not. He stayed as he was for a moment more, watching as Cavan Sheridan closed his eyes and drifted off, this time, obviously, to a more natural sleep.

Jack straightened and looked across the bed at Samantha, who merely gave a gentle lift of her eyebrows, as if to ask what he intended to do with the gift . . . the time . . . he had been given.

Gifts of Gold
and Grace

'Tis grace itself, this letting go of yesterday,
The relinquishing of old days and old ways
To make room for the gift of God's tomorrows.

CAVAN SHERIDAN,

FROM *WAYSIDE NOTES*

NEW YORK CITY

On the following Monday, Samantha was visiting Cavan Sheridan, along with Rufus and Amelia, when Jack strode into the ward.

It was late afternoon, but the man certainly did not look as if he had spent the day at the office. Samantha couldn't stop a smile at his jaunty air and his light, almost dancing, step as he approached. He was his usual natty self—impeccably groomed, freshly barbered, and dressed to the nines in an elegantly tailored gray suit and a silk neckcloth in a shade of lustrous pearl.

He was carrying something—a rather thick letter, so it appeared. As he walked up to the bed, his greeting took in everyone, but his smile seemed just for her.

"I hope you're getting good and tired of playing the slugabed, boyo," he cracked to Cavan Sheridan, who, although still obviously weak and in some discomfort, was propped up by a flock of pillows at his back. "I'll grant you only a few more days, and then it's back to work for you!"

As he spoke, he waved the letter he was carrying in Samantha's direction. "And for you as well, Mrs. Harte—we have company coming, you see."

Samantha wondered what on earth he was talking about, then realized—"You've heard from your brother!"

"Indeed. As it happened, the letter's been lying about the house since last Friday, but with all the fuss and confusion, I'd forgotten to read it until this morning. It seems we have a wee boy and girl coming across very soon now—and my troublesome brother even remembered to send along the copy for their story."

He stopped, studying Cavan Sheridan for a moment before going to stand alongside him. When he spoke again, he dropped his voice and put a hand to the boy's good shoulder. "And you must brace yourself, Sheridan, for the rest of the news in my brother's letter will surely astound you." He paused. "Your sister has been found, lad, and even as we speak, is more than likely on her way to America."

Jack had the satisfaction of seeing Sheridan's eyes grow wide enough to pop as he delivered his news. For once, he thought wryly, the boy was actually speechless.

"Aye, it's true," Jack assured him. "Apparently, she traveled to Galway after the big storm, and that's where Brady came upon her. It seems he has worked things out so she and the children can travel together, with your sister looking after the youngsters."

"Terese . . ." The boy breathed her name like a prayer. His eyes suddenly filled, and for a fraction of a second Jack feared the news might have been too much for him. Perhaps he should have waited until the lad was stronger.

He *had* withheld a less joyous portion of the announcement. The bitter fact that the girl was with child as a result of an attack would have to wait until Sheridan was well enough to bear the whole story. For now, let him rejoice over the *good* news. The rest could come later.

The lad looked about to weep. Jack released him, fumbling in his pocket for a handkerchief, just in case.

"Is she . . . is she well, then, sir—Terese?"

Jack chose his words carefully. "It would seem from my brother's letter that your sister is quite healthy. The children, however, sound a bit frail."

He gestured again to the letter. "When you're feeling stronger, you can read it all for yourself. But for now, you must concentrate on getting well as soon as possible. I can't have my newest reporter working from his bed. It wouldn't do at all, don't you see? You are needed at the office, and the sooner the better.''

"Sir?" The puzzled frown on the boy's face gave Jack more satisfaction still.

"Why, didn't you hear me, lad? It has occurred to me that you will prove far more valuable with a pad and pencil in your hands than sitting on a driver's bench. I'm putting you on the *Vanguard*'s payroll as soon as you're able to come back to work." Jack paused, then added, "And lest you think this has anything to do with your injury, it does not. I had already made the decision before you pulled that fool stunt on Friday night."

"Mr. Kane—what have you learned about the shooting? Have the police found the man yet?"

Jack shook his head. "No, but they're doing what they can. They've little to go on, of course, with the bounder disappearing as easily as he did, but they have some of their best men on it."

Jack had his own suspicions about the affair, but this was not the time to voice them. Even though a hired gun would hardly seem the sort of thing a man like Turner Julian would resort to, he couldn't afford to dismiss the possibility out of hand. But as he had told Avery Foxworth, there was no denying that he had made some enemies. The truth was, it could have been *anyone* behind that gun.

"Jack—*Mr. Kane*—?"

Jack turned to see Samantha blushing furiously at having used his given name in front of the others. He grinned at her discomfiture. *"Mrs. Harte?"* he said with deliberate emphasis.

Her eyes flared a little, but being Samantha, she regained her composure nicely. "Have you considered—what if he should try again?"

It had occurred to him, of course, and he supposed he had to allow for the possibility. But Jack thought it unlikely that a second attempt would come so soon after the recent failure. Still, her concern pleased him.

Rather than alarm her, however, he dismissed the question with a wave of his hand. "Well, I suppose we shall simply have to outfit Sheridan here with a suit of armor, now won't we?"

Jack laughed at her thoroughly outraged expression. "Don't fret yourself, Samantha. Despite what you may have read in the newspapers—" he grinned—"our police department is not without resources. Besides, I've already looked into the matter of a private investigator as well."

He turned back to Sheridan. "About your sister, lad: She'll be needing a place to stay once she arrives, and even though you won't be driving for me by then, I rather like the idea of having my body-guard close by, all the same. So I thought we might partition the room above the stable and make a place for the two of you, for now at least. The room is large enough, and it will give you time to save a bit of money for something larger.''

Sheridan shook his head, as if somewhat bemused by the offer. He pushed himself up as much as possible, extending a hand to Jack. ''How can I ever thank you for all you've done, Mr. Kane?''

Jack's gaze flicked from the lad's hand to his bandaged shoulder and chest. ''Well, now,'' he said, grasping Sheridan's hand in his, ''it seems to me you have already made a right proper job of it.''

⚜

Before Jack escorted Samantha from the ward, Amelia surprised him by pressing a parcel into his hands. ''What's this?'' he said, looking down at the package wrapped in brown paper.

''Happy birthday, Jack,'' she said. ''I bet you thought we'd forgotten all about it, didn't you, what with all the commotion?''

Jack looked at her, then laughed. ''Actually,'' he admitted, ''I'd forgotten it myself. So what is this, then?''

''Well, why don't you open it and find out?'' she teased, linking arms with Rufus.

''I will indeed.'' Jack glanced from one to the other, then at Samantha. He felt somewhat awkward, for it was a rare occasion of any sort when he received a gift. But Amelia was clearly expecting him to open the package as they watched, so he began to tear at the string.

His fingers were clumsy as he worked to free the contents from the paper wrapping. For a moment he could do nothing but stare at the elegantly fashioned vest—obviously one of Amelia's own creations.

His throat tightened treacherously as he held the garment up for all to see. It was a resplendent effort, woven of carefully blended shades of deep crimson and burnished gold, finished with precise gold stitching. Jack found himself pleased beyond imagining.

''Amelia—I am . . . I don't know what to say!''

''Well, now, that's a first,'' Rufus said, ignoring his wife's punch in the ribs.

Samantha stepped closer to inspect the vest, smiling up at Jack as if she sensed his discomfort as well as his pleasure. ''Oh, Amelia, this is absolutely lovely!''

''It is indeed, Amelia,'' Jack seconded. ''I confess I have always envied Rufus his handsome vests. I can't thank you enough.''

He went to her and kissed her lightly on the cheek. When he would have stepped back, however, Amelia stopped him with a little tug on his sleeve. "I've been working on this for a long time now, but after our talk last Friday, I was determined to get it finished for your birthday."

Jack frowned. "Last Friday?"

"Friday evening," she said. "In the sewing room. Remember what I told you about the 'cloth of heaven'?"

Jack nodded slowly, wondering what she was getting at.

"Well, I want you to promise me that every time you wear this vest, you'll think on that little talk we had—about what the Lord can make of your life if you'll just let him have his way. I want your word on it, Jack Kane."

"Do I have a choice?" Jack said dryly.

"You always have a choice, brother," Rufus put in. "It seems to me that Amelia, she's just doing her part to help you make the right one."

THE ATLANTIC, OFF THE COAST OF IRELAND

Terese Sheridan stood on the deck of the *Providence,* taking a last look at Ireland. She pulled her emerald cloak more tightly about her shoulders, trying not to think of the night Brady had bought it for her. At the same time, she attempted to shake off the melancholy that had engulfed her since early morning. She reminded herself how fortunate she was to be up here, on deck, where she could breathe in the fresh air, rather than suffering belowdecks. That was one thing she could thank Brady for, at least—by paying the extra passage money, he had spared her and the Madden children the rumored horrors of steerage.

She would thank him for nothing else, that much was certain. She glanced behind her, where wee Tully Madden was hobbling up and down the short distance of the deck to which Terese had confined him. She watched him for a moment, feeling a tug at her heart for the limp that slowed his little-boy gait. His cheerfulness seemed not to suffer, however; each time he caught Terese's eye, he favored her with a quick smile.

Tully's older sister, Shona, stood close to Terese's side. Terese could feel the girl's eyes on her but did not turn to look. Those large, haunted eyes with their sorrowful blue gaze discomfited Terese. The child seemed to be always staring at something, yet seeing nothing.

Despite her resolve to put the past behind her, her gaze—and her thoughts—returned to the fading coastline in the distance. For another moment, Terese allowed herself a brief memory of Inishmore and all that she was leaving behind: her home—the only home she had ever known—her mother, her da, her sisters . . . Brady. . . .

Her heart wrenched at the thought of Brady, but it was a pain kindled by anger. She had promised herself she would never again think of him without remembering his betrayal, his rejection. She would get over him by despising him.

Only the thought of Jane Connolly brought any real sadness to her spirit. Poor Jane, trapped forever in her chair by the window, looking out upon a world of which she could have no real part. At the end, she had been kind, kinder than Terese would have had any right to expect. That last evening before her departure, Jane had added an extra week to Terese's wages.

And she had given her the ring.

Terese held out her hand and looked at the gold ring Jane had pressed upon her the night before she left. "'Twas made right here, in the Claddagh," Jane had told her. "It belonged to my mother, who passed it to me. My daughter wore it for a time, but she left it behind when she married and left the Claddagh. You wear it now, girl. Wear it to America, and remember Jane Connolly, who gave it to you. Remember me and the Claddagh—and remember Ireland. For Ireland is not only where you come from, Terese Sheridan—Ireland is what you *are*."

Terese lifted her hand to study the ring. The *Fede* ring—the "faith ring," Jane had called it—displayed two hands holding a heart surmounted by a crown. Cast in fine gold, its tradition was one of love and friendship, honor, loyalty, and the hope of future glory.

It was the only piece of jewelry Terese had ever owned, and she touched it now, turning it a bit so that the two hands and the heart were clearly visible.

Finally, she raised her eyes from the ring for one final look at her homeland. In that moment, she placed a hand over the child who grew within her and quietly gave voice to the longing of her heart.

"Please . . . merciful Savior . . . let my child be born to a better life in America . . . a life of hope instead of hunger . . . and freedom instead of fear. . . . A better life, Lord, please . . . a better life. . . ."

Then she turned . . . turned her back on Ireland, on all her yesterdays. And as she turned her face to the west, to America, she lifted the hand bearing the Claddagh ring, lifted it in farewell to the old life . . . and in salute to the new.